"I KNOW THE MANNER OF MAN YOU ARE!"
ALYS SAID HOTLY.

"I know far too much of your passion and its demands!" She met Burke's gaze in challenge, willing him to tell her the truth.

"Do tell," he urged silkily.

"Would you have halted your touch had we not been interrupted?" she snapped, hating the catch that appeared in her voice. "Or would you have had your way with me fully before you abandoned both me and Kiltorren for all time? If you have returned to right the omission, know that I shall never be fool enough to cede to your touch again!"

Burke's eyes flashed, but Alys did not note the warning before he had caught her about the waist. At his abrupt move, she lost her balance and tumbled against him. Alys could not look away from the resolve in Burke's gaze. Indeed, she could not seem to summon the strength to move, not even when his lips hovered above her own.

"Alys," Burke chided in a low voice, "you should be well enough acquainted with me to know I can never resist a challenge. We shall touch again, and often. Upon that you have my solemn pledge. . . ."

HIGH PRAISE FOR CLAIRE DELACROIX'S
THE PRINCESS
THE MAGICAL DEBUT NOVEL IN THE BRIDE QUEST TRILOGY

"EXQUISITE! A marvelously beautiful tale of love!"
—*Bell, Book and Candle*

"READING *THE PRINCESS* IS LIKE SIPPING VINTAGE
WINE—DELECTABLE!"
—*Rendezvous*

"[Claire Delacroix] has a magical, lyrical style of writing
that captures the reader from the first page. Add mysterious
secret treasure, as well as several murders, to this
wonderfully passionate romance and you have an exciting
medieval that's not to be missed."
—*Old Book Barn Gazette*

"THE ESSENCE OF FAIRY TALE, FABLE AND
LEGEND!"
—*Romantic Times*

"DELACROIX CAPTURED ME WITH THE FIRST
SENTENCE . . . and left me wanting more! Her musical
style of writing transformed this story into a bard's tale of
knights, quests, mystery and love."
—*All About Romance*

A proud maiden, she vowed never to love again— until he rode back into her life.

Dell books by Claire Delacroix

The Bride Quest: The Princess

The Bride Quest: The Damsel

The Bride Quest

The
Damsel

Claire Delacroix

A Dell Book

Published by
Dell Publishing
a division of
Random House, Inc.
1540 Broadway
New York, New York 10036

The trademark Dell® is registered in the U.S. Patent and Trademark Office.

ISBN: 0-440-22588-4

Printed in the United States of America

Published simultaneously in Canada

March 1999

10 9 8 7 6 5 4 3 2
OPM

For Christine Zika,
who wanted a
Cinderella tale

Prologue

Kiltorren Castle, Ireland
April 1172

BURKE DE MONTVIEUX CRESTED A RISE, REINED IN HIS destrier, and stared at the scene spread before him. He had ridden hard for three days, pushing his steed to the limits of the beast's endurance, Brianna of Tully-mullagh's challenge in his ears.

'Twas true enough that Burke had not departed upon the bride quest Brianna had issued to the three brothers Fitzgavin with the enthusiasm the lady thought her command deserved. Nor had he brought her a gift that he truly believed would win her heart—because Burke had no desire for Brianna's affections.

For 'twas Alys of Kiltorren who haunted Burke's dreams.

Burke's guilty awareness of his unchivalrous behavior had taken him back to Tullymullagh, only to find Brianna happily wed to his elder brother, Luc. It had seemed to Burke that matters would end there, but Brianna was not so readily satis-fied with a mere apology—she not only demanded the truth, but insisted he set matters to rights.

Brianna had sent Burke upon his own bride quest, not only to seek the lady who still held his heart but to win her hand.

Now his objective lay before his very eyes and Burke's heart pounded in trepidation of what he might find. He paused and surveyed the estate he had not seen these two long years.

Castle Kiltorren clung to the craggy west coast of Ireland, its moss-encrusted stone walls rising from the rock as if they always had been thus. With the fey moodiness of early spring, clouds swept in from the west to blanket the sky in pearly silver as the air turned chill. The sun hung low over the horizon, an angry red glow that pierced the clouds and painted the sea with a ribbon of light.

It had been two years since Burke had last seen the squat tower of Kiltorren, three years since a maid's sparkling eyes had captivated his heart beneath that tower's shadow. Twice he had been here, twice he had found naught but heartache at Castle Kiltorren. A deluge of memories swept over him.

The summons to tournament could not have come at a better moment, for a decade beneath his father's command had left Burke prepared for a new challenge. He was in need of frivolity, yet he was not alone in answering the Lord of Kiltorren's call.

Burke was, however, alone in noting that lord's niece, Alys of Kiltorren.

The lord Cedric and his lady wife, Deirdre, were arrayed in their finest to meet the arriving party of knights, jewels flashing on every finger in the summer sunlight. The way they pushed their two daughters forward made their true objectives more than clear, although those two young women were scarcely worthy of note.

One had been spared no indulgence in her garb and was ornamented far beyond her family's station, her tiny eyes taking greedy note of the calibre of each knight's steed and entourage. The second seemed terrified to be singled out thus and spent the better part of the ceremonies staring at her hands.

But one lady was there, standing to the back of the party, not part of the servants yet not of the family proper. She stood with the dignity of a queen, her proud pose in marked contrast to the way the family ignored her very presence.

And once he drew near and looked upon her, the lady's gentle beauty snared Burke's interest fully. Her heart-shaped face was as sweet as that in any bard's tale, her full lips looked in dire need of a smile. The unadorned indigo of her fitted kirtle showed her slim curves to advantage, for she was as tall and slender as a keen blade. An errant curl of her wavy blond tresses had escaped her veil and danced against her cheek in the breeze, as if 'twould beckon to Burke.

But a single glimpse and Burke knew he must know more of this lady. Impatient with introductions, he nodded hastily to Lady Deirdre, her daughters Malvina and Brigid, then turned his finest smile upon Lord Cedric when that man appeared to have said all he intended.

"Is this lady also of your family?" Burke asked smoothly, and gestured to the beauty behind.

The lady in question flushed in a most beguiling way. Lady Deirdre's eyes flashed. Malvina—the spoiled one—grimaced.

"She is but a niece," he declared. "A mere ward of the family, devoid of dowry and unworthy of note."

Burke thought precisely the opposite and did not take pains to hide his conclusion. "Surely 'tis not too much to ask the honor of making her acquaintance?"

Lord Cedric scowled, then turned a fierce glare upon his niece. Her eyes widened slightly, and, too late, Burke saw that she would be the one to bear the burden of his curiosity.

Then she stepped forward and Burke cared for naught else.

"My niece," Lord Cedric supplied testily. "Alys of Kiltorren." His wife sniffed in ill-concealed disdain.

Clearly unused to such attention, Alys flushed and smiled when Burke kissed her knuckles. Her hand trembled slightly within his, and Burke resolved in that very moment to pursue this lady. He would know more of her, he would prompt her laughter, he would discover why her family thought her worthy only of disregard.

Burke sighed and rubbed a hand across his brow, wishing he had not been so young, so trusting, so certain that naught could stand between him and the course of love.

For he had sought Alys in every corner of the hall, each exchange convincing him yet further that she was a woman of merit. Burke had coaxed her laughter early and had felt a thrill of victory beyond that won on any field when her eyes sparkled at his jest. Those eyes were of the most wondrous shade, a marvelous golden brown flicked with specks of sunlight that seemed to dance when Alys laughed.

And her eyes had glowed when Burke had claimed his first kiss from his lady fair. But Alys had kissed the ardent knight back, and it took no more than that encouragement to see Burke smitten.

There had been more sweet kisses and more laughter, more stolen moments than Burke could name, each one putting him more securely beneath the lady's spell. For the first time in all his days, Burke had fallen in love.

And it seemed his regard was returned.

Until the day in the stables. Burke scowled at the distant keep, knowing he would never forget the fleeting moment that had changed all.

Burke found Alys in the stables that warm afternoon. 'Twas not by accident, for he had been seeking her, though he feigned that he but stumbled upon her. Alys, of course, saw through his ploy.

She was consigned to some ignoble labor, no doubt to keep her out of sight, but even in such circumstance, the lady shone like a jewel. She smiled at the sight of Burke but would hear naught of him taking the labor upon himself. Burke lingered; indeed, he could not tear himself away from her presence. Just the sight of Alys made Burke's heart pound, the barest glimpse of a smile made him long for another of her sweet kisses.

On this day Alys's hair was tied up and her kirtle worn thin. It gaped around the fullness of her breasts in a most intriguing way; her ankles flashed beneath the hem. 'Twas clear the gown was a remnant from years before the lady's figure bloomed to perfection. Burke hated that she must bear such indignity and knew there must be some way he could see matters set to rights.

When she made to heft a full bucket of slops, Burke could bear the injustice no longer. He strode to her side and swept the full bucket out of her grip. "Where do you take this?"

Alys's eyes widened. "Burke, you cannot! 'Tis unfitting!"

" 'Tis more unfitting that you perform such labor," he said grimly. "You have but to tell me where."

"But you are a guest!"

"And you are a lady." His determination must have shown, for Alys shook her head and smiled.

She folded her arms across her chest and regarded him, a teasing glint in those golden eyes. "You, sir, are most stubborn."

Burke grinned and put down the bucket, taking a step closer. The lady's eyes gleamed as she evidently guessed his intent, and she took a playful step back.

'Twas clear she had no objections, and Burke grinned as he easily backed her into the wooden wall of the stall. "And you, my lady fair, are most fetching." He lifted one hand to the soft curve of her jaw, but Alys laughed aloud.

"In this?" She gestured to her tattered kirtle and wrinkled her nose playfully, then laughed anew. "Burke, is it your wits you have lost or your sight?"

"It is my heart that I have lost," he confided, trapping Alys within the circle of his arms. 'Twas not the first time he had cornered her thus, and Burke saw anticipation light her eyes.

"Incorrigible," she charged, a dimple appearing in one cheek. Her eyes sparkled merrily and Burke could see the flutter of her heartbeat at her throat. He touched her creamy flesh with a fingertip, liking well how she caught her breath, and let it wander along the edge of the ill-fitting kirtle.

"Tempted," he acknowledged, and ran that fingertip across the ripe curve of her breast when it tried to escape her kirtle.

Alys gasped. Burke let his palm graze her nipple, and when she whispered his name, he could not resist her any longer.

Burke bent his head and captured the lady's lips beneath his own even as his hand slid beneath her gown to caress her bare breast. She surged against him, her hands slid into his hair, and Burke had caught her fully against him for the first time. She was all sweetness and softness, both strong and supple, and Burke wanted naught but to make this woman his own.

The recollection even now could make Burke's mouth go dry. He could taste Alys still, he could feel his heart hammering, he could smell the straw heated in a summer's sunlight. He could see the shine of wonder in Alys's marvelous eyes.

And he could feel the curve of her breast beneath his hand once more, the taut nipple jutting against his palm.

Yet that single sweet kiss had been their undoing. In that very moment, the stable door had been kicked open to hue and cry, lord and lady and half the household pouring in to demand an accounting. Burke closed his eyes against the recollection of their din. He hated the memory of his own failure to conjure some manner of suitable explanation.

He felt again his anguish when Alys flushed scarlet and—to Deirdre's muttered accusation "whore!"—fled the stables, clutching the front of her kirtle.

Little had Burke known that he would never see his Alys again.

Aye, he had tried to pursue her, but without success, for the family had barricaded him in that stall. Burke scowled with recollection. It had been nigh half a day before he broke free of their incessant questions, and that only because he roared he would wed the woman, if only to silence them.

His declaration had both silenced them and sent them away to consult among themselves. Alys, it seemed, was not interested in any such match, for the word came that evening that she would have none of his proposal. Indeed, 'twas said she refused even to see him again. Burke was sent from Kiltorren's gates, caught in an unfamiliar maelstrom of emotion.

An older knight had informed Burke he would grow to be glad that all had finished as it had. In his youth and uncertainty, Burke had dared to hope that Alys's choice might truly be for the best.

A mere year away from Castle Kiltorren had only proved the strength of Alys's grip upon Burke's heart. She haunted him, she occupied his dreams, he fancied he heard her laughter in the thousand murmurings of any crowded hall. Finally, Burke had returned to Kiltorren, newly determined to see the lady, either to destroy her hold over him or to hear rejection from her own lips.

But Lady Deirdre and Lord Cedric had confessed that Alys was gone, they knew not where. Burke's disappointment had nearly taken him to his knees, and he had left this place yet again with a heavy heart.

Now, as he eyed the village and the fields from the crest of the road, all those old feelings coursed through him. He noted that the holding had changed little, and certainly not for the better. Burke could not help but wonder whether all would be the same within its walls.

Could Alys have returned?

Could she yet be unwed?

Would a confession of love have earned a different response from Alys three years past? Brianna insisted 'twould make all the difference, her certainty giving Burke new determination to return and seek the truth from his lady fair.

Suddenly Burke heard the gatekeeper's cry of warning and realized that twilight fell across the land. His heart leapt and he gave Moonshadow his spurs, determined to pass beneath Kiltorren's gates before they closed for the night.

Indeed, the sun already dipped dangerously low.

Chapter One

GOOD EVENING, ALYS," GODFREY SAID AS ALYS passed beneath the shadow of Kiltorren's gates. She struggled to hurry, knowing that 'twas time to close the portal, but was unable to move very quickly with the sack of flour she carried.

The goats scurried around her ankles, bleating and nudging at her knees. Edana the goatgirl skipped past her, calling a greeting with typical cheer, shooing the goats that complained mightily about her haste through the gates.

Alys hoisted the flour higher despite the ache in her back, permitted herself one uncharitable thought about her aunt's incessant demands, then managed a smile for the kindly keeper.

"And a good evening to you, Godfrey."

That man's brow furrowed in concern as he eyed the sack. " 'Tis too much of a burden for you," he said, "and no labor for a lady born."

Alys put the sack down inside the gates and wiped her forehead. "Mercifully, the kitchen is not far from here." She summoned a brave smile. "I shall manage, Godfrey, as ever I do."

But the older man shook his head in disapproval. " 'Tis not right. Why, your grandsire must be rolling in his grave . . ."

Before Alys could warn the keeper of his impertinence, the thunder of hoofbeats rang in her ears. She turned in the same moment that Godfrey did, only to find a great black warhorse galloping toward the gate.

'Twas a destrier of flawless ebony with a mane of midnight silk, a proud beast of rare size.

Indeed, Alys had seen its like only once before.

"Hold!" the knight roared, riding closer. "Hold the gate!"

Alys's mouth went dry in recognition. She blinked, certain her eyes would prove her wrong, but the knight pulled his steed to a halt before the gates with a flair she well recalled. Every servant and peasant milling inside the gate halted to stare, Alys as good as invisible within their ranks in her simple garb.

The knight doffed his helmet and shook out his black hair as the steed stamped impatiently. Aye, Burke de Montvieux had returned to Kiltorren.

Alys's heart simply stopped. She stood as if struck to stone by his unexpected appearance.

For Burke was not only here, he was far more handsome than Alys remembered. The years had etched attractive silver threads at his temples. His jaw was square, his nose aquiline, his eyes that silvery blue that seemed to pierce straight through artifice.

There was a new terseness in the line of his firm lips, and his eyes narrowed in shrewd assessment of Godfrey. Burke's shoulders seemed even more broad, his physique more superbly muscled than the man who stubbornly occupied Alys's dreams. There was a sense of command about this knight that had not been there when last she saw him.

"I am Burke de Montvieux," he declared, the very sound of his voice setting Alys's heart to hammering. "And I ride on an urgent errand to Castle Kiltorren."

"Aye?" Godfrey stepped deliberately into the middle of the gateway and propped his hands on his hips. The stalwart gatekeeper was not a small man, and his disapproval was tangible. "And what might that be?"

"I come," Burke confessed in a low voice threaded with humor, "at the Princess Brianna's behest."

An uncharacteristic pang of jealousy shot through Alys, though she tried to stifle her response. She knew Burke was a man of charm, a knight well used to successfully courting the affections of noblewomen. She should not be surprised that he served the will of a legendary beauty.

"Aye?" Godfrey demanded in a most unwelcoming manner.

"Aye." Burke grinned outright and arched one dark brow. "I come to Kiltorren in search of a bride."

Alys gasped aloud. Surely it could not be so! The small sound she made was all that was needed to draw Burke's eyes her way.

The knight caught his breath in a most satisfactory way. Alys thrilled to see recognition light his eyes even as Godfrey dispatched a runner to the keep.

"Alys!" Burke murmured, and swung from his saddle with an enthusiasm that could not be denied. " 'Tis truly you!" His eyes glowed with a heat Alys well recalled, a warm smile curved his lips. "I cannot believe this good fortune!"

Burke closed the distance between them with a few long strides. He captured Alys's hand and pressed a gallant kiss upon her knuckles with an intensity that fairly melted her knees.

Just like Heloise's favored tale, her hero cared naught for her humble circumstance. Burke had not abandoned her, he had not left her shamed as Aunt maintained.

"Good day, Burke," Alys whispered, unable to find any more fitting greeting. Her pulse fluttered and she felt herself flush beneath his perusal. Burke doffed his gloves and lifted one strong hand to her cheek, the warmth of his fingers making Alys tingle in recollection of his tenderness. His gaze seemed to devour the sight of her, and she chided herself for ever doubting his intent.

Burke bent his head, clearly intending to kiss her in a

most suitable manner, and Alys rose to her toes to meet him midway.

"It seemed too much to hope that you might be here as well," he murmured, his breath warm on her lips.

"As well?" Alys asked, startled.

Burke smiled down at her with the confidence she well recalled. "As well as your cousins. I *knew* they would yet be unwed." He winked but Alys drew back.

"You did not expect me to be at Kiltorren, yet still you came here for a bride?"

"Aye, I was quite certain you would be gone." Burke's smile did not waver. "Indeed, 'tis most wondrously convenient."

Convenience did not fit with the romantic tale as Alys knew it.

Indeed, the pieces fell into place with alarming speed. Burke came to Kiltorren for a bride, convinced that she would not be here.

Which could only mean that Alys was not a candidate for that position. Just as Aunt had long insisted, just as Alys had feared, this knight found her a fitting mistress but not a fitting bride.

"You shameless cur!" Alys slapped Burke's handsome visage as hard as she could, then spun away, cursing her own foolish hope and blinking back her tears.

"Alys!" Burke shouted, but she would not listen to anything he might have to say.

Indeed, she fairly tripped over her skirts in her haste to retreat. Alys snatched up her basket, strode a distance away, then spun to shake her finger at the astonished knight.

"Do not even think of laying your hand upon me again!"

No doubt he would have rolled her to her back three years past without a qualm if they had not been interrupted, and now he only savored the *convenience* of having her available while he courted her cousin.

Oh, she could just spit.

Burke halted, looking like a man who faced an incomprehensible foe, and Godfrey watched them both with narrowed eyes. "Alys, what is this? But a moment past, you were prepared to welcome my embrace."

"But a moment past, I misunderstood the fullness of your intent!" Alys retorted, the heat rising in her words. Indeed, her cheeks must be burning crimson they were so hot. "You may have forgotten what passed between us—"

"Alys," Burke interrupted, his words low and beguiling. "I forget *naught* of you."

The intimacy of his tone stopped Alys's tirade cold. She swallowed and stared back at him. The sensuous gleam in Burke's eyes made her flush spread to her toes.

Instinctively she wanted to trust him, even knowing what trouble he had caused her in the past. Alys's resolve wavered dangerously as Burke took a step closer; her heart pounded.

"Indeed, my lady," he continued smoothly, his gaze filling with affection, " 'tis the prospect of your smile alone that brings me back to these gates."

That fulsome lie broke the spell.

"Oh!" You *lie*! You just declared you did not even expect to find me here!" Alys danced backward, infuriated at herself for even thinking of believing in him again.

Burke's smile faded with a nearly audible snap. He frowned, looking suddenly boyish. " 'Tis true, I *knew* you would not be at Kiltorren . . ."

Alys propped her hands on her hips, letting challenge filter into her tone. "Then what is this nonsense of my smile?"

Burke stepped closer, his eyes gleaming. "I fully intended to seek you out, Alys."

"*After* you wed one of my cousins?" she asked, still stung by his claim that he came in search of a bride. "Or perhaps during your engagement? How very gallant!"

Burke's eyes flashed silver. "Alys, that is not what I meant.

You misunderstand me!" He shoved a hand through his hair and glared at their very interested audience. He leaned closer and dropped his voice. "Alys, we must have a moment alone . . ."

"You will have no moment alone with me, of that you may be certain." Alys took a backward step, wanting only to put distance between them. How many times did this man have to disappoint her for her to realize that he was *not* the knight of her dreams?

Burke visibly gritted his teeth. "Alys, the truth has gone astray in this. We must have a moment . . ."

But Burke would have no opportunity to finish his plea, for the family entourage spilled suddenly out of the keep. Aunt's voice carried all the way to their ears, the shrillness of her tones making the goats scatter into the far corners of the bailey.

"Burke de Montvieux!" Lady Deirdre cried. "It truly is you! Hasten yourself, girls, hasten. 'Tis Burke, the most eligible knight ever to have crossed our threshold!"

Alys turned in time to note her aunt snapping her fingers at her eldest daughter. "Malvina! Straighten your circlet. And square your shoulders!"

Malvina did as she was bidden, her greedy eyes shining at the sight of the new arrival. "Burke!" she crowed, nearly stumbling over her rich skirts in her haste to reach the knight's side. "Is it true you have come for a bride?"

'Twas evident enough who Malvina thought that bride should be.

But then Malvina believed that all the goods of this world should rightly be her own. Typically, Alys's cousin dressed in garb far too ornate for a simple day, her jewels sparkling, her cloak fur-trimmed. Alys noted that Malvina had already begun to test the strength of the new garment's seams.

Aye, she knew well enough who would have to mend the garment. Again. 'Twas not in Malvina's nature to deny herself any treat—nor that of her parents to deny their eldest any trinket.

"My boy, I knew you would return for one of my beloved and beauteous daughters!" roared Alys's uncle, Cedric of Kiltorren. His bulk slowed him slightly in the procession, and his hasty breathing became audible as he drew near.

The gleam in Cedric's eyes was unmistakable. Alys shook her head, knowing that her uncle had spied another gift fitting for his beloved daughter.

Indeed, she almost felt sorry for Burke.

But mostly she felt ill. Oh, she should have had the wits to know better than to believe a romantic tale had come to life! Burke was not the noble Aucassin of Heloise's tales—he was but a man, interested in his own satisfaction. Though she had once nearly succumbed to his charm, she would not repeat the error.

"Your bride arrives," she informed Burke coldly. "I would not deign to keep you." And Alys lifted her chin and swept away as regally as she could, despite her tattered garb and the weight of flour on her hip.

"Alys! Do not leave!"

Alys frowned and hefted her burden higher, deliberately ignoring the knight. She ducked through the swirl of fine wool and trailing hems edged in fur that already closed around the arrival, without any of her family noting her passing.

But Burke called out. "Alys! Halt!"

Despite herself, Alys found her heart give a little skip of pleasure that he noticed her departure.

Then she called herself seven kinds of fool and continued without stopping.

After all, *this* was the knight to whom she had nearly surrendered her maidenhead. *This* was the man who had whispered sweet tales in her ear. *This* was the man who compromised Alys in her aunt's eye, then rode away untroubled by what he had done.

And left Alys to bear the brunt of Aunt's wrath for three years.

That was not chivalrous in the least.

'Twas no consolation that the sweet heat of Burke's last kiss had never faded from Alys's thoughts. Oh, she was once a fool for loving him, twice a fool for submitting to his kiss, and thrice a fool *still* to be yearning for him. She was supposed to be older and wiser, to know better than to trust a man's beguiling kisses and sweet pledges.

Had she learned naught? Alys stormed across the bailey, as disgusted with herself as with the new arrival.

"Alys! I would speak with you!" Burke roared. Alys flicked a glance over her shoulder to note how he tried to ease his way free of the throng that had surrounded him, but without success. Burke raised a hand to beckon to her.

And Alys enjoyed turning her back upon his summons, striding to the kitchen, her chin held high.

Convenient. Alys growled the word beneath her breath, even as tears blurred her vision. 'Twould be a cold day in hell that she was fool enough to spend a private moment in Burke de Montvieux's company again.

***

'Twas clear to Burke that something had gone awry, for his sweet Alys was angry with him.

Indeed, his jaw stung with the weight of her conviction.

And where had she conceived of the idea that he meant to court her cousins? Did she imagine that her spurning of his proposal had driven him to that? Burke could not imagine that any setback could force him to such extremes, though the very evidence of her fury convinced him that Alys was not without regard for him.

Nay, she still loved him, or else she would not have cared who he wed. 'Twould take but a moment to explain the truth to her and have her tipping her face up for his kiss once more.

Burke could not wait to do precisely that.

But now he was cornered. Deirdre had effectively trapped

him against the gates, and Burke recalled how he disliked this woman and her manipulative ways.

He glanced in the direction Alys had fled, only now seeing the import of her clothing. She had been attired in a kirtle so worn 'twas nearly rags held together by will alone. Indeed, it seemed her status in this household had only worsened in his absence.

It angered Burke that Alys's family would treat her with such disregard. He forced himself to mind his manners, knowing that churlishness of any kind would only hinder his quest for Alys's hand.

"Lord Kiltorren." Burke acknowledged the man with a slight bow.

"Welcome, Burke de Montvieux! Welcome to our abode." Cedric gestured to the three women clustered around him. "You do recall my family?"

"How could I forget?" Burke bent low over Deirdre's hand and kissed her knuckles, letting them make what they would of his dry comment. "A pleasure, Lady Kiltorren."

Deirdre sighed audibly, cast a significant glance at her spouse, then dug her elbow into Malvina's ribs. The girl, no more attractive than she had been before and considerably more rotund, stepped forward and grinned. What could be discerned of Malvina's hair was as fiery an orange as a sunset, her complexion as pale as milk.

'Twas not her figure, nor even the fact that she shared her father's startlingly vivid coloring, that Burke found offensive. 'Twas the clear evidence of Malvina's greed. Her gaze ran over Burke's steed and his garb as if she would assess its value on the spot.

"Sir, you must recall our charming daughter Malvina." Deirdre pushed her daughter forward.

Mother and daughter together did not look in the least like blood relations. Malvina was so pale and plump, while

Deirdre was dark and thin. The older woman was constantly in motion, and one had a sense that she grasped at all within reach.

That, at least, they had in common.

"Of course," Burke murmured, then bent over Malvina's heavily beringed hand.

"And Brigid." Deirdre almost forcibly hauled her younger daughter forward. The girl blushed scarlet and stared stubbornly at her toes, her attempts to ease backward earning her a sharp smack.

He felt sorry for the child, who clearly would have preferred to miss this introduction. Brigid was far prettier than her elder sister, though she could not hold a candle to Alys's beauty. The freckles upon her nose made her look young, and the end of her braid was a darker auburn than her sister's.

Brigid's eyes were wide, her stare not unlike the trusting glance of a steed. She was clearly not possessed of Alys's keen wits nor indeed that lady's spirit, Burke guessed. Likely this youngest was oft trampled by her mother. Young Brigid did not appear to have any confidence in either her appearance or herself.

'Twas no wonder. Burke decided to redress that imbalance and salvage something of merit from this ordeal.

"Fair Brigid, how enchanting to meet you again," he said as he bent over her hand. "Your beauty has only blossomed in the years since last we met."

He heard Brigid inhale, but noted that her face turned yet more crimson.

When he looked up, Cedric was rubbing his plump hands together gleefully. "Is it true, then, what the runner declared? Have you come to Kiltorren for a bride?"

Deirdre urged her daughters forward and smiled hungrily.

Burke smiled. "Aye, I ride at the command of Princess Brianna of Tullymullagh, who bade me seek a bride."

Cedric coughed awkwardly into his hand. "And have you a particular maiden already in mind, sir?"

Burke slanted a glance to the older man, instinctively guessing that a declaration of his suit for Alys would be poorly timed. "Aye, I do, but with your leave, I would keep my own counsel for the moment." And Burke spared the lord his finest smile.

Of course he was misinterpreted, which was precisely what Burke had planned.

"Ah!" Cedric declared with a wink. "The boy would confirm his recollection before declaring his suit! No harm in that, no harm at all. Come, come, you must stay within the keep proper. Godfrey! Find someone to tend our guest's steed!"

"Aye, my lord." Godfrey cranked down the gate, whistling for a stablehand as he did so. Darkness seemed to have descended quickly while they talked, for the night had fallen like a curtain around them. The light spilled from the hall portal like a beacon.

"With your grace, I shall go to the stables myself. I fear Moonshadow can be skittish at times."

"Good, good." Cedric's voice boomed. "Then perhaps you might join us for a late repast?"

"We should all dearly love to hear of your grand adventures these past years," Deirdre added.

"No less the tournaments you have won," Malvina said. Brigid flicked a glance to Burke, then studied her hands once more.

Burke almost agreed to the meal, seeing no way clear of that obligation, when a wicked thought came to him. He wanted, after all, to have an audience with a woman deemed no better than a servant.

Which meant he should require a servant's assistance.

And there was one matter requiring aid that would fit

Burke's agenda perfectly. It could be no coincidence that 'twould be a reasonable request at this point.

Burke scanned his mud-spattered chausses and creased tabard with apparent ruefulness, then met his host's regard. "I fear that I am in no condition to come to the board, Lord Cedric. Indeed, I have ridden hard these three days and nights to reach Kiltorren."

"In haste for a bride," Deirdre breathed, her eyes gleaming.

Cedric snapped his fingers. "We shall summon you a bath while you see to your steed. 'Twill all be ready when you return to the hall. And still there will be plenty of time for our repast."

"A fine idea," Burke declared. "However, I have one concern."

"What is it?"

"You may have anything in our power to give," Deirdre declared.

"Your wish," Malvina contributed huskily, "is our command."

No doubt the girl thought her expression beguiling. Burke would not be the one to tell her otherwise. He cleared his throat and looked back to Cedric. "I lost my squire last year and have not yet had the heart to replace him. Is there someone in your household who might aid me with my hauberk?"

"The ostler is able," Cedric declared heartily, but Deirdre jabbed her elbow into his side. He looked at her, clearly startled, but she smiled for Burke.

"Husband dear, 'twould hardly be fitting for one of common birth to aid a knight as esteemed as our guest." Her smile broadened in that predatory way Burke already knew to beware. "Sadly, sir, there are none of noble lineage in our keep save ourselves." She stepped back with a grand gesture that encompassed her children. "Either of my daughters would be pleased to aid you."

"Mother!" Malvina protested immediately.

Brigid looked as if she might faint.

And Burke was not so much of a fool that he did not see Deirdre's true intent. She should never have suggested that a maiden of the house aid a knight in his bath, but clearly desperation had driven her to extremes.

Aye, if he accepted this offer, Deirdre would claim whichever daughter he chose had been compromised by being alone in the bath with him, thereby forcing Burke's hand.

Burke did not intend to play that game.

And he truly did not wish to have *Deirdre's* aid in his bath.

"Dear lady, your offer is most generous," he said smoothly. "However, I would not risk sullying the reputation of either of these maidens, nor would I expect you to lend your hand to such menial labor." He forced his voice to remain level, even as he hastened to make his suggestion. "Was that not your niece here at the gates just moments past?"

Deirdre's smile reappeared. "Perfect!" she declared, then nodded to Burke. "She is just the one to aid you. It shall be done."

With no concern for Alys's honor at all. Burke instinctively knew they would not consider Alys compromised for having aided him in the bath. He gritted his teeth and hoped none could tell.

Deirdre curtsied low, then glared at her daughters when they did not immediately follow in kind. Two clumsy curtseys were executed, then Deirdre grabbed her daughters by the elbows and marched them back to the hall. Her tirade of admonition was too low for Burke to hear the words, but he could well guess the content.

"Women," Cedric mused, then beamed at Burke. "Marvelous creatures, are they not?"

Some are, Burke thought, and with that he headed off to the stables.

Chapter Two

LYS'S ANGER DESERTED HER AS QUICKLY AS IT HAD arisen, leaving her feeling like a naive fool. She, of all people, should have known the price of believing a man's sweet lies, for she lived it every day. She swept the kitchen floor and fought against the weight of her disappointment.

Aunt Deirdre, of course, was quick to gloat.

"Alys!" Aunt's shrill call echoed through the kitchen, setting each and every servant there to grimacing. Even the goats bleating in the bailey fell silent momentarily.

"Have you heard the news?" Aunt asked none in particular. "Burke de Montvieux has come to choose between my daughters for his bride." She smiled. "Clearly he is a knight of discerning eye."

Or he has lost his eyesight completely, Alys thought.

"How may we aid you, my lady?" Cook asked politely.

" 'Tis my niece I would summon." Aunt's smile turned cold as she surveyed Alys. "Our guest knight would bathe. Naturally, a man of such nobility could not be aided by one of common lineage, and he has no squire with him." A smirk tugged at the older woman's lips as she surveyed Alys. "He has requested *your* aid."

"Mine?" Alys blinked, but Aunt merely smiled more broadly. Alys heard Cook catch his breath and Edana gasp, even as she stepped forward to argue. "But, Aunt, I cannot aid a knight at his bath! 'Twould be completely inappropriate!"

But her aunt looked untroubled. "Should it be any consolation to you, Burke showed tremendous concern when Malvina impulsively offered to aid him." Aunt dispatched a smile around the room, no doubt granting Alys time to accustom herself to this new and unwelcome task. "He was most chivalrous in expressing concern for her maidenly modesty, no less for her reputation. Indeed, I believe he fancies her."

Then Aunt's gaze locked with Alys's own. " 'Tis telling that he recalled you only when I confessed our lack of servants with noble blood. Then he *specifically* requested your aid."

Alys was startled that Burke should treat her so shamelessly, but Aunt ignored her and spun to leave, her kirtle flaring out behind her. She paused on the threshold and glanced back, her eyes glittering.

"Perhaps the man has need of more than a bath," Lady Kiltorren declared. " 'Tis clear enough that he knows how to have his needs satisfied discreetly, no less who should fulfill them."

Aunt would not, Alys told herself. She *could* not.

But Aunt did. Worse, she punctuated her demand with a piercing look to her niece. "I told you before, Alys, that what was bred in the bone would out in the flesh, and here you have the proof of it. The daughter of a whore should ply her mother's trade without undue difficulty. See that our esteemed guest is not disappointed, Alys, or I shall be very *disappointed* in you."

With that, Aunt was gone.

Alys's mouth worked in silence for a moment, so great was her anger. 'Twas one matter that Burke desired her, yet quite another that her guardian would endorse his lust!

"I will not do it!" she cried.

The silence in the kitchen was deafening, then Cook began

to dice parsley with a vengeance. He was a tall and muscular man, as bald as an egg. "Nay? Then what will you do?"

His question made Alys pause to think. To defy Aunt was not without consequence, and she cursed Burke thoroughly for putting her in such a quandary. Alys hauled buckets from the corner, filling them before she could change her mind.

"I shall do Aunt's bidding and give this knight the bath he demands, no more and no less." Alys splashed water on the floor in her annoyance, but she did not care. "I will not roll to my back for any man before I am wed, be he knight or knave!

"Burke de Montvieux will have neither what he expects nor even what he wants of me." Alys ladled water grimly. "Indeed, 'tis time the man knew exactly what I think of his deeds," she declared as the staff in the Kiltorren's kitchen cheered.

The bathing chamber was a warm room, situated as it was behind the bread ovens set in one wall of the kitchen. Those ovens seemed to radiate heat long after the bread was finished baking, and Alys had always thought her grandfather's design most clever. 'Twas not unpleasant that the room always smelled of fresh bread.

There were no windows in the bath chamber and the ceiling was low. A pair of wooden tubs deep enough for a man to immerse himself to the shoulders stood in the middle of the stone floor. The room had need of a good sweep, for it was seldom used in these days since her aunt and cousins had taken to bathing in their rooms. Alys filled the tub with hot water, then set to work as it steamed.

'Twas true that few knights visited Kiltorren, though *no* knight had ever come this way without a squire. That was a scheme of Burke's, Alys knew it well. No knight, especially one of Burke's wealth and success, rode without a squire, if not several. The man meant to seduce Alys fully, and that before he took his bride. Perhaps he would even expect her to continue providing his pleasure afterward. No doubt Burke had abandoned his entourage in the last village.

Alys swept and fumed at this knight's cavalier disregard. She had been sorely deceived by this man's charming manners and smooth persuasiveness before, but his deeds told of his true intent. Burke was not the knight of her dreams and Alys would not surrender to his touch.

'Twould be best to make that inarguably clear.

Alys halted and smiled at a sudden wicked thought. She could ensure that this bold knight was at her mercy, a most tempting prospect indeed. That would turn the tables upon him, for Burke was always one to hold a situation in the palm of his hand.

Aye, then when she had her say, Burke would have no choice but to listen. Alys chuckled under her breath at the tempting prospect, pivoted to sweep the last corner, and froze.

For the knight in question leaned in the doorway.

And Alys's resistance to him began to crumble the moment she met his silvery gaze.

This was no good sign.

Burke's arms were folded across his chest, a wry smile twisted his lips, and he was watching her with that intensity that made her tingle from head to toe.

"Ah, Alys," he murmured, the very sound of his voice prompting her heart to race. "How can you be even more fair than I remembered?"

The words brought Alys back to her senses as naught else could have done. His compliment could have been paid to any maid, and, indeed, Burke uttered it so smoothly that she had no doubt he was confident of its success. She would show this man the value of his charm!

But she would have him where she wanted him first.

Alys smiled with all the sweetness she could muster. "I

must get more water," she said with a softness she was far from feeling. "Perhaps you might begin to disrobe?"

Burke flashed a smile and then caught her arm with gentle fingertips. His touch launched a shiver across Alys's flesh. She caught her breath yet she could not pull away.

Indeed, his gaze seemed more piercing when they stood so close. Alys's mouth went dry.

"Alys," he whispered. "Would you be so kind as to bolt the door on your return? I would not have us interrupted."

While he claimed what he desired of her. The request was yet more evidence that she had read his thoughts in truth. Heloise had oft said that it was the mark of a woman of sense never to make the same mistake twice. She would heed that advice on this day.

Alys stubbornly kept her smile in place. " 'Twas my thought exactly," she managed to say. Burke might have pulled her closer, his gaze falling pointedly to her lips, but Alys hauled her arm from his grasp. She hastened to the kitchen, knowing he watched her retreat, but did not look back.

Her heart was hammering and her hands were shaking, though Alys could not say whether 'twas because of the warmth of Burke's touch or the boldness of what she meant to do.

She certainly would not admit that she had hoped for three long and lonely years that matters had been otherwise than they had seemed, that Burke had had good reason to abandon her, that Aunt had been wrong and that Burke would return.

Aye, her knight in shining armor would still come one day to Kiltorren, but Burke was clearly not that anxiously awaited man.

'Twas better to know the truth, even if it did sting.

❖

Burke frowned, uncertain what to make of Alys's manner. She was no longer angered with him, yet she had ducked the kiss she must have known he intended to share. There were shadows lurking in the golden depths of her eyes, and Burke had an unwelcome sensation that he was responsible for their presence.

'Twas confusion at root, no more than that. He had done naught to insult or hurt Alys, and she soon would know the truth of it. Burke's lips curved in a smile of anticipation as he imagined the kiss they would share then.

Indeed, should his fortune hold, he and Alys might have all resolved between them before leaving this chamber. Burke could announce their betrothal at the evening repast and they could leave Kiltorren at first light.

'Twould be perfect.

Burke whistled to himself as he unbuckled his belt and laid his scabbard aside. He doffed his tabard, flexing his shoulders beneath the weight of his mail. Contrary to his earlier comment, Burke had no intention of burdening Alys with the task of removing his hauberk. The chain mail was simply too heavy.

And, ye gods, the woman had worked hard enough in Kiltorren, by the look of it. Burke doffed his boots, knowing he could shed the mail on his own. He had done it oft enough in the past year.

Burke pulled the hauberk up to his underarms, working it free of the padded aketon he wore between mail and chemise, then bent over, almost grasping his own ankles. He wriggled his shoulders and the hem of the hauberk slipped over his neck, the hard mail rings landing against the back of his head. Burke rolled his eyes at the indignity of it all, glad 'twould shortly be done. He gave his shoulders a shake.

And naught happened.

His mail was caught on the aketon.

Burke muttered a curse and stood up, quickly discovering that the hauberk was not prepared to fall back into place either. It was fairly wrapped around his neck, snagged on that cursed aketon, and hanging over his head like a monk's snood. Burke could not even put his arms down; his elbows were trapped around his ears. He bent over with a growl and set to some serious squirming, determined to work his way free in short order.

'Twas thus, of course, that Alys found him. He knew 'twas her by her surprised laughter. Indeed, Burke had always striven to make the lady laugh, but not at his own expense!

" 'Tis hardly amusing from this perspective," he said with a growl.

"Oh, I might argue that," Alys said easily. " 'Tis not often you are found at disadvantage."

The thread of humor lingering in her tone rankled. "And what does that mean?"

"Only that you are a man who sees his own desire fulfilled, if naught else."

Burke did not know what to make of that comment. He heard the bolt slide home and was relieved to know that, at least, none other would see him in such ignoble circumstance. 'Twas not precisely the way he had hoped to meet his lady, but there was naught for it now.

"Alys, you have but to pull the mail free of the aketon to see it fall clear away."

There was a stillness in the chamber, as if she considered him. "And that would be . . . convenient?"

"Alys, this is no prank," Burke said sternly. He had little patience with her teasing in this moment. He wriggled with vigor, his teeth clenching when the cursed mail did not move. "Surely 'tis not too much to ask for a simple gesture of assistance in this . . ."

Alys crossed the room to stand before Burke, then moved no further, as if she wanted to ensure he could see that she did naught. He studied her through the tunnel of chain mail, and she returned his gaze evenly.

And she did not lift a hand. Indeed, Alys folded her arms deliberately across her chest, the move emphasizing the soft curves of her breasts.

"On the contrary, sir," she said solemnly, "it seems to me that you have no right to expect anything from me, after all you have done."

Burke blinked. "What nonsense is this?" He fidgeted but made no progress, his temper rising with the obstruction of both hauberk and maiden. "Alys, I have done naught amiss!"

Her eyes flashed golden. "Naught amiss? You abandon me in shame, you return to court my cousin, you expect me to submit to your touch immediately upon your arrival, and, failing *that*, you would ensure that my reputation is completely sullied!" She arched one fair brow. "Truly, if that is naught, I should hate to see what you consider to be a deed of merit."

Burke could not even think with the weight of the mail caught over his head. Indeed, Alys might have been speaking in tongues. He wriggled with new persistence and something tore. Certainly his temper was wearing thin.

A pox on this hauberk!

"Alys, you make no sense. 'Twas *you* who sent me from Kiltorren's gates, if you care to recall the truth of it."

"I? *You* left! And that with nary a word to me." Alys leaned closer, her eyes snapping. "And you can well imagine what my aunt made of that, after she found us with *your* hand on *my* breast!"

Burke exhaled in frustration, then fought to keep his tone even. "Alys, 'twas a misunderstanding . . ."

"Aye, 'twas that!" the lady declared. "For I believed you would treat me with honor."

"I did!" Burke cried. 'Twas she who had spurned his suit,

after all. "What else was a man of honor to do after all that occurred but depart?"

Alys gave a short hoot of laughter. "No man of honor would conduct himself as you have done."

Burke fixed his lady with a steely glare through the tunnel of his mail. 'Twas hardly a position in which a man could make a concerted appeal to a woman, but it seemed he had little choice. "Alys, I believed that there was tenderness between us, that my regard for you was returned in kind . . ."

"Aye!" Her eyes flashed like amber in the sun and she stepped closer, but only to shake a finger at him. "You desired me, 'twas clear, and I was fool enough to believe 'twas more than a mere rutting you desired!"

Rutting? He was no barnyard animal!

"What vulgar nonsense is this?" Burke bellowed, writhing with newfound vigor against the mail.

The aketon tore, the hauberk moved, and Burke shook it over his head with a snarl. It clattered to the floor just as Alys jumped away, and Burke gave the unworthy pile of metal a hearty kick.

Then he glared at the woman backing away from him and propped his hands on his hips.

'Twas time to have the truth of it.

"What is this nonsense you spout, Alys? 'Twas no rutting I desired of you, and you know it well."

"Hardly that!" the lady replied, her eyes snapping. "Even now you would try to compromise me while you court my cousins."

"I am not courting your cousins!"

"Nay? Then why did you return to Kiltorren?"

"For a bride, Alys, I told you well."

"And you also confessed that you did not expect me to be

here." Alys glared at him. "Which can only mean that my cousins are sole candidates for that role!"

"Nay, Alys, I came for *you*!" Before she could protest, Burke hastened to clarify. "I meant to find word of you and seek you out. I meant to make *you* my bride." He stepped closer, offering his hand to the wary damsel. "Alys, you know that I am a man of honor."

"Nay, I do not." Alys danced backward defiantly, her eyes snapping in a most intriguing way. "There was no honor in your pursuit of me three years past, and so there can be none now."

"No honor?" Burke shoved a hand through his hair. "What, then, of my offer for your hand? How is that a dishonor to you?"

"You made *no* offer for my hand!"

"I most certainly did!" Burke did not know how she could deny this simple fact. " 'Tis not a matter a man readily forgets."

But Alys was clearly unconvinced. She tossed her braid over her shoulder, lifted her chin, and eyed Burke so pertly that he longed to kiss her senseless. He certainly did not recall that she had fired his blood so thoroughly before.

"Perhaps you have confused your many courtships with those days at Kiltorren," she suggested with soft challenge. "I have no doubt you have found much success in noblewomen's chambers."

Burke shook a finger before her, not at all caring for the tone of this conversation. "There has only been *one* proposal to cross my lips, Alys, and only one that has been spurned."

"Aye?" She arched a brow. "And to whom did you propose?"

" 'Twas to you!" Burke bellowed.

Alys leaned closer and whispered the charge. "Liar!"

"I am no liar!" Burke roared, half believing that volume would make her listen. "I offered for your hand in good faith."

Alys was unpersuaded. "That cannot be true," she said crisply. "For surely I would have known of such an offer."

Burke was incredulous. "You did not hear of it?"

The lady shook her head. "Because there was none."

How could this be?

Burke lowered his voice in appeal, sensing that something was amiss. "But, Alys, I assure you that there was! I offered for you, I swear it. I grant you my word of honor."

Alys rolled her eyes but, before she could speak, Burke stepped forward and snatched her shoulders. She caught her breath and her eyes widened, as reassuring a sign of her awareness as could be. She was soft beneath his hands, her pulse fluttered at her throat, and the sweet scent of her skin inundated him.

Something had gone sorely awry and Burke meant to repair it.

And then he would have that kiss.

"I made that offer, just as surely as you spurned it," Burke insisted, willing Alys to believe him. "I pledged for your hand, I offered to wed you three years past." He felt a measure of his own hurt filter into his words. "Truly, Alys, I thought you would have the dignity at least to refuse me yourself."

Alys frowned and uncertainty filtered into her gaze. "But . . ."

Burke needed no more encouragement than that to press his appeal. He pulled her closer, noting how she leaned toward him, and sensed success in the wind. "Alys, I would see a return to that sweet afternoon. I would begin again . . ."

Alys's eyes flashed and she ducked from beneath his hands, quickly putting the steaming tub between them. "Aye! But you would fully make a whore of me this time!"

"What?!" Burke lunged after her, wanting to shake some sense into this infuriating woman his Alys had become. The lady suddenly scooped up one of the buckets she had brought.

The water within spilled slightly over one side at her hasty gesture.

" 'Tis icy cold, sir, and likely not the bath you desire," she warned with a surety of herself that Burke could not ever recall witnessing in her before. "Keep away from me or you shall wear its contents."

Burke folded his arms across his chest and surveyed this unexpectedly bold damsel. He had no doubt she would do as she threatened.

Truly his Alys had changed.

And truly she was much, much more interesting than the sweet maiden he recalled.

Ye gods, but Burke was glad he was right! 'Twould be a fine battle to win, for this Alys would kiss like a goddess once she knew he had done naught wrong. Their reconciliation would be well worth whatever price he paid.

But the issue remained—how could she not have known of his proposal? It made absolutely no sense . . .

Unless her family had lied to her.

Burke caught his breath in certainty that he had guessed the truth. Indeed, they did not treat Alys well in any other matter; why should this be different? If that were true, was it so very surprising that Alys had lost her faith in him?

Burke wished with sudden fervor that he had never been so trusting as to leave without hearing the lady's refusal fall from her own lips.

What other lies had been told of him and his deeds?

Burke propped his hands on his hips and leaned across the steaming tub to hold Alys's steady gaze. "I would know the fullness of the crimes for which you hold me accountable."

"You have forgotten them already?" Alys asked mildly.

Burke felt his lips thin. "It would seem that I am ignorant of them." He lifted a brow in turn. "Or, perhaps, *innocent* of them."

"Innocent," she echoed, and a playful smile unexpectedly curved her lips. "I hardly think that innocence would be one of your attributes, Burke."

Burke could not help but grin at the truth of that. "To be falsely charged is perhaps not quite the same as to be innocent," he conceded.

Alys chuckled as if she wished she could stop herself, then bit her lip. She sobered and eyed him with sudden solemnity. "You had best have your bath before it grows cold."

'Twas an abrupt change of topic, but Burke recognized the good sense of it. And he *was* in dire need of a bath. Perhaps that was what offended his lady.

Burke eyed Alys, not at all certain he could predict her response in these days. "And then you will tell me of this?"

Alys held his gaze. "No doubt I will tell you more than you have any desire to know."

Fair enough. Burke nodded approval, shed his torn aketon, then hauled his linen chemise over his head.

He flicked a glance to Alys who watched him warily, and his voice turned gruff. "Turn around. 'Tis not fitting for you to see a man fully."

Alys cast him a challenging glance. "I thought you had no care for my reputation."

"You thought wrong," Burke retorted.

"Then why request to have me here?" Alys set the bucket down with a thump and propped one hand upon her hip. " 'Tis no place for a maiden. How could you compromise me thus?"

"I would not compromise you!" Burke insisted. " 'Twas the only place I could think that we would be undisturbed and where none could hear our words." Alys's skepticism seemed unaffected by this claim, so Burke willed his determination to show. "Your honor is the concern of none beyond myself."

She seemed surprised by his vehemence and momentarily

at a loss for words. Burke felt more irritable than he could recall—'twas one matter for a man's deeds to be found wanting, quite another for the lady of his heart to judge him harshly when he had done naught amiss.

Burke frowned pointedly at the lady in question when he reached for the drawstring on his chausses. He was almost surprised when she did his bidding and turned away.

Burke dropped his chausses and climbed into the tub, soothed as the warm water closed over him. Indeed, 'twas enough to dismiss his foul mood and rekindle his usual optimism. He *would* persuade Alys of the truth, and then she would welcome his return with open arms.

Indeed, Burke had never failed at achieving any goal before, let alone one of such import. Why should his fortune change now? Once he knew the crimes for which she held him guilty and the lies she had been told, Burke could refute them with the truth.

'Twould be simple.

"Tell me, Alys," he invited gently. "Tell me what is amiss."

But the lady darted around the tub. She picked up all of Burke's garments, unbolted the door, and cast them out into the corridor with unrestrained glee. Burke watched Alys in astonishment, momentarily distracted by the way her faded blue dress clung to her curves and her bare feet flashed beneath the worn hem.

When she spun to face him, Burke was startled that the lady's eyes suddenly shone with mischief. Her expression put him so in mind of a younger Alys that he did not immediately understand what she had done. Indeed, that dimple fleetingly returned.

Then Alys shot the bolt home with a victorious gesture and Burke frowned.

Why had she cast out his clothes?

"And now," she declared triumphantly, "you are completely

at my mercy, sir." Before Burke could comprehend her actions Alys picked up a bucket of water once more. She advanced upon him with a determination that seemed a bad omen for his immediate future.

"What is this you do?" Burke demanded, half rising from the tub before he recalled her maidenly innocence.

And his own aroused state.

He sat down with a splash, his gaze falling on the flash of her feet beneath the hem of that cursedly short kirtle, and matters became worse. If only he had some garb! He felt his eyes widen as she hefted the bucket, her expression one of resolve.

Verily, he was trapped.

Something clearly had gone awry, but Burke did not know what. After all, 'twas not like *his* Alys to be so unpredictable.

But his Alys was locked away inside this intriguing stranger, this woman who defied and challenged him, and prompted his desire in ways that his maiden had not.

"Now, Burke de Montvieux," Alys confided with a little smile that made Burke's blood quicken despite his predicament, "I shall tell you precisely what you have done, no less what I think of your deeds."

And Burke realized that he had made a miscalculation, no less one that might prove most dire.

To Alys's surprise, she did not feel nearly as victorious as expected when she had Burke cornered. 'Twas just his infernal charm working upon her resolve, she knew it well.

And indeed, he did not even *look* cornered, which was most unsatisfactory.

For a fleeting moment, alarm had flashed in his eyes, then Burke settled back in the tub with an indulgent smile. The man looked supremely in control of the situation, even though he sat nude in a tub of water, devoid of garb and completely at her whim. He watched her carefully, though Alys imagined a dozen plans of action were already forming in his mind.

But she would not be deterred. Alys stepped closer. "Three years past, you kissed me in the stables."

Burke arched a dark brow and settled back into the tub, his eyes narrowing as he considered her. The water swirled about him, steam rising from the surface of the water. The sight of his broad, bare, and tanned shoulders did little to bolster Alys's resolve.

"Aye, that I did." The admission fell readily from Burke's lips. Indeed, he looked untroubled. "As I recall, you, my lady fair, did kiss me back."

Much to Alys's irritation, the knight looked bemused.

Burke leaned forward and braced his elbows on the rim of the tub, a devilish glint dancing in his eyes. "Indeed, if 'tis another kiss you desire, Alys, you have but to ask." He grinned and Alys's heart skipped a beat. " 'Twould be my pleasure."

"Your pleasure is precisely the issue between us!" Alys dropped the bucket to shake a finger at this suavely confident knight. "You took advantage of my innocence and my trust."

"You enjoyed those kisses as well, Alys."

Alys flushed at the truth of that. "But you took advantage of the fact that I knew naught of knights of your kind!"

Burke's eyes flashed and he leaned forward with new intensity. "My *kind*? Why does that not sound complimentary, Alys?"

Alys tipped up her chin proudly. "I refer to rogue knights, who take their pleasure and care naught for the consequences."

At that, Burke took umbrage. He straightened and his dark brows drew together. "I am no rogue knight!"

"Nay? Would you have halted with fondling my breast had we not been interrupted?" she demanded, hating the catch that appeared in her voice. "Or would you have had your way with me fully before you abandoned both me and Kiltorren?"

"Alys!" Burke's expression turned shocked, and Alys was glad she knew how readily he lied. "I never abandoned you . . ."

"Nay, you have returned to finish your seduction while you court my cousins." Burke caught his breath, but Alys could not halt now. "What of this demand that I service you in the bath? How can you imagine that the hall will not be full of tales as a result?"

"I care naught for servants' tales!"

"I *do*! Did it occur to you to consider my honor in this? I must live in this hall, I must survive beneath my aunt's thumb, and when she calls me 'whore,' I assure you 'tis not without consequence."

"Alys, I would never dishonor you."

"That seems an empty claim after you have done precisely that!" Alys dared to lean closer and dropped her voice to a determined undertone. "My aunt made much of my loose morals these three years, as any fool might imagine, and I have learned the price such a charge does bear. Do not imagine that I shall indulge your whim, for I know now the manner of man that you are."

"Do tell," Burke invited softly. He was dangerously still, his eyes glinting, and Alys knew the satisfaction of having captured his attention fully.

"Incorrigible, impossible, and not to be trusted," she declared, leaning ever closer to make her point. "And know, sir, that I shall *never* be fool enough to believe you, let alone cede to your touch, ever again!"

Burke's eyes flashed, but Alys did not note the warning before he had caught her about the waist. At his abrupt move, she lost her balance and tumbled against him. There was no time to fear she might fall, for Burke caught her protectively against his chest. Her hip was perched on the edge of the tub, Burke's arms were wrapped around her, her kirtle trailed into the bathwater.

And Alys could not look away from the resolve in Burke's gaze. Indeed, she could not seem to summon the strength to move, not even when he inclined his head, not even when his lips hovered a finger's breadth above her own.

Because she knew what he intended to do.

And despite all her fine words, Alys wanted naught more than that kiss.

Curse him.

"Have you had your say?" Burke murmured. Alys remained silent.

"Then I shall have mine," Burke declared with low resolve, his gaze unswerving. "You should know me well enough to know I can never resist a challenge. We shall touch again, my lady, and often. Upon that you have my solemn pledge."

Burke smiled, that slow crooked smile that had always stolen away Alys's breath.

Her breath did indeed abandon her, as if she knew naught of this man who held her in his possessive grip, as if she knew naught of the price of wanton urges. Her heart pounded in anticipation of his touch, and Alys hated herself for being her mother's daughter.

"You are, after all, my own lady fair," Burke continued so deliberately that Alys's mouth went dry. "I have won you before and I shall win you once again. And that, Alys, you may rely upon."

Alys had time to catch her breath and no more, before Burke's lips slanted purposefully across her own.

Chapter Three

BURKE'S KISS AWAKENED A DRAGON WITHIN ALYS THAT she would have preferred to leave slumbering until her dying day.

Indeed, his kiss was everything she remembered and more. Burke was gentle, as always he had been, his touch both strong and tender. He coaxed her response, the cursed knave, and made her want him with an unruly desire. That unwelcome desire gave credence to Aunt's tales of Alys's legacy from her mother, tales Alys would have liked to prove false.

To Alys's embarrassment, 'twas Burke who broke their embrace, Burke who lifted his head and stared into her eyes. "I beg your pardon for being so bold," he said softly, his thumb tracing a line along her rib. "But I could resist you no longer." He smiled warmly down at her. "Or perhaps I had to assure myself that the sweet maiden of my dreams yet existed."

As ever, his compliment recalled Alys to her senses.

"Rogue!" She swatted Burke's shoulder and bounded from the side of the tub, retreating a good half-dozen steps before she halted.

Oh, Alys would not think of how many women had heard the same fine words fall from this man's lips, she would not think of the ranks of willing maidens who had warmed his bed! And she would *not* join those women's numbers, however *convenient* this knight might consider that possibility to be.

Alys wrung out her kirtle and glared at the man responsible for her turmoil. "You are overly confident in your charms!"

Again that beguiling smile lurked on Burke's lips, and his eyes glowed as he surveyed her. "Truly, Alys, I have wanted another taste of your lips every day and night of these three years."

'Twas precisely the wrong lie to make, if Burke intended to placate her. "Aye?" Alys challenged. "Then 'tis most odd you never troubled to travel this way again!"

Burke frowned. "I do not understand."

"Nay! Nor did I!" she snapped. "You lied to me! You told me fine tales and, in the end, they meant *naught* at all! How could you simply leave?" She turned abruptly away, not wanting the knight to see the tears that had risen in her eyes.

"Alys, there must be some mistake," Burke insisted, the determination in his voice making her yearn to believe him once again. Oh, she was weak! "I came back—"

"There *is* no mistake!" Alys interrupted. She whirled to face him, letting her words fall in haste. "You departed immediately after we were caught in the stables and never turned back this way all these three years."

Burke shook his head like a great bear. "Alys, you have misjudged me and you must let me explain."

"Save your pretty words," Alys retorted, "for your deeds tell all that needs to be told."

Burke scowled and flung out his hands, his composure slipping once more. "Aye! That they do!"

"Aye!" Alys shouted at him. "And what were those deeds?"

"What indeed?" Burke roared in his turn. "I invite you to examine them!"

"You took advantage of my innocence, then abandoned me, compromised, within my guardian's household!"

"I did no such thing!" Burke shouted, then bounded to his feet. "I offered for your hand."

"Not to me."

"Nay, for you declined even to speak to me!"

Alys gasped that he should cling to this wild tale. "Nay, Burke, you made *no* such offer! You left immediately, I was told without even a backward glance!"

Burke jabbed his finger through the air. "And you never troubled to see the truth yourself! Ye gods, Alys, did it not mean enough to you to be *certain*?"

"Enough to *me*? I meant *naught* to you beyond the satisfaction of your lust."

"My lust is of no import in this!"

"Nay?" Alys pointed to the knight's erection. "But it attends nonetheless!" And with that, she scooped up the bucket of cold water at her feet and cast its contents directly over the knight.

Burke's mouth dropped open in shock, and he blanched.

And then he bellowed like an enraged bull.

"That is ENOUGH!" he thundered, and lunged for Alys.

Alys did not wait to see what Burke would do.

She ran.

She flung back the bolt, ripped open the door, then fled toward the many servants crowding the portal to the kitchen as the door slammed closed behind her.

Their eyes were round with curiosity and 'twas clear that some of the argument—or at least its volume—had been overheard. Edana stood with a bucket of creamy fresh milk, one hand covering her open mouth, her eyes wide.

"ALYS!"

Alys was halfway down the corridor when Burke kicked the bathing chamber door open. It crashed back against the wall and Alys could not help but look. Burke's eyes flashed, his jaw was set, and Alys could not keep her unruly gaze from slipping lower.

It seemed the cold water had had little effect. Her gaze fell to the muscled strength of his legs, then over the broad expanse of his chest, and Alys caught her breath.

God in heaven, but the man was alluring! Alys looked up in time to see Burke realize that he not only had an audience but that he was completely nude.

The anger faded immediately from his features and he rubbed his brow, a rueful smile curving his lips. Though he had bellowed fit to shake the foundations of the keep, his fury was gone as swiftly as the wind.

'Twas only now that Alys realized she had never seen Burke angered before. He was always the heart and soul of diplomacy, his manners impeccable, his even temper unassailable.

Yet she had made him yell.

Indeed, he had prompted her to shout back as she never did. Alys wondered at that, even as she felt a peculiar tingle of pleasure.

If naught else, she had his attention.

"Ye gods, Alys," Burke murmured intimately. "You do have a way of compelling me to forget myself."

Alys blushed scarlet to hear so close an echo of her own thoughts fall from this charming knave's lips. She had to fight her temptation to return his smile.

Burke—curse his perceptiveness!—clearly noted that she was not completely successful in doing that. Their gazes locked and held for a breathless moment, then the knight scooped up his discarded clothing. He paused on his return to the bathing chamber, his chemise held before himself.

"I would ask one favor of you, my lady fair," he said softly, continuing without granting Alys the chance to respond. "I have listened to your charges against me, have I not?"

"Aye," Alys conceded warily.

"Then 'tis only fitting you reciprocate and grant me the opportunity to defend myself." Burke lifted one brow, as if he sensed her desire to refuse him. " 'Twould only be fair."

What was not fair was the way Alys's heart began to pound at the prospect of spending time with this knight once more. She knew full well that she could not trust herself to resist any appeal he made, particularly if he punctuated his sweet tales with even sweeter kisses.

'Twas doubly unfair that his request was most reasonable.

Well aware of the servants clustered behind her, all avidly attending every word, Alys tossed her braid over her shoulder and struggled to look unaffected by Burke's appeal. "I have labor to perform," she declared archly, "and no time to indulge the whim of a visiting knight."

"A pox on your labor!" Burke retorted. "You must at least hear out my defense. You have but to name the place and I shall be there." His eyes narrowed. "Alys, I swear it to you."

His very intensity nearly made Alys agree, but she caught her words in time. "You are quick to make pledges this day," she charged instead.

And Burke smiled that slow sensuous smile, dissolving Alys's resistance yet further. "Yet I would willingly pledge more to share the honor of your company." He stepped forward, his charm resolutely in place despite his lack of garb. "Meet me, Alys," he requested earnestly. "Meet me and let there be truth between us."

Oh, Alys was tempted, but she forced herself to consider the facts. The truth simply could not show Burke to advantage. For if he had offered for her hand, why had she not known of it? Her aunt certainly would have welcomed an opportunity to be rid of her.

And similarly, Burke's tale of returning here could not be credited. Alys had never left Kiltorren in all her days; if Burke had ever ridden through those gates again, she scarcely could have missed that fact. How would he explain that to his own advantage, without concocting a lie?

Curse her curiosity! She would grant him naught!

"I cannot linger and listen to your tales when there is much to be done," she said haughtily, and turned to leave.

"Alys!" Burke cried, and she could not help but glance over her shoulder. "Have no doubt, my lady," he insisted, his voice so low that Alys had to strain to hear the words. "We *shall* speak of this again. All is far from resolved between us."

Alys lifted her chin, emboldened by the distance between them. "Nay, sir, 'tis not. Your apology is long overdue."

"Fear not, Alys, you shall have more than your due of me." Burke's grin flashed, his eyes darkening with intent. "I swear it to you, damsel of mine." Then he ducked back into the chamber, leaving Alys gasping.

She was *not* his damsel!

Nor would she ever be!

Alys willed her blush to fade as she drew near the crowd outside the kitchen.

Edana giggled. "Oh, Alys, to be the damsel of such a man!" She sighed and her cheeks pinkened with what must be wicked thoughts. She set down her bucket with a sigh of satisfaction. "How could you deny him *anything*?"

But before Alys could respond, her aunt's cry carried from above.

"Alys? ALYS? Do not imagine that I did not hear our guest!" The others shrank away from Alys, dread lighting their eyes. At the echo of advancing footfalls, the entire retinue in the corridor suddenly disappeared. "What have you done to anger that knight?"

Alys's heart sank to her toes and her mouth went dry. Indeed, Burke had made her forget herself in more ways than one.

※

Deirdre was not pleased and she did not care who knew it. She stormed down the corridor betwixt kitchen and bathing chamber, not surprised to find her niece awaiting her. The girl held herself proudly, but her eyes betrayed her fear.

Alys *should* be afraid, after what she had done.

Oh, it had been years since Deirdre struck this one, and 'twas not for lack of cause that she had abandoned her willow switch. Yet again Deirdre considered that what had happened that last time had been but a coincidence, not an ill omen, and that 'twas time she lifted the switch again.

She was sorely tempted to fetch it now, for this one had a talent for making Deirdre's most treasured plans go awry.

Alys backed into the wall but did not look apologetic in the least. "You called me?"

The cheek of the child was annoying beyond all. Deirdre strolled closer, still deciding how she would punish Alys. The girl had to learn that she was not in command of her own fate—and she certainly could not be permitted to mar the most promising opportunity to ride through Kiltorren's gates in years.

"I heard our guest," Deirdre said tightly. "He seemed *most* displeased. Did you fail to grant him satisfaction, Alys?" She deliberately let her voice drop. "Have you defied me *again*?"

Alys's rebellious manner only intensified, the flash in the girl's eyes doing little to improve Deirdre's mood. "I did not bed him and I will not bed him, regardless of what you and he think of the matter!"

"Fool!" Deirdre felt her lips thin. "Your impertinence could send him away! Do not imagine that I will suffer the loss of a bridegroom for Malvina, regardless of the price!"

"Malvina is welcome to Burke de Montvieux," Alys retorted.

Deirdre halted her advance to consider her ward, so surprised was she by this claim. She had always thought that Alys had an affection for this knight—no less than he had one for her.

"What is this?"

"I see no reason why my chastity should be sacrificed in pursuit of Malvina's match," Alys declared. "Burke and Malvina are welcome to each other—the matter has naught to do with me."

Except that an Alys compromised was an Alys unfit for nuptials for all time, a most tactically appealing proposition. Deirdre had suspected that a full sampling of Alys's charms might satisfy the knight's unwelcome interest in her ward.

But now Alys seemed to have changed her mind about their guest.

The unlikely sound of a man's whistling burst into the corridor in that moment. It carried quite distinctly from the bathing chamber. Deirdre's fury eased, for it seemed that all could not be completely lost if a man were cheerful enough to whistle.

Indeed, Burke de Montvieux could not be preparing to leave Kiltorren in displeasure. Deirdre studied her niece, considering that she might have been too quick to see two birds dead of one stone.

Perhaps the situation could yet be saved.

"If you will not satisfy Burke's lust," Deirdre declared quietly, "then you must *never* be found in his company. I will not have three virgins contesting for the man's attentions."

"I have no desire of Burke's attention!" Alys straightened with a nearly audible snap. "And I have already decided to avoid this visiting knight."

"Indeed?"

"Indeed." The girl's resolve could not be doubted.

Deirdre could not quell her smile. In this case, it seemed that absence had not made the heart grow fonder. Burke clearly had spurned Alys, and the way the girl took insult could be readily turned to advantage. Aye, Malvina would easily make a conquest of this man if Alys kept out of sight.

Deirdre fixed Alys with a glare and named her condition. "You will not be found in the company of this knight as long as he lingers at Kiltorren."

"I do not intend to seek him out," Alys replied haughtily. "Though I can hardly answer for whatever he might do."

"If he seeks you out, then you will leave his side," Deirdre insisted. "You will not share his company, under any terms."

Alys's chin lifted. "I have *no* desire to share his company."

'Twas not reassuring the way the girl's cheeks pinkened at this assertion, and Deirdre decided to leave naught to chance.

"You have defied my explicit order and you must pay a price," she informed her ward. "You shall labor all this night if necessary, ensuring every floor in this hall is spotless. When you are done, you will scrub the fireplaces until the stone looks newly fitted. And then you will cut and carry enough strewing herbs that every chamber smells of springtime."

'Twas an enormous task and Deirdre paused for a moment to watch her niece comprehend its scope. The girl's shoulders sagged minutely, then squared once more.

Oh, she would pay good coin to see this one surrender in defeat.

"Defiance is not welcome here, Alys, nor is it an attractive attribute in a young woman." Deirdre snarled. "Remember that your presence is tolerated in this household in these less than prosperous times only out of my keen sense of family duty. Am I understood?"

Alys's lips tightened. "Clearly."

"Then you had best be about your labor," Deirdre concluded as she pivoted to leave, "if you mean to sleep at all this night."

◈

Burke strolled into the great hall, well prepared to present his defense to Alys. She could not avoid him at the board, that much was certain. His gaze danced over the dais and he was disappointed, not by the paucity of the feast spread there but by the absence of a certain woman.

Malvina squealed and darted to his side, pressing herself against him in a bold manner and gazing up at him in admiration. "Oh, Burke, you look so fine this evening! Might I call you Burke? It seems so formal to use any other address." She batted her eyes, then dropped her voice low. "Or would it be forward of me to call you my lord?"

"Most forward," Burke retorted. "And most inappropriate. I should think your mother would have much to say about such familiarity upon our short acquaintance."

"Of course, of course!" Deirdre enthused, her smile giving Burke the sense that she would gobble him up alive, granted half the chance. "We must recall our manners, girls!" She pinched Brigid and that girl stepped forward, obviously intending to curtsey but falling over her full kirtle instead.

Burke gallantly caught her hands. Brigid straightened, looked at her hands upon his with terror, then pulled them away. She flushed crimson and stared at her toes.

"Did you injure yourself?" he asked. The girl said naught, though Burke waited politely. Brigid looked to her mother, whose lips thinned.

"Answer the man, child!"

Brigid swallowed and turned an appealing gaze on Burke. He smiled slightly, wanting only to reassure her. Her color rose and he shortly discerned the difficulty.

"N-n-n-nay." Brigid spit out the word finally, then squeezed her eyes shut in mortification and fled for the board.

Malvina grinned at her sister's departure, then sidled closer to Burke, her breast rubbing against his arm. Deirdre took note of Malvina's familiarity but did not chide her daughter. Cedric simply beamed.

They were without doubt a most curious family.

"She is an idiot," Malvina confided, nodding to her sister.

Burke flashed a cold glance downward at such uncharitableness. "She is charming."

Malvina's mouth gaped open and she scowled.

That would give her something to think about. Burke extricated himself from Malvina's clutch and bowed to his host and hostess. "I must thank you again for your hospitality."

Deirdre's lips thinned. "And I must apologize for your *difficulties* in the bathing chamber."

"I had no difficulties. All was most admirable."

Deirdre laid a hand on Burke's arm, leading him to the board. "You are too polite, sir. But in a keep of this modest size, a body cannot help hearing a man who is sorely vexed."

"I cannot think of what you mean," Burke commented, wondering how much of his argument with Alys this woman had overheard.

Deirdre laughed lightly. "Oh, you do not fool me, sir! I know that you found my niece most trying."

"On the contrary," Burke said smoothly. "I found her companionship most amusing." He cast a pointed glance over the small group. "Indeed, I had looked forward to enjoying her company this evening. When is she to join us?"

Behind him, Malvina hissed through her teeth. Deirdre inhaled sharply and looked as if she had just taken a sip of sour wine. "She will *not* be joining us."

"Whyever not?"

Deirdre's features sharpened. " 'Tis not her place in the hall."

Burke was not prepared to let the matter go so readily as that. "Indeed? Yet you yourself have confessed that she is the only other nobly born inhabitant in Kiltorren." He arched a brow in response to Deirdre's sharp glance. "Where I was raised, 'twould only be appropriate that she ate in the hall."

Deirdre's lips pinched so tightly that they nigh disappeared. "This is Ireland, sir, and our customs are markedly different from those in a French court."

"Aye, I can see as much." Before any could take insult, Burke turned his most charming smile upon his host. He had not donned his finest this night for naught—and he was not a man who readily abandoned his chosen course.

Burke would see Alys this evening.

"Surely 'twould be no trouble to indulge my custom in this?" he suggested. "I would imagine that all would enjoy Alys's company this night."

There was an awkward silence that made Burke suddenly fear that 'twas more than maidenly avoidance that kept Alys from the hall. "Is your niece ill?"

"Aye!" Deirdre smiled sunnily, a move obviously intended to cover a lie. "She lies ill with a catarrh." Malvina grimaced. "Indeed, we must leave her alone, lest one of us contract the illness. Come!" She waved Burke toward the board, Malvina scampering past to take her place. "Let us eat."

Burke did not move. "I had no idea a catarrh could attack a body so very quickly. Indeed, the lady seemed hale not long ago."

"Oh, Alys is prey to the slightest illness!" Deirdre laughed. "She is a most fragile creature."

"Yet it must have taken marked strength for a woman to haul that basket back to the kitchen this afternoon," Burke felt compelled to observe. "It seemed most heavy for a woman so slender."

"Oh! Alys lies about her health to avoid joining us," Malvina added. "And about her burdens as well. She would elicit sympathy from all."

"Indeed?"

"You must not be insulted!" Cedric declared. "Alys is tempestuous, there can be no doubt about it."

"Capricious." Deirdre rolled her eyes. "And unreliable."

"Vexing." Cedric winked.

"And quite decidedly lazy," Malvina concluded with satisfaction. "Why, just this morning, she positively dawdled over hauling the water for my bath."

Brigid frowned as she eyed her family. "B-b-but Alys is always nice t-t-to me," she argued. Her eyes were filled with an anguish that told Burke he was being deceived.

"Well, then," he said with a smile for the younger daughter of the house, "perhaps we two might persuade the lady to join us."

Brigid flushed again, even as her mother stepped between her and Burke. "That is not necessary," Deirdre argued with that cold smile. "I would not pamper the girl unnecessarily. She has been summoned to the board and if she chooses not to join us, then that is her choice. She craves attention, as you must have guessed, and I would give her no more than her measure."

'Twas lies, all lies, and Burke knew it well. Alys cared naught for attention—did she not stand back when her family openly ignored her? Though she might indeed be vexing to him, she was neither capricious nor lazy nor unreliable.

But before he could protest anew, Deirdre fixed him with a sharp glance. "Indeed, sir, I can only marvel at your persistent interest in my niece. I thought you welcomed our hospitality while you reacquainted yourself with our daughters."

"Alys was most angered earlier," Burke said, guessing the direction of his hostess's thoughts. " 'Tis only chivalrous to assure that I have not given insult to any maiden."

Deirdre snorted. "You have my assurance that Alys is not insulted, no less that she is scarcely a maiden fit for your attention. The tales I could tell you of her parentage . . ." She shook her head as if she could not bring herself to utter them, and Burke fought his anger at this injustice.

Deirdre smiled. "But enough of such sordid details. Here you have ridden to Kiltorren for a bride, and the only two eligible candidates await you."

"Aye, you cannot have already decided to seek your bride elsewhere!" Cedric boomed. He clapped one hand on Burke's shoulder. "Indeed, my boy, you have scarcely had the chance to note how my daughters have blossomed these past years. Come, come to the board!"

And Burke realized he had little choice in this matter. Deirdre was either too shrewd or too fixed on her own objectives to countenance his overt interest in Alys. If Burke were not to be ousted from Kiltorren before he managed to capture Alys's hand, he would have to make a good performance of courting Malvina.

'Twas a galling proposition but Burke summoned his best smile. Mercifully, the ends did justify the means.

"I can only accept your compelling assurance, my lady Deirdre." Burke bowed. "Indeed, I must thank you for setting my concerns at ease, that I might better enjoy your daughters' graces."

Malvina and Deirdre smiled of one accord, Brigid flushed yet again, and Cedric urged Burke to take the place between his two daughters. Burke sat down and Malvina promptly laid a hand upon his thigh. Indeed, he jumped at her unexpected familiarity.

"You must tell us," she urged, her breast pushing against his arm, "of all the bold adventures you have had since leaving our gates. How many tourneys have you won?"

Burke made to move the girl's hand but caught Deirdre's hawklike gaze. In the nick of time, he checked his impulse, closing his hand over Malvina's own and raising it gallantly to his lips.

"Your wish is indeed my command," he murmured, then set her hand firmly on the board. "I can only hope the tales do not disappoint, for you are surely a maiden of cultivated tastes." Malvina giggled and eased closer, her leg pressed against the length of his own.

Ye gods, but 'twould be a long evening.

Alys worked as she had never worked before. She scrubbed and she swept and she hauled water until she ached clear to her bones. And then she scrubbed some more. She cleaned ashes from the kitchen hearth and hauled bucket after bucket of soot out of the keep.

She avoided the hall with a vengeance, being certain she did not even glance toward the dais when she crept through the shadows to the stairs. Fortunately the torches were lit only near the dais, and she doubted that any noted her passing. Once in the solar above, she could hear a familiar rumble of masculine laughter carry from below, interspersed with Malvina's giggles.

It did not sound as if the man were *not* courting her cousin.

Alys gritted her teeth and cleaned both solar and smaller chambers with a savage thoroughness. Sweat trickled down her back and ashes stained her skin, the shadows of the night fell within the hall, but still she labored.

And still she strained her ears, unable to deny the temptation of listening for a certain knight's voice. Each time she heard Burke chuckle, she scrubbed harder.

He was clearly enjoying Malvina's company this night, she thought waspishly, and showing no disappointment in her absence. Not courting Malvina, indeed. The man bent the truth to his own advantage, that much was clear. Alys swore softly and cleaned.

But no matter how hard she toiled, Alys could not drive Burke de Montvieux from her thoughts. Not his touch, not his voice, not his charm, not the gleam in his silver-blue eyes when he so readily granted her his word.

Even though 'twas a lie.

Alys knew 'twas her own weakness for this knight at root. After all, she *knew* that a man's touch could lead only to downfall, she *knew* more than enough about the legacy of being a whore's bastard daughter, she *knew* that Burke himself had sorely disappointed her once before and undoubtedly tried to do so again.

Yet when Burke fixed his intent gaze upon her—or worse, touched her—she simply forgot. 'Twas madness to let a man so muddle her thoughts, but even the awareness of that did naught to diminish the power of Burke's allure.

Nor did it temper her burgeoning curiosity.

For Alys could not keep herself from wondering what tale this man would tell, if given the chance. Was it possible that there was another explanation for Burke's long-ago departure?

Would he tell a lie, designed to ease between her thighs and no more? Or could there be some angle of the truth that Alys did not know? The possibility that Burke might be innocent of the crimes she laid at his door tormented Alys throughout that night.

And 'twas not only because she prided herself on being fair.

Then the good chance that she was an idealistic fool tormented her yet more. Truly, she had listened too intently to Heloise's tales all these years!

And she had promised Aunt, after all. Alys returned to the kitchen with her army of buckets, her chin held high when a silence descended on the dais as she passed.

"It seems that Alys makes a marked recovery from her catarrh," Burke commented dryly. Alys noted that Malvina nearly draped herself across the man's lap and he did naught to challenge this familiarity.

Did his pride demand that every woman fall at his feet?

Aunt laughed and made up some lie even as Alys gritted

her teeth. A catarrh? 'Twas typical of that woman to tell some tall tale to excuse her behavior. Alys set to cleaning the kitchen, half hoping that a certain knight would seek her out before he retired.

But gradually the keep fell silent, and footsteps echoed on the stairs. Alys caught herself listening for a solid male tread, her vigor deserting her when she heard Burke leave the hall for the stairs, not the kitchen.

Oh, she was an addlepated fool!

'Twas only once they were all gone that Alys dragged her buckets into the great hall itself. The room seemed vast and cold now that 'twas deserted and the fire burned down to glowing coals. The floor stretched on for eternity, but Alys dutifully scrubbed as snores and the scampering of mice filled the keep.

She cursed her aunt a few times for good measure, then cursed Burke for tangling her thoughts. She cursed her mother for being so foolish as to submit to a man's seductive ploys.

If her mother had not succumbed to temptation, then Alys would not have been bastard-born, her mother would not have died of a broken heart, and Alys would not be on her knees, cleaning Kiltorren's floors.

Then she cursed herself for being so very tempted to repeat that same woeful mistake. The truth was all too clear, with no winsome dreams, or romantic tales, or charming men to cloud Alys's view.

But what *would* Burke say if she granted him the chance? Even knowing she should not, Alys was itching to know.

When the dawn's first fingers crept into the hall, Alys was done with her cleaning. She stood and stretched her back, surveying what she had achieved with no pride of accomplishment. Alys ran a tired hand over her brow.

Heloise oft said that curiosity could lead to the downfall of innocents, and Alys reluctantly acknowledged the truth of that. However wrong 'twas, whatever manner of lies he might offer, she sorely wanted to know what Burke would say in his own defense.

And there was only one way to satisfy her burning curiosity. Alys was going to have to grant the man the hearing he requested. 'Twas a risky proposition, given the pledge she had made to her aunt, but perhaps the deed could be concealed.

First, Alys would cut the strewing herbs and finish this cursed task. If Dame Fortune smiled upon her, Aunt would not rise soon and would be so busy checking Alys's labor once she did arise—seeking fault, as always—that she would not immediately note Alys's absence.

Or her defiance.

For this would be the last time Alys would speak with Burke, without doubt. The man was right in this, at least. He had listened to Alys, and 'twas only fair she listen to him.

At least that was the excuse she granted herself to seek him out. Alone in the garden with knife in hand, Alys fervently hoped she could keep her wits about her and hold fast against Burke's allure.

'Twas not heartening to know that 'twas a slender chance, at best.

Chapter Four

B Y THE TIME ALYS HAD STREWN THE HERBS ACROSS every freshly cleaned floor, 'twas nearly midmorning. She had heard Burke's whistle earlier and knew he was awake. Ensuring that both Aunt and Malvina were yet abed, she embarked on her furtive mission.

But Burke was not in the hall or the kitchen. He was neither in the armory nor the bailey. Alys thought he might have gone riding but found his destrier still in the stables. The great steed nosed in his feed bin as Kerwyn murmured to him, brushing his flank. Neither glanced up at her.

Alys paused in the dappled sunlight that filled the corridor running alongside the stalls and glanced down the length of the stables. She seldom came here, her labor keeping her within the hall, and the smell of the place made her thoughts turn to a long-ago afternoon. Her footsteps were drawn to the far end, almost of their own accord.

There the stalls were no longer in use. Each step put the noise of steeds and stablehands farther behind her, but memory echoed in Alys's mind. Nigh feeling the weight of the slops pail in her hand, she smiled in recollection of Burke's appearance.

Aye, he thought he had fooled her that afternoon, that she did not guess from the flash of his eyes that he had been deliberately seeking her.

In those days, Burke had been so easily read.

Or so she had thought. Alys's smile faded.

She paused outside the very last stall and debated the whimsey of what she wanted to do. She glanced back over her shoulder to assure herself that her folly would not be witnessed, then stepped into the stall.

'Twas just the same. Motes of dust danced in an errant sunbeam, the smell of hay and dung, leather and horse-flesh filled her nostrils. Alys heard the distant sound of stomping hooves—granted, farther and fewer than once they had been—and took another step into the stall's shadows.

It had been exactly here. Alys closed her eyes, leaned back, and let herself recall the sweet ardor of Burke's kiss. Indeed, she could fairly taste the urgency she had felt in him, the way her blood had leapt at his touch.

Oh, how she had loved him!

Or how she had *believed* she loved him. But the man Alys loved was Aucassin from Heloise's tale, the bold and handsome knight who cared naught for his lady love's lowly status and stopped at naught to win her hand. Aucassin was faithful beyond all, chivalrous and prepared to sacrifice all for the cause of love.

But Aucassin was not real. Alys had simply confused her favored tale with the truth. She shook her head and spun to leave.

'Twas then Alys realized she was not alone.

She caught her breath to find Burke leaning against the far wall. The shadows had nearly swallowed him, though his gaze shone even in the darkness. And he was more still than Alys would have believed possible.

And he was very real. Burke was watching her, there could be no doubt of that, his arms folded across the broadness of his chest. His slow smile made Alys tremble to her toes.

'Twas clear he had spent time in the stables already this day, for his fine boots were mired. Burke had discarded his tabard, his white linen chemise emphasizing the strength of his shoulders and the golden hue of his tan. His hair was tousled and he looked almost as he had so long ago.

Alys's heart skipped a beat as she acknowledged, if only to herself, that Burke was far more breathtaking than he had been even three years past.

"Dare I hope," he asked softly, "that you seek me?"

Alys felt herself flush, but she did not drop her gaze. "Aye," she admitted, though her mouth had gone dry. "It seemed only courteous to hear you out."

Burke seemed to find this claim amusing. He pushed one hand through his hair, leaving those dark waves in even greater disarray. "Then it seems I owe much to courtesy," he commented, a thread of humor in his tone.

Alys's heart took a traitorous leap when he straightened. She took a hasty step back, finding the stable wall too close behind her for comfort.

She shook a warning finger at Burke, fear of her own response to him rising quickly. "You remain there. I came to listen, and naught more than my attention will you have of me."

Burke leaned back against the opposing wall. "You have no bucket of water on this day to force your edict," he noted mildly.

Alys lifted her chin in challenge. "You say you are a man of honor. I but grant you the chance to prove it."

He considered her in a silence so charged she could not catch her breath. "Touché," Burke said finally, then his gaze flicked over the stall. "It has changed little here."

Alys felt defensiveness of her family's failing fortunes ease into her tone. "There is little to change in a horse stall, and, indeed, this end of the stables is seldom used these days."

"Mmm." Burke frowned. "We parted here and 'tis from here that I would begin to tell you what transpired." His gaze swivelled to hers. "I trust you recall that day?"

Alys felt a lump rise in her throat as she remembered the humiliation of their parting. " 'Twas the last I saw of you. 'Tis all I need to recall."

"You fled."

"And you did not pursue me," Alys charged, hearing the heat of an old wound in her words.

Burke shook his head, a vestige of frustration crossing his brow. "Your family would not permit it! They cornered me here, like a ferret doomed to die, much as they cornered me at the gates yesterday. 'Twas chaos, all accusations and demands, and irritating beyond all." His glance flicked to her again. "I wanted only to speak with you."

"I was in my chamber."

"Aye, so I was told." Burke looked grim. "In those days, your family at least feigned concern for your honor, though I did not see through their pretense then. When I offered for your hand . . ."

Alys raised her hand to challenge this falsehood. "Burke, you could not have offered for my hand!"

Burke's eyes flashed. "I *did*! That very day. I said I would wed you, and I made clear my honorable intent. Indeed, 'twas only once they heard my offer that they let me pass," he continued, no small measure of anger underlying his words. "But your family insisted upon presenting my petition. They returned to me almost immediately and said you would not hear of my offer. I was told that you refused even my presence."

Alys felt her lips part in astonishment. Not only had Burke offered for her hand, but he thought she *spurned* his suit?

"I waited a day," Burke continued bitterly. "I repeated my petition, but your family brought your dismissal to me once more."

There was heat in his words, heat and hurt, the intensity of it making Alys wonder. Surely this passion could be no lie?

Though still it made no sense.

Burke stared at his feet. "I confess that I was uncertain what to think. I did not know much of love and marriage, I certainly knew naught of such happiness as I had known in your presence. An old knight told me I should be pleased not to have to bear the burden of young foolishness. I did not know whether he spoke the truth."

Burke sighed. "And so I left, as I believed you had bidden me to do." He lifted his gaze to Alys and his eyes seemed to glow with his intensity. " 'Twas my first mistake. I should have insisted that I be granted such a rejection from your own lips."

Alys did not know what to believe. Indeed, her troublesome heart urged her to take Burke's side.

"I returned to my father and rode in battle with him," that man continued, "enduring at each turn the matches my mother would have me make. But 'twas odd, Alys, for I could not help but compare each of these women with you—and each time I found them lacking. To my dismay, time did naught to erase your allure. I awakened thinking of you at the oddest times. Gradually I realized that what burned in my heart for you might never fade."

Burke paused and frowned, his voice dropping low. "And so a year after my departure I returned to Kiltorren in the hope that I might persuade you to accept my suit."

Now, that *was* a lie!

"You did not!" Alys declared, angry that he would toy with her thus, and more angered that she could be so readily deceived.

Burke's gaze locked with hers. "I *did*, Alys. I was here that spring, but you were not."

" 'Tis impossible! I told you that I was born at Kiltorren and have always lived within these walls."

"You were not here," Burke insisted grimly. "Your aunt declared that you had fled the keep, that they knew not where you had gone. Your family expressed great concern and begged that I send them word if ever I caught a glimpse of you."

He arched a brow as though dubious of what he would say. "It seemed they were sick with worry."

"But that makes no sense at all!" Alys protested. "I have never left Kiltorren."

"Then where were you, Alys?" Burke demanded. He flung out his hands in frustration. "I do not lie to you, *I was here.*"

"But I would have known if you were here. I would have seen you!"

Burke shook his head. "I do not know the solution to the riddle, Alys. I know only what I saw and what I was told. I did not see you here, and so I left, hoping at least I might find you in my travels."

He swallowed and kicked his toe against the deadened straw. "And that was my second mistake, for I never did lay eyes upon you before returning to Kiltorren this time."

Alys shook her head in exasperation. "Clearly, because I was here all the while!" She propped her hands on her hips to survey him. "What do you intend to gain by lies when I grant you the opportunity to share the truth?"

Burke's glance was steady. "Alys, it seems we both have been served with lies at Kiltorren, and not from each other."

He appeared so convinced of this that Alys paused to wonder. 'Twas not really startling to imagine Aunt lying to her.

Alys frowned. "But Aunt would have told me of any proposal, I am certain."

"Would she have?" Burke mused. "She was quick to tell a tale of your illness last evening."

"Oh, 'tis not because of any faith in her honesty that I defend her." Alys folded her arms across her chest and smiled wryly. "She would be only too glad to be rid of the burden of my presence, you may be certain."

"Indeed?" Burke did not seem to think this as much of a certainty as Alys did. His glance danced over her garb, and Alys realized that she must be filthy beyond all. "They have had a healthy measure of toil from you, there can be no doubt of that."

"I have been told that I must earn my keep."

Burke's eyes flashed. "As your cousins do?"

Alys bit her lip and eyed the knight warily. Though she had had mutinous thoughts all her life, 'twas awkward to discuss them so openly with another. "I suppose 'tis only natural that my aunt and uncle favor their own blood."

"You *are* their own blood!" Burke cried. He paced the width of the stall in obvious frustration. "You are of the same lineage as your cousins." He appealed to her with a glance and an outstretched hand. "Have you never asked yourself why their lives differ so much from your own?"

"Aye," Alys admitted uneasily. "Aunt says she did not wish me to become proud, as my mother was."

Burke snorted a disdain that could not be misconstrued. "Your aunt is well aware that you are the loveliest of the three young women in her care," he declared flatly. Alys's heart fluttered at the compliment stated as bald fact. "She is concerned for her own, 'tis true, but at your expense."

But there was another factor, one that Burke did not understand and one far more critical.

"Nay, we are not equal, for I am bastard-born." Alys felt her cheeks heat as she admitted to this. "My mother brought shame upon Kiltorren and her father's name. Aunt would not see me repeat my mother's error."

But Burke folded his arms across his chest, clearly not giving this morsel of information the due it deserved. "Alys, the noble blood of this house runs in your veins, regardless of how you came to be in this world. Kings and queens acknowledge their spawn from the wrong side of the linens, and Kiltorren is no king's prize. Your mother may have erred, but her moral debts are not yours to pay."

"But Aunt says I carry the whore's taint."

Burke swore and spat in the straw, his condemnation of such thinking more than clear. "Alys! Ask yourself what your aunt wins by so abusing you!" He tapped his thumb, counting off his points. "She sets her own daughters at advantage, for they are never compared to you while you wear a servant's garb."

Burke marked his index finger. "She has a maid without the need to train or compensate or see to the marriage of that maid. Indeed, I have no doubt you serve all three of them." He counted off another finger, not granting Alys the opportunity to acknowledge that truth. "She has another pair of hands in the kitchen with no additional mouth to feed, which is no small thing if the keep does not prosper."

He stepped closer, tapping his third finger heavily with his opposite index finger. "But there is another reason, of that I am certain, for such bitterness cannot be without a root."

"There is my taint . . ."

"There is no such thing as this whore's taint!"

"But Aunt insists . . ."

"She *lies*!" the knight declared savagely. "Your aunt takes exception in your very existence, Alys, regardless of what you do or say. I mean to discover why."

Alys frowned and looked away, fighting against Burke's persuasiveness. Oh, she knew he spoke the truth about Aunt's malice, but what of the rest?

Burke stepped forward in that moment and caught Alys's chin between his finger and thumb, forcing her to meet his gaze. She was achingly aware of his hand braced against the stall beside her shoulder, of the scent of his skin, of the glow in his eyes, the light touch of his finger and thumb on her chin. Her heart pounded at the awareness that she alone held his attention, that she alone was what he desired.

She could not have stepped away to save her soul.

"If all truly was as I tell you, Alys," Burke whispered, his gaze searching hers, "would you have put your hand in mine three years past?"

Alys swallowed at the very possibility. She could not imagine that Burke could feign such intensity, and in this moment, she could not credit any possibility that he lied.

Indeed, she wanted to plead with him to take her away from Kiltorren, under any terms. Alys wanted once again to have the dream of Burke being her knight, her lover, her Aucassin.

But Alys had pledged never to repeat her mother's error, the error at the root of all her troubles. And Burke said naught of marriage in these days, even if once he did.

Alys realized the omission in time. Indeed, 'twas clear—despite Burke's claim—that he came to court Malvina.

"But what if 'tis *not* true?" she whispered unevenly.

Burke caught Alys's hand before she could step away and placed her palm over his heart, his own hand holding hers firmly there. His flesh was warm, even through his chemise, and his pulse pounded beneath her hand. His hand engulfed hers and Alys was seized by a longing for more of his touch so intense that it weakened her knees.

"But, Alys, 'tis the truth."

"What about Malvina?"

Burke grimaced. "Alys, I see only you." His gaze bored into hers and his voice dropped to a persuasive whisper. "I swear it."

When Alys hesitated, Burke bent and brushed his lips across hers. She might have pulled away, but his heartbeat leapt beneath her fingertips.

Alys was beguiled by this small sign that her touch was not

without effect upon this bold knight. She stared up at him and could only watch as he bent to touch his lips to hers once more. And she trembled with desire when his lips closed over hers. He tasted of warmth and the ale with which he had broken his fast. He was warm and gentle as always he had been.

Alys added "irresistible" to her list of this knight's traits just as her eyes closed. Her lips parted and she stretched to her toes, surrendering to the moment and his embrace.

Burke groaned and caught Alys against him, his hands gripping her waist with a surety that made her forget all her objections. His kiss was tender and thorough, his touch making Alys's pulse leap in turn. Alys opened her mouth to him and arched against him, hungry for all he could give.

When his strong fingers eased beneath her chemise and cradled her breast, Alys caught her breath. Burke slid his thumb leisurely across her nipple, the move sending shivers through her from head to toe. He broke their kiss when she gasped, winked, then bent, cupping her breast to lift it to his lips.

And Alys, staring at the ebony tangle of his hair, flooded with the pleasure of his teasing lips, abruptly realized the folly of what she did. The measure of a man was in his deeds, not his fine words, nor even his kisses.

"Nay!" she cried, and pushed him away, noting only the astonishment in his eyes before she fled.

"Alys!" Burke called, but Alys did not look back. She picked up her skirts and ran, as much from Burke as from her own wanton urges.

Oh, she was her mother's daughter, there could be no doubt of that!

"Alys!" Burke roared, his shout echoing over the bailey. "This matter is not done between us!"

Alys could not risk halting to listen to more of his persuasive tales. She fled for sanctuary, her heart fluttering like a wild thing seeking to escape her chest.

Yet when she had nearly reached the kitchen portal, Alys realized that Dame Fortune had not smiled upon her this morn.

Aunt stood there, her murderous expression making Alys's footsteps falter. "You have been in his company again," she charged.

Alys halted but could not lie. "Aye. Just this once." Dread uncoiled in her belly when Aunt's eyes narrowed. " 'Twill be the last time, I swear it to you."

Aunt's brows rose. "Disobedience is disobedience, Alys, be it once or a thousand times."

Alys glanced back to the stables occupied by a knight she did not dare to trust. There was no sign of him.

And there was no one else in this keep who would aid her, for any price, at least not any longer. Indeed, she would not ask it of any, after what had happened before.

But that would not happen again. Alys forced her breathing to steady, looked to Aunt, and decided that she could bear another dose of hard labor.

She stepped forward, her chin held high, not guessing that she had sorely underestimated her aunt's wrath.

Cedric was waiting in the solar when Deirdre returned from the kitchen just before midday. He had that anxious demeanor that foretold his wanting something of her. Deirdre took pleasure in denying him her immediate attention, knowing 'twould trouble him all the more.

If naught else, she had swung that willow switch with vigor this morn. There were a pair of new blisters on her palm, one broken at the force of the beating she had given her niece. But her hand would not have gone soft if she had not laid the switch aside two years past.

'Twas the price Deirdre must pay for bowing to Cedric's superstitious nonsense.

As that last time, Alys had not made a murmur of protest, she had not cried out, she had not wept, she had endured with the will of a martyr. 'Twas infuriating beyond anything else the girl might have done. Deirdre had momentarily forgotten herself in her quest for a response, hence the blisters.

But her hand would heal.

As, undoubtedly, would Alys.

One matter was assured—Alys would not be drawing Burke's eye away from Malvina in the next few days. Deirdre smiled. 'Twas all the time Malvina would need to capture their guest's heart. A pair of blisters was a small price to pay to ensure her eldest's match.

Cedric folded his arms across his chest and eyed her warily. "Where have you been?" he asked.

"In the kitchen," she said breezily, and opened her trunk. "Are the girls arrayed in their finest? I would have them sparkle in this knight's presence."

"Aye, they are." Cedric took a step closer, his brow furrowing. "What detained you, Deirdre? 'Tis unlike you to be late to the board when we have a guest, no less an eligible knight."

Deirdre smiled tightly. "Cedric, you would not have the fare be any less than our best, would you?"

But Cedric was not to be swayed from his course. "It does not take that long to declare that the good ale be uncasked or that a new wheel of cheese be presented. You have been making mischief, unless I miss my guess."

"Cedric!" Deirdre feigned indignation. "I would never . . ."

But she had no chance to finish, for Cedric caught at her right hand. He turned it palm-up, as if knowing what he would find, and looked Deirdre dead in the eye.

"You have been at it again," he accused. "I thought we had agreed after the last time."

Deirdre lifted her chin. " 'Twas deserved."

"Aye?" Cedric looked skeptical. " 'Tis hard to believe that

Alys could have any opportunity to make any sufficiently deserving mischief. You work the girl too hard, Deirdre."

"Oh, Cedric, spare me your sympathetic nonsense!" Deirdre snatched her hand back and bent over her trunk, blindly rummaging for a kirtle.

"Do you not recall what happened before?" her spouse demanded with rare insistence. "You will call the wrath of God upon us once more with your deeds!"

"I recall it well enough, though you would overstate the matter. The old woman would have fallen ill, whether Alys was struck or not."

"You cannot be certain of that."

Deirdre spared her spouse a glance. "I see no one falling in a fit this day."

Cedric folded his arms across his chest. "Perhaps we should send a runner to Heloise and see how she fares."

Deirdre turned her back upon his nonsense. "You listen overmuch to the priests and I have listened overmuch to you. There is naught to be lost in teaching Alys her place in this keep. That last event was but coincidence and has been given doubly its due. And truly we are well rid of the old harridan. She grew tedious."

"You cannot know how the hand of the Lord moves in all of this." Cedric huffed. Deirdre, knowing her expression was hidden from him, rolled her eyes.

Enough was enough. She was not going to cease running her household simply because some old maid fell down frothing and twitching. Indeed, she had only to look at the defiance that had bred within Alys in these past years to justify her choice.

But Cedric, of course, would never listen to simple reason.

Deirdre let her voice run high, deliberately changing her tone and mode of attack. "Is it not enough burden to know that I was only second best to Isibeal, without having you fawn over her child? Do you wish she was yours? Do you wish my sister had parted her thighs for you? Do you pretend that Alys is yours? Is that why you insist on turning a blind eye to her many faults?"

The accusation worked as well as it ever did. Cedric was immediately contrite. "Nay! Deirdre, 'tis not so!" He framed her shoulders in his hands, as if he would will her to believe him. "I never favored Isibeal and I do not want any daughters beyond our own. 'Tis you, only you, who holds my heart."

Deirdre sighed and tried to look mollified. "Truly? Then why do you so favor her child?"

Cedric frowned. "I do not favor her, but she is our ward . . ."

"Cedric, the child expects to earn her keep here," Deirdre interrupted crisply. "Indeed, we all must make sacrifices since the crops are less than prime." She glanced up in time to see Cedric flush.

" 'Tis not my fault," he mumbled, but they both knew that he was far from an adept landowner. " 'Tis the wrath of God . . ."

Deirdre did not give him time to take that thought to its conclusion. She leaned into his embrace and pressed herself against him.

"Of course not, my love," she whispered. "But 'twill be your fault if we do not make the most of this knight's visit to our abode." She straightened and touched his cheek. "Think of it, Cedric! Burke declared he has come for a bride. We must seize this chance to see one daughter's future assured!"

Cedric still looked troubled. "But Alys did not need to be whipped . . ."

"Did she not?" Deirdre propped her hands on her hips and surveyed her spouse, marvelling yet again at his lax wits. "Have you eyes in your head? She is pretty, too pretty, even in tatters. Have you ears in your head, Cedric? Did you not hear the knight call after her from the gates when he arrived?"

Cedric's brow furrowed. "I suppose . . ."

"You *know*!" Deirdre punctuated her point with a tap on her spouse's chest. "She vexed the man. Cedric, he might have ridden directly out of our gates, and I cannot believe he would return if he left again. What of your daughters' lives then? Would you see them languish as spinsters at Kiltorren forever? Would you see them barren and unwanted all their lives? Would you die happily knowing that they would perish without your protection? Ireland is not the safe land it once was, Cedric, and we both know that rogues roam the hills, seeking estates to make their own."

"Well . . ." Cedric shuffled his feet.

"And you know that I have better instinct with these delicate matters of marriage than ever a man might have." She straightened primly. "And this day she did defy me, breaking her oath made only yesterday. 'Tis not fitting." She paused. "You *did* pledge, long ago, that you would cede to me in domestic concerns."

Cedric looked sufficiently uncertain that Deirdre knew she was close to having her way. She twined her arms around his neck and pressed herself against his body, hoping for the thousandth time that her daughters appreciated all she endured for their sakes.

"Trust me, Cedric," she whispered in his ear, then kissed him fully. "Trust me in this matter, my love, and let me see to all."

When Cedric's arms closed around her waist, Deirdre knew that victory was hers. "You always know best, Deirdre," he murmured.

❈

Kiltorren's kitchen had a pair of great fireplaces on the wall below the bread ovens. Both were large enough to hold a spitted deer over the flame and a boy to turn the spit. Between the two of them was a niche for firewood, which had long ceased to be used for that purpose. Lady Deirdre had decreed that no wood be burned beyond that used for the cooking of the meals themselves and kept a scrupulous inventory of the woodpile.

Indeed, the wood was under lock and key, only a certain count of logs and tinder entrusted to Cook's care each morn.

This niche was always empty and had become the coveted spot to sleep, for the stone retained some heat from the fire for many hours. On cold evenings there were fights among the servants as to who would claim the space for their pallet, and none slept there two nights running.

Except when Lady Deirdre took the willow switch to Alys. Then there was no argument as to who should have the favored spot.

Alys lay on her pallet in that niche though 'twas only past midday, dimly aware of the familiar concerned faces clustered around her. The kitchen bustled with the demands of laying the main meal upon the board, though on this day 'twas a markedly quiet bustle. Alys's back ached with the sting of the switch, and only now, out of Aunt's sight, did she permit herself to weep.

It had hurt infinitely more this time than the last, and Alys knew her aunt intended as much. She could not help but think of that last ugly confrontation, of her mother's beloved maid Heloise rising to defend her, of all that had followed. Alys had never believed that Aunt would repeat her abuse after that day, but clearly she had been wrong.

Alys bit her lip, distracted from her pain by the sudden realization that today was the day she should visit Heloise. How would she manage the walk? And how could she hide the damage Aunt had wrought?

Would Heloise respond as she had the last time?

Cook knelt before Alys even as she worried, his amiable face drawn with concern. "A brew for you," he whispered, sliding a steaming crock toward her. " 'Tis one my mother made for bruises."

Alys managed to smile for his thoughtfulness. " 'Twill no doubt make me sleep."

Cook smiled in turn. "Clear through tomorrow's midday."

Alys pushed the brew aside. "I cannot drink it then. I promised Heloise that I would visit this day. She will be sorely troubled if I do not appear."

"And more worried if you appear like this," Cook insisted.

Alys frowned and considered the brew. "She may not notice," she suggested hopefully.

Cook snorted. "One cannot tell what she will notice in these days. But, Alys, 'twas seeing you beaten that put Heloise where she is on this day. You cannot go."

"I could not bear that she have another attack," Alys admitted. "But, Cook, she grows fretful when I am detained."

"Do not trouble yourself over the matter." Cook patted her hand. "I shall send Edana—goodness knows she will concoct some tale or another about your absence." He winked. "Though no doubt her ladyship will not play a favorable role in that tale."

Alys looked at the older man. "Edana will not mind?"

Cook smiled. "You know how she loves to take her goats afield."

Alys smiled in relief. 'Twould be fine. With luck Heloise would scarcely note the exchange. The elderly maid could be unpredictable in these days, and sometimes Alys was not even certain Heloise knew she was there.

Other times the woman's wit was as sharp as a freshly honed blade. But Dame Fortune had done naught for Alys of late—perhaps her caprice was satisfied for the moment.

And either way, Alys was in no condition to walk to Heloise's isolated dwelling on this day. She took a deep breath, reassured, and drew the cup of brew closer.

"Drink deeply, child," Cook urged. "I only wish I knew that

tale Heloise always told to you so that I could sing it to you. It always soothed you."

"Nicolette and Aucassin," Alys supplied, her smile turning winsome. "I know it well enough, Cook. Perhaps I shall hum it to myself." The older man nodded and straightened, though Alys knew he would keep a watchful eye over her.

She sighed and winced at the ache in her back, knowing she had never been so exhausted in all her days. Alys sipped Cook's brew and silently told herself her very favorite old tale.

> *Once, far afield, there lived a man*
> *With wealth and fortune to his hand.*
> *He had one son, a tall, strong man*
> *The handsome knight named Aucassin . . .*

Alys had barely begun the numerous verses when the herbs in Cook's brew took effect. Her eyes drifted closed, her thoughts filled with the gallant tale of two lovers true, and in her sleep, Alys smiled.

Chapter Five

URKE CAME TO THE MIDDAY BOARD IMPATIENT TO
finish what he and Alys had begun. Indeed, a mere
nod from his lady would have him presenting his
suit. If he could find her before the meal, he could secure her
agreement and they could make the nearest town by dusk.

But Alys was not readily found. Indeed, she was not in the
hall, even engaged in some petty labor. He could not hear her
voice, even from the women's chambers above.

Had he underestimated her response? Burke had thought
Alys uncertain, shy, perhaps startled by the passion in his
touch. At worst, he had assumed that she had been reminded
of the trials that had ensued when they last had embraced in
that same place.

But could she be deliberately avoiding him?

Nay! Burke could not permit that, not before the truth was
laid out between them.

Deirdre took her seat, her daughters filing dutifully into
place, and indicated that the meal should be served, though
there was still no sign of Alys. There was a quiet in the hall
that pricked Burke's senses. Indeed, it seemed that Cedric
avoided his glance.

Something was amiss, Burke could fairly smell it.

And he was nigh certain it had to do with his lady.

"Where is Alys?" he asked as lightly as he could manage.

"She does not join us, of course," Deirdre declared, her sharp tone indicating that the matter was closed. She smiled coolly. "Tell us, Burke, of the wonders of Paris."

The knight's unease only increased at his hostess's manner. She spoke too crisply and was too quick to change the subject. "Perhaps Alys should join us," he suggested carefully. "Indeed, it seemed she labored so intently last evening that she could not have had time for a meal."

Deirdre turned a cold stare upon him. "Again you show marked concern for those beneath your station."

Burke smiled with an equal measure of frost. " 'Twas part of my knightly pledge to ensure the welfare of those who cannot defend themselves."

Cedric caught his breath tellingly at those words and Burke straightened in alarm.

Had Alys been in need of defense?

Cedric frowned at the board, but Deirdre shrugged as if naught was unusual. "I have told you that the girl does not come when she is summoned, and a search would only appeal to her vanity."

The serving lad looked up from his task. His gaze flicked to meet Burke's, then averted quickly. When the boy's footsteps faded, ominous silence again flooded the hall. 'Twas as if all knew something he did not, and Burke did not care for the sensation in the least.

"Nonetheless, I will fetch her," he said firmly. "Where might I find the lady?"

"You cannot!" Deirdre declared.

"You should not!" Cedric insisted, half rising from his seat.

"You must leave her to her labor," Deirdre insisted. They were too intent on changing his course, their response only setting Burke more determinedly upon it.

"Where is she?"

All four of them stared back at him mutely.

"Where is Alys?" Burke demanded again. "Is it such a puzzle to know where your ward might be within your own keep?"

They eyed him uneasily.

Burke rose from the board and cast his napkin upon it. "Surely there is some corner she favors?"

But still the family said naught. Burke snorted in disgust at their indifference and strode from the hall, heading for the kitchen. 'Twas, after all, where Alys had been headed when last he saw her.

And 'twas likely to be where the servants congregated and slept. Indeed, he would not be surprised if this lot dispatched Alys to the very stables. He and Alys could not be away from this wretched place soon enough!

"NAY!" Deirdre cried from behind him, but Burke cared naught for what she thought of his actions.

Burke's lips set grimly. If he had to tear this keep apart stone by stone, he would find Alys before he sat at the board again.

Cook was just easing an ill-gotten log onto the fire when the door to the kitchen was abruptly shoved open. He jumped, dropped the log on his toe, and spun guiltily to face certain retribution.

But 'twas the visiting knight who stood on the threshold, not the lady of the keep. Indeed, that knight's broad shoulders fairly filled the portal, and his expression was dangerous enough to make Cook fear for his considerable hide.

"Where is Alys?" he demanded, much to Cook's astonishment.

With the great worktable in front, Cook realized that the knight could not see the niche where Alys slept. Then he wondered what this fierce man wanted with Alys, especially after she had argued so heatedly with him the day before.

Cook was not prepared to see Alys abused twice in quick

succession. He took a deep breath and stepped forward with all the boldness he could muster. "You will not learn from me!" he declared. "I will not let another lay a hand upon her this day."

"Another?" The knight's eyes narrowed and his voice dropped dangerously low. "Alys has been harmed?"

Cook folded his arms across his chest. "Aye. 'Tis hardly news."

The knight's eyes flashed with anger.

"Burke, come back to the board!" Her ladyship's honeyed tones echoed down the corridor. The knight winced in precisely the same manner as most of the servants when they heard their mistress's sharp voice, then slammed the door behind himself with a vengeance.

Cook decided that he could like this man.

"Where is Alys?" the knight demanded. He stepped forward, his gaze steady. "I swear to you that I have no intent to harm her."

Cook knew concern when he heard it. He gestured to the niche and noted the shock that crossed the knight's features at first glimpse of Alys.

Her cheeks were marked with the streaks of her tears, strands of her golden hair had worked free of her braid and hung loose over her shoulders. Her skin was still stained with soot from the night before.

The knight stepped forward as Cook watched, knelt beside Alys, his hand hovering just above her shoulder as if he could not comprehend what he saw.

"She has just fallen asleep," Cook confessed, coming to stand behind the knight. He wondered whether this man saw the sweet vulnerability of Isibeal's daughter, whether his gut clenched as Cook's did to see this woman abused.

Or whether he noted the telltale bloodstain on the threadbare blanket cast over Alys's slender shoulders.

"What happened?" the knight asked softly.

Cook lifted the blanket, his heart swelling when the knight caught his breath. The gashes left by the willow switch were marked in thin lines of blood across Alys's back. The wounds were visible even through her torn kirtle, and they had already swollen. Alys would be sore on the morrow, but Cook knew that she would not reveal that to any.

If naught else, a solid slumber would aid her healing.

"Who is responsible for this abomination?" the knight demanded.

Cook shook his head, torn between his responsibility to the lord who held him in thrall and his desire to see justice served. His dismay must have shown in his expression, for the knight landed a heavy hand on his shoulder.

"You do not have to say it," he murmured, his piercing gaze filled with understanding. "I realize your position." He looked back to Alys. "Her family does her a great disservice."

Cook heaved a sigh. "I cannot agree more."

The knight's gaze ran over the accommodations Cook had made, then he bent and swept Alys gently into his arms. She did not awaken, thanks to Cook's concoction, but settled against the knight's shoulder with a sigh.

"I thank you for your compassion." The knight's voice was low with approval when he turned to face Cook anew, Alys safely nestled against his chest. "I do not mean insult, but she needs a proper bed."

"You speak aright, sir, but I had only the pallet."

"Burke! Here you are!" Lady Deirdre burst into the kitchen, Malvina and Lord Cedric close on her heels. The false smiles on their faces turned to shock when they saw Alys in Burke's arms.

"It seems that Alys has been hurt," Burke said coldly, accusation evident in the hard glance he turned upon the family.

Lady Deirdre lifted her chin and was bold enough to feign

ignorance. "Indeed? How very sad. Cook can see to her welfare. Come, Burke, our repast grows cold."

"My apologies, but my appetite has waned," the knight retorted. He crossed the room with long steps, holding Alys with such care that Cook had a distinct sense that the tide had finally turned in this keep.

And for the better.

"But where are you going?" the lord demanded. "Surely you do not intend to leave Kiltorren?"

"Say 'tis not so!" Malvina implored.

"Where," Lady Deirdre asked icily, "do you intend to take my niece?"

"She has need of comfort." The knight did not smile when Malvina giggled, his stern glance silencing the girl. "I should see her sleep in a bed more fitting of her birthright."

Lady Deirdre sniffed. "We have not a spare mattress in all of the keep."

"Then she shall have the one granted to me," the knight countered smoothly. "If you might excuse me?" He shouldered his way through the door.

"But, Burke, you cannot do this!" Lady Deirdre finally cried.

The knight did not halt, his footsteps echoing in the corridor.

Lady Deirdre nudged Lord Cedric hard and that man jumped. "Nay! I cannot permit it!"

When they trotted after the knight, Cook crept to the door on silent feet and peered after the party.

"Halt!" Lord Cedric cried.

The knight pivoted to face them anew, his expression no less stony. "Do you spurn my concern for this noblewoman's welfare?" he demanded. "Do you dare to suggest I discard my sworn pledge to protect all those unable to protect themselves? A man's word is the measure of his worth, is it not, Lord Cedric?"

The lord scuffed his boot against the floor, looking to his spouse for the right answer before he nodded. "Aye, that it is."

"Then I shall see this noblewoman cared for in fitting circumstance."

"You cannot keep my niece in your chamber!" Lady Deirdre huffed.

The knight arched a brow. "But I could have bedded her in the bathing room without complaint? Your concern for your niece seems less than consistent, Lady Deirdre."

The lady of Kiltorren sputtered, and Cook covered his smile with his hand. Indeed, this knight reminded him of the old Lord of Kiltorren, a great lord and father of both Lady Deirdre and Lady Isibeal. There had been a man worthy of service! It could be no small thing that this knight resembled the old lord, no less that he championed Alys, babe of that man's favored daughter.

"Have you a maid to send to her side?" the knight asked, clearly expecting to be granted his request. "The lady needs care."

Cook dared to raise his voice in the silence that met the knight's question. "Fear not, sir, I shall send Edana when she returns to the hall."

"And I shall remain with the lady until that time." The knight smiled, solely for Cook. "I must thank you again for your assistance. What is your name?"

Cook, despite his years, felt his cheeks heat to be the center of attention. But there could be no fault found in answering a simple question from a guest. "Beauregard, sir."

The knight's smile broadened. "And rightly named you are, good man, for your sight is clear."

"But, Burke, wherever shall you sleep this night?" Malvina demanded.

"I shall join my steed in the stables."

And with that the knight spun to carry his burden toward the stairs, apparently oblivious to the outcry behind him. Lady Deirdre muttered something beneath her breath, then lunged after him, her voice high with appeal.

And Cook turned back to his kitchen, more delighted with affairs at Kiltorren than he had been in quite some time.

Alys was surrounded by softness, enfolded in a warmth alien to her. 'Twas luxurious even to dream of such comfort, and she fought against the persistent ray of sunshine that heated her cheek as though 'twould urge her to abandon sleep.

Nay, she was safely ensnared in her wondrous dream, and Alys would not surrender that pleasure readily. She nestled deeper beneath a thick coverlet, wiggled her hips against the fullness of a feather mattress, and sighed contentment. 'Twas a perfect dream. She envisioned herself wrapped in her dream lover's secure embrace and smiled as her memory conjured a familiar masculine scent. 'Twas one that unfurled a heat in Alys's belly and sent her toe sliding across the linens in search of Burke's warmth.

At least, 'twas but a dream, and that already confident knight of Montvieux would never know how Alys secretly longed for his touch. She buried her nose against the fine linen of her chemise and tried to drift deeper into sleep.

But Burke's scent was so strong there that Alys's eyes flew open.

And she realized suddenly that this was no dream. Her back ached from the twitch of Aunt's wicked willow switch, yet still she reposed in a fine bed.

What was this?

Alys noted the angle of the sunlight, frowning as that made even less sense. 'Twas late morning. Belatedly, she recalled downing Cook's brew. Had she slept a few hours or an entire night and day? Alys could not understand that she had been left to sleep for so long.

Let alone that she had done so *here*.

What trick did Aunt play on her now?

Alys scanned the room suspiciously. The bed was broad, the mattress plump, the coverlet thick and warm. She was alone, alone but for that errant ray of sunlight that eased its way through the shutters and fell across the pillows.

Alys rolled to her back, frowned at the canopy overhead, the four great bedposts, the heavy draperies, and suddenly realized where she lay. 'Twas the guest chamber so rarely used, the one that overlooked the bailey and stables.

'Twas the bed she had made ready for Burke.

Alys sat up with a start, her hair falling unbound over her shoulders. Her heart skipped a beat when she noted saddle-bags propped against one wall. Alys knew well enough who had ridden through Kiltorren's gates with such fine leather bags. They could not be mistaken for those of anyone else, given their remarkable workmanship—the mark of a distant Italian city—and their insignia.

'Twas the lion rampant and three lilies, the same mark of Montvieux that graced Burke's tabard.

Alys shoved one hand through her unbound hair. The neck of the chemise gaped, the sleeves fell over her hands, and she looked at the garb for the first time.

'Twas a man's chemise, wrought of linen finer than any she had known.

And Alys knew, without doubt, to whom it belonged. Her eyes widened in dismay. She could not have slumbered with Burke—could she? Alys peeked beneath the fine white chemise and found naught encouraging, for she was as nude as the day she had been born.

Oh, this tale grew less promising with every moment! She

was in Burke's bed, nude but for his own chemise, and he had not abandoned his quarters.

That she recalled naught of how she had come to be in the man's bed, or even what had occurred afterward, was far from heartening. Alys felt the residual thickness on her tongue from Cook's concoction, and tried to clear her thoughts.

Surely she could not already be compromised?

That single thought had Alys scanning the linens in a panic, seeking the evidence that her maidenhead had been lost. The bedding was blissfully unmarred, but Alys was far from reassured.

The man had a scheme, she knew it well.

A merry knock sounded on the door and Alys spun to find Edana peeking around the wood.

Alys did not wait for a greeting. "Edana, you must tell me—what has happened?"

"Oh, Alys, 'twas *wondrous*!" Edana bounced into the room, her gestures broad in her enthusiasm of reliving events. "Cook said you had only just fallen asleep when your knight strode in the kitchens demanding to know of your whereabouts."

Alys folded her arms across her chest, disliking how her heart stirred to this tale. "He is not my knight, Edana," she insisted, though the case was difficult to make, kneeling in the man's bed, garbed in naught but his chemise, her hair spilling loose over her shoulders.

" 'Tis not what *he* says," Edana declared. "And 'tis not what Cook says. Your knight fell to his knees beside you, then swept you in his arms. He granted you his chamber, despite her ladyship's protests, and sat beside you until I came."

Alys studied the room uneasily. What would Aunt have to say about this? Naught good, she could well imagine.

"He was most concerned for your welfare," Edana bubbled. "Indeed, he gave me an unguent for your back from his own belongings and insisted you wear his spare chemise, since yours was in tatters. Oh, you should have seen his eyes!" Edana fairly bounced in her excitement. " 'Tis like a fine old tale! Alys, are you not the most fortunate woman in Kiltorren?"

Alys was not nearly certain of that. There would be a price to be paid for this, of that she had no doubt. She swallowed the lump in her throat with difficulty. "Where did he sleep, Edana?"

"In the stables." The goatgirl grinned. "Truly there was never a more gallant man to cross the threshold of Kiltorren. He asked most urgently after your welfare this morn and insisted you be left to sleep undisturbed."

Alys sat back cautiously. Edana's version of events did indeed sound like an old tale come to life, but Alys knew 'twas not.

Truly, naught could have painted Burke's intent more clearly than this! She had been deposited in the man's own bed, in a chamber he had not abandoned, and he was in haste for her to heal. 'Twas obvious enough that Burke intended to take his pleasure with her. If ever he had spoken of nuptials before, 'twas clear he had no such plan this time.

Despite his fine words, Alys's suspicions were painfully true.

Then she recalled a deed left undone and was anxious for another cause. "Did you go to Heloise?"

"Yesterday," Edana confirmed. She sat down beside Alys and bobbed lightly on the mattress, her eyes widening at its softness. "You have slept clear through the night and the morning. Cook says 'tis his brew at work, though on a bed like this, 'tis scarcely any wonder to me that you did not wish to awaken."

"How was Heloise?"

"Well enough." Edana wrinkled her nose. "She did not believe my tale, though 'twas close to the truth."

That was enough to take Alys's thought from her own troubles once more. "Why? What did you tell her?"

Edana lay back across the mattress and sighed appreciatively. "I could sleep a week in this bed."

"Edana!" Alys let her frustration slip into her tone. "What did you tell Heloise?"

The goatgirl sat up, her red-gold braid tumbling over her shoulder, her expression unrepentant. "I said that her ladyship had set you at an impossible task and you dared not disappoint." Edana grimaced. " 'Twas the wrong tale to tell, for Heloise grew most agitated."

"Did she fall ill again?" Alys demanded.

Edana shook her head. "Nay, she muttered a great deal and I could not discern her words." She flicked a glance to Alys. "She told me that she was not addressing me when I asked. In the end, I pledged that you would visit her shortly."

Alys stretched her shoulders and was surprised to find how much they had already healed. If naught else, Burke's unguent had aided her, and she grudgingly admitted it had been gracious of him to offer it.

Even if his desire to see her healed had a selfish root.

No doubt Burke would demand a token of her esteem for his thoughtfulness, a kiss that would quickly turn to his advantage. 'Twould be like him to be so incorrigible, so quick to press any advantage in his pursuit. Her pulse leapt, but Alys knew better than to follow its urgings.

She dared not risk meeting him this day.

"I shall go this very day to see Heloise," Alys declared, and smiled for Edana. "I would not have her worry."

Edana's brow puckered with concern. "But are you certain that you should? Cook insisted you should rest, and your knight was most intent that you remain in his bed."

In *his* bed? Those unwelcome words were all the encouragement Alys needed to get up.

" 'Twill do me good to be out in the air," she insisted. She quickly peeled off Burke's chemise and reached for her own humble undergarment, deliberately ignoring how rough the cloth was in comparison.

Indeed, Alys smiled when she noted it had been carefully mended already. "Edana! Is this your labor?"

"Your knight wanted me to ensure that you were undisturbed this morn and there was little else to do here. I mended your kirtle as well," the girl confessed shyly. "Though my stitches are not as fine as yours."

" 'Twas most thoughtful of you!" Alys ran her fingertip across the repair. "And all the more appreciated for I know how you dislike a lady maid's employ." She gave the girl a quick kiss on the cheek and Edana flushed.

"I do this willingly for you," Edana said with a stubborn set to her chin. "But never for *them*."

Would that Alys had such a choice. She sighed at the unwitting reminder and donned her garb, determinedly humming Heloise's tale beneath her breath.

She could not be away from here soon enough.

Alys descended to the hall and, grateful to find it empty, hastened onward to the kitchen. Cook inquired after her sleep and she reassured him with a smile, setting to the task of packing some foodstuffs for Heloise. They argued briefly about Alys's intention, but Cook quickly resigned himself to the fact that she would go, with or without his endorsement.

"If you must go, then take this treat for Heloise, with my regards." Cook handed Alys a warm loaf of bread, his manner telling her that 'twas of the finer flour. Alys tucked it into the depths of the basket, then cut a measure of the new wheel of cheese. She worked quickly, determined to be gone before Burke could come upon her.

But Alys was not quick enough to avoid another.

Malvina strode into the kitchen in obviously poor temper, her voice rising in a whine. "Alys, why did you sleep so very late? My favored kirtle is in need of mending and I would have it done before the midday meal."

Alys did no more than glance up before she continued what she had begun. "I cannot tend to it now, Malvina."

Her cousin pouted. "Whyever not?"

"Because I am on my way to visit Heloise," Alys explained patiently. "I shall do the mending when I return."

"But, Alys! I would wear it for the midday meal!"

"Surely you could don it as it is," Alys observed. One look confirmed 'twas the kirtle she had mended a week before and Malvina had worn it just once since that time. "It cannot be so badly damaged as that."

"But I want it *perfect*!" Malvina wailed. " 'Tis a hue that favors me, you said so yourself, and I want to look my very best for Burke."

Alys froze, not liking the sound of that. "For Burke?"

Malvina smiled. "Aye! He has been most charming to me these past evenings, telling me tales of his adventures and coaxing my laughter in a most chivalrous manner. And last night, last night, Alys, he kissed my hand with such ardor that I nearly swooned."

Alys blinked. So much for Edana's tale that the knight had been consumed with concern for *her* last evening. Clearly his attention was easily won. "Burke kissed you?" she asked woodenly.

Malvina smiled. "Aye! I am certain he would have kissed me fully if Mother had not been hovering so close. The man's eyes had a gleam in them that made me tingle clear to my toes."

Oh, Alys knew that gleam, as well as its potency. She had no doubt that Malvina embellished the facts, but still there must be a kernel of truth in her tale.

Malvina was not that imaginative a soul.

"And his touch!" Malvina shivered with the thrill of recollection. "He touched my chin so gently, despite his strength. I could have denied him naught!"

Alys knew that sensation better than she might have preferred and did not appreciate knowing how broadly the knight spread his charm. She jammed a pair of apples into the basket, her ears ringing with the recollection of Burke's laughter two nights past.

He had been enjoying Malvina's company while Alys toiled, which lent credence to her cousin's tale. And he had not seemed inclined to peel Malvina from his shoulder.

It seemed the man must have every woman panting for him to suit his considerable pride. Alys swallowed and blindly shoved a napkin atop her basket's contents.

Malvina continued, apparently oblivious to the impact of her words. "Oh, Alys, Mother is certain the knight means to offer for my hand. So you see, I cannot risk looking less than my finest."

"I cannot do this now, Malvina."

"Nay?" Malvina leaned closer, her eyes bright. "Alys, I shall tell Mother if you deny me. She would be most vexed with you."

Alys straightened and held her cousin's gaze for a telling moment. She was not afraid of her cousin, who did little but whine when her will was not fulfilled.

"What else do you imagine Aunt could do to me?" Alys asked coldly, then hefted her basket, wincing at the pain across her shoulder.

"Alys, are you certain you should go?" Cook asked quickly.

"Of course. Heloise is worried." Alys forced a smile. "I cannot let her fret, and she will only be reassured by my presence."

Cook frowned at the truth of that and turned reluctantly back to his onions.

"That is a lie! You only do this to deny me," Malvina charged.

"I told you that I would repair the kirtle later."

"You must repair it *now!* Do it first, before you go—that old harridan can wait."

Alys stiffened at Malvina's disregard for everyone besides

herself. "Nay, for once in your days, *you* will have to wait."
And she pivoted, heading for the portal with purpose.

"You only want to keep me from charming Burke utterly
and completely," Malvina cried. "But you cannot do so, Alys,
'tis too late for any dreams you might have had of him."

Alys halted halfway across the floor, unable to keep herself
from looking back. "I have no dreams of Burke de Montvieux."

"That is not what he says! Oh, he told me all about you,"
Malvina declared, her tone scathing. "Indeed, we had a fine
laugh over the way you so obviously long for his touch. You
are a wanton, Alys, and our guest is most embarrassed by
your manner." Malvina flicked the hem of her veil over her
shoulders. "In truth, he asked for my aid in dissuading you
from your pursuit."

Alys set the basket down heavily. "I have never pursued him!"

Malvina chuckled. "Truly, Alys, do you believe that no
one notes the way you sigh when he looks your way? Your
blushes do not go unnoticed, you may be certain of that.
Mother even confided that she had forbidden you to see Burke,
hoping only to preserve your virtue, but it seems your mother's
taint is overstrong."

"Nay! That is not true!"

"Alys is the daughter of a whore," Malvina chanted child-
ishly. "Alys was born to be a whore."

"Isibeal was no whore," Cook muttered angrily.

"Aye, she was!" Malvina lifted her chin, her gaze bright.
"Even a chivalrous knight is prey to a man's desires, Alys.
You have pushed Burke overmuch, and now he will grant you
what you so clearly want." She smiled, looking very much
her mother's spawn. "Mother says that men are weak when it
comes to temptations of the flesh. Surely you cannot make
naught of the fact that you slept in his bed?"

Alys held herself stiffly. "Edana said the knight was concerned for me."

"Aye, he spoke of your needing *comfort*." Malvina laughed as Alys's cheeks burned, then shook her head. "Ah, Alys, do you not see how pathetic you are?"

"It seems I owe you thanks for making the matter clear," Alys said frostily.

"Make no mistake, Alys," her cousin declared with a shake of her finger, "you shall find yourself out of Burke's bed as quickly as you were dumped within it, with naught to show for it but a rounding belly." Malvina sneered. "Just like your mother. The man knows for what you were wrought."

"You are wrong!"

"Aye? Mother says that men believe that bestowing their seed is a great gift—but 'tis where they put their *ring* that matters."

Malvina looked pointedly at Alys's bare fingers. Alys could not keep herself from hiding them in the folds of her kirtle.

" 'Tis odd, I note no ring on your hand," Alys commented.

"*Yet.*" Malvina smirked. "Knights do not wed bastard serving wenches, Alys." She laughed. "No doubt Burke and I shall share a jest over your foolish hopes at the midday board."

Alys's heart thudded in her chest.

"Mend my kirtle now, Alys," Malvina invited, tossing the offending garment onto the table, "and I shall permit you to attend my nuptials with Burke." She paused, letting her scornful glance drift over Alys. "Even if he has had you as his whore."

Alys snatched up her basket angrily. "Mend it yourself!" she cried, and flung herself out the kitchen door.

Burke was impatient beyond anything he had known.

He knew that Alys needed her rest, but still it vexed him to linger in this cursed place. Indeed, he would have simply carried her away while she slept, but he was quite certain his lady would have much to say about that.

He would have her agreement first.

Burke concertedly avoided Deirdre, not trusting himself to

hold his tongue over what Alys had endured the day before. Indeed, the sight of those marks marring his lady's soft flesh could not be pushed from his thoughts. He fervently wished he had a healer's skills, not merely some unguent, to ease those marks away.

He would have sat diligently beside her all the night long, ensuring that she slept well and undisturbed, but Alys's charges of his disinterest in her reputation had cut deep. 'Twas true enough that such a course would have prompted chatter, though Burke would have cared little for that.

But Alys cared. Out of respect for his lady's desires, Burke stayed away.

It nigh killed him.

His mood was not improved when Malvina came to seek him out. He and Kerwyn were occupied with the cleaning of Moonshadow's hooves, a task the destrier tolerated poorly and one that, in all honesty, was not even due to be done.

That 'twas better than doing naught said much of Burke's mood.

"Burke! Where *are* you?"

The sound of Malvina's voice made Burke wince and Kerwyn chuckle. "I believe the ostler has need of me," the stablehand said with quiet mischief, earning a dark glance from the knight.

"Abandon me to her and you shall regret it," Burke muttered through his teeth. "I shall hunt you down and wring a penance from your hide."

"Ah, but this lady's presence is a heavy penance in itself," Kerwyn retorted, his eyes dancing. "I must weigh the cost of lingering against any threat you make."

Burke chuckled despite himself at the truth of that. "You can ride the beast, if you only remain."

"Aye, if he will permit me." Kerwyn scraped at the hoof Burke held and Moonshadow shuddered in agitation. The destrier twitched and fought once more to pull his foot from the knight's grip. He whinnied when he failed and Burke tightened his grip.

"Finish it quickly!" he bade the stablehand, feeling Moonshadow's temper rise. 'Twas time to be done with this labor or abandon it.

"Burke! Here you are!" Malvina appeared suddenly at the end of the stall. Her shadow slanted into the tiny space and a deluge of exotic perfume wafted before her. Moonshadow's nostrils quivered dangerously and Burke knew trouble was, quite literally, in the wind.

"Leave it be and step away!" he instructed tersely.

"Done!" Kerwyn cried in the same moment and darted backward, his hands in the air.

Burke released the stallion's hoof just as Moonshadow threw back his head in fury. The steed kicked hard, narrowly missing both men, and swung his hip against the wall of the stall, clearly intending to flatten those who tormented him. Kerwyn swore as Moonshadow's weight landed solidly against the wall a mere arm's length in front of him.

"He must like you," Burke teased. "For he missed."

The stablehand laughed in his relief but the stallion exhaled mightily. Moonshadow had not had his say fully as yet, and Burke took a wary step back.

To his astonishment, Malvina appeared betwixt him and his steed. He had nigh forgotten her presence, but clearly that omission was not to go uncorrected.

"Burke," Malvina chided with a sly smile, clearly oblivious to the furious steed behind her. "How can you so ignore me when I have sought you all the day?"

Moonshadow fought the tether and the bit. He lifted one heavy foot and Burke spied trouble just before it happened.

Chapter Six

MALVINA, LOOK OUT!"

Burke caught the girl with one arm and swept her out of harm's way in the nick of time. Moonshadow kicked directly where she had been, his tolerance of perfume limited at the best of times. The destrier stamped, flung his weight against the opposing wall of the stall, snorted and fumed.

Then, apparently satisfied that he had made his opinion clear—or that his tormentors had retreated sufficiently—the stallion settled.

He blew insouciantly at the contents of his feed bin, scattering hay in every direction. Clearly pleased with his deeds, he acted for all the world as if naught were amiss.

Burke breathed a sigh of relief. The beast would not willfully hurt another, but there was always a chance of his miscalculating his weight and strength.

'Twas then Burke realized that Malvina still clung to him. He stepped back, trying to set a distance between them.

But to his chagrin, Malvina wound her arms around his neck. "Oh, Burke, you saved me from dire peril! How wondrously gallant!"

"Anyone would have done as much," the knight said grimly, working a little more diligently to extricate himself.

"But you *did*," the girl breathed, landing a wet kiss on his cheek. Burke met Kerwyn's gaze and nearly laughed, for the stablehand—safely out of the girl's view—puckered his lips in a swooning mimicry of the daughter of the house.

Burke tried to look stern. "Malvina, you must not make much of little."

"How modest you are." Malvina purred, and rubbed her breasts against him. " 'Tis no small thing to be so brave a man as you."

Burke refrained from commenting that 'twas her own foolishness that had placed her in jeopardy.

"No doubt your father would have been sorely displeased if my steed injured you," he said with a cool smile. He deliberately broke her embrace, then stepped away.

The girl was not so easily deterred as that. "I think we should seal the moment with a kiss," she suggested. "Mother constantly asks me about the course of your suit."

With those words, Burke knew he had to find some means of escape that would not reveal his utter disinterest in Deirdre's eldest.

And he was fortunate enough to find it.

"Ah, Malvina! Your kirtle has been mired." Burke grimaced as if this were more dire, hoping against hope that she would see fit to change. "Malvina, you should not have sullied your garb with a visit to the stables," he said with a winning smile. "Perhaps if 'tis cleaned immediately, there will be no stain."

Kerwyn smirked, but Malvina's brow darkened as she examined the mark upon her skirt. She laid her fingertips on Burke's arm and leaned closer as the knight fought his urge to recoil. "I shall not be long. Wait for me!"

Malvina trotted to the stable doors, and Burke ran one hand through his hair in relief.

"One can only hope that it takes her half the day to choose her garb," he muttered, and Kerwyn laughed aloud.

Edana came into the stables just as Malvina left, the two passing in the portal. The goatgirl uttered a greeting, but Malvina brushed past, her nose in the air.

Kerwyn straightened as Edana headed toward them with a pert smile. The goats, stalled beyond Moonshadow, began to bleat as if they knew she drew near.

"I am coming, ladies!" she called with a cheerfulness Burke found far from his own mood.

"Good morning, Edana," Kerwyn said with surprising formality. The girl flushed and returned the greeting.

But Burke eyed Edana. "I thought you minded Alys." He surveyed his surroundings impatiently. "Indeed, if the lady would only awaken, we would be gone before that one returns."

"But she *is* awake," Edana declared. "That is why I come for my ladies."

"She is?" Alys was awake and she had not sought him out? Burke frowned. "Is she well? Does her injury still plague her? There is more of the unguent, if she has the need."

"She is well enough. Indeed, she has gone to visit Heloise." Edana graced Kerwyn with another warm smile, and the stablehand grinned foolishly. Then the goatgirl headed for her wards, her hips swaying.

But Burke blinked, unable to credit her tale. Alys had awakened in his bed and left, without even thanking him for his concern? 'Twas unlike his lady to show such a lack of manners.

And how could Alys not have desired to see Burke as ardently as he wished to see her this day?

A less confident man might have been insulted, but Burke knew there was still some issue between them. Alys was avoiding him, he had guessed aright. Why else would she take such an unnecessary mission upon herself in this moment?

Burke propped his hands on his hips and turned to call

after the girl. "And who is this Heloise? Where might she be found?"

"The anchorite," Kerwyn supplied instead. "She lives in the stone hut on the point. 'Tis a good few miles along the coast."

"Miles? Alys was to lie abed this day!" Burke protested. "She was to heal, not walk miles alone!"

Edana shrugged. "Alys insisted on visiting Heloise. She was supposed to go yesterday but could not in the end. I went in her stead, but Alys worries about Heloise."

With a pert smile, Edana opened the latch and the goats spilled noisily into the corridor. She patted them as they passed her, greeting each by name, Alys's doings clearly the last matter upon her mind.

Burke gritted his teeth. He had not surrendered all to win naught. Nay, he would not countenance Alys's avoidance. She would hear him out, and she would hear him out on *this* day.

"Fetch Moonshadow's saddle for me, if you will," Burke requested of the stablehand, who still stared after the goatgirl. "And point me in the direction of this anchorite's abode."

"Burke! I am coming!" Malvina cried from the keep. "The mark was removed with but a bit of water and I am again at my finest."

Burke deliberately ignored the stablehand's smirk. "Kerwyn, make haste, if you value your hide!"

"Empty threats," Kerwyn teased, but he fetched Moonshadow's saddle so quickly that Burke had no complaints.

◈

Alys paused and caught her breath. She saw Heloise in the distance, crouched, staring at the pebbles that covered the ground, her head cocked to listen.

'Twas going to be one of those visits.

Alys sighed, summoned a smile, and waved. Heloise had always recognized her, but each time Alys visited, she feared the worst. The older woman's thoughts grew progressively more muddled as time passed.

"Good day, Heloise!" she called with a cheer she was not feeling, then lifted her skirts and made her way closer.

The older woman looked up and squinted into the sun. Though another might have been startled, Alys barely noted in these days that one side of Heloise's face hung slack and expressionless, or that her right arm was nigh useless. She had learned to focus upon the other half of the older woman's visage, where still Heloise's smile curved her lips and her eye sparkled.

"Alys!" The older woman hobbled past the crude stone hut that now was her home, her quick steps ample evidence of her concern. 'Twas not easy for her, for still her right leg fought against movement. "What has she done to you?"

"Naught, Heloise, naught," Alys lied, putting an arm around the woman's shoulders before she could see even the mending upon Alys's kirtle. They did not need to repeat the past this day. " 'Twas some whimsy of a task Aunt granted me, no more than that. You see? I am here, hale and hearty." She kissed Heloise's cheek. "You have naught to fear for me."

Heloise shot a sharp glance her way. "Aye? Did she set you to scrubbing the hall with one fingertip?"

Alys laughed and declined to elaborate. "How are *you*?"

"Well enough, if not for *them*." Heloise looked back to the pebbles and frowned.

"Them?"

The older woman leaned closer, her eyes gleaming. "The stones! They are speaking, keeping me awake all the night with their chattering." She sighed. "They grow louder each and every day so that I cannot bear their din. Listen to them!"

The older woman stared fixedly at the pebbles in question. Alys held her tongue, as 'twas clearly what she was meant to do, but discerned naught beyond the typical whistle of the wind, the crash of the sea, and the cries of the seabirds.

She jumped when Heloise looked sharply at her once more. "Well?"

Alys shrugged. "I cannot hear them."

Heloise clicked her tongue in agitation.

'Twas clear that solitude was addling the older woman's wits, and Alys felt a surge of anger that Aunt had insisted the older woman be removed to this place. 'Twas a poor prize for years of loyal service. Heloise was too old to be left alone, too frail to be subjected to the dampness of the wind from the sea, too forgetful to ensure her own welfare.

Indeed, Alys had no doubt that Heloise had let the fire die again.

"How fares your hearth?" she asked, trying to distract the older woman from the stones. "Cook has sent you some lovely bread, and we could melt a piece of cheese atop it."

Heloise's gaze brightened, then she frowned in confusion. "There is no hearth here."

"Of course there is." Alys took the maid by the hand and led her to the stone hut. 'Twas dark inside, no glimmer of a coal upon the flat stones placed for a fire.

The firewood Alys had collected upon her last visit was either still there or Edana had replenished the stock. Clearly, though, the girl had not known that she must start the blaze for Heloise. Alys left Heloise to peruse the contents of the basket and collected some wood, then struck a flint.

Heloise, as always, cried out at the first sight of a spark. For some reason, she associated the fire with events leading to her fit, regardless of what Alys said of the matter.

Perhaps that was why she left the hearth untended.

" 'Tis all over, Heloise," Alys said crisply, coaxing the first tinder to burn. " 'Tis in the past and can hurt neither of us any longer."

"Let me see your back," the older woman said suddenly.

The fire caught as Alys glanced up. "There is naught to

see," she argued, wondering at this unexpected demand. Heloise's eyes were oddly bright. " 'Tis long healed and you know it well."

Heloise shook her head. "The stones say nay."

Alys felt the hairs on the back of her neck prickle at this oddly accurate claim. She straightened, ensuring she faced Heloise. "The stones are wrong," she asserted. "Would you have some cheese and bread?"

Heloise considered her for a long moment. "You are well?"

Alys smiled. "I am fine."

But Heloise shook her head, clearly troubled by her memories. She squatted down and rocked on her heels in agitation. "She should not do this, she should not hurt you, she should not disserve the memory of Isibeal. Ah, Isibeal!"

As was often the case when the maid was agitated, she fingered a chain around her neck that Alys had never seen her remove. There was a pendant upon it, though Heloise guarded it jealously and never let any look upon it. Alys assumed 'twas a token from her family, or perhaps that of a love gone astray.

"Isibeal!" Heloise whispered, and began to cry. "I failed her in this one important deed. She bade me care for you, protect you."

"And so you did." Alys crouched before the older woman and pulled her into a loose embrace. "Heloise! 'Tis because of you and your love that I grew so straight."

Heloise bit her lip and abandoned the pendant to touch Alys's cheek. 'Twas as if she had to prove Alys's presence to herself, and Alys ached at the older woman's uncertainty.

"There is no reason for concern," Alys crooned. "I had an onerous task that kept me from visiting you, but 'tis done, and I am none the worse for wear."

Heloise stroked Alys's cheek, her gaze filling with an affection that reminded Alys of the maid's younger days. "Sweet like Isibeal," she whispered.

Alys held Heloise while the fire flickered to life, unable to avoid thinking that their roles had been transposed. She could remember Heloise holding her close in reassurance—and knew how much those embraces had meant to her.

Heloise finally shook her head, gave the pendant one last rub, then tucked it into her chemise with fumbling fingers. "Has your knight come for you yet, Alys, as Aucassin came for Nicolette?"

"Nay." Alys forced a smile and cut the bread, well aware of how Heloise watched her.

"Are you certain?"

Alys took a deep breath. She met Heloise's gaze and decided to ask. No one would know, especially a certain cocksure knight. And this was the only person she knew she could trust.

"Heloise, do you remember a man, a knight, named Burke de Montvieux? He came to Kiltorren three years ago."

Heloise shook her head. "I was here then, I have been here since Isibeal died."

Alys shook her head, well accustomed to Heloise's uncertainty over timing of events. Her thinking had been much muddled by her fit. Though it had cleared markedly, still some matters were confused. "Nay, you were still at the keep then. Isibeal died when I was only a babe, and you know you told me tales every night for years. That was at the keep."

The older woman chewed her lip.

"Heloise, do you remember that tale we used to sing?" she asked. Alys began to sing the familiar chanson, fully expecting Heloise to join the words.

"Once, far afield, there lived a man
With wealth and fortune to his hand.
He had one son, a tall, strong man
The handsome knight named Aucassin.

Aucassin's father, he did fret
For he did want his son to wed.
But no bride would that knight accept,
For he loved only Nicolette.

Nicolette had a beauty pure,
Though her parentage was not assured.
Raised humbly by a childless brewer,
Her sweetness won her knight's amour.

When Aucassin would not deny
His lady or seek another bride
His father did the brewer advise
The maid must vanish or die."

"Aye!" Heloise crowed, her voice rising high and clear as she began to sing in turn.

"But Aucassin searched without cease,
He sought his lady on seven seas,
His banner snapped upon the breeze,
Graced by a lion and three lilies."

Alys stiffened, oblivious to the melting cheese that dripped into the fire with a sizzle. There was only one insignia she knew with a lion and three lilies. And this verse echoed rather too strongly of Burke's insistence that he had sought Alys far and wide.

What *did* Heloise remember?

"This is not the tune as you taught it to me."

Heloise grinned, the firelight painting her features with an uneven light that made her disfiguration even more marked. She seemed more intently present than she had been in years.

"The stones say 'tis how it should be sung now."

The hairs prickled again on the back of Alys's neck, but suddenly Heloise spied the toasted cheese and bread. Her face lit with pleasure and she reached impatiently for the bread, chattering of her love for cheese. Once again she was naught but a confused older woman in need of Alys's care.

The moment was gone, but Heloise's unexpected verse would echo long in Alys's thoughts.

The sun was sinking low when Alys climbed from Heloise's hut and turned to wave farewell. But the older woman had already forgotten her. Heloise was bent once more over the stones, her head cocked. Alys watched her for a long sad moment and resolved to come more often.

She wondered whether Aunt could be persuaded to let Heloise back into the hall. If naught else, the elderly maid would be warmer and better fed than she managed on her own.

Aunt. The very thought of confronting her was sobering. Perhaps Alys should retire to this hut and care for Heloise herself. Undoubtedly the feud between the two older women was a bitter one. Alys sighed, frowned, and turned to trudge homeward, only now acknowledging the ache in her bones.

She had done too much this day, that was certain, but there had been no choice. Heloise had her alone to rely upon, and truly, Alys's debt to her mother's maid was not small. She would do anything for Heloise.

Perhaps even challenge Aunt.

Alys glanced up, gauging the distance to the keep, and caught her breath.

For a knight stood silhouetted against the brightness of the sky, his destrier grazing beside him.

Burke was clearly waiting for her.

Alys willed her heart to slow and tried to continue on as if the sight of him, waiting, did not trouble her in the least. Her lips twisted with the recollection of Malvina's claim that they laughed together over her desire for the knight. Whether 'twas true or not, Alys resolved that Burke would see no evidence of her wayward yearnings this evening.

'Twould do the man good to have some doubt of his appeal.

Burke knew the very moment that Alys spied him.

She had been trudging tiredly along the stony coast where no path was discernible to the eye. He had waited impatiently, his boot tapping, knowing that he had no place invading the solitude of an anchorite, yet anxious to assure himself that Alys was well.

The way she walked when she finally appeared did little to reassure Burke. She was exhausted, 'twas evident, yet still she intended to walk the few miles to the keep. He did not know whether to kiss her or kill her over her reckless disregard for her own health.

Then Alys spied him. She straightened as if bracing herself for a battle—or deliberately hiding her fatigue—lifted her chin, and strode in his direction with purpose. And Burke found a smile of anticipation curving his lips.

Oh, he liked the fire that had been kindled in his lady love.

Alys's eyes flashed when she drew near him, though she neither halted nor glanced his way. 'Twas left to Burke to turn and match his steps to hers. Moonshadow, his reins hanging slack, ambled behind.

Burke felt as much as saw Alys's sidelong glance.

"You wait for me."

"And have all afternoon."

Alys sniffed. "Surely Malvina made more pressing demands upon your time."

Aha! Suddenly Burke understood the reason for the lady's irritation and that made him smile. "Are you jealous?" he teased.

"Not I! I merely heard you courted her," Alys said tightly. She strode with a vigor that belied her stated indifference, and Burke was vastly cheered by this. "Indeed, she insists your offer for her hand will come shortly."

"And she is sorely mistaken," Burke clarified. Alys looked to him in surprise, and he smiled. "Alys, why are you walking all this distance on this day? I had intended for you to remain abed."

"In *your* bed!" Alys corrected. "Aye, there is little import to be missed in that. Did you expect me to welcome you between my thighs for your aid?"

"Nay! I am a man of honor . . ."

Alys pivoted smartly to face Burke, her eyes snapping. "Yet 'tis your deeds that continually make trouble between us. What am I to think when a knight deposits me in his bed, nude but for his chemise, and does not abandon those quarters?"

Burke folded his arms across his chest in annoyance. "I slept in the stables. Did Edana not tell you as much?"

"Aye. But the presence of your saddlebags indicates your intent to return."

"They indicate naught beyond the fact that I forgot them." Burke leaned closer and let his voice drop low. "Alys, I was concerned for you. Did you not think to seek me out this day? To thank me? To set my fears to rest?"

Alys studied him for a moment, as if wanting to believe him but not daring to do so. Then she shook her head and continued on her route. "I understand that you are anxious that I heal, that you might have your pleasure."

Burke strode after her, infuriated by this tale. "Who told you such nonsense?"

Alys lifted her chin. "Malvina claims you two are confidants."

"Malvina." Burke swore softly. "The truth is as likely to fall from that one's lips as a volley of pearls."

"I saw you and I heard you, making merry at the board with her," Alys retorted. "And there is no lie in that."

"And what am I to do?" Burke flung out his hands in frustration. "Your aunt and uncle insist I must have come to court your cousins."

"Fair enough. 'Twas what *you* said when you arrived."

Burke chose not to argue that. "They already have threatened to cast me out over doubts of my intent. I must make a show of courting Malvina, at least until you grant me a fair hearing."

Alys slanted a glance his way. "Consider yourself to have had it."

"I have *not*, for still you think poorly of me and I have done naught to earn that," Burke said with a growl. "Alys, it seems I can do naught aright in this. I granted you solitude this morn, because you declared that I did not give enough care to your reputation within the hall. So, out of deference to your concerns, I did *not* sit in that chamber all the night long and ensure you were undisturbed."

She glanced up, but Burke did not cease. "And my reward for this is that your family have the opportunity to pour poison into your ears, which you believe at my expense!"

"Fairly spoken, but your deeds do little to reassure me that I have misinterpreted you in truth." Alys pivoted to walk ahead of him, obviously untroubled by his frustration.

And Burke's annoyance faded to naught when he noted a thin trickle of fresh blood staining her kirtle.

He lent chase, concern making his voice low. "Alys, you have opened your wounds again." When she did not halt,

Burke caught at her arm and turned her to face him. "You have done too much this day, as I feared you would."

Alys shook her head. "It matters naught. Indeed, I had no choice."

"Surely this Heloise could have waited another day."

But Alys shook her head firmly. "Nay. Edana told her some tale and she was fretful for my welfare. I had to come." She took a deep breath and summoned a smile. "I shall be back at the hall soon enough, if you permit me to continue, and, with some fortune, will not have too much labor to do."

"You jeopardized your welfare to see her fears laid to rest," Burke murmured, awed by her selflessness. "Alys, you must show yourself more mercy."

His lady shrugged, her cheeks pinkening slightly. "I would not see her have another fit."

Burke cupped Alys's chin, forcing her to meet his gaze. "And I would see you healed in truth. 'Tis the same concern for a loved one that drives us both, Alys."

Her expression turned assessing. "What of Malvina?"

Burke grimaced. "I have told you the truth, as always I have done. I would ride from the gates with you at this very moment, Alys, and never glance back to Kiltorren again." Uncertainty lit her golden eyes and Burke leaned closer, intent on securing his victory. "Alys, 'tis you alone who holds my heart, you alone who haunts my dreams."

"Oh!" Alys rolled her eyes, pulled herself away from his touch, and marched ahead of him once more.

Burke flung out his hands and bellowed, feeling cheated of his prize in the last moment. "What did I say?"

"Oh, Burke, whenever I come close to believing what you pledge, you make some preposterous compliment that cannot be believed," the lady complained, her irritation clear. "Do you make the same sweet promises to all the women whose affections you court?"

"Alys, there is only you!"

She cast him a skeptical smile. "Indeed. It sounds as if you have practiced that claim as well."

Burke growled and matched steps with his lady once more. He forced himself to pursue matters on another front. " 'Tis a sorry state of affairs when a man finds himself jealous of the time his lady spends with an old woman." He took a deep breath. "And truly, this place vexes me beyond all."

"Not just me?" Alys teased unexpectedly.

Burke chuckled despite himself, enjoying her quick wits. Aye, she saw right to the meat of the matter, and he liked that well. "You have had a role in my frustration, Alys, no doubt. All the same, I would apologize for my poor temper."

They walked in silence for a few moments.

"Tell me of this old maid," Burke invited finally.

"Heloise is not that old," Alys said, her tone carefully neutral.

"Who is she?"

"She was my mother's maid."

"And how did she come to be an anchorite?"

" 'Tis not pertinent, Burke."

"On the contrary, you speak her name with affection," he insisted. " 'Tis of great import to me to know of those you love."

Alys considered Burke as if this thought had never occurred to her before. "Heloise raised me as her own when my mother died," she admitted. " 'Twas she who defended me from Aunt, at least until they two did match wills several years past."

Burke frowned. "Was she here when I came?"

"Three years past, she was yet in the hall. You may recall her, though she tended to stay in the shadows."

And those few words alone did prompt Burke's recollection. "The older woman, with silver in her chestnut hair," he said with a snap of his fingers. "She was sparsely built. She said very little but gave an impression of great strength."

"That was Heloise."

Burke grinned. "And I recall that she oft looked daggers at your aunt."

Alys obviously tried to fight her answering smile, but her eyes sparkled. "That was she."

"She did not look to be a woman of God."

"Nay, she was a handmaid then, albeit one who grew older. Until the day I vexed Aunt overmuch—"

"Doubtless you did naught wrong," Burke interjected.

Alys sighed and frowned. "Nay, I broke a favored trinket of hers and she was not inclined to let the matter be. 'Twas the first time she whipped me."

"The first time?" Burke heard anger ripple in his voice. "This then is typical? How often has she raised a hand against you?"

"There has only been that time and this."

"Once is too much," he muttered. "What stayed her hand?"

" 'Twas Heloise. She leapt to defend me and Aunt, in her fury, turned upon her. She struck her and Heloise fell to the floor in a fit." A shadow drew across Alys's features, and Burke guessed the memory was both vivid and painful. " 'Twas horrible to watch, for she was in great pain, but none knew what to do." Alys shivered but did not pull away when Burke caught her hand in his. " 'Twas dreadful to stand by and do naught, but I could not help her."

"No one could have." He squeezed her fingers reassuringly, guessing how her thoughts would turn. "Though no doubt you felt responsible for this."

Alys swallowed and then nodded with reluctance. "Aye, in a part of my heart, I do blame myself, for if I had not defied Aunt . . ."

"If you had not been the daughter of the woman Heloise served with such dedication," Burke interrupted with vigor, "she would not have felt compelled to defend you from such injustice."

Alys met Burke's insistent gaze.

"Heloise loved you, so she defended you," he continued with conviction. " 'Tis your aunt who was wrong, and your aunt alone, for no one should be struck as you have been."

Alys frowned. "I only wish Heloise had not suffered."

Burke ran a thumb across the back of Alys's hand and urged her to walk closer to him, encouraged by her trust.

"And what did she suffer?"

Alys sighed. "When her fit subsided, one side of her body was without sensation. She could not move her arm, nor her leg, and her face was slack upon that same side."

Burke nodded. "I have seen this once, and that time it did ease away."

"So did Heloise's affliction fade, though still a vestige of it lingers. She cannot use that hand with any dexterity, and she limps. Her smile does not travel fully across her lips." Alys frowned. "And her thinking is not so clear as once it was."

"Why then is she out here, left alone to the elements? 'Tis unfitting for a woman in such a state. She should be sheltered within the hall, where others could aid her."

"Aye, she should!" Alys straightened in indignation. "But Uncle declared 'twas the hand of God that struck down Heloise, that He used Heloise as a tool to intervene in Aunt's dark deeds. Uncle insisted Aunt never strike me again, lest she attract God's wrath once more, and so she did not."

"Until yesterday."

"Aye." Alys swallowed. "Aunt did not take well to Uncle's dictate. She insisted that if God worked through Heloise, then Heloise must be fully pledged to His will. At her command, Heloise was cast from the hall and moved here"—Alys raised her voice to a mimicry of her aunt—"that she might live in solitude and contemplate God's mysteries in peace."

Burke snorted. "That she might fall ill and die, or at least not interfere with Deirdre's plans again."

Alys met his gaze solemnly. "You have called that aright, but Heloise is stronger than might have been expected."

Burke studied his lady, thinking the same might be said of her. "It seems your concern for Heloise grows greater."

Alys winced. "She is forgetting to tend the fire," she admitted in a low voice. "I fear 'tis a bad portent. And she is more confused than before. I fear she will forget to eat or to ensure her own welfare. And none come this way but me."

"You would have her return to the hall."

Alys nodded. "I wish I could persuade Aunt to welcome Heloise."

Fear shot through Burke at the very possibility. He grasped Alys's shoulders, pulled her to a halt, and turned her to face him. He had no doubt that she would do battle for this elderly maid and disregard any cost to herself.

"Alys, you cannot challenge your aunt, not after what she has just done!"

"Aunt cannot do worse to me and Heloise needs my aid." Alys turned an appealing look upon the knight that melted his heart. "Burke, understand that I owe her much for all the years she cared for me. I cannot let her perish out here alone! 'Tis wrong by any accounting!"

"Heloise may need aid," he said firmly, "but it does not have to be from you."

"But there is no one else who cares for her."

"But I care for you," Burke insisted. "I shall raise the issue with your family." He looked Alys steadily in the eye, willing her to believe him. "Not you."

"You would do this? Aunt will be most vexed."

"All the more reason for me to take this cause." Burke smiled slowly and squeezed her shoulders. "Do you not understand, Alys? I would do far more to win the sweet treasure of your smile, and even more again to win your hand within mine."

But Alys bit at an unwilling smile. "Burke, you must cease with these overwrought compliments."

"What did I say?"

"Sweet treasure of my smile?" Alys made a face. " 'Tis too rich for even a minstrel's taste!"

" 'Tis praise fairly won!"

Alys laughed at his indignation. " 'Tis a compliment too fulsome to be believed!"

But Burke did not smile. "And your belief in me is the issue that lies squarely between us, is it not?" he asked softly.

Alys sobered and looked away, the truth needing no confirmation.

He studied her for a long moment and had to ask. "Did your Heloise remember me?"

Alys caught her breath. "Her memory is addled."

Heloise did not recall him. Burke felt disappointment as keenly as a blow. 'Twas clear enough that the woman's endorsement of his suit would have gone far to win favor in his lady's sight.

"A week, Alys," he insisted. "Grant me a week to win Heloise's return to Kiltorren's keep."

Alys eyed him and Burke saw a flicker of hope dawn in those amber depths. Then she nodded abruptly. "One week."

Burke noted suddenly how his lady sagged beneath his hands. 'Twas as if relief stole the last of the fight within her. He recalled that trickle of blood and knew he could not permit her to do yet more. "Alys, you must ride back to the keep."

She glanced to him, then to Moonshadow, her alarm at the prospect more than clear. "There is no need . . ."

"There is every need. You have done far too much this day. You know that your wound is open again." He turned her and frowned at the mark of the fresh blood, relieved to see that there was no more. He saw no reason to tell Alys as much.

She should be back in bed, his or any other.

"I will not ride that beast," the lady insisted with a flick of her braid.

"You will ride that beast or I shall toss you over my shoulder," Burke retorted, letting her see his resolve. Alys's eyes widened slightly and he was pleased that she believed something of what he said. " 'Tis your choice—one of us shall carry you."

Alys lifted her chin. "I would walk."

"Sadly, that is not among your options."

And Alys smiled unexpectedly up at Burke. "You are most stubborn."

Burke felt his brow arch high. "And you would know naught of such a trait, of course."

Alys laughed aloud, her eyes sparkling merrily, and Burke felt a surge of victory beyond anything he had known. "I choose the steed, then, for you are most unpredictable."

"On the contrary, there is none more predictable than I."

The lady's smile faded, though whether 'twas at his words or the prospect of riding Moonshadow, Burke could not say. He fitted his hands around Alys's waist, deliberately ignoring his urge to taste her sweet lips first, and lifted her to sit side-saddle.

When he set her down, Alys's eyes widened in shock and she clutched the saddle in obvious fear. " 'Tis so high! I shall fall."

"You will not fall. Moonshadow will not permit it."

"He will have naught to say about it when I lose my balance and plummet from his back."

'Twas true enough that his saddle was not wrought for a lady and that Burke's stirrup dangled far beneath Alys's toe. Her perch would be solid enough, though, for the destrier moved at a leisurely rolling gait.

"You have only to grip the saddle." Burke took the reins and urged the beast forward, not missing his lady's gasp of terror. He looked back to find her complexion ashen and her knuckles white as she bumped awkwardly on Moonshadow's back.

And Burke immediately understood the problem. "Have you ever ridden before?"

Alys made a choking laugh. "And where would I ride a destrier, if even there was one to be found at Kiltorren?"

Aye, she had said she had never left the estate.

Burke slowed his pace to walk beside her, the stallion perfectly content to stroll without direction. "You must be one with the horse, Alys, and let yourself be carried with his rhythm."

"I cannot!"

" 'Twould happen of its own accord, if you were not so frightened."

She shot him a dark look. " 'Tis only sensible to be frightened when you are about to fall as far as I. I shall break every bone within my body for your stubborn insistence."

Burke could not help but chuckle at that.

" 'Tis not amusing!" the lady charged, her own lips curving in an unwilling smile.

"Nay, 'twill not be amusing on the morrow. You will be sore indeed, if you do not heed my advice."

"This is impossible! I shall walk instead."

" 'Tis the steed or I who will bear you."

Alys fired a mutinous look Burke's way that was far from flattering. "Then I shall take the bruises."

"You shall have no bruise if you heed my advice." Burke laid one hand on the back of her waist to emphasize his point. He pushed her with the rhythm of the steed's walk. "Roll with his gait, Alys. 'Tis simple enough. Do not fight the rhythm."

She frowned and clearly tried to do his bidding, though still she was stiff with fear. Burke realized that Alys was almost within the circle of his arms, her buttocks beneath his hand and her legs nearly against his chest. He could have plucked her from the saddle and held her close, the very knowledge making his heart pound.

The lady's delicate feet hung bare before him, tormenting him with their perfect femininity. They were tanned on their tops and dirtied on the bottom, so achingly fragile that Burke longed to spend the rest of the day tickling her toes.

Alys shook her head, apparently oblivious to the direction of her companion's thoughts. "Yet you insist this will do less damage to my hide than a leisurely walk. Burke, you would torment me!"

'Twas naught compared to how she tormented him.

Burke glanced up, intending to make some quick remark, but was snared by the laughter in the lady's eyes. The dimple that so fascinated him flashed in her cheek and she looked young and mischievous once more.

Burke could not help but stare. Alys held his gaze for an endless moment and it seemed he could not breathe. Her gaze fell to his lips, her own lips parted, and Burke could resist her allure no longer.

Before he could question the wisdom of his intent, he pulled Moonshadow to a halt, cast the reins over the steed's neck, and put his foot in the stirrup.

"What is this you do?" Alys asked breathlessly, even as he swung into the saddle behind her. Burke clamped one hand around her waist and pulled her back against him, not caring if she felt the evidence of his own torment.

"You must forget your fears," he said softly, then raised one hand to Alys's jaw. When he turned her face to his, he saw anticipation lighting her eyes and knew he was not the only one longing for a kiss.

'Twas the only encouragement he needed to continue.

" 'Tis my duty, Alys, to ensure you are injured no further," Burke murmured, then lifted one brow. "I must do my best to distract you."

Alys gasped as if she guessed his intention, but she did not pull away. Burke captured her lips with his, his eyes closing when she trembled, then leaned back against him. She parted her lips and he fanned his fingers wide, spanning the slenderness of her waist, even as his kiss deepened.

Alys murmured something against his lips, then arched against him. She abandoned her clutch upon the saddle to turn more fully into his embrace, her hands landing on his shoulders. Moonshadow continued undeterred as Burke kissed his lady thoroughly.

'Twas a long time before he lifted his head, and when he did they both were breathing quickly. The shadow of Kiltorren's keep was surprisingly near, though Burke did not want to surrender Alys's company as yet. The lady dropped her gaze, even as Burke noted that they both moved now with the rhythm of the steed.

"You see, Alys," he said with amusement, "you had only to forget yourself to ride with ease."

The words made Alys straighten with a vengeance. "Aye, I have forgotten myself in truth," she declared with unexpected heat, then turned a tearful glance upon Burke. "No doubt you and Malvina shall amuse yourselves well this night with the tale."

She flung off Burke's grip and jumped for the ground.

"Alys! Nay!" Burke snatched at her but missed. To his relief, Alys landed without injury, for she was quick to flee toward the hall.

But Burke did not intend to let her escape so quickly as that. "Alys!" he roared, giving Moonshadow his heels.

Chapter Seven

LYS RAN, CERTAIN THAT SHE WOULD NOT BE FAST enough to evade Burke. She scrambled over the low wall, knowing he would have to ride all the way to the gate, yet doubting 'twould be time enough to give her much advantage.

Hearing Moonshadow's hoofbeats as the beast rounded the wall, she raced to reach the kitchen portal without looking back. Burke swore and Alys glanced back to see him leap from his saddle. She lunged for the door and was snatched up just as her foot brushed the threshold, a strong arm locked around her waist.

"Put me down!" Alys wriggled and found herself deposited with her back against the wall. Burke glared, then leaned closer. "Do not even think of kissing me!" she insisted wildly, and the knight stiffened, then retreated slightly.

"What is this?"

"Do not kiss me, do not lay a hand upon me, do not so much as touch me again!"

Burke exhaled as if regaining his even temper. "But whyever not?" He smiled with all his usual charm and his voice dropped low. "You savor my kisses as much as I savor yours, my Alys."

'Twas not comforting how readily his smile melted her

defenses, and her own weakness made Alys more angry. "I do not!" she retorted. "Your touch addles my wits."

"There is no need to think overmuch when all proceeds well between us," he said, and eased closer.

Alys planted her hand in the middle of Burke's chest to halt his advance and fought to ignore the thunder of his heart. Oh, he was far too experienced at seduction! "Kisses make me forget that you are not the man for me."

Now Burke frowned. "Of course I am."

"Of course you are *not*." Alys folded her arms across her chest and struggled to catch her breath.

Burke leaned his weight against the hand he braced over Alys's shoulder, clearly intent on not letting her escape, but not touching her either. She refused to feel satisfied that he ceded to her request.

He propped his other hand upon his hip and considered her. "Your heart belongs to another?" The very idea clearly displeased him. "Who is this man?"

Alys straightened proudly. "I do not know."

Burke chuckled and shook his head. "Alys, you would spurn me for a man you have yet to find?"

"I know you are not the man for me, because you do not care for me in truth."

His eyes flashed anew. "What is *that* to mean?"

"Oh, you desire me, that much cannot be misconstrued." Alys spoke quickly, before she could consider the wisdom of what she did. "You cloud my thinking with kisses and compliments fall so readily from your lips that I know you have used them oft before. Your intent to seduce is more than clear."

Alys looked into Burke's eyes, her heart stirring at how avidly he listened. "But I would have more than desire between myself and the man of my dreams."

"But . . ."

"But naught! You pursue me in every corner of this hall . . ."

"I seek to persuade you of my sincerity."

"You intend to compromise me."

"Never!" Burke looked grim. "Determination yields results, Alys, as I have seen over and over again. Determination won you before and 'twill win you again."

"I am not a gate to be besieged," Alys retorted. "And my desire is of import in this. You are concerned to see *your* desire fulfilled and naught more than that."

"That is not true! I would treat you with honor, and you know it well."

"I know no such thing. Indeed, your pursuit has won me naught but trouble from my aunt and no doubt prompted endless gossip in the hall."

Burke growled something under his breath. "Only because you are too cursed stubborn to leave this place!"

"Why should I leave?"

Burke flung out his hand. "Why should you stay?"

"Kiltorren is no paradise, that much is true, but at least I am fed." Alys folded her arms across her chest, refusing to meet the knight's perceptive gaze. "And there are those who rely upon me."

Burke's brow darkened dangerously. "Surely you imagine I would offer you more than a regular meal."

"Aye, pleasure abed, as long as it suited you."

"My affections would not fade!"

"How can you know?" Alys challenged. "You are much concerned with chivalry, Burke, and that is telling." She shook a finger beneath his nose, certain she had hold of the truth. "Indeed, if I were not in such dire circumstance, would I attract your eye?"

The knight scowled. "Of course! You are my lady fair!"

"*Why*, Burke? I have naught to offer a man like yourself.

I have no dowry, no inheritance, not even an influential but penniless family. There is no reason for you to court my affections."

Burke visibly gritted his teeth. "Save that I love you."

The words made Alys's heart skip a beat but she knew better than to believe him. "How can you love me?" She spread her hands in appeal. "What truly do you know about me, save that you desire me?" Burke paused and Alys knew she had named it aright.

"Nonetheless I do," he insisted.

"Aye?" Alys lifted her chin. "Then tell me three things you love about me. And not a one of them some compliment that could be granted to any woman hungering for your attention."

Burke looked completely flummoxed. His gaze fell to her lips, then swept over her figure, lingering oddly upon her bare feet. He frowned, then met her gaze again.

Quite uncharacteristically and most tellingly, this man with his quick praise seemed at a complete loss for words.

Alys would not consider how disappointed that left her.

Instead, she tapped Burke on the chest. "One day a man will come to this hall as Aucassin came for Nicolette—he will love me, he will court me, and he will wed me. I will leave with him, secure in the certainty that he will not abandon me when his desire wanes, but love me for all his days and nights." She met Burke's gaze steadily. "No less than that will do."

And Alys ducked beneath the astonished knight's arm, leaving Burke de Montvieux to ponder that.

And ponder it, Burke did.

He stared after Alys, stunned that his pursuit could have gone so amiss. Stolen kisses and ready compliments had won the affections of more than one lady in Burke's experience.

Trust Alys to be immune to his charm.

Burke scowled and kicked at the stones in the bailey, glowering at his surroundings. Curse his facile tongue for abandoning him in a moment of need! All would have come aright if he had been able to summon the right words, but Burke had not been able to see beyond Alys's many charms.

And he knew that two graceful insteps and the sweet softness of her kiss would not satisfy those three qualifications for his love. Alys spoke aright—she was not a tower to be besieged but a quest that proved most challenging to win.

Even as Burke paced the stables, another knight rode far, far to the east of Kiltorren. His party closed upon Warwick, a last stop before returning to Normandy, the keep's silhouette rising against the darkness of the sea. The sun was sinking low in the west, the first stars beginning to twinkle overhead.

Millard de Villonne doffed his helmet and let the warm breeze ruffle his hair. He deliberately dropped back from the group of knights, abandoning the rumble of their conversation, as he tipped back his head to study those stars.

He needed a moment to call his own, a moment to face his disappointment. His nephew looked after him, but Millard deliberately ignored the boy.

Yet again Millard had gone abroad, yet again he had sought some glimpse of the woman who still held his heart. Yet again Millard had found naught of her. Each time his feet touched upon a new shore, his hope was rekindled and his love seemed to burn with a new flame. This time had been no different—either in that kindling or the fact that he had found naught of his lady.

Millard closed his eyes, the starlight an unbearably vivid reminder of one magical night, a night some twenty years in the past.

She had whispered to him that night as they lay together and watched the stars wheel overhead, and he could still hear the soft conviction of her words. She had confided, with the trust of a young first love, that a world with such marvels as those stars could only be a perfect place.

A lump rose in Millard's throat at the recollection, for their world had proven far less than perfect.

Millard had never imagined, especially not that night while he was caught in the fullness of the lady's love, that he would live out his days alone. He had never imagined that the starlight would grant his last glimpse of his lady, that the dawn would steal her away from his side.

Forever.

Millard frowned and forced his eyes open, determined not to dwell upon his loss, and did so just in time to see a star shoot across the heavens.

Like an impulsive child, he dared to wish upon it.

Millard wished with all his heart that he would find some hint of his Isibeal's fate, some sign of what had become of her. No less, he wished for that sign before he returned once more to the hollow echo of his own massive hall.

'Twas nonsense, yet just the act of wishing made Millard feel younger than he had these many years. 'Twas unlike him to be impulsive, unlike him to indulge in foolishness.

Perhaps his lady love was closer than he thought. Isibeal had been a great one for whimsy. Millard shook his head at that and gave his steed his spurs, bracing himself for his nephew's anxious and irritating demands.

Nay, Millard's world was a far cry from perfect.

'Twas best he reconcile himself to the truth of it.

By the evening repast, Burke had devised his new line of attack. Alys had, after all, told him that the truth of a man's character lay in his deeds.

'Twould be deeds then she would witness in plenty.

"Burke!" Deirdre cooed when he first set foot in the hall. "I have not laid eyes upon you all of this day." She hastened to his side, casting a sharp glance to Malvina. That girl smiled and scampered to Burke's other side. Deirdre laughed, the sound high and false. "Indeed, I feared you had abandoned our hospitality."

Burke saw his opening and did not intend to waste it. He looked to the lady of the keep and let his eyes narrow. "Indeed, I must admit I had considered it."

"What?" Malvina choked.

"What?" Deirdre squawked. "You said you came to Kiltorren for a bride. You have yet to choose either of my daughters!"

"Aye, but matters here have changed, and I must reconsider my position."

Burke seated himself at the board and—intent on letting Deirdre panic as long as possible—smiled a greeting at shy Brigid. She was already seated, though she said naught to him. Her eyes widened at this fleeting attention, then she went back to staring at her entangled hands.

"Reconsider?" Deirdre repeated, looking most distressed.

Cedric made his entry at that point, booming a greeting to one and all. "Ah, Burke! You join us again. Deirdre was most concerned about you."

"So she has said," Burke acknowledged.

Deirdre crossed the floor and seized her husband's elbow. That man looked alarmed when she nearly dragged him toward Burke, no less when her voice dropped to a hiss. "He means to reconsider his suit," she confided. "For once in your life, *do* something!"

Cedric granted his wife a surprisingly harsh look and she flushed slightly. Then he coughed, smoothed his tabard, frowned, went to the board, and took his seat. The women hastily dropped into their places, Deirdre all ears. The wine was poured, the meat and bread served. Burke decided, for the moment, to leave the issue of Alys's attendance aside.

Indeed, his plan should see all set to rights.

Finally Cedric looked to Burke when it seemed he had no other options for delay. "Why would you reconsider?"

Burke smiled, nodding when a servant offered him a chalice of wine. He acted supremely unconcerned, knowing full well that it would drive Deirdre to a frenzy. She was already tapping her fingers upon the board with impatience.

'Twas a kind of vengeance, Burke thought, for all that woman had done to Alys.

"I must think of progeny," he said carefully.

"Both of my daughters are young and healthy," Deirdre asserted. She snapped her fingers. "Stand up, girls, turn around! We shall call a physician, if need be, to satisfy your concerns."

"Mother!" Malvina protested, Brigid naturally so appalled at the very idea that she was scarlet-faced and silent.

But Burke frowned in thought. " 'Tis not what troubles me," he confessed, waiting until the whole family leaned closer. "I worry that there may be a taint in the lineage of Kiltorren, a weakness that could pass to my own sons."

"Alys!" Deirdre muttered through gritted teeth.

Burke looked up, as if surprised. "Nay, Alys seems to be the only one spared of this trouble."

All four looked blank.

"What do you mean?" Cedric asked, Deirdre's piercing glance no doubt prompting his question.

" 'Tis most odd, for there seems no good reason for the ailment at all." Burke scanned the hall at his leisure, as if he sought the proper words, knowing that the entire family hung on his every breath. "Has your family ever been cursed?"

Cedric frowned, but Deirdre shook her head. She fired a glance at her spouse and he shook his head in turn.

"Has any forebear died unshriven?"

They shook their heads in unison, their expressions perplexed.

"Heretics in the family?" Nay again, much as Burke had

suspected. "Pagans? Any who broke a pledge before the Lord?" They were completely puzzled by this point, but Burke leaned back and fingered his chin like a man powerfully concerned. "Yet there 'tis, all the same. Most troubling."

And he began his meal.

"There *WHAT* is?" Deirdre demanded shrilly. "What is it that you see?"

Burke glanced up, considering each of them in turn. " 'Tis astonishing that you all are completely unaware of it," he murmured, knowing full well they all would hear his words. "Nay, it can be no good omen."

They waited with bated breath.

Burke sipped his wine, then set his chalice down firmly. "Perhaps I erred in coming to Kiltorren," he pronounced. "Perhaps I should not have sought a bride here."

"Nay!" Deirdre cried. "There can be no mistake, there is no mistake. You have but to tell us of our omission and we shall see it set to rights, I grant to you my word."

Burke shook his head. "Nay, it cannot be fixed so readily as that."

"We shall see it repaired, whatever it is!" Deirdre insisted.

"Aye, your will shall be done!" Cedric assured Burke. He patted the younger man's shoulder. "Any matter of import between men of honor can be resolved."

Burke tried to look surprised. "Indeed? You would endeavor to set my concerns at ease?"

"Of course!" Cedric boomed. "You have but to tell us of the trouble."

Burke toyed with his food, admitting in his heart just how much he was enjoying this. 'Twas doubly pleasing in that it might benefit Alys.

He sighed, then slanted a glance to Cedric, lowering his voice as he leaned toward that man. "I am concerned at the import of a family that shuns their own blood."

Cedric blinked. "We shun no one."

A flicker of anger lit within Burke that they still could not see their omission, but he forced himself to remain calm. "Indeed? And I had thought Alys your niece."

"Alys!" Deirdre laughed in her relief and sat back. "Alys hardly counts!"

Burke frowned at his trencher and pushed it away. 'Twas no lie that he had lost his appetite. "You see?" he murmured to Cedric, not managing to veil the anger in his tone. "There 'tis again."

Cedric's eyes widened in alarm. "It is true that the child is blood," he admitted heavily. "But—but . . ."

"But she requests the labor," Deirdre interjected.

"She expects it," Malvina added.

"Indeed, Alys understands that 'tis only fitting she toil to earn her keep within Kiltorren," Deirdre said. " 'Twas beyond good of us to take her in, and the girl understands the cost of that. 'Tis her willing contribution to the prosperity of the keep."

Burke was stunned that the woman could make such arguments without hesitation.

The very fact made him burn with fury to see Alys's circumstance changed. " 'Tis unfitting for a child of the house to labor like a serf—and yet more unfitting that none of you finds the matter troubling."

Burke shoved to his feet as they stared at him in stunned silence, and his words were briskly spoken. " 'Tis clear I erred in coming to Kiltorren. My apologies for wasting your hospitality." He bowed to his host and hostess. "I shall leave at first light."

Of course Burke had no intention of doing any such thing, at least not without his Alys—who admittedly seemed somewhat disinclined to accompany him as yet.

But the family of Kiltorren did not even guess his true intent.

Burke made it halfway across the floor before most of the shocked foursome behind him leapt to their feet.

"Wait!" Deirdre cried.

"Aye, halt," Cedric echoed.

"Do not leave me, Burke," Malvina cried.

Deirdre found her feet when Burke hesitated, and she fairly flew across the floor to his side. Her features were drawn with anxiety, her smile that of one eager to please.

"I must thank you," she declared breathlessly. "You are right, we have been wrong. I cannot imagine how we failed to see our error! We shall restore Alys to her rightful position. Please, sir, will you reconsider your departure?"

Burke barely managed to hide his smile of satisfaction. He frowned deeply to cover his response and scanned the four hopeful faces. "I do not know. 'Tis so unseemly . . ."

"I shall cease Alys's labor," Deirdre promised. "Save as a maid, of course."

Burke arched a brow and that woman recanted.

"Of course you speak aright. She shall have only such duties as are fitting."

"Duties like Malvina's," Burke suggested softly.

Hatred flashed through Deirdre's eyes. She smiled hastily, though the light of her smile did not reach her eyes. "Duties such as Malvina's," she agreed through teeth Burke guessed were gritted.

"I have never seen a servant garbed so poorly," he commented. "Even the beggars of Paris have more to call their own."

Deirdre's nostrils fairly pinched shut, she inhaled so sharply. "She shall have a new kirtle."

"Shoes and other frippery," Burke supplied with a winning smile. "As befits a lady of the house."

Deirdre eyed him coldly. "We shall do what we can in our reduced circumstance."

He let his smile broaden. "Of course, 'twould be most unfitting for a lady of lineage to slumber on the kitchen hearth."

Deirdre lifted her chin. "We have not another chamber."

" 'Twould be my pleasure, then, to cede the chamber granted to me to the lady's comfort. As a man of war, I am much used to simple accommodations and shall take to the stables."

Burke turned his smile upon the entire family. "Indeed, it does my heart good to see this trouble so readily dismissed. Perhaps there is indeed prospect of a bride at Kiltorren."

He pivoted and made to leave the hall, then paused as if struck by a thought. "There is, of course, one other small concern."

"What?" Deirdre snapped.

"I hear tell of an anchorite living on the perimeter of Kiltorren, an aged woman once in your employ."

"Aye, Heloise." Cedric stepped forward. "She is most pious."

"Ah, and an honor 'tis to have a woman pledged to God upon your holding."

"What of it?" Deirdre demanded.

Burke shrugged easily. "Perhaps 'tis my natural inclination to be concerned for the plight of women"—he smiled with all his charm—"but it seems to me unfitting that an elderly religious woman would be left to the wind and the rain."

" 'Tis her pledge, to endure adversity for her love of God," Deirdre said coldly.

"Indeed?" Burke met Cedric's gaze. "Though what misfortune might her demise bring upon Kiltorren if the Lord perceived that passing to be untimely? The hand of God does work in mysterious ways."

He waited to see the flash of fear in Cedric's eyes before stepping away. " 'Tis not my concern, of course, and Lady Deirdre has already noted the differences between Irish estates and those French. No doubt my sensibilities are unwelcome."

"Of course not!" Cedric boomed. "I have long been concerned for Heloise's welfare."

But Deirdre turned on her husband in fury. "We have no accommodation suitable for a religious."

"We shall make do," that man insisted with rare vigor. "The knight speaks aright and surely we have no need of further misfortune at Kiltorren."

"We shall discuss this matter privately." Deirdre turned a dark glance upon Burke, and he was glad he had assured Alys's welfare first. The Lady of Kiltorren was not taking well to his interference in her plans.

Burke bowed deeply and left the hall, sensing that he had pressed his fortunes far enough this night.

Alys had scarce abandoned the storeroom in pursuit of a bit of food than Aunt appeared in the kitchen. Alys took a wary step back, but Aunt continued on her course undeterred.

She clucked her tongue over the state of her niece's kirtle. "Alys, where do you find such rags?" she chided. "Truly, you must think of presenting yourself more fittingly. Do you mean to shame us all?"

Alys frowned at this unexpected accusation. "You granted it to me but a month past, and 'twas not in much finer condition then."

"Such impertinence!" But there was no heat in Aunt's words. Cook and Alys exchanged a puzzled glance. "And why, Alys, do you insist upon slumbering here? 'Tis somewhat beneath your station and makes us look less than honorable."

Cook snorted and earned himself a sharp glance from his lady that had him turning back to his labor.

Alys folded her arms across her chest, not trusting her aunt's new manner. "I had thought you wanted me to sleep here."

"Oh, Alys, where do you find such nonsense? I will hear naught of your protests, nor any tales of the friends you harbor in the kitchen. Truly, what has seized your thoughts that you fraternize only with the servants?" Aunt leaned closer. "They are common-born, Alys. You forget yourself."

"I forget naught!" Alys began to argue at the injustice of that, but Aunt seized her arm and hauled her from the kitchen.

"Come along, come along. God's blood, Alys, but you have need of a bath." She wrinkled her nose, then roared at the steward to summon a bath.

Alys fought her aunt's grip, wondering what the woman intended for her now.

"Do not even think to return to your labor," Aunt chided. "We shall find some embroidery to occupy your time. Perhaps Malvina will teach you."

That halted Alys's struggles. "Embroidery?"

"Aye, *embroidery*, Alys. I would think you might have heard of such noble pursuits." Aunt called for that bath to be hastened as they crossed the threshold of the room that had been Burke's. Alys noted immediately that the knight's saddlebags were gone.

Before she could blink, Malvina—who surrendered naught to anyone—presented her with a plain yet fairly new kirtle. 'Twas the shade of goldenrod.

" 'Twas cut too cheaply for me by that fool seamstress," she declared. "But you are all bones, Alys, 'twill no doubt suit you well enough."

Alys blinked. Someone had infested Kiltorren with strangers who looked as her family but did not act as them.

"Bathe yourself," Aunt declared with a gracious smile. "Indeed, Alys, I cannot believe you have let matters go for so very long. And do teach this Edana child all that you know. 'Tis time enough you learned your role in this place and dressed appropriately, and time we all had a *decent* maid."

"I did not choose my role in this keep," Alys began to argue, but Aunt waved off her words.

"Details, Alys, are not of import."

With that Aunt and Malvina scurried away.

When the door shut behind them, Alys shook her head. She surveyed her surroundings, incredulous that she would call this chamber her own. She was to live like a noblewoman!

And then she grinned, for she could hazard a guess as to the only one who could have wrought such a change in her circumstance. Alys could not help but wonder what Burke had said to see his will so smoothly done.

The man was incorrigible! Alys bounced on the bed and laughed aloud. Oh, she did not care what Burke had said, did not care that she would be cast back to the kitchen as soon as he departed. Alys would savor this change as long as it lasted.

But the knight was sorely mistaken if he thought she would express her gratitude with earthy favors.

"Woho!" Cook declared with a rap on the door. Alys sat up to find his eyes twinkling. "Our guest ensures you win your due. I like the man better with every passing day!"

"He seeks his own end, Cook, 'tis no more than that."

Cook might have said more, but Cronan the steward brushed past him. The steward beckoned the lads from the kitchen, who rolled a great tub into the tiny chamber. He indicated the placement of the tub, nodded with thin-lipped approval, then snapped his fingers to demand the water.

"Quickly, quickly," he rasped, his voice as dry as dust. One white brow arched slightly, and he presented Alys with a cake of soap. "Your mother favored this," he conceded with a minute bow of his head, and then he swept from the room.

Alys lifted the cake to her nostrils and was treated to a wondrous smell of fresh flowers, a scent she liked but could not name. She let the newly arrived Edana smell it and the girl's eyes widened in delight.

" 'Tis marvelous!" Edana clasped her hands together. "Fitting of a lady true!"

Two girls carried candles and braziers in that very moment, their lips curved in smiles. Alys was quickly surrounded by the servants she had labored beside for so many years. They smiled and hugged her, kissed her cheek, and some even bowed low before her. They were laughing, each and every one, so pleased with her good fortune that Alys was nigh moved to tears.

Indeed, she wanted only to savor the moment and to sing.

Millard sat in the crowded hall, not in the least bit interested in the entertainers frolicking there. The meal was fine enough but already he chafed to return to his holdings.

'Twas a desire born as much from the urge to be rid of his nephew as anything else. Truly, Millard wished he had not been so readily persuaded by his sister to bring the boy along.

Indeed, Talbot had already made a considerable dint in the host's wine. His manners were appalling—they only grew worse as he drank more and became uncharacteristically bold.

At least the boy was intimidated by Millard when he was sober.

As if to emphasize that point, Talbot winked at his uncle, reached to pinch the buttock of a serving wench, and spilled the entire contents of his chalice upon the floor. Worse, the girl lost her balance and the pitcher of wine she carried was spilled immediately afterward.

'Twas a shocking waste.

Millard snatched his nephew's tabard and hauled the young knight up from the floor, depositing him with force upon the bench once again. "Witless fool!" he charged in an undertone.

"Uncle, 'twas an accident!"

" 'Twas folly and 'twas rude," Millard corrected. "Wine is cursed expensive in this land, yet our host brings forward the wealth of his cellars to show homage to the king's own party."

He cast a scathing glance at his dejected nephew. "And you cast it upon the floor as if 'twas as plentiful as piss in the stables."

Talbot hung his head. "I am sorry, Uncle."

"You are always sorry," Millard observed. "Yet naught changes in your behavior. Truly, you are as reliable as a child of five summers. Did you learn naught in training for your spurs?"

Talbot poked at his empty chalice. "Maman said there was no need."

"No need!" Millard inhaled sharply. "What manner of nonsense is this?"

His sister had always been indulgent of her younger son—indeed, Millard suspected this alone was the boy's trouble. Though he was nigh upon twenty years of age—a full-fledged knight no less!—'twas hard to think of Talbot as anything other than a child. He had been indulged for too many years to deny himself anything at all.

Millard's attempts to address this deficiency inevitably resulted in hostility from Talbot and a stream of recriminations from his sister. Still, he could not leave the matter be.

Aye, Millard knew well enough what plum his sister hoped to win for her youngest son. He would be damned to hell if he did not try to make a silk purse of this sow's ear before 'twas too late.

"How could your mother maintain that there was naught of merit to be learned in your training?"

Talbot shrugged, then summoned the beatific smile that worked him free of most trouble he found. If he had not been such a handsome lad, Millard had no doubt he would have already felt the weight of his own inadequacies. "Maman knows best, Uncle."

"Does she indeed?" Millard snapped. "And who will save your sorry hide when your Maman is not hovering over you, determined to make all you have done wrong come aright?"

Talbot blinked, began to speak, but then evidently thought the better of it.

Millard sat back with a grunt of satisfaction. At least the boy ceased to believe that he could comment openly about inheriting all Millard had built.

Indeed, his sister's presumption grated on the older knight. He had once been a younger son, he had once been without inheritance, he had once lost the lady he loved for the lack of a sliver of land to call his own. Yet Millard had labored—in the wake of his loss, 'twas true—and he had built himself a holding far beyond the wealth of the one his elder brother had inherited.

And he would not willingly drop that prize into the lap of this sorry excuse for a man.

Unfortunately, because of that lack of an heir, Millard had little choice. He was snared by his own principles, trapped by his own refusal to wed another when still he might find his lady love. Indeed, he could never care for another woman the way he loved Isibeal, Millard knew it well. And he would insult no woman with a faint shadow of the love he knew himself capable of feeling.

He would have all, or he would have naught, and naught looked to be the winning choice.

A minstrel took the floor and Millard bent his attention upon the young man, as much as an excuse to ignore Talbot as to hear the tale.

But the minstrel's tale, once it had begun, fairly stole the old knight's breath away. Millard craned his neck to capture each and every word, hope rising with every stanza.

'Twas beyond belief, but his wish upon that star had come true.

Chapter Eight

TALBOT WAS QUITE PLEASED WITH HIMSELF. NOT ONLY had he coaxed more wine from the serving wench, but she had consented to sit by his side. She was a comely creature, all curves and dimples, more than enough to keep a man's hands full.

She perched beside him, filled his chalice at regular intervals, and was not concerned about the roving of his hand. Talbot was quite certain she was the perfect woman for him.

At least for tonight.

Even better, his crusty uncle deigned to ignore what he did. There was naught worse, to Talbot's mind, than to be the focus of his uncle's attention, for that man was demanding beyond all.

If only Millard would show the good grace to die soon.

'Twas a mark of his uncle's disregard for Talbot that he not only lived but continued to amass yet more wealth and keep it greedily to himself. 'Twas as if Millard tempted Talbot with what that man could not have, at least not yet.

The minstrel sang a triumphant closing stanza about the cursed maid of Kiltorren, and the serving wench sighed into Talbot's ear. "Is it not terribly romantic?"

Talbot had not troubled to listen to the tale, but he smiled for her all the same. "Wondrously so," he agreed, then gave her buttocks a hearty squeeze. Romantic tales, he well knew, could make a maid lusty.

But Talbot would have no chance to test the truth of that.

Millard snatched his sleeve, the older man moving so abruptly that Talbot nearly lost another chalice of wine. "Did you hear that?" he demanded, his eyes blazing as if they were aflame.

" 'Twas some tale, no more than that," Talbot declared with all the scorn he dared to muster.

That man inhaled quickly. " 'Twas no mere tale! 'Twas *my* tale!"

"Truly?" the wench asked, her eyes wide.

Millard's gaze dropped to the breasts spilling out of her bodice, then rose to her face. "Find yourself a decent kirtle, child," he said with more gentleness than he ever summoned for his own blood. "There are those here who might misinterpret such a display of your many charms."

She smiled, then raised a hand to her bodice, flushed, and fled.

Talbot stumbled to his feet and called after her, but to no avail. He snorted disdain. "Thank you, Uncle, for that!"

"You have no time to rut with a serving girl. I have a task for you."

Talbot rolled his eyes and made to sip his wine. "You always have a task for me, Uncle, and 'tis always one at which I fail to satisfy."

The chalice never reached his lips, for Millard snatched it away and dropped it on the board with a thud. Before Talbot could grab it again, the older man grasped a fistful of his tabard and gave him a shake.

"You will not dare to fail at this task," he said with a growl, casting Talbot away from him as if the merest touch was offensive. "Or you shall have no chance whatsoever at seeing any trinket fall from my hand to your own."

Talbot blinked as he found his footing, the delightful lan-
guor of the wine abandoning him in a heartbeat. "If 'tis of
such import, why not do the deed yourself?"

"Millard!" came a cry from across the hall. "We parlay at
your convenience." Talbot watched his uncle wave and give a
nod, then the weight of that man's attention was upon him
once more.

'Twas not a pleasant sensation.

"My liege lord has need of my presence," Millard acknowledged through his teeth. "And if you understood anything of
the pledge you have taken, you would know the import of
that." His eyes narrowed. "Indeed, Talbot, if I had my choice,
I *would* go in your stead, but the choice is not mine."

Talbot straightened at the implied insult and brushed down
his tabard with care. "You know you can rely upon me,
Uncle."

Millard scoffed. "I know no such thing, but I have no alter-
native. Did you listen to the minstrel?"

"Nay! Such nonsense is for women alone."

"Such nonsense will decide your fate. This minstrel sang of
a maid of Kiltorren, a beauteous woman abandoned by her
lover true."

" 'Tis a common enough tale." Talbot shrugged and tried to
reach for his chalice.

Millard neatly interrupted his gesture. " 'Tis an uncommon
tale in its details. You will go to Kiltorren, you will ride out
this very night, and you will find this maiden."

Talbot looked up in astonishment, but there was no mistaking the resolve in his uncle's gaze. The old man had lost his
wits. "Uncle! 'Tis naught but a tale!"

" 'Tis rooted in truth and I know it well."

This was madness! "But I do not even know where this Kiltorren lies."

Millard arched a silver brow. "Had you listened, you would

know 'twas on the west coast of Ireland, that the waves of the sea crashed upon its very walls. You would know that the Lord of Kiltorren was blessed with two daughters, the eldest of whom he dispatched to Paris to find a fitting match. You would know that she was a blond beauty unrivalled in that town so filled with blond beauties."

Talbot's uncle, in this moment, looked every measure the ferocious warrior. Talbot eased away from the older man.

Millard's lips tightened. "Had you listened, you would know that she fell in love with a knight, a man with no holding to call his own and no hope of a holding because he was the younger son. You would know that she was compared to the legendary beauty in the tale of the unicorn, the maiden so sweet and innocent that she tamed even the ferocious unicorn, a beast deemed to have no heart of its own before it succumbed to her charm."

Talbot's mouth went dry as his uncle fingered the unicorn rampant embroidered in gold upon his deep-green tabard. Indeed, there were elements of this tale that were too familiar for comfort.

"And you would know that she returned to her home in shame," Millard continued, his voice softening over the words, "her belly ripe with her lover's child. A *child*!"

There was an intensity about his uncle's manner that made a shiver of dread roll over Talbot's flesh.

"You have heard the tale before?" he dared to ask.

"I have *lived* it," Millard retorted. "I have sought this woman in every corner of Christendom for nigh upon twenty years, though clearly I missed this Kiltorren."

He turned that boring gaze upon his nephew. "You will go there in my stead. You will find this maiden, you will find her child, and you will bring them both directly to me. If you fail, do not trouble yourself to darken my threshold ever again."

Millard paused, looking as forbidding as only he could. His voice dropped dangerously low. "Am I understood?"

Talbot fought to make sense of what he had just been told, he struggled to see his way clear of this dawning sense of betrayal. After all he had done for Millard, his uncle would deny him an inheritance upon this bard's tale?

'Twas unfair!

Talbot levelled a cold glance at his uncle and dared to voice his objections. "I am to ride to an estate which may or may not exist, I am to retrieve a woman who has no name, I am to seize a child who may have never seen daylight and who may or may not be your spawn, and if I fail, you will grant me naught?"

"Precisely," his uncle agreed with satisfaction. "But the woman's name is Isibeal."

Talbot knew his eyes boggled.

"I can wait for you no longer than a fortnight," Millard continued with crisp authority. "If circumstance permits, I myself shall ride to Kiltorren before that time and meet you there."

Millard frowned. "Do not be so foolish as to fail, Talbot. This is a matter of great import to me." Before his nephew's incredulous gaze, Millard turned, his cloak swinging behind him, and strode to the chamber where his liege lord would parlay.

The older man was apparently unaware of the indignation rolling through his nephew. Talbot rose to his feet and lifted his fist as if he would cry out at such injustice, but then his hand fell limply to his side once more.

For truly, Talbot did not have the audacity to challenge his uncle openly. He dared not risk that man's wrath while there was still a chance of making Millard's holdings his own.

This Isibeal and her child, though, were another matter.

Nay, Talbot would not play so willing a part in retrieving Millard's heir, not at his own expense. He drained his chalice in one gulp and bent his thoughts to the question of how he could appear to follow his uncle's bidding without undermining his own ambition.

There had to be a way.

If Isibeal or her child yet lived, that fact must be changed. And it must be changed before Talbot returned to his uncle's side, or before that man appeared at Kiltorren.

Talbot dared not linger a moment.

Alys lay in the great soft bed and stretched. 'Twas different indeed to not labor all the day long. On this night, for the first time in many nights, she did not fall into slumber as soon as her head hit the pallet.

'Twas wonderful. Alys surveyed her new chamber yet again, smiling. She folded her arms behind her head and listened to Edana snore. And she permitted herself to dream.

Perhaps she would grant Burke a kiss—just one—to show her appreciation for the change he had seen made to her circumstance. Alys's toes curled as she guessed how he would respond. Burke would smile a slow smile of delight when he lifted his head. His eyes would shine that silver blue that stole her breath away; he would touch her jaw with a gentle fingertip and send her pulse racing.

Something rapped against the shutters, and Alys jumped at the sudden sound. Her eyes flew open, though silence reigned again.

Another rap followed. This time Alys saw something roll across the floor. She crept from the bed and felt in the shadows.

'Twas a pebble, rounded by the sea.

A third hit the shutters and rolled before Alys could think of how it had come to be flying through the air.

Then a low voice supplied the missing detail. "Alys!"

She smiled despite herself. 'Twas Burke, there could be no doubt of that.

"Alys, are you awake?"

Alys knew she should not respond, but still she did. She opened the shutters and let in the indigo of the night. The sky was full of stars, the wind from the sea hinted of rain. Alys leaned out the window, her loose braid falling over her shoulder, and was not surprised to find a knight staring up at her from the bailey.

"How could I sleep when 'tis raining pebbles?" she demanded playfully, and cast the stone back toward him.

Burke caught the missile with a flourish, then clutched it to his heart. "A token from my lady fair," he crooned, then his smile flashed.

It seemed safe enough to return his smile with so much distance between them. "You are drunk!" Alys charged laughingly.

" 'Tis true enough." He executed a sweeping bow. "I am besotted with the vision of loveliness before me."

Alys choked on her laughter, knowing she should not encourage his nonsense.

"The moonlight gilds the tresses of my lady fair, the stars dance for her alone . . ."

"Oh, Burke, promise me that you will never seek employ as a bard," Alys interrupted with a smile. "The company would cast eggs at your head."

He chuckled then and propped his hands on his hips. "Truly, your concern for my welfare touches my heart, Alys. I shall treasure this hint of progress in my suit."

Alys chuckled in turn. "You grasp at the wind, sir."

Burke shrugged amiably. "You grant me little choice." His smile faded suddenly. "Come down, Alys. Come talk with me."

"I cannot talk with you in the moonlight!" Though Alys sounded shocked, 'twas not the suggestion as much as its appeal that troubled her.

"Whyever not? You already do as much and 'twould save much shouting if you joined me here."

"Aunt would not approve!"

"Indeed, she might compel us to wed without delay for such shocking behavior! That would be a calamity." Burke feigned dismay so thoroughly that Alys chuckled again. "Come down, Alys," he entreated again. "Come walk with me so that your aunt cannot overhear."

Alys glanced to the silvery quarter moon, to the stars filling the sky, to the man waiting hopefully for her response. 'Twas a night made for dreaming, and Alys could not deny herself this one moment.

Would it harm anything if she had a walk in the moonlight to recall for all her days and nights?

"I shall come." Alys shook a finger at the knight below when he grinned to so readily win his request. "But you shall not steal kisses, nor will you regale me with nonsensical compliments."

Burke blew her a gallant kiss as his response, and Alys knew better than to trust him in this.

But for this one night, she did not care. Indeed, her fingers trembled as she fastened her kirtle. She crept past Edana and fled down the stairs on silent feet, telling herself that her haste was only to ensure that none heard her passing.

But even Alys knew that was a lie.

Burke could not believe his good fortune when Alys appeared in the shadows of the kitchen portal. He had not expected her to join him, he certainly had not expected her to laugh at his jests.

He captured her hand in his, savoring the way she shivered when he kissed her knuckles. Alys glanced back over her shoulder in trepidation, but Burke touched one fingertip to her lips.

"They all sleep," he whispered. "And none will know what we do. Believe me, Alys, I will not permit your aunt to raise her hand against you again."

There was such hope in her lovely eyes that Burke was sorely tempted to sweep the lady away this very night, but he knew he had to win her agreement first. He smiled, but she shook her head and pulled her hand from his.

"You will not be able to stop her, once you have left Kiltorren," Alys said flatly. She brushed past Burke and walked toward the sea wall.

Burke quickly matched his steps to hers. " 'Twill not be an issue when you come with me."

Alys cast a glance his way. "I pledged long ago to not repeat my mother's error, Burke, so do not try to change my thinking."

Here was a key to his lady's secrets, Burke was certain. "What error was that?"

Alys smiled. "She trusted a man, probably a charming one, and to her own detriment. I have inherited much from her, according to Aunt, but I do not want to repeat such a mistake."

"Tell me of her."

But Alys shook her head. "You did not summon me out here to hear the tale of my mother."

"Perhaps I should have. 'Twas you who insisted I should know more of you."

Alys turned to face him then, her expression indulgent. "Oh, Burke, you are the most cursedly determined man that I have ever met. Do you ever take nay for an answer?"

Burke grinned. "Not when the stakes are of such import as this."

Alys studied him for a long moment, her gaze searching. Burke hid naught from her, though he did not know what precisely would reassure her doubts. The wind came in gusts from the sea, ruffling his chemise and lifting the lady's hair; the moonlight painted her features in ethereal silver.

"How is your new chamber?" he asked.

"Most fine," Alys admitted with a smile, her eyes twinkling

with mischief. "I suppose you would demand a token of appreciation?"

Burke grinned. " 'Twould not be unwelcome."

The dimple he adored made a fleeting appearance, then Alys leaned closer. She placed one hand on his chest as if to restrain him from demanding more than she offered, then brushed her lips across his jaw. "I thank you," she murmured.

Burke closed his eyes, stunned by the heat that flooded through him from that one featherlight touch. 'Twas the first time Alys had ever kissed him of her own volition, and the realization made his heart pound.

He felt her move away, and his eyes flew open in time to note the pale splendor of her feet flashing as she hoisted her skirts. She climbed the rubble remaining of the seaward curtain wall. Burke stood transfixed for a long moment, both by her kiss and her fine ankles.

Alys fired a glance back Burke's way when she reached the low summit of the wall. "What ails you?" she asked. "You look to have been struck to stone."

Burke grinned and decided not to confide that a part of him had indeed turned as hard as stone.

"There is mischief in your eyes," the lady accused with a smile.

Burke laughed. He leapt to the top of the wall, caught Alys in his embrace, and kissed her fully while he yet had surprise upon his side. Alys parted her lips beneath his own, the sweetness of her kiss nearly undoing Burke's resolve. He caught her close and kissed her deeply, loving how she leaned against him, how her arms slowly crept around his neck.

It seemed the moonlight had unfettered his lady's soul.

Finally Burke lifted his lips from hers, knowing that soon he would not be able to stop his embrace. He swung Alys into his arms and leapt to the sea side of the wall. Then he strode toward the smooth darkness of the sandy beach, certain that all would shortly be put to rights between them.

"Put me down!" the lady insisted.

"You will injure your feet upon these stones," Burke said evenly. " 'Twould be most unchivalrous of me to abandon you to such a fate."

"Again you cite chivalry as your justification. Burke, how can you not see that 'tis my situation alone that attracts you?"

"I love you, and 'tis *that* which sends me in your pursuit."

"You *desire* me," Alys corrected. She squirmed as they reached the wet stretch of sand, proving that assertion so true that Burke set her reluctantly on her feet.

"But 'tis not enough, Burke," she insisted, her voice low and imbued with no small measure of determination. "Not nearly enough." Alys held his gaze tellingly, then stepped past him, walking down the beach.

Burke stared after the lady for a long moment. She insisted he did not know enough of her, that his ardor must be measured by deeds. Now he would learn more of the lady. He cast his mind over all she had said, then strode after her, disregarding the likely damage to his boots as he stepped into the surf. They walked side by side, until finally Alys looked his way.

"I accept your challenge to learn more of the lady who holds my heart," Burke said, over the steady pounding of the surf. "Tell me a tale of yourself, Alys."

The lady was somewhat less than cooperative. "There is naught to tell."

"Nay? What of your mother's error?"

Alys's lips thinned. " 'Tis what made me a bastard."

"You told me this already." Burke arched a brow. "Do not imagine that this fact troubles me."

"My father may have been a common serf."

"Do you know his identity?"

Alys shook her head.

"Then he might just as well have been a king." Burke grinned. "You could have been stolen away by pirates when you were a babe, as Nicolette was."

Alys halted and stared at him. "You know that tale?"

"Of course. Though you sang it more beautifully than I have ever heard before." Burke smiled. "You have a fine voice, Alys."

The lady flushed and did not seem to know what to do.

"What happened to your mother?"

Alys sighed and frowned across the endless sea. "She died just after my birth. Aunt insists 'twas of shame, though Heloise said 'twas of a broken heart."

"Your mother's error was to love?"

The lady glanced up, her bright gaze impaling Burke. "My mother's error was to love a man who served her false."

Her head bowed with the weight of this inheritance and she might have turned away, but Burke caught at her shoulders.

Here indeed was the key to the puzzle, the reason why she did not intend to trust him. Burke was not about to lose the chance to learn it, and he was certainly not prepared to let Alys's mother's error stand in the path of his courtship. He touched one finger to Alys's chin and compelled her to meet his gaze once more.

"Tell me, Alys," he entreated. "Entrust me with this tale."

Alys bowed her head. Burke's hands were warm and reassuring on her shoulders. She felt her defenses crumble beneath his patient silence and knew that on this moonlit night, her resistance to him was dissolving like salt in the sea.

This was a tale Alys had never shared before, a whispered secret she had learned at Heloise's knee. "If I tell you this tale, will you be satisfied this night?"

Burke's smile flashed like quicksilver. "Nay, I will not be

satisfied until your hand is securely within mine, and that for all time," he declared, then offered Alys his hand.

She considered his outstretched palm for only a moment before putting her hand upon his. Alys felt for the first time since Heloise fell ill that there was another she could rely upon, if only for this one night. They turned as one away from Kiltorren's keep and Alys cleared her throat.

"My mother was the elder of two daughters born to my grandparents, the first Lord and Lady of Kiltorren. She was named Isibeal, her younger sister is my Aunt Deirdre. 'Twas my grandfather who built Kiltorren, and 'tis said that he was a man of rare diligence and determination."

"Did you know him?"

Burke's thumb moved across the back of Alys's hand in a leisurely caress. With Kiltorren behind them, 'twas easy to imagine that they two were alone upon this coast. It seemed the night could last forever, and Alys half wished that it would.

"I was young when he died." Alys smiled softly. "I recall that he bounced me on his knee and sang Norse ditties to me."

"He was not of Ireland?"

"Nay, he was a Norseman. There is a tale that he came raiding on this coast with a shipload of his countrymen and, with one glance of my grandmother, he was smitten."

"Ah, then you come by your allure honestly."

Alys flushed. "Whatever the truth, my grandfather never returned to his homeland. He labored for the local king and won the approval of my grandmother's family. Finally he earned the right to build a holding and he chose this place."

"Why? 'Twould not have been the first choice of many."

Alys smiled. " 'Tis said he could not bear to be out of sight of the sea. Indeed, he was a man that seemed to fill any space he occupied, a man that should be outside in the wind. I can still hear the way he bellowed and the way he laughed, and recall that he had an enormous silver beard."

Alys glanced to her companion to find a similar smile gracing his firm lips. "He sounds the perfect grandfather."

She shrugged. "Perhaps I have created him in my memories, I am not certain." She sobered. "But it seems to me that the hall rang often with laughter in those days. Perhaps I was merely too young to notice otherwise."

"Hmm. My mother has been known to declare that we are oft overly quick to dismiss the recollections of children, or indeed their understanding of all around them."

'Twas a surprisingly sombre comment, and Alys found herself glancing at Burke.

He smiled crookedly. "Do not look so astonished that I have a mother, or even that she has a wisdom about her."

Alys smiled. "You have never mentioned her."

Burke sobered and looked away. "She is . . . *formidable*." Then he glanced at her again with an affectionate glint in his eye. Alys wondered whether 'twas for her or his daunting mother. "But, please, continue with your tale of your own mother."

"You are not bored?"

"Far from it. I am intrigued to learn of the woman who brought you into this world."

Burke's gaze was so warm that Alys had to look away in her turn. "Well, here there is a parting of the tale, for Heloise told of it one way while Aunt tells almost the perfect opposite."

"I would hear the version of Heloise," Burke said quickly.

" 'Tis far prettier."

"And undoubtedly closer to the truth."

There was little to argue with that. Alys frowned at the waves sliding before her and retreating again. She considered the distant silhouette of Kiltorren, only now realizing how far they had walked.

'Twas stunning to realize how much she did not want to go back. All the same, Alys knew there was little choice. She turned deliberately and strolled toward the keep, welcoming Burke's presence beside her.

"Heloise maintained that my mother was beauteous beyond all. She declared that Isibeal was as fair as a flower, her hair like gilded sunlight. She said my mother's laugh could coax a smile from the most dour guest and that my grandfather adored his eldest above all else."

"I knew Heloise would have a finer tale," Burke murmured. "Gilded sunlight," he then mused, and cast a sidelong wink Alys's way. "I shall have to recall that phrase."

Alys had no doubt he would, though she would not consider further than that.

"For you see," she continued, "my grandmother had died while Mother and Aunt were young. Heloise said that Isibeal was the only one who could entreat my grandfather to smile. He retreated to his chamber after his loss, and my mother persisted in visiting him each and every day. 'Twas six months before he emerged, another six before he smiled, by all accounts, and by then they two were inseparable."

"How old was she?"

"I do not know. Eight or ten summers, by all accounts."

"Then this is the root of your generous nature," Burke mused.

Alys glanced to him in surprise.

" 'Tis true, Alys," he declared with a smile. "You grant the benefit of the doubt to all, you are loyal beyond expectation. Clearly your mother showed the same trait."

Alys continued, feeling that Burke discerned overmuch in this tale. "When it came time for my mother to wed, my grandfather found no man in all of Ireland suitable for his beloved daughter. He was determined to find her a spouse beyond all others.

"So my grandfather dispatched her to the care of distant cousins in Paris and charged them to find her a suitable spouse."

Alys bit her lip but could not stop the words. "Heloise said that Cedric was compelled to wed Aunt because he owed Grandfather a debt and no one else would have her."

Burke laughed aloud. "I think I might like this Heloise."

"Oh, she has a bitter tongue when she does not favor another, and she does not favor Aunt."

Burke's grin did not fade. "Then I quite definitely would enjoy her company. You must take me to visit her."

Alys chose to ignore this suggestion. "So my mother was sent to Paris and introduced to all and sundry. 'Twas there she met Heloise. Heloise was nobly born, though the last of six sisters and at the bottom of her own father's list of obligations. My mother knew little of fine Parisian manners, and in the course of Heloise's instruction, they two became friends against all convention.

" 'Twas at the king's own court that Heloise says my mother met my father. My father was a knight, by Heloise's telling, a chivalrous man though stern of bearing. Apparently he was so bent upon his business at the court that he scarce noticed they two. My mother, though, noted him immediately and brazenly introduced herself. She showed no fear of this man who was known to be a merciless warrior. Heloise says 'twas that audacity alone that snared his eye and her beauty that held it.

"And once he looked, Heloise insists, he could not look away."

"Two more traits you gain from your mother," Burke murmured. At Alys's questioning glance, he smiled wryly. "A rare resolve and a beauty more compelling than might be believed."

Alys felt herself flush. "You do it again!"

"Ah!" Burke smiled mischievously. "You are stubborn yet fetching, then."

And Alys could not quell her certainty that she had preferred his first, though more flamboyant, compliment. God in heaven, but the man had a way of addling her wits!

"At any rate," she said primly, "my mother's guardians thought little good of this match. It seemed the knight was a younger son and destined to inherit naught at all. Certain that my grandfather would eye any resulting match poorly, they tried to keep the pair apart, but to no avail. They met often, they courted secretly, Heloise said they fell in love."

"Did he have a name?"

"It was never told to me."

"They must have been intimate."

Alys forced a smile. " 'Tis how I came to be."

"Indeed." Burke searched her features and seemed to choose his words carefully. "Yet the knight's suit was never accepted—it could not have been, if you are illegitimately born."

Alys shook her head. "My mother came home in shame, pregnant and without a betrothed. Heloise said she met my grandfather while he was bellowing in rage. My mother insisted that her lover would follow and do the honorable deed of asking for her hand."

Alys turned to look out over the ocean.

"He did not come," Burke suggested with quiet compassion.

Alys shook her head. "Not a word came from him. My mother lived but a year after I was born. Heloise said that once I was weaned, she surrendered all will to live."

Alys sighed when Burke said naught. "Heloise remained at Kiltorren, despite the fact that she had no family or friends here in my mother's absence. She raised me as her own."

Burke's lips tightened. "She defended you in this household in your mother's absence. What of your aunt's version of events? You said 'twas less flattering."

"Aunt always insisted that Isibeal was oft confused and readily deceived by the words of men. My mother was pretty but simple, according to her tale, indeed even more simple than Brigid. My mother shamed herself, then she made up tales about my father."

Burke's eyes flashed in anger. "That is wicked nonsense to tell a child!"

"You do not know which tale is true!"

"I know that Deirdre holds a malice toward you, a malice that I have no doubt was born of your grandfather's favor for Isibeal."

"But . . ."

"But naught, Alys! By your own word, your aunt was wedded by compulsion, while only the finest would do for her favored sister! No wonder she is bitter—such a fate would vex even a woman born with a sweet nature." He raised his brows. "And I heartily doubt that Deirdre ever suffered that affliction."

"But, Burke, 'twould be like Heloise to change a tale to see me smile."

"Because she loved your mother and was loyal to her friend's memory," he insisted. "Because she cherished the dream of her friend's great love. Because she loved you and she wanted you to know the truth."

Alys frowned. "But if my father truly loved my mother, why did he not follow her?"

Burke spread his hands. "There could be a thousand reasons . . ."

"Nay," Alys declared forcefully. "There can be but one." She pulled her hand from the warmth of Burke's. "He used the lie of love to steal her maidenhead, then once he had had his due, he abandoned her and me."

They reached the portal to the kitchen and paused. The knight studied Alys for a long moment, and she feared that he saw more than she would prefer he glimpse.

"And here is where you take your lesson," he suggested quietly. "That a knight's claim of love is not to be trusted."

Alys lifted her chin. "I have the wits to make a better choice for myself than my mother did."

But Burke shook his head. "Nay, Alys. All you will win upon this course, even with your wits about you, is solitude." He smiled slowly. "Mercifully, I have taken it upon myself to persuade you that you are wrong."

While Alys fought to find an argument to that, Burke bent and brushed his lips across her brow. 'Twas a measure of that man's cursed charm that every word that fell from his lips made her doubt what she already knew.

To Alys's mingled relief and disappointment, he did not press his advantage. She watched as Burke strolled to the stables, her thoughts churning and her brow tingling from his touch.

Burke turned in the portal of the stables. "Sleep well, my Alys," he called softly. "I shall dream of you sleeping in my chemise." And he kissed his fingertips, ducking into the stables with a wink.

Alys bit back her smile. The man had an impossible charm! If only she knew whether to trust him.

But that, she feared, was not something she ever would know with certainty. Alys lifted her skirts and turned for her chamber, never guessing that she was not alone in the kitchen.

Chapter Nine

WHEN THE SKY LIGHTENED THE NEXT MORN, ALYS rolled over in the soft bed and sighed contentedly. Edana still slept on a pallet before the single coal glowing feebly in the brazier, as the first golden rays of sunlight slanted through the shutters.

But to Alys's surprise, Brigid hovered on the threshold, the tangle of her dark auburn hair hanging loose over her shoulders. She was clad only in her chemise and looked on the verge of tears.

Alys swung out of bed in a heartbeat and crossed the cold floor. "Brigid, what is amiss?"

Edana started, even at Alys's low tones, and jumped to her feet, hastily coaxing that coal to a flame. Brigid bit her lip and considered the two, her gaze finally meeting Alys's again.

"M-m-mother said I c-c-could not call you again," she admitted, her tears welling. "B-b-but my hair!" She touched the cascading tresses and her tears spilled. "W-who will help?"

Alys gathered her cousin into a tight hug and led her toward the bed. "Of course you can call me. You know I love to braid your hair."

Brigid's hair had a will of its own, its wild curls having no interest in being tamed. It was beautiful, thick and glossy, and Alys had never seen the like of its auburn color. But Brigid was terribly self-conscious about the glory of her hair, thanks to Malvina's jealousy.

Malvina called Brigid's hair "witch's tresses" in a cruel childhood taunt, demanding to know whether Brigid was a witch or perhaps a faerie changeling. Brigid had been horrified by the thought, but Malvina had compounded the damage by telling the ever-trusting Brigid of the havoc a witch could wreak by unbinding her hair.

Ever since, Brigid had been adamant that her hair be safely braided away at every moment of the day. Brigid was not the brightest soul, but she could be stubborn once she had hold of an idea—and it troubled her deeply to believe that she could in any way bring misfortune upon others.

She was so distraught this morn that Alys's reassurance fell on deaf ears. "B-b-but Mother said . . ."

Alys stifled a rebellious condemnation of her aunt's insensitivity. "Aunt is too cautious in this," she counselled. "Have you brought your favorite comb? We shall quickly make some order of it all and have it safely braided away."

"N-nay!" Brigid pulled herself from Alys's embrace. "M-m-mother said nay!"

Alys took her cousin's hands in hers and kept her voice low. "Brigid, you must heed me. If I do not braid your hair, who will do it?"

Brigid bit her lip, looked at Alys, and her tears fell. 'Twas clear she did not know the answer, and equally clear how much that troubled her.

Alys cursed her aunt silently, but turned a smile on Edana. "Brigid, do you know Edana from the village?"

Brigid eyed the girl solemnly while Edana bowed her head. " 'Tis a great pleasure to meet you, milady."

Twin spots of color lit Brigid's cheeks, just to find herself the center of a maid's attention. "Hello," she mumbled, and gripped Alys's hand more tightly.

Alys gave those cold fingers a squeeze and leaned closer to her cousin. "Aunt says that I am to teach Edana to be a fine lady's maid. I could teach her to braid your hair, just the way you like it, and Aunt would surely find that fitting."

Brigid's whole countenance brightened. She even managed a small smile. "T-t-truly?"

"Truly! Would you like that?"

Brigid's smile broadened and she looked shyly at Edana as she nodded. Alys put out her hand and Brigid slipped her favored comb onto Alys's palm.

"Your hair is so lovely," Edana declared with a characteristic smile. Brigid flushed, but the compliment obviously pleased her.

Alys showed Edana how to ease the comb through Brigid's hair. "You must begin at the ends and progress slowly up each length, for it tangles terribly and will not be rushed into order."

"Ooooh," Edana whispered in awe as she took the first lock in her fingers. " 'Tis so very soft!"

Brigid giggled, then blushed, but still she let Edana make order of her hair. She flicked a glance to Alys, then tentatively covered her cousin's hand with her own. "C-c-can you talk to me again? Mother always s-s-said you had labor."

Alys felt a pang of guilt. She wished that she had discerned Brigid's loneliness sooner. 'Twas not easy for Brigid to talk to others, and there had been a time when she and Alys talked so often that Brigid's stutter had begun to fade.

'Twas only now that Alys realized it had become worse again.

"All has changed now, Brigid." She sat on the bed beside her cousin and took her hand. "We shall talk as once we did, and perhaps once more you will grow less shy."

Brigid slanted a surprisingly knowing glance Alys's way. "And perhaps my s-st-stutter will go away again."

"Perhaps." Alys smiled encouragement. " 'Tis a matter of practice, and you know, 'tis worse when you are afraid."

Brigid nodded solemnly, then bestowed a sudden sunny smile on Alys. "I am g-g-glad that B-B-Burke came back again."

Alys did not understand the connection and her puzzlement must have shown, for Brigid tapped one finger on their interlaced hands. "H-h-he made Mother let you b-b-be here." She deliberately took a deep breath while Alys accepted her cousin's endorsement of Burke's deeds.

But Brigid's next words stole Alys's breath away.

"I liked him b-b-both times he came before."

Alys blinked, but Brigid smiled. Surely there must be a mistake! "*Both* times he came before?"

Brigid nodded easily.

Alys shook her head. "Nay, Brigid. Burke came only for the tournaments Uncle Cedric planned. 'Twas three years past."

Brigid nodded happily. "And then ag-g-gain," she asserted. "The n-n-next year."

Alys sat back, stunned to have Burke's claim confirmed. She wondered whether her cousin was confused, but then Edana leaned forward.

"I remember that," she affirmed. " 'Twas but a year after the tourneys and he rode through the gate on that great black horse, those blue caparisons flapping in the wind. 'Twas like an old tale come to life."

Brigid nodded agreement, her eyes shining recollection. "Handsome," she declared, then blushed at her own boldness.

"Oh, he is indeed!" Edana agreed, the pair collapsing into giggles. "Have you ever glimpsed such a finely wrought man? And noble!"

Brigid nodded happy agreement.

"There is a man who could steal my heart away and be welcome to it," Edana concluded with a sigh.

Brigid sighed dreamily, but Alys frowned. "I do not understand. How can it be that he was here and I did not know it?"

The pair sobered and stared back at Alys, Brigid reaching suddenly to grasp the comb from Edana's busy fingers. She held it out toward Alys, the missing tooth glaring in its absence.

This was not an ornate comb, but one carved simply of wood. Its virtue in working Brigid's tresses lay solely in how frequently it had been used and how smooth the wood had been worn.

"N-n-naughty Alys," she whispered, her eyes filled with sympathy as she shook the comb.

And Alys gasped.

'Twas only too easy to recall how Brigid had come by the comb. Alys had inadvertently broken that tooth when this had been Aunt's comb. This was the broken treasure that had precipitated Alys's first beating, the crime at the root of Heloise's fit and the event that had cast the entire keep into chaos. Alys had forgotten naught of the terror of that night, no less of the challenge of moving Heloise to her hut and tending that woman's recovery for weeks afterward.

But she had forgotten precisely *when* the deed occurred.

Two years past, in the spring. And 'twas then—according to Brigid—that Burke came again to Kiltorren's gates.

God in heaven, he had *not* lied.

Alys could not summon a breath.

Aunt had soon afterward discarded the purportedly prized comb, Alys recalled. Brigid had found it among the refuse in the kitchen and, with her usual compassion for all objects and small creatures, could not bear to see it cast away for lack of a tooth.

Brigid was always taking the smallest things to heart, retrieving a wilted flower discarded in the garden, setting a beached mollusk back into the waves that it might swim away, saving the pebble that lodged in her shoe in the belief that it desired to come home with her. 'Twas an endearing trait, and a mark of the sweet simplicity of her nature.

And she had liked the knight *both* times.

But why had Burke abandoned Kiltorren so quickly on that visit? If he truly returned to sweep Alys away, would he have taken nay for an answer so readily? Would he not have stormed the keep, scoured the countryside, and sought her out?

Would Aunt not have willingly pointed him to Alys, if only to be rid of her ward?

But what if Burke were right? What if Aunt had lied, both to her and to him, against all expectation? Could he be right in his belief that there was more to Aunt's animosity than Alys knew?

Deirdre had lain awake half the night, planning her strategy, and by morning she had concocted a scheme that she was certain could not fail. Indeed, once her annoyance eased with her defiant niece, she knew precisely what must be done.

Alys was weak when it came to this knight's company, and clearly not even a beating could encourage the girl to avoid his company. But Alys must be kept from Burke's side if Malvina was to succeed. Fortunately, the knight had already shown that he could be manipulated by his particular weakness.

Deirdre dressed with particular care, lingering in her chamber to be certain that she would make an entrance. She swept down the stairs and smiled to find her daughters and ward breaking their fast together.

Perfect.

"Cronan!" Deirdre called. "Perhaps you might summon our guest and ensure that he does not miss our repast." Alys smiled in anticipation as the steward bowed and left upon the errand, though Deirdre knew that smile would not endure long.

She would ensure as much. Alys would learn not to trifle with Deirdre, one way or the other.

"Good morning, Mother!" Malvina said. Deirdre spared a kiss for her eldest, delighted with the richness of the girl's garb. "I trust you slept well. I slept with the angels last eve, with Burke's sweet pledges ringing in my ears."

Deirdre could not stifle her smile of victory. How she loved when Malvina followed her bidding. Alys's lips tightened and she seemed suddenly very interested in her crust of bread.

Deirdre took her seat at the board with a majestic flourish. "What pledges, my darling?"

"Oh, Mother, 'twas marvelous. I swear the man spends all the day thinking only of how to court me better." Malvina smiled at her companions and Alys's expression turned grim.

"Do tell," Deirdre urged.

"Why, yesterday morn—after you departed, Alys—Burke summoned me to the stables to steal a kiss. He made some excuse about the temper of his steed to catch me in his arms!" Malvina sighed. "He looked deeply into my eyes and insisted he loved me alone, then he kissed me with an ardor that left me breathless . . ."

Alys spread honey upon her bread with a purpose the task did not require.

" 'Tis not how you t-t-told it before," Brigid said irritably.

Deirdre glanced up in surprise. "And what would you know of the matter?" she asked. "You were not there!"

"The t-t-tale changes with each t-t-telling," Brigid insisted.

Malvina grimaced. "You are jealous, 'tis no more than that. You know that Burke favors me and we shall be wed. He told me that I and I alone held his heart."

"N-n-nay. He d-d-did not." Brigid looked mutinous. "He w-w-would not."

"You know naught of him!" Malvina cried, bounding to her feet. "I am the one he courts. I am the one he will wed! You should have heard his ardor! Once he had gathered me close, smiled down upon me, and whispered his pledge of undying love, he kissed me with a passion that made me shiver."

"He d-d-did not the l-l-last time," Brigid muttered.

Malvina spun. "Do you call me a liar?"

Brigid lifted her chin with rare defiance. "Aye."

Malvina's eyes flashed. "You wish only that Burke had eyes for you, but he does not, for you are naught but a little mouse. The man sees quality and desires me alone. Mother says as much."

"Yet he grows ever more passionate in each telling of the tale," Alys said in defense of her younger cousin. "One must wonder whether the truth was not ardent enough."

"One must wonder whether there are other maidens with eyes above their station," Deirdre interjected coolly. Brigid flushed and stared at her hands. Alys colored similarly, but she squared her shoulders and did not drop her gaze.

Malvina drew herself to her full height. "You will regret that impertinence! You will not even be welcome at the wedding. I will never welcome either of you at my gates, once I am Lady of Montvieux!"

And the knight of Montvieux, at that crucial moment, set foot into the hall. Deirdre watched his expression change from delight to dismay, his gaze moving from Alys to Malvina as he belatedly understood what was said.

Deirdre rose smoothly to her feet. "And here is none other than the man whom we discuss," she purred. "Do join us, Burke. We are having a most lively discussion of your courtship of Malvina."

The knight swallowed and looked somewhat discomfited. "My courtship?" His gaze flew to Alys once more and he did not hasten to the board. 'Twas unlike him not to be supremely confident! Deirdre knew she had not forced this exchange a moment too soon.

"Aye." Deirdre feigned surprise. "Surely I have not misunderstood your intent to win my eldest daughter's hand?"

Cedric descended the staircase just then and his voice boomed across the hall. "Surely you do not toy with the affections of my child?" He frowned in a most ferocious manner, and Deirdre decided she must reward him for his unwitting aid.

"Do your kisses mean naught?" Malvina demanded. "And your pledges of undying love?"

Burke looked between the three of them, his manner that of a cornered cat. "I certainly would not intend to deceive anyone . . ." he began, but Cedric took a menacing step forward.

"Declare yourself, sir, and do so now. You cannot linger within this hall and persist in kissing my daughter without making an honorable offer for her hand."

"But I did not kiss her!"

"Oh, he lies!" Malvina charged. She raised a hand to her mouth, as if she would weep, her lips trembling dangerously. "Father, he toys with my affections!"

"Say 'tis not so!" Deirdre demanded.

"Aye, state your intentions for my daughter's hand!" echoed Cedric. "Or I shall turn you out of this keep and set the dogs at your heels until you are run clear from Ireland. Did you lie about coming to Kiltorren to seek a bride?"

Burke's brow furrowed. "Nay, of course not!"

Cedric folded his arms across his chest. "We have dallied enough and you have had time enough to confirm your choice. Name your bride and name her now."

The knight, tellingly, looked to Alys.

"Do tell, Burke," Alys urged, her tone tempered with steel. 'Twas clear the man won no favor in that corner.

Burke frowned, he looked to Cedric, he glanced at Malvina, then his gaze locked with Deirdre's. She certainly did not imagine how his eyes turned a frosty silver or how his jaw set, before he turned to Cedric with a smile.

"Of course I court Malvina," he said flatly. "You guessed aright from the start."

Cedric grinned, then stepped forward to shake the knight's hand. Malvina gave a cry of delight and launched herself across the hall to embrace the knight. Brigid pouted, but Deirdre smiled yet again when Alys pushed away from the board and strode from the hall, her chin held high.

The knight looked after her for but a moment before Malvina dragged him toward the board. "We must plan our nuptials in grand detail," she enthused. "But first, a betrothal ceremony. We shall have to invite everyone of our acquaintance and Father will host a wondrous meal. Perhaps we should have tournaments and you could compete with my colors . . ."

Alys and Brigid sat glumly in Kiltorren's garden, which flourished in a small courtyard attached to the kitchen. Neither of them had borne Malvina's planning long, though in the silence of the garden, Alys had naught to do but think about all Burke had said. She watched Brigid embroider a band destined for a hem or cuff and hated that the knight had fooled her again.

"He d-d-did not say it," Brigid repeated. "And he d-d-did not kiss her."

"Maybe not," Alys said, then studied her cousin as an unwelcome thought struck her. "Does it matter to you, Brigid, if Burke courts Malvina?"

Her cousin's scarlet flush was all the answer Alys needed.

Brigid busied herself with her embroidery, her cheeks burning, as Alys stared at her. 'Twas one thing for Burke to toy with her, but Brigid had no means to defend herself against the man's allure.

Surely he would not take advantage of Brigid's innocence?

A man cleared his throat just then and Alys's head snapped

up. Burke himself leaned in the portal, his arms folded across his chest, his expression bemused. There was a determined glint in his eye, though, that warned Alys he meant to see something done this day.

"I have been searching for you," he said softly.

"Malvina and Aunt will not approve." Alys rose to her feet and placed herself between the knight and her trusting cousin before she even realized that she did as much. Burke took a step into the garden, his gaze running appreciatively over her. Alys straightened at his obvious approval.

" 'Tis not the best hue for you, but we shall do better in Paris," he said with an easy smile that rankled.

"I will not go to Paris with you," Alys retorted. "My situation is not so dire that playing mistress while Malvina is wife would be appealing."

"Alys!" Burke looked exasperated. "I am not going to wed Malvina!"

"I kn-kn-knew it," Brigid muttered to her needlework.

Reminded that they were not alone and knowing Burke would have his say, Alys led him to a far corner of the garden. "How odd. I heard you say precisely that just this morn."

"Nay, I said I courted her. 'Tis a far cry from a proposal."

"Oh, you play with words!" Alys shook a finger at the smug knight. "You know well enough that Aunt and Uncle believe you intend to wed her!"

"Aye, and you know well enough that I had no choice but to answer as I did."

"Since you have been kissing Malvina."

"I have not!" Burke was clearly frustrated and Alys found she enjoyed the sight. "The girl makes much of naught—'tis you alone I kiss."

Alys arched a brow. " 'Twill not happen again."

Burke growled something uncomplimentary beneath his breath and took a determined step closer. "Alys, you must understand that I had no option. If I had not said my intent was to win Malvina, they would have cast me from the gates! You heard your uncle. And if I was not at Kiltorren, then I could not pursue your reluctant heart."

Alys folded her arms across her chest, resolved not to be swayed by the knight's apparent sincerity. "So you lied."

Burke waved off the thought. " 'Twas not truly a lie."

"You told them you courted Malvina, yet you do not," Alys retorted, her demeanor stern. "That, Burke, is a lie."

"Alys! 'Twas merely a small falsehood."

"Small or large, a lie is a lie."

" 'Twas a convenience, no more, no less. You make too much of too little. 'Twas for the greater good!"

Oh, this man was too quick to turn anything to his own advantage. Alys was not prepared to let him escape so readily as that. "So, one may readily lie for the greater good."

Burke shrugged. "Aye, when one must."

"Aha!" Alys leaned toward him, her gaze bright. "Yet you expect me to trust you."

"Of course I do!"

"Then how, Burke, am I to know when the greater good is being served and when you are telling me the truth?"

"Alys! You know I am a man of honor."

"I know no such thing. Indeed, you have just confessed to being a liar." Alys argued. 'Twas quite enjoyable to put Burke in a corner, for he always seemed to hold the upper hand.

" 'Tis not the same," he insisted grimly. "Not at all."

But Alys spread her hands. "Burke, if you do not tell the truth, then how am I to know when to believe your tales?"

"But I have always told you the truth!" Burke insisted.

"By fortune or design?" Alys tilted her head to survey him. "Just now in the hall you admitted you told a falsehood in my presence."

"Alys!" Burke snatched at her shoulders, his eyes gleaming.

She caught her breath to have his will so surely bent upon her. "I pledge to you that I have never deceived you."

Beneath the heat of his regard, Alys's resistance eroded dangerously. Indeed, she knew now that Burke could well have returned while she tended Heloise two years past. In this moment, she could not think of a lie he had deliberately told her, which was little help. Alys fought to keep her wits about her, but Burke smiled that wondrous smile and slid his thumbs persuasively against her shoulders.

Irresistible, indeed. Every thought seemed to have abandoned her at the first brush of those thumbs. She completely forgot her cousin's presence as she stared into Burke's eyes.

"Did they not give you shoes?" he murmured.

"Aye, old horrible ones."

"Surely you could have worn them still?"

Alys seized on this practicality. She stepped away and pulled up the hem of her kirtle to reveal her ankles and bare feet. She wiggled her toes against the moss-encrusted flagstone. "But I *like* to be barefoot in the summer."

When she glanced up, Burke's eyes had darkened and he looked as agitated as she had felt beneath his touch. Certainly his breathing was uneven and his jaw was clenched. Alys looked back to her toes, but there seemed to be naught amiss there.

'Twas most unlike Burke to be silent.

She eyed the grim knight warily. "What is amiss?"

He looked once more to her toes, then shook his head, summoning a smile that did not mitigate his expression. "Ye gods, Alys, but I will win your trust if 'tis the last thing I do."

"It may well be that," she could not help but tease.

Burke grinned. "Deeds you demanded and a deed you have, Alys."

Alys took a step back. "I thanked you already."

His smile widened. "Most enchantingly. And you chal-

lenged me to learn more of you, which I have done." Burke
eased closer, his manner confidential. "There was a third challenge you made, though, one that I would answer this day."

Alys watched as Burke tapped his thumb with purpose.

"Loyalty," he said firmly, and without further preamble.
Alys caught her breath, knowing precisely what argument he
made. "There is not a man alive who would not welcome a
woman by his side with such fierce loyalty as burns within
you, my Alys. That is *one*."

Oh, Alys was in trouble. Burke was not even touching her
and she could barely summon a coherent thought. A lie had
only just fallen from his lips in the hall, a lie by his own admission, and Alys was feckless enough to fancy she could
discern the difference in his manner between then and now.

She was a fool. The man knew his own assets well and
plied them with merciless ease.

But she still wanted to believe him. Alys's mouth went dry
when Burke's vivid gaze did not swerve from hers. He did not
smile, but touched his index finger.

"Compassion. 'Tis the mark of a noble heart to show such
concern for those weaker or in more dire straits, a sign of
great character to put one's own troubles aside to aid another.
'Tis compassion that takes you to Heloise with such dedication, Alys, and I do not miss the import of that."

Burke paused as Alys swallowed. "That is *two*."

God in heaven, but he was exceeding her challenge as
never Alys might have imagined. A trembling began in her
belly when Burke took another step, his attention fixed upon
her. There was only an arm's length left between them when
he marked the next finger.

"Fortitude," he declared softly. "And this is the greatest of
them all. The same flame that melts wax forges steel, Alys.
Though you have borne much in this place, still you rise to a
challenge, still your spirit is undiminished, still you walk with

the dignity of a queen. 'Tis no small thing for a man to know that his lady will be undaunted by whatever fortune is cast across their path."

But Alys felt far from strong in this moment. Indeed, her knees threatened to buckle beneath her weight. That tremble grew to a roar, yet she could not even break Burke's gaze, let alone turn away.

"That is *three*." Burke took the only step remaining, bringing them toe to toe. Alys tipped up her chin to hold his gaze, caught the scent of him, and saw that beguiling smile begin to curve his lips. He captured her hand within the breadth of his and raised it to his lips.

"Those are but three of the reasons I love you, Alys," he murmured with such resolve that she could not doubt his claim. Her heart began to thunder and Alys knew she was lost.

Burke opened her hand and pressed a burning kiss to her palm with exquisite slowness. He leisurely closed her fingers over the embrace, each one in succession, the warmth of his own fingertips sliding over her skin in a deliberate caress. He met her gaze once more as he kissed her knuckles, but even then he did not release her hand.

"This change in garb favors you, but truly, Alys, I would see you garbed as richly as the queen you are."

She would never be able to deny the man anything he asked in this moment. Isibeal's ghost hovered more closely beside her daughter than ever before.

Even knowing that she was cursed with a wanton's urges, even knowing that Burke had likely spoken precisely thus to Malvina just a day past, even knowing that naught but trouble would come of this in the end, Alys knew she would succumb.

Indeed, there was naught else she wanted but the man's kiss. Burke leaned closer, his eyes gleaming. Alys found herself rising to her toes.

Then Aunt's voice rang through the keep. "A-LYS!" that woman shouted. "Where are you? I have need of you—Alys!"

And the web of enchantment Burke had spun was instantly shredded.

Alys straightened and stepped away, all too readily imagining what Aunt would have to say of this. She pulled her fingers from Burke's gentle grasp, but felt oddly cheated. 'Twas the only evidence of her wanton nature that she needed.

"Alys! You cannot go!" Burke protested.

"I must, I must," Alys argued wildly, picking up her skirts to hasten across the garden. "My aunt summons me."

Burke's eyes flashed. "Your aunt can go to hell!"

And Alys chuckled despite herself, glancing back from the threshold. "Oh, I have no doubt that she will," she murmured, and Burke grinned in turn.

"Stay, Alys."

But Alys shook her head. "I dare not."

'Twas not easy to turn her back on the knight's appeal, but Alys managed the deed. Barely. She fled down the corridor, half fearing she would change her course if she did not run with all haste. She had come dangerously close to temptation, of that there could be no doubt.

And there was even less doubt that Burke would tempt her again.

Alys wished she knew that she would be strong enough to deny him.

❖

Yet again Burke could fairly taste how close he had been to success. Aye, he had seen Alys's expression soften, he had glimpsed the welcome in her golden eyes.

And he had been robbed of his lady's kiss, no less the chance to offer for her hand with all the ceremony such an offer demanded. Her footsteps echoed on the stone corridor, then faded to naught. Burke bowed his head, shoved his fingers through his hair, and wished that his lady could be more readily won.

But then she would not be Alys.

Indeed, he admired how she clung to her convictions. Burke knew that once Alys cleaved to him, once all her doubts and questions were set to rest, that loyalty would be his alone.

Surely that was an objective more than worth a pitched battle.

But he had come so close! Burke swore with rare thoroughness, forgetting that he was not alone. Indeed, he started when a tiny voice cleared beside him. He glanced to find Brigid hovering behind him, her cheeks burning, her gaze downcast.

"I t-t-told Alys you w-w-were here t-t-twice," she admitted. "D-d-do not be angry. She c-c-could not have known."

Burke's curiosity was prompted and his annoyance faded. "Why not? Where was Alys when I returned?"

Brigid's gaze danced to the portal, then back to Burke. She gestured cautiously toward the seat.

Burke smiled softly. "I would be delighted to join you and most pleased to hear anything you can tell me of your cousin."

Brigid flushed scarlet at his attention, but she immediately perched on the bench. She looked up expectantly at Burke, a hopefulness in her gaze that could not be misconstrued.

And Burke understood fully.

She sought his company for the same reason he sought out Alys's companionship. But Brigid was young, and truly she knew naught of the man he was. 'Twas but a case of girlish infatuation.

Burke had no desire to wound Brigid, so 'twould be best if

he were honest with her. False hopes could only hurt more in the end.

Burke seated himself beside her, leaving a discreet distance between them. First, he would listen to all Brigid had to say, then he would explain to her how matters lay.

Aunt's demands were readily satisfied. Indeed, Alys had the sense her aunt merely wanted to keep track of where she was. Still puzzling over this, she was halfway back to the kitchen before she realized that Brigid had been left alone with Burke.

She gathered her kirtle in two fistfuls and quickly walked back to the garden. But naught seemed awry.

Alys paused in the shadows of the portal when she found knight and maid seated in the sunlight. Burke sat well apart from Brigid, his manner much as one would take with a child.

"So, Alys erred in breaking the tooth of a comb, your mother saw her punished for this crime, and 'twas then that Heloise intervened." The tight line of Burke's lips told Alys what he thought of this deed. "Heloise fell ill and was moved to the point, Alys tending her there for some weeks. That is why she was not in the hall when I came."

Brigid nodded quickly, then flicked her fingers toward the gates. "Y-you left, Alys returned."

As simple as that, and Alys had never known. Only now she realized the real reason for the runners Aunt had sent to ensure she remained longer with Heloise—at the time, she had thought it an uncharacteristic concern for the older woman.

But Aunt was never uncharacteristic, and never concerned for Heloise.

Burke had been here and Aunt strove to keep him for Malvina.

This time, however, the knight seemed to share that

objective—at least in Aunt's presence. But what was the truth of Burke's intent?

Burke arched a dark brow as Alys wondered, his expression hinting that he thought little good of this revelation. "It seemed I erred in sending word of my arrival ahead, for Alys paid the price," he muttered, and Alys's eyes widened.

Aunt had *known* he was coming? A horrible dread took root within her. Alys had wondered at the time how a humble comb could prompt such a vicious response.

Aunt had used the comb as an excuse! Clearly, Alys's beating had been intended to remove her from view but had borne unexpected fruit in Heloise's attack.

Alys could have wept that Heloise had suffered so much for Aunt's selfish goal.

Burke frowned at his boots for a long moment before his toe began to tap. "Why was she beaten this time, Brigid? Do you know?"

"N-n-naughty Alys."

Burke was consummately patient though the girl was flustered. "But why, Brigid? What sin did she commit?"

"Alys b-b-broke her promise." Burke lifted his brow, inviting more, and Brigid took a deep breath. "T-t-to not see you."

Burke's brow darkened ominously. He pushed to his feet, he paced, he shoved a hand through his hair, and he muttered something that Alys was quite certain Brigid should not hear.

" 'Tis all my fault!" he declared in vexation. " 'Tis my pursuit that brings the lady such punishment. But *WHY*? Surely Deirdre would be glad to see Alys gone?"

Aye, that was exactly the riddle that Alys could not solve. Burke sat down heavily, and she knew his mind worked like lightning. He spoke aright in this one thing—there must be another piece to the puzzle.

But Alys forgot her own concerns as Brigid suddenly reached for the knight's hand. "I-I-I-I like you," she confessed. Alys took a step forward, halting only when the knight smiled gently.

Would he be kind to Brigid?

Or would he take advantage of her trust?

What could Alys do to intervene?

Burke captured Brigid's fingers, even as Alys watched, and pressed a chaste kiss to her fingertips. Brigid's eyes widened with wonder.

"I thank you, Brigid, for you honor me with your honesty," he said in a low voice. "Indeed, if my heart were not already captured by one lady, I would be honored by your esteem."

He set her hand back in her lap as Brigid stared at him and Alys eased back into the shadows. "But, as you doubtless know, a man can grant his heart but once, if he grants it fully."

Brigid clasped her hands together and leaned toward the knight, rapturous at this romantic tale. "Who is she?"

Alys nearly gasped aloud. 'Twas the first time in a long while that she had heard Brigid utter a full sentence without stammering.

And Brigid did not even note that she had done it.

Burke glanced up abruptly. Alys saw the flash of surprise cross his features. So he had noticed as well.

" 'Tis not evident?" he demanded, amazement in his tone.

Alys's heart warmed that he pretended 'twas Brigid's question alone that surprised him. Brigid shook her head, her eyes shining.

Burke shook his head in turn. "Ah, but I should not be so bold as to utter the lady's name before she accepts my suit."

Brigid rolled her eyes and smiled. "Tell me!"

"I should not."

"You must!" Brigid wrinkled her nose. "It cannot be Malvina."

Burke echoed her expression, making Brigid laugh. "Nay, not she."

"I knew you did not court her! Tell me."

Burke looked from side to side and Alys drew back into the shadows. " 'Tis a secret!" he whispered, and Brigid's eyes sparkled. Alys bit back her smile, unable to tear herself away from the sight of this bold knight being so gentle with a maiden's heart.

Oh, there were times when this man was too good to be true.

"Tell me!" Brigid insisted.

Burke grinned. " 'Tis my heart we discuss here! If I share the tale, then you must pledge to keep this secret for me."

Brigid smiled and made a cross over her heart with one fingertip, then touched that fingertip to her lips. "Secret," she whispered.

Burke leaned his dark head close to Brigid's and dropped his voice yet lower. "The lady is here at Kiltorren," he confided.

Brigid poked him when he took too long for her taste. "Tell me!"

" 'Tis your cousin, Alys, who holds my heart," Burke admitted. " 'Twill be hers for all time."

Alys's felt her heartbeat falter before it began again to race.

Later she knew she would doubt that she had heard aright. Later Burke would make some charming comment that could not possibly be true, some lover's words that made Alys feel as if she were only the current candidate in a long, long line of women that stretched both before her and would continue after she was forgotten.

For that was the trouble with Burke. He was so handsome, so charming, so utterly alluring, that Alys could not believe that she—or any other woman—could hold his attention for all time.

'Twould be against the odds, indeed.

She forced herself to note that he made no mention of nuptial vows, except when compelled to do so about Malvina, and felt disappointment swell within her. And indeed the knight himself confessed that a lie did not count in pursuit of the greater good.

The greater good would always be to his advantage, she was certain. Nay, Burke was not her Aucassin, even if he did fill that knight's shoes in her dreams.

Alys folded her arms across her chest. No doubt that even if she ceded to Burke, his interest would fade once she was no longer in distress. It might not happen for years. But one day a beautiful maiden would catch his eye and Burke would be gone, as surely as if he had never been by her side.

As surely as Alys's own father had been.

Or Burke would take a wife in truth. The very thought chilled Alys's blood. She could not imagine being forced to share Burke's attentions with another for all her days and nights—another, perhaps like Malvina.

Nay, Alys would rather have naught than hold a dream doomed to be shattered. She would not repeat her mother's error.

Alys would not die alone, pining for a lost love.

Chapter Ten

RIGID GASPED AND SAT BACK. "ALYS!" SHE REPEATED, then clapped her hands over her mouth in horror.

" 'Tis a secret!" Burke teased. His manner was as playful as one would be with a younger sibling, and Brigid giggled. She repeated her pledge with her fingertips.

Then her mouth drooped with dejection. "Why not me?"

Alys bit her lip at the sight of her cousin's vulnerability. She nearly stepped forward, but Burke took Brigid's hand again in his.

Alys watched as he turned the full weight of his charm upon her cousin. "Brigid, there is a special bond between a man and a woman meant to be together. They know each other when first their eyes meet, they understand that each was made for the other."

"Love," Brigid said with a shy smile.

"Aye, love 'tis and no match should be without its flame." Burke looked down at her hand, his expression pensive.

Brigid smiled. "I want love."

Burke smiled at her. "Then I am not the man for you. There will be such a man, Brigid, and he will cross your path when you least expect him."

But Brigid's smile faded and she shook her head sadly. "Not me. I will not be able to talk to him."

"That is not true," Burke insisted gently. "You have just spoken to me."

Brigid glanced up in alarm, her eyes flew open as she realized what she had done.

Then Brigid flushed anew and fixed her gaze on the ground. "I c-c-cannot do it again."

"Of course you will," Burke maintained. "You are a lady of charm, a lady of beauty, and one day a man will be as awed by you as you will be of him." Tears shone in Brigid's eyes, and Alys blinked back a few of her own. Burke gave Brigid's fingers a squeeze. "Wait for him, Brigid. You deserve no less."

Alys spun and flattened her back against the wall, biting her lip to fight her tears. Far from taking advantage of Brigid's truth, Burke had behaved with a rare gallantry.

And his chivalry had made Brigid forget to stutter. 'Twas no small thing, and Alys knew she must thank him, whatever the toll he demanded in return. Alys heard Burke clear his throat and peeked around the corner again.

The knight grinned as he braced his elbows on his knees. "So, Brigid, can you help me win Alys's affections? I shall need aid if I am not to make difficulties for my lady with your mother."

But Brigid did not smile. She shook her head. "Nay."

"Why not?"

"She is not allowed."

Alys frowned in the same moment as Burke.

"What nonsense is this?" he asked, his voice rising slightly. Alys took a good look, but Brigid was not intimidated by his increasing volume.

Nor apparently by the flash of his eyes.

Brigid tapped a fingertip. "First, Malvina." She indicated herself. "Then Brigid." She smiled sadly for Burke. "*Then* Alys." She shrugged. "But no one wants Malvina." Brigid kicked her feet. "We wait and wait and wait but no one comes."

And no one ever would, Alys realized with a start. She would never be free of this place, by Aunt's dictate! 'Twas unfair!

Burke had already leapt to his feet. "Who made this demand? Who insisted that Alys could not wed at her choice?"

Brigid opened her mouth, but Burke held up a hand to silence her. "Nay, Brigid, I can guess the truth readily enough." He spun and headed for the portal where Alys was hidden, the grim look of him enough to make her heartbeat skitter. "What I do not understand is *why* I did not know."

And Alys knew from whom he would seek the truth. It seemed rather a poor excuse not to have even known. She picked up her skirts and turned to flee, hoping to take advantage of the fact that neither knew she was there.

Dame Fortune, once again, did not play Alys's game.

Alys heard Burke mutter her name, then the thunder of his footsteps as he gave chase. She was not even out of sight when he rounded the corner, and he paused to bellow, no doubt certain she could be readily caught.

"Alys! You listened!"

Alys spun to a halt, turning to face him proudly. He would catch her and she knew it well—she would rather face him here. "Aye. I wanted to be certain you treated my cousin with honor."

Burke's eyes gleamed as he advanced upon her. "You secreted yourself in the shadows! You eavesdropped upon us."

Alys could not argue with that.

Burke took a dozen quick strides to bring them toe to toe, his voice dropping to a low silky tone that melted Alys's knees. He smiled down at her, looking like a cat who had cornered its prey. "Why, Alys, you *deceived* us both."

He had her there and Burke knew it well.

Alys looked past him to the portal to the garden, then flicked a glance to Burke's eyes. Even in the shadows, he could see her slow flush.

" 'Twas only for a moment," she said tentatively.

" 'Twas a deception." Burke found himself enjoying this change of circumstance. "Indeed 'twas a manner of *lie*."

"Only a small one," Alys argued.

"A *small* lie?" Burke granted her a skeptical glance and spoke with deliberation. "But I understood there was no difference between a small and a large lie."

Alys glared at Burke but did not abandon the field. Ye gods, he loved that she was so quick of wit. She folded her arms across her chest and looked him in the eye. " 'Twas for the greater good."

Burke grinned. "Ah! I have heard much of the greater good this day."

Alys swore with a thoroughness unexpected. "You are a most vexing man," she muttered impatiently. Burke could not hold back his chuckle. Alys glanced up, then her lips quirked with laughter as if she guessed the direction of his thoughts and could not stop her response.

"There seems to be much of that trait hereabouts," Burke teased, and was rewarded by a glimpse of the lady's own smile.

"An epidemic," she agreed, and Burke laughed aloud.

Then Alys propped her hands upon her hips and regarded him cockily. " 'Twas a lie, I admit it. There! Are you satisfied?"

"Far from that," Burke mused. "Though perhaps a token of your esteem would soothe me."

"A token . . ." Alys frowned, then her eyes widened in understanding. The twinkle dancing there revealed that she was not so horrified as she might pretend. "I shall not kiss you as penance for being protective of Brigid!"

Burke sighed with mock resignation and leaned against the wall. "Ah, then I fear I shall not be satisfied any time soon."

And Alys laughed. Her fingers rose to her lips as soon as the sound bubbled forth. Her eyes danced with mischief and her dimple not only appeared but lingered.

"So you did listen," Burke concluded with satisfaction.

"Of course I listened. I do not know what to expect from you." She eyed him warily. " 'Twas a pleasant surprise."

Burke supposed that was a compliment. "Then you must have heard Brigid."

"Aye."

"Did you know of this dictate?"

Alys shook her head, clearly unhappy with the revelation.

"And there lies the root of your aunt's concern. For if you wed and had a son, that son likely could challenge Deirdre or her daughters for Kiltorren when Cedric passed away."

Alys did not argue his thinking. "Especially if neither of Cedric's daughters wed."

"Aye. 'Tis appallingly simple." Burke shoved a hand through his hair. "Your aunt would keep you from wedding, she would insist upon this nonsense of Isibeal being a whore so that you would not even be tempted to bear an illegitimate child."

Alys's smile tightened and disappointment lit her fine eyes. "My own blood would see me die alone, unhappy and untouched, merely to ensure their own legacy for another generation."

Burke held her gaze. "For the sake of Kiltorren."

She studied him for a long moment. Burke knew he did not imagine the glimmer of hope in her eyes. "And what do you say of that?"

An easy question. " 'Tis wrong, of course!"

But Alys's eyes narrowed. "And?"

Burke gestured helplessly. "And it cannot continue."

Now Alys frowned. "And?"

"And *what*?"

"And what would you do about it?"

Burke flung out his hands. "Take you away, of course, with or without your aunt's permission. Alys, you have only to say the word and we will leave this keep behind us. We could be gone before midday!"

"And I could repeat every error my dame ever made before nightfall." The lady growled in frustration. "How could you expect so much of me for so little?" She pivoted smartly and marched away, leaving Burke dumbfounded.

"Alys! I am yours!"

" 'Tis not enough!" the lady cried. "I am not such a witless fool that I would grant my all to a man who offers naught but a honeyed tongue!"

And Burke felt a shiver of dread.

How could Alys know that he had spurned his hereditary estate? Did she care more about such matters than he? Did she not believe that he could win a king's ransom at the tourneys?

Did he not have enough to offer his intended bride? Too late he recalled that the lady *had* insisted that at Kiltorren, she was at least certain to be fed.

Nay, she could not have so little faith in him as that!

But Burke was not entirely certain of that.

"Do not be so quick to dismiss the merit of a honeyed tongue," he called after her for lack of anything better to say.

Alys laughed in a spurt born of surprise, then glanced over her shoulder. "Incorrigible," she declared, then disappeared into the kitchen.

"Tempted," Burke answered grimly. "Frustrated and alone." He folded his arms across his chest and glared after Alys. How could she not trust him to ensure her welfare?

'Twas insulting.

"She likes you," Brigid murmured from behind him, and Burke turned to find the girl watching.

Burke shoved a hand through his hair, took a deep breath, and considered the array of obstacles before him. " 'Tis true you must be wed first?"

"Malvina," Brigid insisted, her gaze troubled.

And rightly so, to Burke's thinking. 'Twould not be easy to find Malvina a spouse, and Burke had no doubt that Deirdre had tried. Indeed, this seige was proving to have many fields of battle, not a one of them an easy victory.

But the simple truth was that finding Malvina a spouse would not only fulfill Deirdre's condition, but convince Alys that Burke had no intent to wed her cousin.

A deed, if ever there was one.

In that moment, the rain began to fall in heavy drops, sending both knight and maiden inside with all haste. 'Twas fitting weather for the task confronting him, Burke could not help but note.

Indeed, 'twas a good thing he was not a man who was readily daunted.

Burke's mood was markedly less than prime.

Hot with purpose, he had ridden out before midday to seek Malvina's match. 'Twas imperative that he wed Alys's cousins before offering formally for her hand once more. He would not tolerate Deirdre finding any reason to deny him, and he would not leave any doubt in Alys's mind of his proposal or its sincerity.

So he descended upon a keep to the west of Kiltorren, shocking the residents with his sudden and sodden appearance. Sadly, they had no sons available for wedlock and no news of any unmarried men within range.

He begged accommodations and headed out the next morn to the south of Kiltorren, only to have similar results.

On Tuesday he made his way east, his quest yielding naught.

Wednesday took him to Killarney itself and Burke had high hopes for the prosperous town. A settlement of sufficient size, here he was certain there would be young men desiring a nobly born bride, perhaps interested enough to ask few questions of the lady's nature. But it seemed rumors of Malvina's nature preceded him, for more than one nobleman covered his mouth to hide a smile at the mention of Kiltorren.

Burke had the definite sense that Deirdre had trodden this ground before him, and done so many times.

He was so determined to check every possibility, to interview every family with any prospects, that it grew dark before he was done. Burke sought refuge in an inn, not pleased in the least to be away from Kiltorren.

He could only hope that Alys did not pay for the exchanges they had had on Sunday. Burke glared at the ceiling as the locals caroused in the common room below and refused to consider the possibility of failure.

Burke de Montvieux did not fail at any objective.

And he would *not* fail at this one.

'Twas still raining the next morn. Burke rode back to Kiltorren with a heavy heart, the fine steady mist of rain doing naught to improve his mood. Perhaps an answer lurked at Kiltorren itself. Perhaps the steward knew of someone, or the gatekeeper had heard a tale, or the priest in the village could be of aid.

Somewhere in Christendom, there had to be a man desperate enough to make Malvina his bride.

Encouraged at the thought, Burke gave Moonshadow his spurs, never expecting to find the very candidate he sought already standing at Kiltorren's own gates.

Talbot was certain he had ridden to the ends of the earth. Indeed, the ocean rolled beyond the tower of this isolated keep, its surface unmarred by ship or silhouette of distant land. The wind shoved chill fingers through his damp garments, the rain fell without cease. Goats milled behind the portcullis, their inquisitive gazes fixing upon Talbot at intervals, their jaws working incessantly.

He had ridden clear across this cursed island to find a faltering farm.

Indeed, Talbot had slept in places no better than hovels these past nights, he had found no wine, no women, and what passed for song made his ears ring. Last eve, he had bedded down in a field, and awakened cold, stiff, and damp. His squire, Henri, complained constantly, his nasal whine making Talbot long to throttle the boy.

Trust his uncle to send him to this godforsaken corner of the world! At moments like this, Talbot wondered whether his uncle's wealth was truly worth the ordeal of winning it.

'Twas a sign of distress that he could even question such a fundamental tenet.

And now, after all he had endured, the gatekeeper was disinclined to admit Talbot to this cursed keep. Indeed, the man had barred the gates against their arrival and stood now behind the portcullis, his arms folded across his formidable bulk.

Talbot's minuscule measure of charm completely deserted him.

"What in the name of God do you mean I cannot pass?" he asked impatiently. "I am sent on a mission to Kiltorren and I demand admission!" His voice rose in irritation and his mare stepped agitatedly. 'Twas not a fine, even-tempered beast, though Talbot blamed his uncle for that as well.

The man could have bought him the finest stallion, and so readily that he would not even notice the expense of the coin. But Millard had this curious idea that a knight must "earn" his way in the world.

Talbot would much prefer to be *given* his due.

The gatekeeper did not so much as blink. "And I say you shall not have it, not until I have a better explanation for your arrival."

"What nonsense is this? Have you no manners in this foul corner of a yet more foul country?"

The keeper inhaled sharply. "I was born and raised in this corner of this country . . ." he began, a thread of anger in his tone, but Talbot waved off this recounting of family history.

"I care naught for your birthright, unless it ends with my admission to the keep," he snapped. "And a fine bowl of rabbit stew would be welcome, a glass of good Burgundy wine, and a plump willing wench."

"Aye!" Henri agreed with a hearty bobbing of his head. "Wenches and wine would be fine, indeed."

"See to it!" Talbot demanded.

But the gatekeeper squared his shoulders stubbornly and did not move. "We have few visitors at Kiltorren," he declared. "And one cannot be too cautious in admitting armed knights to a holding." He looked Talbot dead in the eye. "I say you shall not pass."

Talbot flung out his hands. "Will you not even speak to your lord? What manner of hole have we found where the nobility are treated like common dirt?"

The gatekeeper smiled wryly. "Perhaps I shall find a moment to speak with him this evening." He shrugged. "Or in the morning."

"In the morning!" Talbot shrieked, his steed shying at the sound. "And what am I to do in that time? Where am I to sleep? And where am I to find a decent meal?"

The keeper shrugged, clearly enjoying Talbot's discomfiture. As if to emphasize the unacceptability of these arrangements, thunder rumbled in the distance and the cold rain slanted down with new vigor. "Killarney is a half-day ride that way," the keeper declared with no small measure of pleasure.

"If you left now, you could reach there before the evening meal."

Talbot swore. He dismounted and stamped his feet, he strode through puddles and kicked muddy water at the gates. His fists were clenched tight, his face was hot, he was filled with the anger of impotence.

And the cursed keeper merely smiled. "Indeed," that man commented, "you do confirm my very worst fears of your intent."

Talbot snarled, but the keeper stepped toward his hut, oblivious to the knight outside his own gates.

The insolence of it all! To be disregarded by a mere gate-keeper was beyond disgraceful. Talbot put his hand on the hilt of his sword and strode to the portcullis, not entirely certain of what he intended to do but determined to see results.

And in that moment, the pound of hoofbeats filled the air. The gatekeeper turned back, his heavy features alight with curiosity. Talbot found himself turning the moment he recognized the gait of a destrier.

Another knight!

But this knight rode alone. How could that be?

Talbot frowned as the silhouette of the arrival drew out of the mist. The man rode with haste, bent over the neck of a steed whose magnificence was not concealed by distance. Indeed, the stallion was so fine and so black, its step high, its coat glossy. 'Twas the manner of destrier Talbot had always desired, and he disliked this knight, simply for riding it, without knowing any more about the man.

Talbot slipped back into his saddle, not wanting to be at a complete disadvantage when this oddly solitary knight arrived.

The man who pulled the black steed to a halt beside Talbot did so with a flourish. His armor left no doubt of his knightly status, neither did his finely embroidered tabard nor his fur-lined cloak. Fine spurs gleamed on his heels, his steed was mud-splattered but wondrously caparisoned. He was soaked to the skin, just as Talbot was, but this knight seemed unreasonably delighted, despite his state.

He had already doffed his helmet and shoved a hand through his dark hair, loosing raindrops like a shower of jewels.

"And who," the knight asked with amusement, "have we here?"

"Sir!" The keeper crowed with delight. "The ladies have been asking after you."

Aye, this knight was cursedly good looking and would give Talbot a contest for the finest wench. Talbot hated him even more.

The knight grinned, a merry twinkle lighting his eyes. "*All* of them, Godfrey?"

The keeper chuckled. "All but one, though I daresay she is more interested in your return than all of that."

This seemed to please the knight, who surveyed Talbot anew. Indeed, he clucked to his steed, that beast prancing around Talbot's own sorry mare in a tight circle.

Even the destrier would not acknowledge the mare, so humble was she. Talbot's ears burned with shame, he gritted his teeth and pretended not to notice this knight's survey.

"This man calls himself a knight," Godfrey supplied. "And would pass my gates without explanation."

"I told you well enough that I had a mission at Kiltorren," Talbot snapped.

"A mission?" the knight inquired silkily.

" 'Tis not to be confessed to any soul who crosses my path."

The knight arched a dark brow, riding behind Talbot to complete his circular survey. Talbot itched to watch the man but did not want to show weakness by turning to look. He stared stiffly ahead, wondering what mischief this knight intended to make.

For there could be no doubt that the man had something on his mind.

"Is your master oft so testy?" the knight asked Henri.

"Aye, sir!" the boy declared, and Talbot clenched his teeth yet tighter at the gatekeeper's quick smile. "Though 'tis worse when he has need of a cup of wine and a wench, as he does now."

Talbot would box his squire's ears for that impudence.

The knight paused beside Talbot. "And what does your wife think of your wenching?"

"I have no wife!" Talbot retorted impatiently. A trickle of rainwater made its way beneath his chemise and ran coldly down his back. "And I fail to see what import that is. I ask only to be admitted to this keep, to find comfort and some measure of hospitality . . ."

The knight's eyes flashed. "No wife! But you must have a betrothed."

"My marital circumstance has naught to do with entering this godforsaken hovel on the edge of the world."

But the knight merely smiled. "Have you a betrothed?"

"None!"

The knight's brows rose. "Indeed?" He surveyed Talbot once more—most insolently to that man's way of thinking—then met his gaze again. "But you must be a knight. You do have spurs and a blade."

Talbot heard an implication that his armament was less than adequate in the knight's words and was immediately infuriated. "Of course I am a knight! I am a *nobleman*! I am in need of hospitality and welcome, a welcome that would be offered more readily anywhere else in Christendom!" he raged. "Must we stand in the rain while you satisfy your cursed curiosity?"

"All these assets, yet no betrothed." The knight rubbed his chin consideringly, as if Talbot had said naught. He turned to the keeper. "Do you think he is foul to look upon, Godfrey? 'Tis not my matter of expertise."

"Nor mine, sir, but I daresay many a woman would take him."

"Indeed." The knight's bright glance swivelled back to the simmering Talbot. "Are you without inheritance, then?"

"Such rudeness! I fail to see what my circumstance has to do with passing beneath these gates!" Talbot ranted. He dismounted and strode through the puddles to grip the portcullis. He gave it a hearty shake but the keeper did not even show the courtesy to look alarmed. "I am Chevalier Talbot d'Annoceaux and I demand that you grant me admission . . ."

"D'Annoceaux!" The knight nodded to the keeper with approval. "A fine family, Godfrey, there can be no doubt of that." He sidled closer. "My mother has oft spoken of an old flame of hers, one Richard d'Annoceaux."

"My uncle," Talbot supplied stiffly and returned to his saddle. "He took holy orders and is currently the bishop of Sainte-Madeleine." He flung out his hands. "Does that win me favor in your eyes?"

"A *bishop*, Godfrey." The knight released a low whistle. "That is not a measure of influence many families can claim."

"Nay, indeed, sir."

The knight leaned closer, and Talbot instinctively did not trust the glimmer of humor in his silvery eyes. "And your father would be?"

"Michel d'Annoceaux, the eldest and heir of Theobald d'Annoceaux, but I fail to see the import . . ."

The knight tilted his head and spoke as if Talbot said naught. "You must then have older siblings."

Talbot inhaled with impatience. "I have an elder brother, whom my father grooms to manage Annoceaux, though even he does not show the audacity to insult my presence as you two . . ."

"Ah! So you are left without legacy. And hence without right to claim a bride." The knight sat back with satisfaction at having solved the riddle, but before Talbot could complain once more, that man turned to the gatekeeper again. "Is it not a shame, Godfrey, to see a young man so full of prospect denied the chance to take a bride?"

"Aye, sir, that it is."

Before Talbot could protest this discussion of his fortunes, the knight turned to Henri once more. "Is your master taken with a single woman?"

"Sir?"

"Does he pursue a lady who has stolen his heart?"

"Nay, sir, he prefers to spread his affections far and wide," the squire contributed with more forthrightness than Talbot believed the situation merited. "My lord is popular indeed among the wenches, though his uncle claims he will have bastards at the gates if ever he wins a piece of land."

The knight was smiling again. "And what manner of wench does he prefer?"

"Plump and willing, sir."

"Henri! Bite your tongue!"

The squire looked chastised but the knight chuckled. "We could assure half his needs were met, at least."

The keeper gasped, then guffawed. "Ah, sir, now I see the direction of your thoughts!"

Talbot had the sneaking sense that he was being mocked, or that the knight played some game at his expense, though he could not fathom what was amiss. 'Twas not an unfamiliar feeling, for he oft felt this way in his uncle's presence.

The difference was that he did not have to humor these two.

Talbot was well and done with this pair and their infernal

questions. "I am delighted to have provided your amusement on this day," he began hotly, gathering the reins into his hands. "But if we are to make Killarney . . ."

"You cannot leave!" the knight protested.

"I will not sit in the rain and be mocked!"

The knight looked contrite in turn. "Godfrey, have we mocked the man? Indeed, 'twas not my intent."

"Nay, sir, we but inquired after his credentials." The keeper braced his feet against the ground and eyed Talbot. "Though we have yet to learn of his errand here."

"I have told you that I ride to Kiltorren on a mission . . ." Talbot began tightly, but the knight interrupted him once more.

"And we should dearly love to hear the details." He smiled. "Do not leave, Talbot of Annoceaux."

At least, matters had changed course in Talbot's favor. "Surely we could adjourn to the keep proper," he suggested, taking no pains to hide his irritation, "and continue this discussion in whatever modicum of comfort could be won here."

"Indeed," the knight said with a slight inclination of his head. "I am certain that Lady Deirdre and Lord Cedric would be delighted to make the acquaintance of a knight of such fine lineage as yourself. Godfrey, if you would be so kind. I shall personally ensure that this guest makes no mischief."

"Fair enough, sir." The keeper, his grin too wide for Talbot's taste, immediately cranked open the portcullis.

Talbot's blood began to boil. This knight had but to ask and his will was done! Talbot deliberately closed his mouth and tried not to resent the differences in their circumstance.

He could loathe this country, for their failure to respect a noble knight, if naught else.

The two knights rode beneath the spiked gate, Henri trailing behind. Talbot could not help but compare his own steed once more to that of the newly arrived knight. Proximity did naught but make the contrast worse and did not reassure Talbot in the least. The black beast must be worth a small fortune.

Indeed, at such close quarters, Talbot could see that this man's blade rested in a fine scabbard far beyond his own means, that the man's boots and tabard and even his very trap was worth a king's ransom.

What manner of man might Talbot have become if he had been granted his due from the outset? What might his life have been if he had been born first, instead of his brother Theobald?

'Twas unfair, there was no doubt of the matter.

"And who are you?" Talbot demanded testily, the comparison and the weather making his tone sharper even than usual.

The knight pulled off his glove and offered his hand. "Chevalier Burke de Montvieux."

Talbot felt the blood drain from his face. By reputation, Burke de Montvieux was a champion, a knight who never lost a seige, a man who had but to desire something to make it his own. His good fortune was legendary—as was his charm, his handsomeness, and his wickedly lethal skill with a blade. Talbot knew that Burke rode with his sire, a sorry excuse of a mercenary, the father as reputed for his savagery as the son was for his grace.

But what was Burke de Montvieux doing here?

Talbot swallowed awkwardly and decided 'twould not be clever to irk such a man. He hastily shed his own glove and took Burke's hand. "I apologize for my comments," he said hastily, but Burke waved off the words.

"It is naught. Indeed, I cannot tell you, Talbot d'Annoceaux, how very delighted I am to make your acquaintance."

Talbot blinked. "Truly?"

"Truly." Burke nodded with vigor. A bevy of sodden goats trotted out of their path, bleating complaint, their bellies muddied and their tits hanging low. Talbot swallowed a grimace of distaste at finding himself in such humble surroundings.

"Are you familiar with Kiltorren at all?" Burke demanded. " 'Tis a rare prize, and I would be pleased to show you its many merits."

Talbot had no eye for agricultural matters, but this place did not seem to be prospering. There was almost no activity in the village beyond. Indeed, the place had the tired look of somewhere abandoned. And no wonder! The estate was more rock than soil. Talbot had yet to hear of crops that flourished in stone. Even the goats had a hungered look about them.

They certainly eyed him overmuch.

But his companion seemed oblivious to all of this. "After all, we have some time before the meal and the company of women beckons us into the hall." Burke turned an expectant smile upon Talbot. "Shall we?"

Talbot looked longingly toward the golden glow spilling from the distant portal, a prospect of warmth and food, women, perhaps wine, certainly greater comfort than he was currently enjoying.

God's blood, he could not believe what he endured at his uncle's command!

But, on the brighter side of matters, this knight's intervention had won Talbot the admission to Kiltorren that he craved. He had but to let the man exhaust himself, then he could seek this Isibeal.

Indeed, Burke might tell him all he needed to know.

Chapter Eleven

WHEN A WOMAN DECIDES TO IGNORE A MAN, MATters proceed much more satisfactorily when the man is present to notice her slight.

Four days without even the prospect of glimpsing Burke was weighing heavily upon Alys. She sat in her chamber, determined to enjoy it for every possible moment before Aunt snatched it away, and found herself often staring out the window.

"You are missing your knight," Edana declared with a sympathetic pat on Alys's shoulder on Thursday afternoon. "And I cannot blame you . . ."

"Burke is not my knight!"

Edana slanted a glance toward Alys, no doubt noting the heat in her words. " 'Tis not the way he tells the tale."

"Burke is mistaken."

"He does not strike me as a man who is oft mistaken. And truly, Kerwyn says he talks of naught but you . . ."

"Kerwyn?" Alys asked, grateful for a chance to change the subject. "And what do you know of what Kerwyn says?"

Edana flushed and spun to face Alys. "Is he not the most wondrously mysterious man that ever you have seen?" she enthused. "Those dark eyes seem to hold a thousand mysteries, and truly, he himself declares that he can tell a horse's secret name with but a glance." She inhaled deeply and danced around the chamber. "I should swoon from a single kiss, I know it well."

Alys smiled despite herself. "Kisses? But a week ago you did not even know the man was alive!"

"Aye, but that was *before*. Did you know that Kerwyn has been here at Kiltorren over two years? I saw him before, you may be certain of that, but was certain such a handsome man must be wed." Edana smiled, her dimples making an appearance. "I have your knight to thank for the clarification."

Alys rolled her eyes. "He is not my knight!"

"Nay?" Edana challenged. "Then why have you sadly dragged yourself about the keep since his departure?"

"He says himself that he seeks Malvina's hand."

"That is not what Brigid told me."

Alys opened her mouth and closed it again. She frowned at the shuttered window. " 'Tis the rain," she said without enough conviction to convince the younger girl.

"Ha! It has never troubled you before."

" 'Tis the lack of labor. I do not know what to do with myself."

"Nonsense! I should welcome a relief from labor." Edana leaned closer. "Do you know that sorry excuse of a girl they summoned from the village has no skill with my ladies at all? They will not permit her to milk them—she was kicked this morning and bawled like a child. If you hunger for labor, Alys, you are welcome to some of mine." Edana surveyed Alys with a frown. "Tell me truly what ails you."

Alys pleated the wool of the gold kirtle between her fingers as she tried to find another excuse, then realized it was beneath her very hand. " 'Tis the kirtle," she declared. "I tire of Malvina's leavings."

Edana pursed her lips. She squinted at Alys's garb, then tilted her head in consideration.

"We could at least improve it," she suggested. "Aye, it could be taken in to fit you better." She bent and turned over the hem. "And there is enough cloth to let the hem down. Indeed, Alys, it might look as if the gown was your own. You are better with such needle tricks than I, but I would help."

"What a wondrous idea!" Alys fetched her needle and thread, delighted at both the prospect of change and something to do.

Working together, the pair made the adjustments more quickly than Alys might have believed possible. Edana retrieved half a dozen short lengths of embroidery she had culled from Deirdre's castoffs, and they managed to piece it all together to add the last increment necessary to the hem. In candlelight, the patching would not be visible.

"We shall make you a lady fair yet!" the maid jested, and Alys laughed. Edana hummed as she braided Alys's hair with care.

No sooner was Alys dressed than Brigid appeared in the portal. She gasped with delight then fled for her own chamber. She returned to shyly offer a gossamer veil wrought of deep gold and a slim silver circlet.

"But, Brigid, this is yours."

"You wear it," Brigid said with a smile. She touched the veil and the kirtle with quick fingers. "Matches." Then she touched her own, the deep blue of her kirtle accented by the pale blue of her own veiling. "I have mine."

Alys thanked her cousin profusely, feeling like royalty as she donned the fine veil and fitted the circlet over the top. She had never worn such finery, and it made her feel both feminine and pampered. Alys did not care that Brigid's hems and cuffs were lavish with embroidery wrought to the proper length, or that her cousin's circlet was set with gems while hers was plain. Malvina's garb, indeed, was yet more ornamented than Brigid's.

'Twas enough for Alys to have her ankles hidden from the breezes, enough to wear a veil like any lady of any hall.

"If only your knight could see you thus," Edana breathed. "He would sweep you up on his great steed and ride away into the night with you."

Brigid smiled sadly. "But then Alys would be gone," she whispered, her smile fading. Her lips trembled, her words faltered anew. "And no one would remain to 1-1-love me."

Both Alys and Edana stared at Brigid, stunned by her conclusion. A lone tear slipped down the younger girl's cheek, and Alys stepped quickly across the room.

"Nay, Brigid, nay!" She pulled her cousin into a tight embrace. The way Brigid clung to her made Alys's own tears rise at her cousin's vulnerability. "I am not going anywhere," she whispered against Brigid's veil. "I would not leave you."

"But Burke loves you. I-I-I will never have a knight to love me."

"Of course you will."

"Nay, Alys." Brigid shook her head and her tears scattered across both women. "I am not c-c-clever enough to have a man. M-M-Malvina and Mother told me."

"That is not true, Brigid." Alys took a deep breath and loathed her aunt for so injuring this maiden. "You will be wed happily one day, I am certain. Did Burke not say that a man would love you?"

Brigid blinked and seemed encouraged. She looked at Alys again, wiping at her tears with her fingertips. "And you will not leave me alone?"

"Nay." Alys smiled for Brigid. "Never."

When Brigid flung herself into Alys's arms with relief, Alys closed her eyes and leaned against her trembling cousin.

By all that was holy, she hoped that Burke had not given Brigid false hope.

Alys was startled to find the knight who loomed large in her thoughts loitering in the hall. She froze on the bottom step, certain how he would interpret the improvement in her appearance. It took no wits at all to see that Burke would believe Alys had adorned herself for him. He would be encouraged, he would woo her with his charm once more.

Alys was not convinced that she could withstand the man's allure.

For she had missed him. She watched him covertly for a moment, letting her heart hammer at the sight of him, knowing he would turn an intoxicating smile upon her at any moment. Alys secretly admitted that she was not only glad to look her best for his return but that she had no desire to avoid him this night.

Burke glanced up in the heart of that realization and smiled at her with his usual sunny confidence. Alys's heart leapt in a way that was quickly becoming familiar. Burke's gaze danced over her, warm with appreciation, and his smile broadened. Alys found herself unable to take a breath when he left his companion to stride toward her.

Indeed, her pulse positively thundered.

"You look wondrous!" Before Alys could think of a response, Burke caught her hand, leaving a burning imprint of his lips upon her knuckles. He lifted her hand high and turned her, and Alys did not doubt 'twas by design she ended up standing dangerously close to him when he was done.

"Magnificent," he whispered, his eyes glowing.

"Burke! You should not utter such nonsense." Though Alys intended to chide him, her words fell more breathlessly than she might have preferred.

Burke smiled into her eyes. "The truth is never nonsense," he murmured, then his smile faded. "Do you still doubt my word, Alys?"

Alys dropped her gaze, surprised when Burke chuckled softly.

"Then might I ask your aid this evening?" he asked. Alys peeked to find an intriguingly wicked gleam in Burke's eyes. "Events might well persuade you of my true intent."

Alys withdrew her fingers, immediately suspicious. "What do you scheme?"

Burke caught at his heart as if struck by a blow to the heart. "My lady, you wound me!"

Alys laughed, for she could have done naught else. "You would make all dance to your tune this night."

"Only for the greater good."

"So you say."

"Alys, listen to me well." Burke leaned closer and Alys could not step away from the gleam in his eyes. "I had to feign pursuit of Malvina to ensure that your guardians did not dispatch me from the gates before I could win your favor. But on this night I bring the man who will take that honor in my stead." Burke indicated the man he had abandoned. "Here is the man for Malvina."

Alys choked back her laughter at this unexpected claim. "You cannot have found a husband for her!"

"Indeed I have." Burke's eyes twinkled. "Though the man does not know his fate as yet."

"Burke, you cannot be so mean!"

"They deserve each other," he said grimly.

Alys had to look. She peered discreetly past Burke's shoulder and studied the dark-blond stranger. He was shorter than Burke, younger, though garbed as a knight. He might have been considered handsome if his lips had not been so tight with impatience.

Indeed, he snarled at his squire as she watched, and Alys had to concede that he shared some trait with her cousin.

"Alys!" Burke chided, his voice low with humor. "Such uncharitable thoughts!"

"I said naught!"

"You did not have to. Your eyes, my lady, tell a thousand tales. I doubt you could tell a lie to save your life. 'Tis another thing I love about you." While Alys tried to accept that, Burke leaned closer, the warm fan of his breath making her shiver. "Indeed, I share your thinking on this. They two seem to have much in common."

Alys looked again, liking despite herself that Burke considered her part of his conspiracy. She enjoyed the intimacy of discussing this with him, of having his confidence, no less the sense that they worked together to an end.

The new arrival had the manner of a petulant, indulged child. His garb was fine, his toe tapped impatiently, his gaze roved the hall. He noticed Alys and surveyed her from head to toe as if she were no better than a whore.

Alys stepped back. Burke pivoted and glared so pointedly at the other knight that the man flushed. Alys felt a thrill at Burke's protectiveness, even as she eased closer to him.

The arrival studied his toe once more.

"A man of ambition with naught to his name," Burke said with a growl, his fine mood dismissed. Alys did not miss the proprietary way he grasped her elbow, nor did she argue over his touch. There was something about this new arrival she did not like or trust. "He will suit perfectly."

"But, Burke, Aunt believes Malvina should wed *you*, and you yourself have pledged to be courting her." Alys felt compelled to make note of the facts. "Neither will be readily persuaded to let you escape."

"Nay?" Burke arched one brow, his manner playful again. "Would you care to make a wager upon that, my lady fair?"

He looked so certain of himself that Alys longed to prove

him wrong. Even so, she could not stop her smile. "I am ignoring you this week," she informed him.

Burke grinned. "Aye, I can tell."

"You would have noted it, if you had not been away."

"Ah, so you did miss me!"

Alys felt herself flush. She might have stalked away from
his cursed confidence and charm, but Burke's smile faded. "I
missed you, my lady fair," he murmured, sincerity shining in
his eyes. "Will you grant me a kiss for my return?"

Alys looked away, knowing she flushed furiously at the very
prospect. She was not faring well in her decision to avoid this
man, nor in her determination to be indifferent to his compliments. Truth be told, in this moment she did not care.

Indeed, she wanted that kiss with a ferocity that shook her
to the core.

"What is this wager of yours?"

Burke's thumb began to slide across her hand in a slow caress, as if he would ease her into agreement before he even
spoke. "That if Deirdre accepts this man for Malvina, you
will meet me in private again."

"I think the prospect most unlikely."

"She will. Of this I have no doubt."

Alys shook her head. "Nay, she would never cast your suit
aside. Burke, you underestimate her will in this."

Burke grinned wolfishly, his voice dropped low. "Then
you, my lady fair, have naught to lose in taking my wager."

There was a challenge in his tone that made Alys wary.
The folded her arms across her chest, wondering what Burke
knew that she did not. "And naught to win," she challenged.
"What shall you grant me if *I* win this wager?"

Burke chuckled. "Your heart's desire," he whispered
wickedly. "Indeed, it might be the same as my own."

'Twas with difficulty that Alys stifled the urge to swat him, but Burke stepped quickly away is af he were not certain of what she would do.

There was some satisfaction to be had in that, at least.

"Well?" Burke demanded. "Have we a wager? Decide quickly, Alys!"

"Aye!" she declared with rare impulsiveness.

Burke's grin flashed. "I assure you, my lady, that you will not regret your course," he murmured, then stepped away.

'Twas as if he fled something—or someone.

In the next moment, Alys knew who.

For Aunt's voice rose behind Alys. "Well! Who is *this*?" The older woman shoved Alys aside without waiting for an answer and strode across the floor, her best smile at the ready.

"Burke!" Aunt cried in honeyed tones. "What a delight to find you returned! And you do us even greater honor in bringing your friends to Kiltorren." She studied the newly arrived knight openly from head to foot.

Evidently Aunt approved, for her smile broadened.

Burke winked at Alys before he bowed, but Alys did not grant him any victory for his quick progress. She knew her aunt could not be swayed from any objective. And Burke and Malvina were as good as wed to her aunt's way of thinking.

Indeed, Burke had played no small role in that conclusion.

"Ah, Lady Deirdre, this knight is but an acquaintance met upon the road. When I learned he was without even a betrothed—such a fine knight as this!—I knew he had to come to Kiltorren."

Aunt's gaze sharpened, even as Burke touched his own brow. "But where are my manners?" he asked of no one in particular. Alys bit back her smile at his antics. "Lady Deirdre of Kiltorren, might I do the honor of introducing you to Chevalier Talbot d'Annoceaux?"

"Chevalier!" Aunt echoed with delight.

"Enchanté," Talbot murmured, and bent over her hand. "You are most kind to lavish your hospitality upon me."

Aunt caught her breath, then pivoted to shout. "BRIGID! Get yourself to my side!"

Alys heard her cousin stumbling down the stairs, that girl's eyes widening when she came to a halt at their foot.

Edana nudged Brigid impatiently from behind. "Go on!"

Brigid took a deep breath and stepped into the hall, then hesitated. Alys wondered whether her cousin felt the same disquietude about this arrival as she.

Cedric trotted down to the hall, bellowed a greeting to Burke, and beamed as he strode across the floor. The Lord of Kiltorren earned himself a sharp glare from his wife when he reached her side. Alys knew 'twas a commentary on the knights' fine manners—as compared to Cedric's own—but her uncle blinked in characteristic confusion at what he had done.

"Brigid!" Deirdre snapped. "Get yourself here!"

Malvina burst into the hall. "Mother! Why must you always make such a hue and cry? We are not deaf, as you surely must know . . ." Malvina shoved past Brigid and Alys, her words faltering to naught as she saw this Talbot standing by her mother's side.

"Oh! Who is that?" she whispered in evident awe.

Alys nearly laughed aloud to see Burke's plan showing such promise already. "A knight Burke brought to the keep," she supplied. "He is Talbot d'Annoceaux."

"Indeed!" Malvina breathed. "A French knight! He is . . . *handsome* beyond all."

Alys's glance slid to Burke, and she noted how his lips quirked. 'Twas as if he were fully aware not only that he had made one convert to his cause but that he had never doubted the result.

But Talbot, Alys noted with dismay, was staring at *her*, not

Malvina. Alys felt her flesh creep, for she had no doubt this knight had not an honorable thought in his head.

Then Malvina tossed her veil over her shoulders. "If I were not already being so ardently courted, I might grant this one the favor of my attentions." She scampered to Burke's side then, laying a proprietary hand upon his arm. "Did you bring me a gift?"

Burke's grin flashed. "In a way," he conceded, and Alys bit back her laughter. Oh, he was incorrigible indeed! "Perhaps you would like to be introduced to Kiltorren's new guest."

Aunt smiled for Burke alone and laid a hand upon his free arm. " 'Twould be so inappropriate, Burke, for your betrothed to be the first to greet a knight new to our household."

Burke's brows lifted in feigned astonishment. "My betrothed? Truly, Lady Deirdre, you proceed ahead of matters. I have but confessed an interest in Malvina—we have not yet pledged any troth."

"You would consider wedding *this* woman?" Talbot demanded, then he chuckled. He cast a glance over the hall. "Indeed, I did not know that Burke de Montvieux had been struck blind."

His rudeness hung in silence for a long moment. Aunt glared at the knight, Cedric cleared his throat in obvious dismay. Burke turned a cold glance on the man.

And Talbot paled.

"Beauty is as beauty does, *chevalier*," Burke said in a chilly tone, "and there is no excuse for a failure to be courteous."

"Of course!" The other knight inclined his head in acknowledgement, but hostility lingered in his eyes. "My apologies to all."

Aunt eyed this man assessingly though Alys knew the very moment that her aunt dismissed him from her thoughts.

For Aunt turned a smile upon Burke, her fingers tapping companionably on the arm Malvina had not claimed. "Burke, you cannot blame me for saving the greater plum for my first-born. And you, sir, are a rare prize for any maiden."

Aunt's manner was flirtatious. Cedric flushed to the roots of his hair, but he did not intervene. "We have all been most dismayed by your absence this week," Aunt purred. "There is no need for you to be coy about your intentions."

Talbot looked bored. "Is there any wine in this hall?"

"Ale, sir, we have good Kiltorren ale," Cedric supplied, as if relieved to have another matter to discuss. "We have a talented alemaster . . ."

"Ale?" The knight grimaced. "How perfectly common. I believe my father's serfs content themselves with ale."

Cedric frowned.

Burke, seemingly oblivious to this exchange, shook a playful finger at Aunt. "With regret, Lady Deirdre, I must confide that you have sorely overestimated my worth."

Aunt blinked, as did everyone else in the hall.

"Aye, Montvieux is worth several king's ransoms," Talbot commented with more than a thread of envy in his tone. "One might easily mistake the precise value of its wealth."

These bitter words seemed to aid Aunt's recovery, and she smiled at Burke once again. "You are too modest, sir! After all, you are heir to *Montvieux*. 'Tis a fine and prosperous estate, as your friend observes, and one that my Malvina will manage with ease."

Burke shook his head and Alys had the distinct sense that he was enjoying himself. "Ah! Now, I understand the root of your confusion. 'Tis true that I *was* indeed the heir of Montvieux."

"Was?" Aunt echoed.

"Was?" Malvina and Talbot echoed simultaneously.

Was? Alys frowned at this unexpected morsel of news.

Burke's smile broadened. "My father and I argued six months past. He has disinherited me as a result." He frowned slightly, though his eyes twinkled merrily. "Did I neglect to mention that? Surely you have heard of the tale, even here at Kiltorren?"

Aunt's face went white then it flooded red. She pivoted, glared at Cedric as if the fault was his.

Burke had not confided this critical detail! No wonder he had been so certain he would win their wager.

And he wondered why she could not trust him fully! Alys would not concede victory readily to Burke, there was no doubt of that. She folded her arms across her chest and watched matters unfold precisely as Burke had insisted they would.

Of course. She would have guessed as much as well, had she known the truth. If indeed it *was* the truth. Had he truly lost Montvieux, or did he simply use this tale to see his will done?

Alys could not even guess and did not like that in the least.

Aunt's voice was tight and her smile yet tighter. "Surely a man of your success must have other holdings . . ."

But Burke shrugged. "Not a one. Indeed, I have naught but my steed and my blade," he confessed. His lips quirked wryly. "What is upon my back and between my ears."

"But you call yourself 'de Montvieux' still."

"I was born and raised at Montvieux and am of that estate, regardless of my status as its pending lord," Burke said coldly. "Surely you cannot imagine that after parting ways so decisively with my sire, I would take the appellation Fitzgavin?"

Aunt straightened. "Surely you and your father will reconcile?"

At that suggestion, Burke's countenance hardened as if 'twas wrought of stone. "Never." His single word was uttered with such conviction that Alys knew this was the truth. "We shall *never* reconcile."

Talbot stared at Burke, clearly aghast. "You willingly ceded Montvieux?"

Burke did not smile. "Aye."

Malvina stepped away from Burke as if the touch of him had suddenly become vile and smiled at Talbot. Aunt looked from one knight to the other, then conjured a smile of unbelievable sweetness for Talbot herself. "Malvina," she said with a snap of her fingers, and that daughter was right beside her.

Talbot became alarmed. "A moment, madame! I am not seeking a bride . . ."

"Nonsense!" Burke interjected heartily, his good humor apparently restored. "A man of such fine family as yours, Talbot, would do the world injustice by not taking a bride and bringing heirs into the world."

The knight stepped backward, though he did not manage to summon a protest in time.

Burke had already turned to Aunt, his words falling fast, his tone confidential. "Do you realize, my lady hostess, that the lineage of Theobald d'Annoceaux, that legendary warrior and confidant of kings, courses through this man's veins? What good fortune to find him on our doorstep! What an honor to have such a man as your guest!"

"But I have come on another quest altogether," Talbot argued.

Aunt, however, needed no further encouragement to corner her wary prey. "Sir," she said sweetly, "my eldest daughter, Malvina."

Malvina flushed and curtsied low, even though her unwilling suitor's chagrin was more than clear.

"But . . ."

"But naught, good sir. You may tell us of your desires after we have shown you our hospitality. Malvina would be delighted to share a trencher with you this night." Aunt flicked her hands toward the table as if she would urge matters onward.

"I could not presume as much . . ." Talbot looked like a man prepared to chew off his own arm to escape a trap.

" 'Twould be an honor," Malvina declared breathlessly.

"Of course, anything for a guest," Aunt confirmed. "Cronan! See what delays the meal." She tapped impatiently upon Cedric's shoulder, her voice dropping to a hiss. "And find some excuse for wine in this place. Our guest prefers *wine*."

Talbot's gaze flicked between mother and daughter in panic. He looked to Cedric, who strode to the kitchen without a backward glance. In desperation, Talbot turned to Burke, but to no avail.

"If you will excuse me, I should like a word with Alys," Burke said smoothly.

Aunt waved her hand dismissively. "Do whatsoever you will. We have matters of import to discuss." And 'twas clear from her manner that Burke's marital fortunes were no longer of interest.

Burke winked at Alys and spread his hands, clearly proud of what he had wrought. A glint in his eye warned her that he meant to collect upon his wager, and her heart skipped a beat in anticipation.

Aye, Alys would keep her bargain and grant Burke the hearing he requested—but she would have the truth from this knight.

'Twas time enough he shared the whole of the tale of Montvieux—whatever it was.

Chapter Twelve

THE STOREROOM HAD SEEMED LIKE A GOOD IDEA AT the time.

After all, it was the best place to hide away from her family and their newly ensnared guest and still be close to Cook and his helpers. There were sacks of grain stacked around the perimeter, the air was tinged with the scents of peppercorns and cloves locked in the spice box. Overhead there were bundles of herbs dried from last summer—meadowsweet and tansy, dill and chervil—each and every one lending their perfume to the crowded room.

For that was the problem—'twas crowded. 'Twas impossible to share the space with a man of Burke's height and breadth without touching him in some way.

But there was naught for it. Burke was settling onto a sack of grain and Alys would not protest the intimacy of the place she had chosen. She sat as far from him as she could and spread the napkin deliberately between them. Within it was half a loaf of bread and some cheese.

Burke had a great mug of ale, though Cook had been willing to surrender only one vessel to them. Alys had no doubt the older man was matchmaking, for 'twas clear he favored Burke.

Burke offered her the first sip with a grim gallantry. 'Twould be the next one that would unsettle Alys, the next one that would either give her the taste of Burke mingled with the ale, or prompt his comment when she avoided the place where his lips had rested.

"Will you tell me of Montvieux?"

Burke turned, challenge bright in his eyes. "Will you believe me if I do?"

Alys managed to find a smile. "I shall try."

"*Try.*" Burke's lips tightened and he stared across the room once more. The silence stretched long between them. Alys almost thought he would not speak, but then his voice echoed with low heat in the little room.

"Alys, you think that I do not understand you, you think that we have naught in common, but that is not true. I see in you a shadow of myself, for you are as surely beneath your aunt's thumb as I was once trapped beneath my father's. It took me long to decide to cast off his demands and it cost me dear, but I cannot look at you without considering how welcome the change felt once 'twas done."

Alys did not know what to say, but Burke continued on, apparently not expecting a response.

"I have spent my life, Alys, endeavoring to please my parents." He studied the contents of the ale mug. "They are people of worldly ambition, their desires tangible and readily identified. They wished me to show skill with a horse. They wished me to become a knight. They wished me to wage war alongside my father. They wished me to win at tourneys. I managed it all, until my father decided whom I should wed."

He sipped of the ale once more, then offered the mug to Alys. She shook her head and he continued to cradle the pottery in his hands. There was an undercurrent to his words that Alys could not name, but his manner was compelling. Indeed, there was no pretense in his manner—he spoke bluntly, leaving Alys no doubt this was the truth.

" 'Twas last year," Burke continued. "My father chose to

join Strongbow's invasion and make a claim within Ireland for no better reason than his own greed. He chose his prey by its wealth and weakness, naught else. Tullymullagh was a fine prize and another piece of property to make his own. I was there for the siege, though I am not proud of what was done there."

Burke clearly felt deeply about this matter—indeed, Alys could fairly smell his irritation.

"Why not?" she asked.

"The inhabitants had done naught to provoke a war. They simply had the misfortune to live in a keep my father desired to make his own. He was more brutal than necessary, as is his wont, and my squire—a boy of eight who had just come to serve me—died."

Burke flicked a heated glance to Alys. "I did not know him overwell, I do not pretend that we were close. But 'twas a waste of a life. I daresay his mother was surprised by the vehemence of my missive informing her of his loss."

"There is a saying of the last straw breaking the steed's back," Alys suggested softly.

Burke shrugged and turned back to the mug. "Aye. I had borne enough of my father's ways. Perhaps I had been obedient too long. At any rate, the loss of the squire and the claiming of Tullymullagh left a sour taste on my tongue."

Burke pursed his lips and sipped while Alys waited. "So you might imagine my dismay when the king came to consolidate my father's claim and my father revealed that he intended Tullymullagh to be mine. Mine! This place of misfortune and greed, of early death and unnecessary cruelty. A gift 'twas, in my father's mind, and all I had to do was wed its princess."

"Brianna of Tullymullagh," Alys whispered, remembering Burke's comment that she had sent him here.

"Aye, Princess Brianna, the Rose of Tullymullagh. All

raised a cup to my good fortune." Burke grimaced. "But I was not prepared to do this thing. I did not know the woman, I did not want her family's holding. I could not conceive of a way to avoid this duty without confronting my father's wrath. Fortunately, the lady was no more enamored of having her spouse chosen for her, and demanded the right to select from all three Fitzgavin sons."

Burke frowned. "My eldest brother, Luc, has never taken any pains to evade our father's wrath. He simply did not care and I had to consider this. While it never occurred to me to defy our father, it apparently never occurred to Luc to obey him. And Luc seemed to have survived well on his own."

Burke looked down into the mug and swirled its contents. When he continued, his voice had softened, a tinge of marvel lingering in his tones. "When Luc arrived at Tullymullagh and first saw Brianna, there was a look in his eyes of such wonder that I was reminded of the day I first glimpsed you."

Alys caught her breath and Burke shot her a crooked smile.

"Aye, Alys, but one glimpse was all it took. I stood in Tullymullagh's hall and I watched my brother. I thought of you and the way you smile, I heard again the ripple of your laughter and I knew the true reason why I could not wed this woman."

Alys's heart was in her mouth. She feared suddenly that Burke would glance at her, that he would see her longing in her eyes as he often did read her thoughts.

But Burke did not. He deliberately set the mug on the floor of the room and leaned back, his eyes narrowing as he stared at the opposite wall. "Then Brianna dispatched the three brothers Fitzgavin upon a quest for her hand."

"What was the quest?"

"She would wed the one who brought the gift to make her laugh loudest and longest."

" 'Tis a curious way to choose a spouse."

Burke snorted. "So said Luc. He refused to go and won the lady's heart as well as her hand. He also won my father's wrath but lived to tell the tale." His expression turned indulgent. "Luc and Brianna are very happy together. She is with child."

"What did you bring her?"

Burke shrugged. "It does not matter. My heart was not in the mission and the lady guessed as much. As did my father, and he had much to say of the matter." His lips tightened and he frowned anew. "He insisted I fetch another gift with haste, he insisted I win Brianna's hand, but I refused."

"You declined your sire's bidding?"

"Aye, and he is not a man who takes well to defiance. He threatened me, and for the first time in all my days, encouraged by Luc's example, I held my ground. Gavin bellowed and I yelled back. Then I left him standing there, stunned at the change in his obedient son."

Burke glanced up at Alys, a bright gleam lurking in his eyes that stole her breath away. "I tell you, Alys, 'twas the most satisfying moment of all my days."

Alys was amazed at his confession. "But your father disinherited you as a result?"

"Aye." Burke held her gaze, his expression deadly serious. "Because I would have no woman by my side other than you."

Alys felt her lips part.

"You may believe it, Alys, or not, as you choose. 'Twill change naught." Burke took a deep draught of ale and seemed disinclined to continue.

Alys could not imagine that anyone would abandon anything for her sake, much less that this man would set aside all he might call his own. Montvieux was a prize, Alys knew it well.

"But what will you do?"

Burke's lips tightened to a line that was yet more fierce. "I had thought to wed, but you show an unholy resistance to the thought."

Alys's heart stopped.

Then it raced anew. Her fingers clenched each other at the conviction in Burke's tone. "I meant, how will you live?"

Burke seemed untroubled by the uncertainty of his prospects. "I shall return to the tourneys. A few good years and I shall have enough to call my own. You need not worry for me."

"But men are injured in the tourneys. You could be hurt!"

Burke almost smiled. "I have been hurt before, Alys. A man must be prepared to make a sacrifice for what he desires." He set the mug aside. "He must even be prepared to face his greatest fear."

The silence hung between them and Alys wondered what fear a knight like Burke might have. He had spurned a legacy with bold confidence, he faced Aunt with determination, he had battled countless foes effortlessly.

"What could you fear?"

Burke bowed his head. "That I shall lose the only battle that ever was of import to me." He turned then, and Alys was startled by the bright glitter in his gaze. "That *you* should refuse me."

Alys could not fathom that she held the power to make this man feel vulnerable, but his vulnerability caught at her heart as naught else had done.

Still, she had to voice her own doubts.

Honesty seemed to be in the wind this night.

"Burke, I am afraid that you only desire me, that there is no more than that between us. I am afraid that desire will have its due and fade away."

Sympathy filtered into Burke's expression but he did not move away. "Ah, Alys, if only I could face your fears for you and show you that they are as naught. You would see, Alys, that what you fear is as substantial as the morning mist."

He made to withdraw, but Alys impulsively put her hand on his shoulder. She might be uncertain of what lay ahead, but in this moment, she did not want her knight to leave her alone.

Not yet.

For that, she was willing to take a small chance.

Burke stared down at her fingers splayed across his chemise. He did not move, as if Alys were a small creature who might be readily frightened and flee.

"Again you touch me of your own choice," he murmured, his gaze intense as it rose to meet her own.

"I seldom am granted a chance."

Burke smiled, lines wrought of laughter creasing his tan around his eyes. "I confess, Alys, that I am not inclined to leave the prospect of your company to fortune." He stroked his thumb across the back of her hand. "I shall try to change in this."

"You will not vow it?" Alys could not help but tease.

Burke grinned outright. "I do not know if I can do it," he confessed. "And I would have you know that when I pledge a thing to you, 'twill be thus."

He sobered, tracing circles on the back of her hand with one warm fingertip. "You must understand, Alys. 'Tis my vocation to pursue any goal with diligence, and with greater diligence still when 'tis of greater import. To stand aside and wait is not a course I know well." He looked up and his voice softened. "I ask only that you do not judge me too harshly if I fail."

Alys could not look away from Burke, she could not take a breath, she could not shake herself loose of the desire that raged within her. She was amazed that this assured man would try to change to ease her fears. Alys could not stop her fingers from curling around Burke's hand. He interlaced their fingers with a slow deliberation that melted her bones.

Alys's gaze fell to the firm line of his lips. Her tongue ran over her lips of its own accord. She watched Burke catch his breath as he watched her. His eyes shimmered like pale sapphires, but he did not move closer.

He was waiting, though it must nigh be killing him, and she loved him for it.

Indeed, Alys knew with sudden clarity exactly what she could do, what she *must* do. There would be naught left unsaid between them. She would face her fear and solicit one kiss from this knight, in this moment when he believed the sun rose and set in her.

Alys moved the napkin out of the way without unlocking their fingers, she slid along the sack of grain. She heard Burke inhale when she raised their interlocked hands to her lips. She kissed his knuckles, as he so often had kissed her own, enjoying the different texture of his skin against her lips and feeling very bold.

"This is for returning to tell me the truth of your first departure," she whispered, her voice uncharacteristically uneven. "Indeed, for insisting I understood the fact of it."

Burke did not move, though a flame lit in his eyes. She lifted one hand to Burke's jaw, her fingers easing over the stubble gracing his chin, her heart pounding. She let one fingertip slide over his lips, and Burke sat as still as a statue.

Alys stretched, her mouth gone dry at her own audacity, and brushed her lips across the warmth of his. "This is for granting me your own bed and treating me with honor."

Burke closed his eyes and exhaled shakily.

To her surprise, Alys found his response to her touch reassuring beyond all. 'Twas good to know that she was not the only one quivering inside.

Alys kissed one corner of Burke's mouth with slow deliberation.

"This is for your gentle manner with Brigid's heart," she

breathed against his flesh. He did not move, though the tension emanated from him in waves.

Alys boldly let her lips graze Burke's as she moved to kiss the other corner of his mouth. "This is for ensuring I had better garb and less labor."

Burke's grip tightened on Alys's hand when she paused before him, their noses a thumb's breadth apart. Still he waited for whatever she chose to do.

Alys smiled and framed his face with her hands. She was shaking yet felt oddly exhilarated. "And this, sir," she whispered, her gaze dancing over his intent features, "is for finding a candidate to become Malvina's spouse in your stead. I would not leave such a bold deed unrewarded."

Alys took a deep breath, then leaned against Burke's chest and kissed him full on the lips.

Sadly, her aim was less than ideal, her technique so poor that she bit her own lip. Alys pulled back in a fluster and felt herself flush scarlet at her own inability to make a memorable moment of something so simple as a kiss. She could not look at the laughter that she knew must light Burke's eyes.

"I am sorry," she whispered disappointedly, her cheeks burning. "You must think me a witless fool . . ."

Burke touched her chin with a gentle finger, forcing her to meet his gaze.

"Practice, Alys, practice is key," he whispered, his eyes gleaming. "Little of merit is won on the first try." That slow smile eased over his lips and Alys's heart began to pound. Indeed, he still looked at her with wonder, as if she alone had hung the stars in the firmament.

"I had to return twice to Kiltorren to seek you, after all," he declared, his lips quirking. " 'Tis my chivalrous duty to leave my services—and my lips—at your disposal."

Alys laughed and almost declined, but the warmth in

Burke's gaze prompted her to try again. She was quite certain she had never blushed so furiously.

But Burke waited.

And his eyes glowed with an affection that made it impossible for Alys to think of doing anything other than kissing him again. She took a deep breath, she leaned closer, then hesitated in her uncertainty.

"Ease into it," Burke advised with a quick lift of one brow. "There is no need for haste." His eyes widened suddenly. "Unless you have another engagement this evening?"

Alys smiled at the way he endeavored to reassure her. "Nay."

"Nor I," he admitted, then winked. "Consider me at your mercy."

Alys could not halt her smile. "You are a rogue, sir!"

"You sound less convinced of it than you were before." The smile faded from Burke's lips. His gaze clung to hers as if he hoped for confirmation.

There was that irresistible vulnerability once more.

"'Tis true enough," Alys acknowledged. She watched Burke's eyes flash, then let her fingers slide down his jaw and over his throat. She nestled closer, then cupped his face into her hands. Alys tried to ease into the matter, as he had bidden her, her lips touching Burke's as tentatively as a butterfly landing on a flower.

'Twas excruciating to let the lady have her way with him.

But on the other hand, 'twas a marvel to have Alys touch him willingly. Indeed, Burke was stunned by the fact that he had won more this night by doing naught than he had gained with his concerted pursuit of the lady.

There was a lesson here and he did not miss its import. For his Alys came to him. She touched him. She kissed him of her own choice.

'Twas an intoxicating development.

Burke closed his eyes when Alys's lips brushed against his own; the warm scent of her made his blood roar. Her innocence was beguiling, her cautious trust humbling. She dared to face a fear, at his urging, and Burke wanted her only to win success. He certainly did not want to frighten her.

Even if he did desire her more than he had ever imagined a man might desire a woman and survive to tell the tale.

Alys's fingertips flattened against his jaw, she sidled closer, her breasts brushed against his chest. Burke's chausses tightened; he dared to let his hands fall to the back of her waist. She was so slender, so supple and strong. Burke closed his hands around her and she did not resist.

Indeed, Alys nibbled on his mouth, the tentativeness of her touch nearly driving Burke mad. She nestled yet closer, her lips moving slowly against his own. Alys's hands slid into his hair and launched an army of shivers over Burke's flesh.

Her lips lingered against his, as if she knew not how to proceed, and Burke permitted himself to make a suggestion. He tilted his head, letting his mouth slant across hers, and nearly moaned aloud when Alys promptly followed suit. Burke opened his mouth, let his tongue touch her lips.

Alys echoed his gesture, the slick heat of her tongue darting between his teeth, and Burke thought he would explode. He inhaled, struggled to contain his desire, and gripped her waist more resolutely. Alys arched, fitting against Burke as if she were wrought for him.

She kissed him more deeply and he responded in kind. She was in his lap before he knew how the deed was managed, her hands gripped the back of his neck, her buttocks wriggled restlessly against his thighs. Burke rolled her to her back atop the sacks of grain before he could think to halt the impulse and Alys kissed him with fervor, her legs tangling with his.

Burke silently vowed to let the lady have her way with him

more often. Aye, he could well discard compliments for all time if their absence won such a prize as this kiss.

Then Alys's tongue cavorted with his and Burke could think no longer. He felt her nipples tighten against his chest and could not resist temptation. His hand rose to cup the ripe curve of her breast. He deepened his kiss when she arched and trembled. Burke's thumb slid across her turgid nipple and Alys moaned into his mouth.

The minute sound recalled Burke to his senses.

He could not prove himself of the same ilk as her father.

Burke disengaged himself with clumsy haste and set Alys deliberately aside. He shoved to his feet and put the width of the room between them, closed his eyes and took a trio of deep breaths.

It did not check his desire markedly. He could still hear her accelerated breathing, he could smell her skin. He licked his lips and tasted her sweet kiss.

Burke did not dare to look at Alys for fear he would not be able to resist her. His own quickened breathing mingled in his ears with the thunder of his pulse.

Ye gods, had he ever felt such raging desire?

When Burke finally composed himself sufficiently to risk a downward glance, the leap of his heart was no reassurance. Alys's lips were swollen and reddened, her nipples strained against the heavy wool of her kirtle. Her cheeks were flushed and more than one wavy golden tendril had worked itself free of her braid to curl softly against her cheek. Her bare feet were tucked beneath her, her kirtle caught around her knees, the very sight kicking Burke's desire to the very moon.

He had only a glimpse of the myriad questions in Alys's golden eyes before she dropped her gaze, the thickness of her lashes brushing her cheeks.

"I apologize for my lack of skill, that I am not practiced

enough to please," she said huskily, and Burke nearly laughed aloud. She had almost destroyed his considerable resolve and she apologized for *inadequacy*?

But then he realized his lady's embarrassment. Burke dropped to one knee to reassure her, but still left a pace between them for he did not trust himself to be closer. Everything within him clamored to finish what she had begun, but Burke did not dare.

He would not sacrifice what fragile trust he had won.

Alys knotted her hands together in her lap, her fair brows drawing together in a frown. She studiously avoided Burke's gaze.

"Alys, look at me," he urged softly.

"I do not know much of such matters. You must think me a fool . . ."

"Alys, your touch inflames me as naught else could do."

"But you pulled away. I must have done something amiss."

"Nay, you did all aright!" Burke let himself smile slowly. "But you have a way of making me forget myself."

Alys flushed anew, though her eyes sparkled and the hint of a smile curved her lips. " 'Twas just a kiss!"

"Aye, a kiss of alluring portent. Do not imagine, Alys, that I could trust myself to savor more of your kiss and halt myself in time." Alys looked so startled by this confession that Burke moved closer and took her hand in his.

She was trembling, just as he quivered inside. 'Twas a powerful love between them, Burke knew it well, just as he knew he would be seven kinds of fool to let this lady escape his side.

"Alys, I pledged to treat you with honor and I will do so, for I understand the import of your mother's experience to you." She parted her lips but Burke lifted one finger to silence her. "I also will find spouses for both of your cousins to prove my will in this. Talbot, I believe, will serve well for Malvina—"

"But he does not desire her. Burke, you cannot simply force people to your will!"

"I have only introduced a possibility." Burke smiled. " 'Twill be Lady Deirdre's manipulative nature that will see results."

"How so?"

"I do not believe your aunt will suffer such an eligible knight to leave this place alive and unwed."

"And what of Brigid?" Alys looked concerned. "Would you compel an unwilling man to wed her?"

Burke folded his fingers around Alys's hand, appreciating how she cared for her youngest cousin. "Nay, Alys, I have a friend, an old comrade, whom I thought of since speaking with Brigid. He is a kind man, a knight who is noble but shy, and one who has been wounded by many heartless beauties. He has vowed never to trust a woman again."

Hope lit Alys's wondrous eyes. "You believe he and Brigid would make a good match?"

"Aye. Ride with me to find out, Alys." The words fell from his lips in haste, for Burke feared that his lady would refuse him this. "Let us ride with Brigid to Paris. We will find this friend of mine, we shall see if they might make a match."

But Alys pulled her fingers from his grip. "I could not leave Heloise." She pushed to her feet and turned away from him, her manner telling Burke success had been snatched away.

"Alys! You cannot spend all your days here because of an anchorite you hold dear!"

"I cannot abandon her, Burke." Alys folded her arms across her chest. " 'Twas Heloise alone who cared for me. I owe her much!"

"But not *all*, Alys." Burke did not pursue his lady, but held his own ground. Her quick glance told him that she was more tempted by his offer than she would like to show, and he endeavored to persuade her without fine words. "Alys, 'tis the only way to find Brigid a spouse, for none come to Kiltorren. And we shall ensure Heloise is back within the hall before we leave."

Alys rubbed a hand over her brow. "But Aunt cannot be trusted."

Burke stepped forward and caught her shoulders in his hands. "I shall resolve this matter with Heloise, Alys," he insisted. She looked up, her gaze searching. "Trust me."

And Alys smiled slightly. She touched Burke's jaw then shook her head, her words falling softly. "Do you not understand, Burke? 'Tis myself I do not trust in this." She stepped away before he could make sense of that and paused on the threshold of the storeroom. "Will you go with me to see Heloise on the morrow? 'Tis a day earlier than I usually go, and she should not welcome a man to her seclusion, but . . ."

"I will go." Burke understood that this elderly woman's endorsement was the only judgment Alys would trust. Ye gods, but he hoped the woman recalled him, or thought well of him now.

"After Mass," Alys murmured, but hesitated to leave.

"Will you consider my suggestion? Think of Brigid's happiness and how she longs to be wed."

To Burke's confusion, shadows haunted his lady's fine eyes. What was amiss? "How can you be assured she will be happy with a stranger?"

"Guillaume de Crevy-sur-Seine is no stranger to me. I trained for knighthood with him. He is the same age as I, a hand shorter, browner of hair and blacker of eye. His hand is steady, he fights well when necessary but provokes naught. His father crusaded to Jerusalem, his mother runs Crevy-sur-Seine since that man's demise, though in truth it is Guillaume's own."

When Alys simply listened, Burke continued. "Crevy is a

prosperous estate, though not wealthy beyond compare. Guillaume has a sister who is wed and has three small children. She and her spouse are vassals of Guillaume's and hold a manor on the holding. Brigid would not want for company in that keep, of that you may be assured, and she would want for naught as Guillaume's bride. They all, each and every one, are good-hearted people."

Burke exhaled. "Brigid could fare worse, Alys. He would never raise a hand against a woman, he does not drink overmuch, he does not make war. I believe that Guillaume would go far to cultivate a lady's love if he found her fetching."

Alys bit her lip. "But will he?"

Burke made an appeal to his lady's good sense. "We can only find out if we travel to his keep. He will not come this far for promise of a bride, not after all he has endured from women. We can only take Brigid there and let her charm do the rest."

"You believe it will."

Burke nodded. "I believe she is precisely the sweet and gentle manner of woman who will capture Guillaume's heart."

Alys hesitated. "And Guillaume is a good man?"

"He is my best friend." Burke stepped closer to secure her agreement, but Alys abruptly shook her head.

"But 'twould not be appropriate for the three of us to travel together." Her words fell flat, as if she made an excuse. "Nay, Burke it cannot be done."

Yet again Burke felt cheated to have her close agreement snatched away. "We shall take a chaperone!" he roared. "Ye gods, Alys, we shall take your cursed aunt if need be! Have you not learned that I will not take nay for an answer?"

She considered him for a moment. Her words fell so quietly that Burke nearly missed them. "And is your will the only matter of import in this?"

Dismay erupted within Burke and yet again he knew he had chosen his words wrongly. "Nay, Alys! 'Tis not so!"

But with a flick of her skirt, his lady was gone.

Burke swore and kicked a sack with such vengeance that the canvas tore and spilled the grain. He shoved his hand through his hair and scowled at his surroundings, his blood still afire from Alys's shy kiss.

Burke sat down heavily on the leaking sack of grain and sighed. Then he bent, scooped up the mug, and drained the ale from it in one gulp. He had surprised his lady, 'twas true, he had not phrased matters aright.

But all was far from lost. As his temper faded, Burke conceded the truth. On this day, he *had* found a spouse for Malvina, which was no small victory. And Alys *had* kissed him, most passionately, of her own choice. He had learned something of the lady, even if he had been slow to put it to use.

Aye, Burke would reflect upon his gains alone.

Chapter Thirteen

LYS LAY AWAKE MOST OF THE NIGHT, ALTERNATELY savoring and regretting her impulsive kiss, calling herself a fool and wondering if Burke would think her wanton. She finally fell asleep just before the dawn, only to awaken out of sorts. 'Twas a sullen grey day, the skies heavy with the threat of rain, and far from the finest weather to set out on the journey to visit Heloise.

But Alys dressed, attended the second Mass, and returned to the bailey with her uncle and Brigid to find Burke awaiting with his saddled steed. The others were apparently still asleep.

Burke's arms were folded across his chest, his dark fur-lined cloak flowing behind him. Alys's heart leapt at the sight of him, no less at the certainty that he waited for her.

"And where are you going?" Uncle demanded.

"Burke takes me to visit Heloise."

"Is this not a day early?"

"Aye." Alys lifted her chin, daring her uncle to deny her.

But Uncle dropped his voice, his gaze flicking nervously to the hall. "This knight speaks aright in one thing—Heloise should not be so far from the hall. God speaks through her, and I would have His counsel closer to hand. Bring her back with you this day."

"But Aunt . . ."

"Will bend to my will in this," Uncle insisted with a certainty Alys was far from feeling. "Go! Hasten yourselves before Deirdre awakens."

Alys was not about to ask twice. She fled toward Burke, who tersely confirmed that he had heard Uncle's command. Certainly Burke's sweet manner had abandoned him this morn, and he looked as tired as Alys felt. Indeed, their poor parting of the night before seemed to yet linger between them.

"Did you sleep?" he asked, and Alys cursed his perceptiveness.

"The wind kept me awake."

Burke snorted. " 'Twas thoughts of a beguiling woman that haunted me." He offered her his hand and Alys knew she would have to ride the beast once more. The steed flared its nostrils as if it thought as little of that as she.

"No kisses," she decreed, and Burke smiled so abruptly that her breath was stolen away.

"Of course not," he agreed, too easily to soothe Alys's pride.

That was that, she decided sourly as they rode from the bailey. She had declined the man's offer in no uncertain terms, and this time Burke had accepted her at her word. There was no reason to be troubled by his choice, not in the least.

Alys lifted her chin to the wind, ignoring how much easier 'twas to match the steed's gait now that she knew to relax. She also ignored the solid weight of Burke's arm around her waist, at least as well as she could.

'Twas a marvel how quickly they reached Heloise's abode and, just in time, for the wind was whipping ominously at the dark sea. Alys strained for some sight of Heloise, but the woman was not to be found.

"Where can she be?" she murmured, surprised when Burke's arm tightened around her waist.

"You will learn to dismount properly this day," he muttered.

"Not leap from a running steed and break your leg." Burke pulled the destrier to a halt, then swung out of the saddle with ease. He reached for Alys, his expression grim, and lifted her to the ground. There was a moment when they stood toe to toe that Alys thought he might speak, but she ducked beneath his arm and ran for Heloise's hut.

"Heloise!" Alys called, her fear rising when only the sounds of the wind and the sea carried to her ears. She scrambled down the rocky slope, slipped, and found Burke's hand beneath her elbow.

"Haste will win you naught but a dip in the sea," he declared. "Have you no care for your own welfare, Alys?" She did not answer, and he did not release her elbow until they were on the level ground before the hut.

Yet still there was not a sound from the hut. The first heavy drops of rain splattered against the stony ground. Alys hurried forward, still calling. The fire was out, which she should have expected, though the wind was biting. Alys ducked through the portal, hoping against hope that Heloise was not too chilled.

Her heart stopped when she saw the elderly woman curled upon the ground as if she had fallen.

"Heloise!" Alys dropped to her knees beside the anchorite, her hands skimming Heloise's face, her hands, her brow. Heloise was warm, though her breathing was faint and uneven. "Heloise, what has happened?" Alys tried to gather the woman into her arms but could not move her weight.

To her immense relief, Burke stepped into the hut and readily brought the older woman to a sitting position. Heloise choked and gasped as she stirred. Burke gently thumped her back.

"Water," he commanded with a sharp glance to Alys. She ran to fetch the ladle from the bucket left to catch the rainwater. By the time she returned, Burke had Heloise's back braced against the wall and was rubbing the older woman's hands within his. Her eyes were open, but her features seemed more contorted than usual. She frowned at Burke as if uncertain who he was. Alys knelt before Heloise with the ladle and the older woman's expression brightened.

"Alys! The stones said you would come." Heloise sipped of the water, then turned her head away from it. She looked at Burke, then eyed his hands rubbing hers. "All cold," she pronounced.

"You cannot feel your hands?" Alys demanded.

Heloise shook her head. "All dead."

"Nay, not dead, Heloise. Chilled. You should not have let the fire die. 'Tis too cold to be without it in these days."

But Alys noted that when Burke set one of Heloise's hands aside to take the other, the first did not move. It lay unnaturally twisted, as did Heloise's legs, and Alys caught her breath in sudden understanding.

She met Heloise's eyes and saw that the older woman knew fully what had happened to her. "The fit came again," she whispered.

"In the night, the dark rider comes." Heloise gasped as if she could not catch her breath, and Alys distrusted the unhealthy pallor of her skin. "The stones, they knew."

"Nay, Heloise, *nay*. No dark rider comes for you." Alys would not permit any such nonsense. Burke slipped away and Alys heard him gathering the tinder for the fire. "Perhaps you heard the horse we rode, naught more than that. We shall make a fire and heat the broth I brought for you. And then you will come back to the keep, Uncle insists, and you will be warm and . . ."

But Heloise frowned. "Nay, Alys. I will never leave here."

"Of course you will! That is why we have come. Burke and I will aid you . . ."

"None can aid me, not even the stones," Heloise said flatly, her gaze keenly bright. "I am dying, Alys."

Tears blurred Alys's vision. "Nay, Heloise, not that." She took Heloise's hand within hers, its chill confirming the unwelcome tale. "Not now, not when all is coming aright."

"I have no choice, child." Heloise wheezed, then labored to take a breath and winced. "The pain will come again, I can feel its portent even now. I have not long, Alys."

The fire flared to life beneath Burke's hands and Heloise started as always she did, the golden light painting her features unnaturally bright. She caught her breath shakily and Alys held fast to her hands, unable to do anything when the color faded from Heloise's cheeks.

"It comes," Heloise declared, her voice uneven. "And quickly. Take the pendant from my neck, Alys."

"Nay, Heloise, 'tis yours. I could never take it."

" 'Tis yours, Alys, your legacy."

"Nay, Heloise, 'tis yours!"

Heloise's features worked and Alys feared the pain rose within her once more. Her hand shook within Alys's grip, but still she forced out the words. "Your father had it cast for your mother as a token of his love."

Heloise gulped a breath and whimpered. Alys clutched her hands, not knowing what else she could do, wishing she could endure the pain in Heloise's stead. She felt Burke hovering watchfully behind her and had only felt so helpless once before.

But Heloise caught her breath. "Isibeal entrusted it to me, that I would grant it to you."

Alys shook her head. "Nay, Heloise. You continue to wear it . . ."

"So some thief will pluck it from my grave?" Heloise demanded sharply. " 'Tis yours, Alys, yours by right." The older woman's voice softened. "If naught else, take it as a reminder of me."

Alys parted her lips to protest anew, but Heloise gave a cry of pain. Her entire body shuddered and her fingers gripped Alys's with painful intensity. Her eyes rolled back and she made a choking sound, even as Burke stepped forward to lend his aid.

There was naught to be done and Alys knew it well, though it still was not easy to watch. The fit subsided, fading to shudders as Alys held fast to Heloise's hand and Burke braced her back.

"Alys, I beg of you," the elderly woman whispered shakily when she could draw a breath. "Let me die knowing I fulfilled Isibeal's trust. Take the token."

Alys's hands were shaking as she reached for the pendant. Without Burke's aid, she would never have managed the deed. He lifted Heloise's head with a care and compassion that wrenched Alys's heart, extricating the chain from the older woman's veil when Alys could never have succeeded.

"Don it," Heloise insisted, her voice rasping. "I would see it on you." Her gaze was bright as she watched Alys do her bidding.

The golden oval was heavy and it hung between Alys's breasts, the metal still warm from Heloise's flesh. Alys took Heloise's hands again as Burke eased the older woman into comfortable repose. He slipped into the shadows, though Alys knew he lingered near.

His very presence gave her unexpected strength.

Heloise breathed laboriously for a few moments, her pain clearly easing. "Isibeal had but one regret," she finally confided.

"Placing her trust too readily?"

"Nay, child! She loved you nigh as much as she loved her knight. Never believe anything else that witch says of the matter. What does *she* know of love? You were wrought in love."

"Heloise, you should not stir yourself so."

But Heloise would not be swayed. "I saw them together,

Alys, I saw their love and 'twas humbling in its vigor."
Heloise licked her lips and Alys offered the ladle once more,
only to have the older woman shake her head. "Nay, the only
thing Isibeal regretted was that she waited."

Alys frowned. "Waited?"

"She waited for her knight to come, because he had
pledged to do as much. When she died, she said she wished
she had not been so proud, that she had pursued love herself."
Heloise fixed Alys with her bright gaze. "The stones want
your promise, Alys."

Alys's nape prickled at Heloise's odd insistence. "What
promise?"

"Your promise that you will pursue love as your mother did
not."

"Heloise—"

"Promise, Alys!"

"Aye, Heloise, I will, of course I will."

No sooner had she uttered the words than Heloise caught
her breath. The older woman arched her back as a spasm of
pain obviously rolled through her and her lips pulled back
from her teeth.

"Burke!" The knight was there already, holding Heloise as
she cried out, murmuring to her, but the older woman emitted
a heart-wrenching cry. She gasped, she shook her head, she
trembled violently. She might have said something, but then
suddenly she sagged against Burke.

And an eerie silence fell in the hut.

Alys waited for Heloise to take another breath. She was certain the spasm would pass, but naught happened. Alys leaned
closer, touching Heloise's throat, seeking a sign of her pulse.

There was naught. Panic rose within her. She stroked
Heloise's face, called to her. But Alys knew the truth even before Burke eased Heloise down and lifted her hands away.

He looked straight into Alys's eyes. "There is naught more to be done."

"Nay! There must be something we can do. We must aid her, we must make her breathe again, we must—"

Burke shook her hands. "Alys, she is gone."

"Nay!"

"Aye."

At his conviction, the tears Alys had been fighting broke loose in a torrent. She wept like a child, burying her face in her hands. She shuddered to her toes, and once she had begun to cry, Alys could not stop. She gulped great gasping sobs, rocking on her heels, and touched Heloise's hand repeatedly. Alys could not believe that the woman who was as close as a mother to her was gone for all time.

She was grateful that Burke left her to her tears, though she did not immediately guess what he did. When Alys eventually looked up, she realized that the older woman now looked to be in repose, a marked contrast to the agitation in which she had died.

To her astonishment, Alys watched Burke slide his hands across Heloise's aged face. The contortion of her dying spasm faded beneath the deft touch of his fingers and thumbs. In the twinkling of an eye, Heloise's features were at ease, as they had been three years past. She looked as if she slept.

Burke glanced up and must have seen the surprise in Alys's expression. "War teaches a man many unwelcome skills," he said softly, then stood. " 'Tis easier if your last sight of her is a peaceful one." He inclined his head slightly, then headed for the door. "I will be outside while you say farewell."

And he left Alys to her mourning.

Cedric was alone in the hall when Talbot strode impatiently across the floor. "Is there any morsel worthy of breaking my fast?" that knight demanded. "Or shall I have to wait until Killarney to eat decent fare?"

Killarney? Surely the man did not intend to leave? Cedric bounded to his feet, knowing his request to Alys would already cost him dear in his wife's eyes. If this knight left before Deirdre arose, there would be hell to pay in this hall.

"Sir, you cannot think to leave!" he boomed. "Why, Cook is just making fresh bread now."

"Aye?"

"Aye, and you will never guess what the steward found in the cellar—a fine cask of apple wine." Cedric gestured to the cask, its discovery naught short of miraculous in his eyes. "You and I shall partake of its bounty."

Talbot snorted. He considered the hall, the cask, then Cedric before he shrugged. "I suppose 'twill hurt naught to see whether 'tis worse than that swill you found last evening."

"Naught at all, naught at all." Cedric gestured wildly to Cronan who mercifully caught his meaning with speed. The cask was opened, two chalices filled, and Cedric breathed relief when Talbot pursed his lips in satisfaction.

" 'Tis not half bad," he conceded.

Cedric settled back, content. "Surely you cannot even consider leaving Kiltorren while there is such fine wine to be savored."

"Indeed." Talbot eyed the contents of his chalice, then fixed Cedric with a bright eye. "Perhaps you could aid me."

"Aye! Anything I can do for a guest!"

Talbot smiled. " 'Tis but a tale I desire. A tale of a woman named Isibeal of Kiltorren."

'Twas not long that Burke waited for Alys, though he would have granted her days if she had needed it. He could see what a blow the woman's loss was to her and could only imagine what 'twas like to witness death the first time with the loss of one held so dear.

He stared out to sea, skipped stones across the water, gauged the changing mood of the clouds. The great raindrops had not lasted, though still the sky brewed. Moonshadow grazed, the quantity of grass so insufficient here that the task fully occupied the steed.

Burke watched the waves, thought of Heloise's solitude, and marvelled anew at Deirdre's cruelty.

He heard Alys's step before she spoke and turned to find her hovering in Heloise's doorway. She looked bruised and uncertain, young and shaken. Her fingers toyed incessantly with the pendant she had not wanted to take.

Burke waited in silence and, with halting footsteps, Alys came to his side, staring out to sea in her turn. He did not know how long they stood there thus.

"Thank you," Alys murmured finally. "I am glad that you are here."

"As am I."

She turned to him, her red-rimmed gaze searching. " 'Tis not new to you."

Burke shrugged. "Though no less tragic, for all of that."

Alys heaved a sigh, her gaze trailing over this lonely point. "I shall never be able to accept that she is not here, waiting for me to bring her fresh bread or melt her cheese." Her lip trembled. "She loved cheese so."

"Aye, you will. 'Twill not come readily, but 'twill come."

Alys bit her lip, her thumb working across the pendant.

Burke thought it time to change the topic. "Might I see it?"

Alys hesitated only a moment before she pulled the chain over her head. She handed it to Burke, clearly reluctant to remove it. "Do not drop it, I beg of you."

"Of course not." Burke wound the length of chain securely

around his fingers. He tipped the golden oval so that the image engraved there caught the light. " 'Tis a unicorn," he said softly, "and a maiden. Like the old tales, when the innocence of a maiden subdues the ferocity of the unicorn, compelling that creature to tamely lay its head in her lap."

Alys nodded. "Can you guess what it means?"

Burke shook his head, examining the motif once again. "Perhaps your father felt that your mother had tamed him— did you not tell me that Heloise said he was reputed to be most fierce?"

Alys nodded again.

"Or perhaps there was a *chanson* on this theme that they favored." Burke winked, thinking the lady in need of a smile. "Perhaps you were wrought in a forest glade."

Alys extended a shaking hand for her token, but Burke stepped closer and lifted the chain over her head. "It matters little what it meant to your mother, Alys," he said quietly. " 'Tis a token of love and an apt reminder of Heloise's love for you."

Alys's gaze clouded once more and Burke caught her in his arms. She wept against him, soaking his tabard with her tears, the sound of her grief tearing holes in his heart. Burke held her close, whispering soothingly in her ear.

When Alys finally lifted her head, Burke shed his cloak and cast it around her shoulders, nuzzling the fur lining against her chin. "Like a queen," he whispered, and was rewarded with a faint glimmer of a smile.

"Hardly that." She sighed, her tears gathering again.

"Should we take Heloise to the chapel in Kiltorren?" Burke asked, not certain how Alys would take to discussion of such practicalities.

She straightened though, looking regal indeed as she shook her head. "She said she would never leave here. In fact, she probably would want to remain with the stones."

"What was that about?"

"She had claimed of late that the stones whispered to her and told her things." Alys met Burke's gaze. " 'Twas uncanny how accurate some of their confessions could be."

" 'Tis often said that the voice of God resonates in all His creations."

Alys nodded, her eyes narrowing as she scanned the site. "She liked it here, against all odds, and certainly more than at the keep. But I cannot imagine how she could stay." The seabirds called and circled above, their cries more than apt reminder of the realities of leaving Heloise untended in the wilds.

"I can seal her hut, if 'tis what you desire."

Alys looked to him hopefully. "Truly?"

"Of course."

The lady nodded with resolve. "I think Heloise would prefer that." Her eyes filled with uncertainty. "But what of last rites?"

"I do not think this anchorite had any sins to confess," he said firmly. "She was a woman of God, Alys, and no doubt as pure as after her last confession."

Alys nodded slowly. "You are right."

Burke touched his lady's cheek. "Have you said your farewell in full?"

Alys blinked back her tears, then nodded vigorously. She kissed his fingertips then turned away, walking a little distance to stare out to sea, swathed in his cloak.

And Burke set to work.

Burke was quick. Alys turned to watch him when she had suppressed her tears once more, and was surprised at how much progress he had made. He fitted stones with precision, his brow knotted as he chose each one in turn, and already she could not even discern where the base of the door had been.

As Alys watched, he finished the stonework, then chinked the stones with the greenery cast up by the sea. Finally, Burke stepped back to appraise his work.

But a few adjustments and he washed his hands, offered Alys his arm, and together they strode back to his destrier. He lifted Alys wordlessly to the saddle, then walked alongside her. Alys glanced back as he led the stallion away and cast her gaze one last time over this place.

In her heart, Alys knew she would never return.

Just as Heloise would never leave.

When she listened closely, Alys almost fancied she could hear the stones murmuring to each other. She turned away then, telling herself to be content that Heloise was at peace, in solitude with her whispering stones.

'Twas perhaps all the anchorite desired.

The wind pressed at their backs as they made their way toward the keep, and Burke was stoically silent. Alys considered the pledge she had made to Heloise, stubbornly ignoring the catch that rose in her throat at the very thought. She realized that what she fought was not Burke, nor his charm, nor even her uncertainty of what might come between them. 'Twas not even a dread of repeating her mother's error, though she had long been certain that was true.

'Twas the fact that she loved Burke de Montvieux precisely as he was.

And she realized that her pledge to Heloise compelled her to do something about that, not merely wait to have her dream fall into her lap.

Burke halted when they reached the low wall on this side of Kiltorren's bailey and fixed Alys with a troubled gaze. "Alys, I would speak to you of something before we return to the hall, though indeed the timing is less than opportune. This day's events will change matters, as always a passing does, and I would have matters clear between us."

He did not touch her, nor did his gaze swerve from hers. Alys almost dreaded whatever he might say.

"You know well enough that I am without holding, without inheritance, without allegiance to a powerful lord," he admitted heavily. "I have precious little to offer, save myself, but I offer all that I have to you, Alys."

Alys stared as Burke continued with quiet intensity. "A few successful years at the tourneys and I would have enough to support a family, to acquire a small holding, to see my wife indulged."

Then he offered Alys his open hand. His fingers were outstretched, his broad palm up, but the choice to take his hand was left to Alys alone. Burke looked up at her, his expression serious beyond all.

"Be that wife of mine, Alys."

Alys did not trust her ears. Though Burke had offered himself before, he had never offered marriage with his heart shining in his eyes, no sweet words upon his tongue. "You would truly wed me?"

"You cannot be surprised, Alys," Burke chided. "I offered for you before, and the choice of a bride is not an issue upon which any man of merit changes his thinking. Brianna dispatched me on a quest for a bride, and only one bride would do." With one last silver glance, he made to pull his hand away. "I ask only that you think of the matter."

"There is naught to consider," Alys said quickly.

Burke looked back to her, his expression so cautiously hopeful that a lump rose in Alys's throat.

"I will marry you, Burke, whether you have Montvieux or not."

His eyes flashed, he snatched her from the saddle and held her close. Alys laid her head against his chest and savored the agitated pounding of his heart, the tenderness of his hand cupping her nape.

"Alys, I shall see that you never regret this," Burke murmured, a waver in his voice. "I pledge it to you."

Alys smiled and reached up to touch his jaw. "I believe you."

Burke seemed momentarily astounded by this, then he granted her a thorough kiss that left her unsteady on her feet.

"Alys, I would not hasten you, but I would welcome having this wretched place behind me." Burk's arms tightened around her. "I do not trust your aunt. 'Tis late this day, but I would prefer not to linger here any longer."

"Nor would I," Alys agreed. "Indeed, there is no longer any reason to stay."

"Shall we leave with all haste?" Burke's gaze was anxious. "We could escort Brigid to Guillaume."

"Aye. I shall fetch her. She will not have much to pack."

Burke kissed Alys with a ferocity that shook her to her core. She closed her eyes against the heat of his ardor and knew that she chose aright. She would pursue love, precisely as Heloise had bidden her, and she would not be left clinging to regrets.

That was the lesson of her mother's life, and Alys had long ago vowed not to repeat her mother's mistake.

She could only hope that her love for Burke would suffice.

No sooner had Alys reached the landing before her chamber than a figure stepped from the shadows to confront her. "Aunt!"

"Aye, 'tis me, though you have kept me waiting long enough," Aunt snapped. "Not to mention another. Where have you been, you ungrateful child?"

Her aunt's unveiled hostility caught Alys by surprise, and she took a tentative step backward. "I visited Heloise. She died this day—"

"And good riddance that is, if indeed 'tis the truth." Aunt

advanced upon Alys, the malice in her features making Alys shrink against the wall. "You think none noted the import of your disappearance with that knight last evening, but you are wrong. You were lifting your skirts, with the same lack of shame as your mother, and do not imagine that I do not know it."

"Nay, Aunt . . ."

"Save your lies! Another knight has smelled the taint upon you, Alys," Aunt declared angrily. "All day long Malvina has been compelled to listen to him crow your praises. 'Tis time you paid your due. 'Tis time you earned your way in this hall, and this time you will not defy me."

Alys's heart began to pound with the fear that she had not fled Kiltorren quickly enough. "What do you demand of me?"

"You know what I want of you! Earn your favor here upon your back, as your mother earned all she won in her sorry life!"

Alys lifted her chin. "I will not!"

"You are tainted and can do naught else." Aunt leaned closer and hissed. "You have no choice, child. Your fate was determined when your wanton mother first parted her thighs and blessed you with the whore's taint."

Alys stepped forward to challenge her aunt. "There is no such thing as a whore's taint."

"Indeed?" Aunt folded her arms across her chest and regarded her niece coldly. "Then why did this knight ask after Isibeal, that whore of this house, and why did he insist that he must have *you* come to him as soon as he learned you were her spawn?" Aunt arched a questioning brow.

Alys did not have an answer for that. "I do not know."

"But I do! 'Tis the taint of a whore that follows you, the rumor of your mother's loose morals that brought this knight sniffing all the way from Paris."

Alys frowned, sensing there was an element missing in

this argument. Her mother had been dead nigh upon twenty years and none had come seeking her before. "But that cannot be . . ."

"But 'tis, Alys, 'tis!" Aunt leaned closer. "The knight lusts for you, he demands your services, he knew from the sight of you that you were born to be a whore. Just as the other one did." She snatched at Alys's arm so suddenly that Alys did not have time to step away. "Your kind cannot be particular if you mean to eat each day. Go and service him."

"I will not!"

"By all that is holy, you most certainly will."

"Nay!" Alys shook her arm free.

"Fool! Listen to me and listen well." Aunt snarled. "This Talbot wants a whore and I want his every pleasure met within the walls of this keep. Malvina fancies him and she shall have him." She gave Alys a shake. "You will ensure that Talbot is pleased or you will be cast from these gates to starve. Am I understood?"

But Alys shook her head, though she was trembling inside at her own defiance. "I will do no such thing. I am leaving with Burke."

Aunt smiled mockingly. "And this knight will wed a bastard child like you? The daughter of a whore? A woman with no dowry? The man may have lost his inheritance, but he still has a lineage that demands its due. He will use you and cast you aside with naught."

"Nay, he will not!"

"Get yourself to the hall without delay." Aunt sneered when Alys did not leap to do her bidding. "Do not imagine that your champion will save your sorry hide with nuptial vows. A knight like Burke de Montvieux sees only one use in a woman like you."

With that Aunt pivoted to walk away.

But Alys straightened in the shadows, determined to have

all clear between them before she departed forever. "Why did you lie to me about Burke's offer of marriage three years past?"

Aunt froze, though she did not turn.

Alys swallowed the lump in her throat. "Why did you lie to me about his return to Kiltorren the year after that? Did you truly beat me only to ensure I did not meet him then? Is that why you expelled me with Heloise?"

Aunt pivoted slowly and Alys felt her dread rise. Her palms were damp and she knew none would aid her here. Still, she had to know the truth. "And why should you imagine that I will believe whatever lie you tell me now?"

Aunt studied her, her own features wreathed in shadows, her expression unreadable. "This, then, is the gratitude I have for raising you as my own after Isibeal's shame. You truly are your mother's child."

"You raised me as a serf!" Alys retorted. "You suffered me here only to wait upon you."

"You deserve no better!" Aunt shouted. "You and your slut of a mother! No man in Ireland was good enough for Isibeal, nay, Father had to send her to Paris for the finest Christendom had to offer. But me, what fate did our darling father store for me?"

Aunt advanced on Alys, her eyes wild. "Naught! Naught but a suitor not deemed fitting to scrape Isibeal's shoes." Aunt jabbed herself in the chest. "I was wed to Isibeal's leavings, regardless of what I had to say of the matter.

"And then what happened?" Aunt demanded, flinging her hands skyward. "Fine Isibeal, she who could do no wrong, *did* do wrong. Amidst her dancing and feasting and fine parties in Paris, Father's darling Isibeal managed to conceive a child out of wedlock. Here, I thought, would finally be *justice*!"

Aunt shook a fist beneath Alys's nose. "But did our doting

father cast her out? Nay, not Isibeal. I would have been flogged until I bled, but she was treated like a queen! She brought shame into this house, and I, I had to wait upon her during her time! 'Twas unfair! 'Twas wrong, but my father cared for naught but his beloved Isibeal."

" 'Tis true then," Alys whispered. "You hate me only because Isibeal bore me."

"Is that not enough?" Aunt gritted her teeth. "I was *glad* when she died," she declared bitterly. "I was glad that Father wept for months, I was glad that Isibeal's lover never did come to her side. She deserved some pain in her life for all that she had caused me."

"And what of Burke?"

Aunt fired a look of such loathing down the corridor that Alys cringed. "What makes you imagine that I would let you make a hell of my daughters' lives the way that Isibeal made one of mine? You could not have a knight when none would have my Malvina, especially one of the ilk of Burke de Montvieux.

"Those tourneys were an expense borne to find spouses for *my* daughters. I could not suffer you to win the prize." Aunt's eyes narrowed. "I have granted you more than your due these twenty years. Go to the hall, Alys. 'Twill be the last debt due between us."

Alys squared her shoulders. "Nay. Any debt is long paid."

Aunt took a sharp breath. "You have grown defiant," she snapped. "Indeed, Alys, we have need of the willow switch again."

Aunt stepped closer, but she had no chance to reach Alys before Alys was struck from the side.

"Bitch!" Malvina screamed, lunging suddenly out of the shadows to strike. Alys's neck snapped back with the force of her cousin's blow and her head hit the wall with a crack that left her dizzy. "You would steal all from me, just as your mother stole all from mine!"

"Malvina! Aunt, aid me!"

"Never." Aunt's words sliced through the shadows like a knife. "Indeed, I see you win only what you deserve." Aunt chuckled softly, then Alys heard her stroll away, humming under her breath.

She was on her own. Alys turned to find her cousin's eyes lit with the same fury that had shone in her aunt's.

"You stole Burke from me with your whoring ways!"

Alys backed away, her hands raised in a plea for good sense. "Malvina, I did no such thing."

"You did, you did!" Malvina's tears fell as fast as her words. "He never truly looked my way because of you, and now, you do the same with Talbot. He has sat at the board, all the day long, talking only of you. He spared no attention to *me*!"

"But, Malvina . . ."

"I want him, Alys," Malvina insisted. "I want Talbot, and you shall not steal him too!"

"But I do not want Talbot . . ."

"I will not heed your lies. And I will not watch you tempt Talbot in my garb!" Malvina cried. She grasped Alys's kirtle at the neck and pulled with all her might. The wool rent right down the front, exposing Alys's patched chemise. Malvina tore it as well, though when Alys made a sound of protest, her cousin slapped her face.

Alys slapped her back, hard. Malvina paused, caught her breath, then lunged after Alys like an enraged bull. The pair went down scrapping furiously, Malvina seeking to inflict damage and Alys wanting only to be free of Kiltorren. Alys knew she landed at least two successful blows before Malvina changed strategy.

"And you will not don my sister's circlet! Or put her veil

against your filthy hide!" Malvina ripped the circlet and veil from Alys's head and nearly pulled the hair from Alys's head in the deed. She shredded the gossamer veiling and stamped upon the pieces. She cast the circlet to the floor with such vigor that it was surely dented beyond repair.

Alys fled for her chamber at her cousin's distraction, but Malvina chased her. She tripped Alys and shredded the carefully pieced embroidery along Alys's hem. "And you will not steal from my own mother, after all the generosity she has bestowed upon you."

Alys snatched at her cousin's ankles and they rolled again across the floor, wrestling and striking whenever they could. Suddenly Malvina bounded to her feet and spat on Alys. "That is better than you deserve, you thankless whore!"

And she fled.

Alys could not believe the assault was so abruptly ended, but she escaped into her chamber and secured the latch before her cousin or her aunt could return. Alys took a shaking breath and leaned back against the door. There was a lump rising on her head and her cheek would be black on the morrow.

Burke was right. They could not be away from this cursed place quickly enough.

Chapter Fourteen

TALBOT PACED THE HALL WITH IMPATIENCE. HE WAS finally alone, though Kiltorren's foul apple wine clouded his thinking. At least, this Isibeal was dead—whether she was his uncle's Isibeal or not—though the confirmation that she had a child was far from welcome.

Could this Alys be the daughter of Millard? The very possibility made Talbot's blood run cold.

But it could not be so. This Isibeal had been a whore, according to those at Kiltorren, which made Talbot doubt that she was truly the Isibeal of his uncle's memories.

For Millard was naught if not rigorously moral. He had never left any question that he might have spawned a bastard in any city. Millard did not employ whores. He did not approve of Talbot's indulgences with whores.

But Isibeal had been a whore, and this Alys was a whore, evidently following the role of her mother. So she could not be Millard's spawn.

Talbot knew only a moment's relief before he realized that his uncle might not let the truth interfere in this matter. Millard had nigh decided that his Isibeal was Isibeal of Kiltorren.

And the child of Isibeal of Kiltorren would be exalted in Millard's eyes, by dint of her mother's name alone. Aye, Millard might well lavish gifts upon this whore, he might take her into his household. Indeed, men were known to become whimsical in their dotage, and Millard was oddly fixed upon Isibeal of Kiltorren.

It could become even worse. Millard could grant this worthless woman his holdings!

Talbot had to sit down to come to terms with that possibility. He breathed with deliberate slowness, bracing himself for what he must do. Even the wine seemed to desert him in this moment, leaving him with little boldness for the task ahead.

Aye, Talbot had already asked for the whore. He was alone in the hall and would have the opportunity to ensure that this Alys met with an *accident*.

The very thought made Talbot tremble. He was not a man of violence, but Villonne, prosperous Villonne was all he had ever desired.

Villonne should be *his*! Talbot drove his fist into his palm and bounced to his feet with newfound resolve. He would not bow to his uncle's will in this, he would take an active role in ensuring his legacy. Aye, he would fight for what should be his by right!

The very words buoyed his ambition, rekindling the power of the wine. Talbot paced the hall with quick steps. Aye, he would *take* what he deserved and leave naught but the bones for any other. Ha! He would command Villonne like a king, he would slaughter any cocky knight like Burke de Montvieux who did not grovel before him. He would be surrounded with wine and luxury and willing wenches for all of his days and nights.

'Twould be perfect, all the more so because 'twas no less than he deserved.

God's blood, but Talbot had need of a woman! Ambition had raised his warrior to full battle, and he decided he would use this whore before she met with her untimely end.

A curvaceous wench hesitated on the stairs in that very moment. 'Twas not Alys, but this one was far more tempting than Isibeal's skinny child could be. Talbot stared, then he smiled, for his fortune already changed.

Attitude was all. He would have this one first.

The woman was cursed with the red hair and pale skin that so many of these Irish seemed to share, but in this light, her hair hung loose over her shoulders like liquid fire. She looked faintly familiar, but they all looked somewhat similar, particularly now that the wine had blurred his perceptions.

He must have seen this one earlier in the hall. Talbot let his smile broaden, wanting her only to come closer.

The woman smiled in turn and strolled across the room. Her hips rolled with the easy seductiveness of an Eastern whore he had once had the fortune to sample.

And she smiled. Indeed, she had already unfastened the neck of her kirtle and now worked the drawstring of her chemise. Her fingers hung with rings, a testimony to her skill. Even the lady of this pathetic keep was not so bejewelled, and Talbot knew suddenly where the lord spent his wealth.

And with such a shrew of a wife, who could blame the man?

Talbot grinned. He liked the idea of bedding the lord's own whore. 'Twas fitting of a visiting king to take the finest for himself and disregard any result. He liked the ripe perfection of the creamy breasts this one revealed, he liked the tentative way her tongue flicked over her lips.

"Would you join me in a quiet chamber?" she asked throatily. "I would not have us be disturbed."

Talbot smiled and took her hand. Aye, she would do very well.

Alys moved with haste. She cast away the shredded kirtle and donned Burke's chemise, the one that Edana had repeatedly forgotten to return, and breathed deeply of his lingering scent. 'Twas as if his protective concern surrounded her, and she closed her eyes, drinking in reassurance.

The door jiggled and Alys jumped in alarm.

"Alys?" Edana hissed. "Why is the door bolted?" The maid fiddled with the latch again. "May I come in?"

Alys touched her bruised cheek. She could not let the goat-girl see her in this state. "Nay, Edana. I have a task for you."

"Aye?"

"Aye. Run to Brigid and tell her to pack with all haste."

"Pack?" Edana squeaked. "You are leaving?"

"Aye, immediately. And—"

"But, Alys, why? Where are you going?"

"Brigid and I leave with Burke, Edana, to find Brigid a spouse." Alys knew she should go to Brigid to explain, but she had to hide her rising bruise and she had naught to wear. "Perhaps you could assist Brigid to pack. Ask Burke how much she can take."

"But, Alys . . ."

"Edana, I have naught to pack, and there is much to be done." Alys considered how angered Burke would be if he glimpsed the blackened eye she was certain she would have in the morning.

She must ensure that Burke did not do something they all would regret. Aunt would demand a penance for any mis-demeanor within Kiltorren's walls. Alys wanted only to be gone, to never have to look back.

"But, Alys . . ."

"Edana, please ask Brigid if she has a kirtle she might grant me for travel and a spare cloak, one with a hood. Make haste, if you please. Burke would leave immediately."

Alys held her breath. She could nearly hear the goatgirl thinking furiously. The latch moved one last time, Edana sighed, then her footsteps faded away.

❖

Edana ran.

She stumbled down the stairs, she tripped over her skirt, she scraped her knee and stubbed her toe, but she did not stop.

For Alys was *leaving*. Edana could not bear the thought of remaining here without Alys, or even Brigid. She fled the keep on fleet feet, not caring who jumped when she raced through the kitchen. The sky darkened already, the bailey was damp underfoot. Edana heard the low murmur of men's voices and raced for the stables.

She found the knight packing saddlebags, deep in discussion with the ostler. The very sight made her heart chill. 'Twas true! Both men looked up in surprise at her sudden arrival, and Edana had to catch her breath before she could speak.

" 'Tis my lady Alys." She gasped.

The knight stepped forward with concern. "What is amiss?"

"She wants to know how much Brigid should pack."

He smiled, then looked at the ostler. "That depends. Is it two palfreys you can spare until we reach the port or three?"

The ostler frowned as Kerwyn stepped out of the shadows.

Edana took a breath, but she had no chance to speak before Kerwyn hailed the knight. "Are you truly leaving?"

"Aye, with all haste. We shall be gone this day."

Kerwyn cleared his throat. "I would travel with you, sir. It seems you could use a squire."

Not Kerwyn, too! Edana nearly cried aloud.

The knight paused. "Are you not beholden to Kiltorren?"

Kerwyn shook his head. "Not I. I am a freeman who labors for his keep. I would welcome the chance to leave this place."

"And I would welcome your hand, Kerwyn, for you are gifted with horses," the knight admitted. "But understand that I cannot offer you much. Perhaps not even the security of a crust of bread thrice daily or a roof over your head. I am without legacy in these days and must tourney to win my own keep. Until then I have naught."

Kerwyn shrugged. "I have lived with uncertainty all my life, sir." His dark eyes glowed. "I would do it in your employ, caring for your fine steed, rather than age unappreciated in this place."

The knight smiled slowly and offered his hand. "Then I welcome your labor, Kerwyn freeman. Know that I will do my utmost to ensure your security and welfare."

"I know, sir. 'Tis why I would travel with you." They two shook hands, then the knight turned back to the ostler.

Edana found her voice. "But what of me?" she cried.

All the men looked to her. Edana's goats stirred at the sound of her voice, or perhaps her dismay. They milled from the sheepfold into the stables, sleepily butting their heads against her knees.

"You?" the knight asked.

"I do not want to remain at Kiltorren if Lady Alys and Lady Brigid depart!" Edana felt her tears rise. "I do not want to stay and be beaten with the willow switch and labor for naught but sharp words." She bit her lip, forced to face one unwelcome truth. "But I am not free."

Edana sat down amidst her ladies, her tears falling. "I was born on Kiltorren. I am beholden to this estate for all my days, as were my parents, as will be my children. I cannot go."

The goats surrounded her, as if they would console her, the eldest doe nuzzling her hand. Edana flung her arms around the gentle beast and curled her fingers in its fur. She cried, hating herself for appearing so weak before these men.

Before Kerwyn.

To her surprise, the knight cleared his throat at close proximity. Edana looked up to find him squatted beside her, his expression grave. "Do you truly want to go with us?"

Edana wiped her tears. "I would hate to leave my ladies."

"But I heard you were a maid now," the ostler interjected. "You may be certain that you will not be cast to the fields again. Her ladyship and Lady Malvina will be expecting your aid."

"Them!" Edana could not stop her grimace, and she noticed that the knight failed to smother his smile.

"Well?" he asked again.

Edana looked to Kerwyn, she could not help it. His dark gaze was fixed upon her, and there was a glimmer there that made her heart skip. "Every journey is both an end and a beginning," he said quietly, and Edana suddenly felt warm all over.

With an effort, she tore her gaze from his and looked to the patient knight once more. "I would come, given half a chance."

Burke smiled and pushed to his feet. "Then I shall endeavor to see it done." He paused to shake a finger at her. "There is no guarantee in this, though. I can only try."

Edana bounced to her feet, unable to suppress the quiver of excitement that ran through her. She had no doubt that if any could achieve this end, 'twould be the man before her. "Aye, sir. But I still need to know how much Lady Brigid might bring."

The knight winced. "Best make it as little as possible." He turned to the ostler, asking after the closest harbor, and was quickly embroiled in a discussion of steeds.

Edana hesitated before running back to the keep. If she did win the chance to leave, she would not be able to speak to her ladies again.

She had best do it now. Edana kissed the top of the eldest doe's head and brushed her hands over all of her flock. When she was done, she stood reluctantly, only to be halted by Kerwyn's gaze upon her. He leaned against the far wall, motionless as a shadow, silent as the night. He was watching her, smiling slightly, as if he waited for her attention. The knight and ostler were gone already, pacing the length of the stable corridor and discussing horses.

Edana held the stablehand's gaze until she was certain she would faint from not taking a breath. Then Kerwyn winked and loped after the other men, leaving Edana staring at his back. Her fingers rose to cover her dawning smile.

An end and a beginning indeed.

◈

While Burke readied the trio of palfreys, the mist rose from the sea and enshrouded Kiltorren, making it seem truly on the edge of Christendom. All was ready quickly, leaving Burke anxious to be gone.

'Twas not long before Brigid stumbled down the stairs to the bailey. She held one end of a small trunk, Edana puffing with the other, and was garbed for travel in plain homespun. Burke relieved the two of them of their burden, setting Kerwyn to the task of lashing it to one steed.

Brigid wrung her hands before herself, her eyes filled with concern. "Is it true?" she asked, her hope undisguised.

Burke smiled for her. "Aye, Brigid. We shall find you a spouse."

"So you can wed Alys." Brigid sighed with satisfaction.

"Aye." Burke had no chance to say more, for Deirdre erupted into the bailey.

And erupt was no understatement. She fairly flew out the portal, her kirtle flaring behind her, her expression fearsome.

"THIEF!" Deirdre raised an accusing finger at Burke and screeched, her voice echoing oddly in the fog. "You would steal my daughter without the burden of marital vows! How dare you bring such shame to my door?"

Brigid shrank back but Burke faced Deirdre squarely. "I would find your daughter a spouse, as you have failed to do," he retorted coolly. " 'Tis clear enough that none are to be had here, so we ride to Paris."

"You cannot do this! You cannot take her away."

"But I will. The lady has given her consent." Burke pivoted with crisp ease and escorted a wide-eyed Brigid to one of the palfreys, murmuring reassurance to her under his breath.

He aided her to mount and left Edana settling her skirts, both women's nervous gazes following him as he faced Deirdre anew.

"I shall see Brigid wed to a good man of good fortune, you have my pledge in that."

The older woman's eyes narrowed. " 'Tis an odd way you have of seeking my endorsement of the match you would make," she complained. "Abducting my daughter to win my niece."

Burke spoke even more coldly than before. "You may well recall that more conventional methods met with little result. And understand, Lady Deirdre, that my interest in Brigid's fortunes stems purely from Alys's concern for her cousin. They both will marry well, despite your efforts."

"You cannot do this!" Deirdre's lip curled. "I shall send word to the king of your deeds! I shall tell him that you abducted my own daughter!"

Burke was not afraid of anything this woman might do. Indeed, now that he knew that Alys would be safely by his side, there was no reason not to speak his mind.

"And I shall counter with revealing yours. Trust me in this, for your king thinks little of those who would deny children their inheritance, even an inheritance as humble as Kiltorren. Such testimony would win you little in the royal court, and still less for your own daughters." Burke smiled coolly. "Go to the king and you shall never see these two wed."

"You are insolent! I should have had you barred from Kiltorren's gates." Deirdre sputtered. "Indeed, I shall not permit you to pass within these walls again!"

Burke did not even raise his voice, so ridiculous was her claim. "You could not stop me, not with the lack of knights you have within your employ. Indeed, madame, you should count your good fortune that I do not covet Kiltorren."

"Kiltorren is my family home and my legacy," Deirdre

cried. " 'Tis a fine abode and you—a man of no estate—have no place finding fault with it."

" 'Tis an adequate enough abode," Burke conceded. "And much could be made of it. My disinterest is wrought of Alys's memories alone. You have tainted this place for her, and although a part of me would delight in seeing you deprived in recompense, I put my lady's needs first."

"Your lady." Deirdre sneered. "Alys is no lady, and I do not believe that you truly intend to wed her. 'Tis a whore you steal from me, and one less mouth to feed, in truth. Take her!" Deirdre flung out a hand. "And take Brigid as well, if she is fool enough to follow your lies."

"Indeed," came a cool voice from the shadows of the portal. " 'Tis lies we leave behind."

Burke glanced up to find Alys hovering on the threshold, though he could not have guessed how long she stood there. A homespun cloak was wrapped over her shoulders, the hood drawn so high against the foul weather that he could not see her features.

"If you leave, then do not return to Kiltorren, Alys," Deirdre snapped. "I will have no space for you, even if you come to beg."

"Do not fear, Aunt," Alys declared with quiet conviction. "I shall never return."

And she stepped out into the bailey toward Burke, her regal bearing making him proud she would be his bride. He offered his hand, closing his fingers over hers when he felt the tremble in her touch. Alys brought no baggage, not so much as a comb, and Burke knew 'twas a decision she made to take naught of this place.

"There is an opportunity here for graciousness," Burke said to Deirdre as he drew his lady close.

Deirdre's lips thinned. "I do not know what you mean."

"Clearly. But your daughter and niece ride out into the

world, blessed only with myself to protect them. It might be suitable—"

"Who else would you take with you?" Deirdre interrupted. "Who else would you steal from Kiltorren?"

'Twas clear that Deirdre cared little for her ward and her daughter's safety. Burke chose to be blunt. "The women will have need of a maid. I can only suggest your contribution to this journey in the person of Edana."

"EDANA?" Deirdre was enraged. "She is a serf! She is the *property* of Kiltorren!"

"Who else would you send?" Burke asked. "Or would you have your daughter scorned at the royal court?" He guessed that this was a weak flank by the way the older woman caught her breath. "Would you have all mock Kiltorren and its daughter?"

Deirdre's lips tightened and she glared at Brigid. "A pox on you for forcing me to this," she declared, and Brigid flushed agitatedly. But Deirdre had already turned back to Burke. "Take her, then, though I suppose that is not the last of it. Why is this stablehand lingering by your side?"

"Kerwyn intends also to accompany us."

"To return the horses?"

"Nay, the ostler will ride out and return with your palfreys. Kerwyn, who as you know is a free man, intends to travel with us."

Deirdre's countenance darkened. "My daughter, a slave and a stablehand, and the ostler gone for days. Do not trouble yourself to ask my opinion of your lofty plans!"

"I shall not," Burke replied, refraining from commenting that Alys was, again, absent from her aunt's list. "You have wrought enough damage as the matter stands."

"Who else do you take? Am I to be left with *anyone* within these walls?"

Burke permitted himself a cold smile. "Look upon the

bright side of matters, Lady Deirdre. You shall have fewer mouths to feed."

Her lips pinched tightly, her eyes flashed, but Beauregard strode out of the keep before Burke could turn away. The cook dropped a sturdy sack before the lady of the keep, and his expression was apologetic.

"I heard of this expedition," he said, his voice a solemn rumble. "And I must offer myself as chaperone to Lady Brigid. 'Tis not proper for two maidens to travel alone with a knight, even one as reputable as Burke de Montvieux."

Deirdre gaped at him. "You would leave as well?"

"Aye." Beauregard's expression set. "I would assure their safety with mine own hands if need be." There was an air about him that told Burke that this man had fought with his hands before.

Indeed, he would welcome Beauregard on this journey.

"But this is highly inappropriate," Deirdre protested. "You are not free! You cannot simply leave. What should we eat?"

Beauregard looked troubled. "But the maidens . . ."

"Have made their choice and will have to bear the burden of the results," Deirdre snapped. "Return to your duties, Cook. I shall expect a fine repast at midday."

But Beauregard did not move. "My lady Deirdre, would you deny me the only request that I have ever made of you?"

"Aye!"

"But your daughter . . ."

"I do not care!" Deirdre screeched. "Get to your labor!"

Beauregard's face fell. He turned aside, then bent to scoop up his belongings, the very image of a defeated man.

Alys sighed softly under her breath and her fingers tightened on Burke's own. He knew well enough that she had an affection for the gentle man and knew also that Beauregard had oft cared for Alys.

"And hasten yourself," Deirdre snapped. "We have a guest in the hall who expects finer fare than you usually conjure."

Beauregard paused for a telling moment when the barb hit its mark, and Burke guessed that he took great pride in his labor. 'Twas not as if Kiltorren's larder burst with fine ingredients.

" 'Tis so unfair," Alys whispered.

Burke impulsively reached beneath his tabard and withdrew a small pouch. He did not have much coin left to his name but this cause was a worthy one.

He withdrew a silver denier, ruefully noted there was but one more, then called the cook's name. The large man turned, his eyes widened, and he snatched the flashing coin out of the air instinctively. He turned it in his palm, then looked to Burke in astonishment.

"Buy your freedom from this place, Beauregard, and join us. I would welcome your companionship."

"Oh, Burke." Alys's voice wavered slightly. "Bless you for this." Burke slipped an arm around his lady's waist and drew her closer, liking how she leaned on his shoulder. 'Twas no small thing for Alys to lean on anyone. Aye, all would be fine, provided Brigid and Guillaume found each other pleasing.

Beauregard clutched the coin. His eyes misted with tears but he grinned like a madman. "I thank you, sir, I *thank* you. I shall see that you never regret this deed!" Then the cook stepped forward, bowed to the Lady of Kiltorren, and presented the coin to her.

Deirdre's mouth worked silently for a moment, then she snatched up the silver. "Begone with you, then, all of you! And good riddance to the lot." She spun and stalked back to the portal, hissing something under her breath.

"Let us go before she thinks again," Alys said anxiously.

"Alys?" Burke murmured, easing her closer. He could fairly taste her distress and knew 'twas more than how Deirdre had addressed Beauregard. But when he would have looked into the shadows of the hood, Alys kept her face averted.

That could be no accident. A chill sliced through Burke with the surety of a knife. "What is amiss? Alys, tell me!"

"I cannot," she whispered, though her fingers clung to his. "Not before we are at sea."

"Alys, what has happened?"

The lady's fingers tightened. "I cannot tell you as yet, but I will. All will be fine once we leave Kiltorren behind. Please, Burke, I ask only that you trust me in this."

"You will tell me?"

"Once we are at sea." A smile crept into her voice. "I pledge it to you."

The change in her tone reassured him slightly. "I will do so, Alys, if you consent to ride with me." He heard the breath of her laughter and his concerns were immediately eased. If she laughed, matters could not be as dire as he had feared.

"Aye," Alys agreed. "Aye, I will."

She would ride with him, she would wed him, she left Kiltorren with him. Burke could want naught else. He lifted Alys onto his saddle with a flourish, then swung up behind her, clamping his arm protectively around her waist. Moonshadow pranced impatiently while Beauregard mounted the second palfrey. Kerwyn helped Edana mount behind Brigid, then swung up himself behind the ostler on the third palfrey.

Burke drew Alys tightly against him, wrapping his fur-lined cloak around them both. The mist changed subtly and a soft rain began to fall as he gave Moonshadow his spurs. 'Twas folly to ride out so late, but there was not a one of them who would have stayed another night at Kiltorren instead. Burke knew he did not imagine his lady's soft sigh of relief when they waved to Godfrey and rode beneath Kiltorren's gate.

Aye, all was finally as it should be.

Malvina awakened from a languid sleep at the sound of her mother ranting in the kitchen. Deirdre slammed pots and pans, shoved furniture, and swore like a sailor.

Indeed, her mother sounded even more vexed than usual. Malvina nestled back against Talbot's warmth where they lay secreted in the storeroom, fearing that her deeds were responsible for her mother's wrath. But Deirdre stomped from the kitchen, her angry footsteps echoing in the hall and finally on the stairs.

Malvina bit her lip and turned to watch the knight sleep, wondering how she would manage this to ensure she won her heart's desire. Surely her knight would do the honorable thing, after the dishonorable things they had done? How she wished she knew! She surveyed him through her lashes, her heart tripping at his handsomeness, and knew one way to have her answer.

Malvina rolled against him, rubbing her breasts against his side in the way that had made him moan all the afternoon, and walked her fingers up his chest.

Talbot grimaced, swatted at her hand, and turned his back to her. "Leave me be, wench." He growled. "My head aches fit to explode and 'tis all from that miserable wine your lord served me. Awaken *him* with your lust and leave me sleep."

Malvina's hand stilled. "Awaken my lord?"

"Aye. I have eyes enough to see that you are his favored whore. Seek your pleasure elsewhere, wench, I have had all I require of you." And the knight settled in to slumber.

Talbot thought she was a whore?

He thought she coupled with her own father?

He thought he was *done* with her?

"How dare you so insult me?" Malvina grasped a fistful of the knight's chemise and shook him back to wakefulness.

"I am sleeping!"

"You will do no such thing before you listen to me!" Malvina retorted. She lifted him slightly by his chemise, then released her grip.

He thunked his head, his eyes flew open, and he frowned. "What is this you do? I shall see you paid for your service."

Malvina leaned over him, her anger clearly evident, for he warily eased backward. "I am no whore, sir," she declared with a precision that could not be missed.

"But—but you came to me and offered yourself," the knight argued wildly. "No woman of decency would do as much!"

"And no man of decency would shame his host by coupling with that man's daughter!"

Talbot blanched in a most satisfactory way. "You are not his daughter. You cannot be his daughter!"

He had not even looked at her. Disappointment unfurled in Malvina's belly, for she had done her utmost to win this man's attention. Indeed, she had thought he greeted her with such pleasure because he was attracted to her.

But 'twas all a lie. He thought her a whore, he thought her innocence was his for the taking.

He had not even noticed her innocence.

"I *am* the daughter of this house," Malvina corrected, her voice shaking with cold anger. "Had you troubled to look my way but once since your arrival, you would have realized the truth."

"Dear God!" The knight dropped his face into his hands. "You are the one they want to force me to wed."

His choice of words did little to appease Malvina. "I am the one you *will* wed," she declared vehemently. "I shall see you account for the taking of my maidenhead, and I shall personally ensure that you pay penance for this insult."

"Maidenhead?" Talbot sat up, shoving a hand through his

hair. What vestige of color remained left his face. "You cannot do that! You cannot force me to wed you!"

"I can do anything. You have erred, sir, and I shall see that you pay the debt due." She stood and shook out her hair, arranging it over her shoulders to look even more dishevelled than it had. As the knight watched in dawning horror, Malvina tore her own chemise, baring her breast.

"Mother!" she cried with feigned dismay. She flung open the door to ensure her voice carried. "Your guest has compromised me!"

"God's blood!" Talbot buried his face in his hands.

Truth to be told, he was rather appealing when he looked so woebegone. Malvina decided that she would ensure he oft felt out of control of his circumstance.

Deirdre, as might have been expected, was quick to reappear. She gasped when she spied her daughter, her eyes rounded with horror in a most satisfying way. "CEDRIC!" she shouted. "Get yourself here!"

Talbot groaned pitifully. Malvina lifted her chin and managed to summon a tear that she hoped was compelling.

"And what precisely has happened here?" Deirdre demanded.

Malvina decided 'twould be a good opportunity to weep. Truly, she doubted that Talbot would correct her version of events.

Indeed, he would not be believed if he did.

"Oh, Mother! I came to the hall to fetch a sip of water and this knave forced himself upon me!" Malvina sobbed as if horrified by all that had transpired.

The knight shook his head. "I cannot believe this."

"What is this?" Deirdre demanded. "He kissed you? He touched you? Tell me the fullness of his familiarity, Malvina!"

"Oh, Mother, the shame of it all."

"Shame?" Deirdre's tone sharpened. "What shame?"

Malvina threw herself weeping into her mother's arms, noting the timely arrival of her father. Perfect. "He stole my maidenhead!" She wailed. "He dragged me to this room and *ravished* me! He took my greatest treasure and now no man will wed me!"

Her parents stiffened. Malvina caught the glance they exchanged, then Cedric strode closer. "Nonsense, my dear. *This* man shall wed you." And both parents turned to glare at the knight in question.

Malvina smiled against her mother's shoulder and sniffled.

But Talbot bounded to his feet. "This is madness! I cannot wed this woman! I *will* not wed this woman!" He pointed an accusing finger at Malvina. "She came to *me*, with her bodice undone and her hair loose! She seduced *me*! She has wrought this situation!"

"Lies!" Deirdre charged before Malvina could.

" 'Tis an abomination that a knight should stoop so low as to blame a lady for his own crimes." Cedric turned a glance of paternal indulgence upon Malvina. "Are you certain that you want such a man as your own, child?"

Malvina wiped at her damp cheeks, surveyed the knight, and let new tears well. "I do not believe there is any choice, Father." Her lower lip trembled in a manner she hoped was convincing. "Indeed, who else would have me?"

And she let a new volley of tears fall, ensuring that she sobbed noisily. Talbot's lips tightened in a way that made him look most beleaguered. The very sight made Malvina's blood quicken.

"Indeed. The man must make rights of his transgression," Deirdre said crisply. "We shall plan the nuptials for a fortnight hence."

Talbot glanced about the kitchen as if seeking an escape. "I cannot be wed in a fortnight. I cannot be wed at all!"

"You should have thought of that before you shamed my daughter," Cedric declared.

"But I cannot take a bride!" Talbot argued. "I have no holding, I have no inheritance." He turned an appealing glance upon Cedric. "Surely you cannot wish to consign your daughter to such an uncertain fate?"

"There is no uncertainty." Cedric was unusually decisive, his tone one that brooked no argument. "Kiltorren has need of a lord to follow me, and a man such as yourself will suit the task well."

"Kiltorren!" Talbot echoed in ill-disguised horror. "I cannot be consigned to this hovel forever!"

"Indeed, you may have new ideas for this holding to improve its lot, for there is always much to be learned from the French." Cedric fixed the knight with a stern glare. "You shall become Lord of Kiltorren, and Malvina its Lady."

"But, but, but you cannot do this!"

"I *can* do this," Cedric retorted. "I am Lord of Kiltorren. You stand in the hall of my holding—indeed, you claimed my daughter's maidenhead within my abode. And you, sir, will not leave Kiltorren without taking a nuptial pledge."

Malvina's mother caught her breath. "Cedric! I have never seen you so . . . *masterful*!"

" 'Tis not a trifling matter, my dear. We cannot allow a guest to bring shame upon our house."

"But I have a quest!" Talbot cried, clearly less content with matters than the other occupants of the hall. "I have a quest that I must fulfill for my uncle."

"Then you may certainly do so," Cedric said calmly. "In a fortnight. *After* your wedding."

"What is this fixation of knights upon quests?" Deirdre demanded. "We are only rid of Burke de Montvieux and his quest . . ."

Talbot's head shot up. "Burke is gone?"

"Aye," Deirdre supplied. "Gone with Alys and half the household on some fool quest to see Brigid wed."

A lump worked in Talbot's throat. He stepped forward in evident dismay. "Alys is *gone*?"

"Aye, should Dame Fortune smile upon us for a change, we shall never see any of them again."

If Talbot was agitated before, that was as naught to his current state. "But nay, this cannot be! She cannot be gone!" He snatched up his belt and scabbard, fastening it about his waist with shaking hands. "Nay, I must find her, I must lend chase!"

"You cannot leave before your nuptials!" Deirdre declared.

"You cannot abandon my daughter in shame!" Cedric chimed in.

"I cannot remain. My quest . . ."

But Talbot got no further before Malvina launched herself out of her mother's embrace. She caught the surprised knight by the shoulders and forced him back against the wall.

His repudiation of her followed by his determination to see Alys was too much to be endured. 'Twas too close to Burke's choice for comfort, but this time Malvina had more at stake.

And she was furiously angry that this man cared more for pursuing Alys than he did for her honor.

"I will hear no more about Alys!" she cried. "Do you think I did not note how you asked after her? Do you think I did not see your gaze follow her, that I did not see she was of greater interest to you than I?"

"Well, I . . ."

Malvina gave him a shake. "How do you think that made me feel, when I was trying to win just a modicum of your attention?"

"I cannot . . ." Talbot had that cornered look that tore at Malvina's heartstrings.

"How do you think it feels to always be the unwanted one? To always be second best? To always be the plain one, the plump one, the unattractive one, the burden upon everyone?"

"I find you neither plump nor plain," Talbot dared to suggest, but Malvina was not prepared to listen to him.

"You wanted me this day," she insisted in a choked voice. "I saw it in your eyes and could not resist it. 'Twas the sweetest gift that ever I have been granted."

"Well, I . . ." Talbot colored.

"How much of a burden do you think it is to know that no one wants you, that no one finds you pleasing, that no one desires you for yourself? To watch every man's glance slide over you to linger on a poor cousin?" Malvina caught her breath and felt genuine tears gather. "To know that you will *never* be good enough, that you will *never* measure up to expectation?"

Talbot blinked. He seemed to consider this, then he looked at Malvina, truly *looked* at her for the first time. His gaze danced over her features and, to her astonishment, he smiled ever so slightly, as if what he saw was pleasing.

"I think," he said carefully, "that I know the weight of that burden quite well."

Malvina stared back at the knight, stunned that they might hold something in common. Indeed, Talbot also looked surprised. He smiled sheepishly and Malvina barely noticed her father send a runner to ensure that Godfrey kept the gates barred.

Chapter Fifteen

I F ALYS FEARED FOR THE ENDURANCE OF HER APPEAL, leaving Kiltorren provided ample fodder for her doubts.

Indeed, Ireland was populated with the most beauteous women she had ever seen. Each village, each keep, each marketplace teemed with flashing eyes and sparkling smiles. Femininity greeted her gaze at every turn, and Alys only began to realize the fullness of the assault Burke faced.

For each and every woman acknowledged him in one way or another. Some shy ones merely glanced his way; the more bold women smiled directly at him, flicked their skirts or toyed with the drawstring of their chemises. He was granted many a sensual invitation even in her presence.

What man could withstand such an assault of temptation, however noble his intent?

Burke, though, seemed almost unaware of the women. His gaze slid over them, and to Alys's surprise, he appeared deafened to their offers. He smiled only for Alys. He was always ready to offer his hand to her, always by her side to explain the wonders of what she saw for the first time.

Alys kept her hood resolutely drawn over her face, consigning the purple majesty that had erupted around her eye to the shadows, and fretted.

Their lack of coin was an issue in the harbor, for every ship wanted payment for passage, particularly since their party was comparatively large. But Burke would not accept defeat. He scoured the harbor, walked the docks, and inquired in the taverns long after the others might have lost hope.

On their second morning in Cork, the Templars sailed into port. 'Twas unusual for the warrior monks to visit into this harbor, and it almost seemed to Alys that Burke's incredible determination summoned them there.

Already the comparatively new order of knights was known for its wealth, and their ship was larger than most in the harbor. They held lands across all of Christendom, and free of ecclesiastical and secular tithes, their prosperity seemed to know no bounds.

They were gathering wool from their scattered estates, wool they would carry to Flanders to be woven into cloth, then sell throughout Christendom. They owned ships, estates in many cases, mills in Flanders, and they commandeered a formidable share of the wool trade.

And 'twas that wool which earned Alys's party their departure. Several of the men on board had been struck ill, and the Templars were short of hands to load the bales. Burke quickly struck a deal with the Templar sergeant commanding the ship. Kerwyn, Beauregard, and Burke would labor for their passage. Burke's last silver denier would combine with that toil to assure the passage of the women and Moonshadow.

Kerwyn immediately set to the labor at hand. He was strong despite his lean build, and the sergeant supervising the loading grunted with satisfaction. Edana watched with such open-mouthed wonder that Alys had to pull the girl away.

Burke saw to the settling of the women before taking up his own task, and Alys knew he intended to assure himself that all was adequate. He offered Alys his hand and, not for the first time, she felt his searching glance upon her hood.

" 'Twill be an arduous journey," he admitted in an undertone. "We halt in virtually every port known en route. But we depart with three damsels and, in the company of men sworn to God's service, we shall arrive with three damsels. 'Tis more than I could be certain of upon any other ship."

Beauregard raised his brows and interjected a gruff comment. "One can only hope these Templars adhere to their pledge of chastity more than to their vow of poverty."

"Ah, but, Beauregard," Burke mused, "I do not believe any of them would be fool enough to challenge both you and me in this."

The cook grinned, then strode off to join Kerwyn.

"Where do we land?" Edana asked. Brigid had already paled, just the rocking of the gangplank clearly unsettling her stomach.

"Le Havre, eventually," Burke supplied. "At least it has the advantage of being closer to our destination."

Alys leaned closer to him that the others did not hear. "That was your last coin, was it not?"

"Aye. I had only two," Burke admitted. " 'Twould have been enough to ensure the arrival of you and me at the tourneys, but I had not planned on a retinue."

"Nor on Beauregard. You did a fine deed there."

Burke squeezed her fingers. "No man with a heart could have abandoned him. And he has long been good to you—'tis important for kindness to know a reward."

"But how shall we travel from Le Havre? Moonshadow cannot bear all six of us!"

"Do not fear, Alys." Burke grinned. "We shall find a way. Indeed, I imagine that you and I shall become quite adept at wringing more from less."

He flicked a glance her way so quickly that Alys barely managed to avert her face in time. His thumb moved across her hand with that leisure that melted her bones and his voice dropped low. "Does the prospect trouble you overmuch?"

There were yet so many obstacles laid before them, but Alys believed that her knight could surmount any barrier. "Nay, Burke." She squeezed his hand in turn. "I trust you in this."

"Alys, we sail as soon as the wool is loaded, by the captain's decree." He brushed his lips across her fingers, sending a tingle over her flesh. "I shall expect your accounting of what happened at Kiltorren as soon as the ropes are cast off. Meet me on the deck once your cousin is settled."

And he turned to stride away. Alys did not argue, even if she did dread his response. At least there was naught he could do about the matter any longer.

❖

The sun was already dipping low when the ropes were cast off. The deck was alive with activity as men made ready to depart. The sails were hoisted aloft, fluttered, then billowed with a snap. Men called to each other, those on the docks waved farewell, Kerwyn, Beauregard, and Burke grinned, their labor complete, and wiped the sweat from their brows. The ship eased farther out to sea, and Burke took a deep breath of the salt-tinged air.

"Farewell, Kiltorren," he whispered. "Farewell to all of you."

He pivoted and found Alys already waiting at the rail, her cloak lifting in the breeze. Her back was to him, her gaze fixed on the coastline fading from view, and Burke strode across the deck to her side. Her hood was pushed back for the first time since they had left Kiltorren, her hair cast into disarray by the wind. He smiled at the way the fading sunlight picked out the gold of her hair and braced his elbows on the rail beside her.

"Gilded sunlight," he murmured. "I knew 'twould fit."

"Ah, Burke, you always seem to know what to say," Alys mused. Burke heard the smile in her voice, turned to face her, and did not know what to say.

Indeed, he gaped at the bruise staining Alys's face.

The blackened eye was not new, its shade already turning yellow around the edges and the purple fading in spots. He would guess its age at three or four days.

Before they left Kiltorren. Burke's hand rose to caress her

cheek, then he feared he would hurt her further if he touched her. His hand fell again to the rail.

Then anger flashed through him. "How did your aunt dare to strike you again?" he demanded, his words low and hot. "I thought matters were clear between her and myself."

" 'Twas Malvina." Alys lifted her hood once more. "And there is naught to be done about it now." She turned to face the horizon again, and Burke braced his hands against the rail, fighting against his unruly tide of anger.

How could she be so composed? He wanted vengeance for what she had endured, and the more onerous the better!

"Why did you not tell me of it?" he demanded. "I would have ensured a toll was paid!"

"I know." And she punctuated that with a telling glance.

"You should have told me."

Alys shook her head, a small smile curving her lips. "I know enough of you to understand that you would have done something rash in my defense," she claimed softly, no censure in her gaze. Indeed, there was a glimmer that might have been teasing in her eyes. "And we should *never* have been freed of that place."

Alys said "we" so easily that Burke could not help but grin. He braced his elbows against the rail and unabashedly studied her. "Have you a problem with my defense of my lady fair?"

"Nay, but Aunt has already won one silver denier too many from your purse."

Burke snorted. "I have a mind to fetch it back again, as a toll for this insult." He caught a glimpse of Alys's alarm and covered her hand with his. "But do not fear, we shall not return there."

Alys smiled fully, her bruise doing naught to diminish her allure. She leaned on the rail beside Burke, her arm brushing against his. "Perhaps I do not understand you as well as I thought," she mused playfully.

Burke could not halt his answering smile. "Indeed?"

"Indeed. I expected you to try to steal a kiss in this romantic moment," she charged, her dimple denting that colored cheek. "Indeed, you have been most reticent of late. Perhaps you are not the man I think you to be."

Burke chuckled. "Perhaps I am a man who has learned that the kiss my lady grants of her own volition is far sweeter than any I might steal." Alys flushed slightly at that, her eyes fairly dancing. "Truly, such kisses as yours are well worth the wait."

"Oh, you have a honeyed tongue," she teased. "Do you regale all the ladies with such glowing accounts of your love?"

"Nay, Alys. Only you." Burke captured her hand. " 'Tis you I love and you alone. 'Twill always be thus, I fear."

"Such a fate," Alys jested, and they shared a warm smile.

Though the lady did not confess a similar affliction. Burke could not help but note her omission.

But he had learned to wait for gifts from Alys, not force her hand.

'Twas a shame the task became no easier.

"Tell me at least that your opponent looks worse."

Alys laughed lightly and wrinkled her nose in a most fetching manner. "I assure you, she will be *sore*."

Burke grinned and caught his lady against him, admiring yet again her fortitude. "You were right in not trusting my response, Alys." He winked at her. "But I would appreciate your not telling all that my impulse was wrong."

The peal of her laughter was all the reward Burke needed.

That and the quick disappearance of Ireland's shore. They watched the gap of the sea grow wider and their thoughts must have turned as one to the shore they eventually would reach.

"So, are your formidable mother and cruel father smitten with each other?" Alys asked.

Burke snorted. "Nay, they two loathe each other."

Alys cast an alarmed glance his way and Burke shrugged. "There is no point garnishing the truth of it. They are mismatched and I understand it became clear soon after their nuptials. My earliest memories are of their battles. They chose to live apart when I was very young and, mercifully, their paths seldom cross. I have no doubt 'tis deliberately contrived."

"Then why do you put such stock in love's value?"

"Because love is what is missing in their marriage." Burke frowned, knowing he had to convince Alys of the merit of something she had never seen. "My father wed always to sate his lust, a lust born as much of carnal desire as his thirst for power. My mother is attractive in her way and also an heiress. He could not resist her and, for a telling moment, she could not resist him."

He pursed his lips. "She insisted upon marriage, though I have no doubt she later wished otherwise."

Burke smiled at a thoughtful Alys. "I am the result of that moment of folly, though all ended soon after my conception. My elder brother, Luc, is the result of an earlier passion of our father's, though that bride had the grace to die and leave him unfettered. My mother would never so indulge a man."

"I am not certain I want to meet this woman."

"I will protect you," Burke pledged, and Alys chuckled.

"Tell me more."

"There is not much more. They lived in a common hell of their own making, until my father dallied with a dancer from a traveling troupe. The resulting toddler arrived at our gates several years later—my brother Rowan—and my mother was so infuriated that she cast my father from Montvieux's gates."

"She did not divorce him?"

Burke smiled in mingled affection and respect. "As I said, she is disinclined to serve the will of others. And my father had no desire to lose the prestige of being associated with Montvieux. In truth, the only thing they agreed upon was that I should inherit the estate of my mother's family."

"They sound most fearsome."

Burke nodded. "When I was a child, I thought all marriages were thus, as children are wont to do. Then I trained for my spurs in a happy household. The lord and lady did not fight, they did not bed others, they did not insult each other, and they lived together in peace and contentment. I could not make sense of this, as you might imagine. The lord himself told me of the power of love, and the evidence of its effects was there before me.

"Over the years I studied couples and quickly discerned that those who claimed love between them were the happiest. 'Tis true that many matches are based on mutual trust, or affection, or respect, or even compassion, and though these may also be acceptable marriages, there is not a one that can hold a candle to a match made in love."

Burke shrugged and looked to Alys again, reassured to find that he had her full attention. "I see naught amiss with being truly happy, and in fact, far prefer it to the opposite. Having come from a marriage filled with strife, I would doubly appreciate one devoid of it."

Alys shook her head. "No marriage is devoid of strife."

"Nay, but those based upon love shake free of it more readily. I have seen it to be so, time and time again."

Alys considered him for a long moment, her eyes filled with questions. "You have seen far more of the world than I," she admitted softly. "Tell me of it."

And Burke was more than content to do precisely that.

◈

'Twas a fortnight before they landed at Le Havre. Alys had no idea there were so many ports—so many people!—beyond the circle of Kiltorren's walls. She was fascinated by their differences and similarities, and she raced to the deck each morning to spend the day by Burke's side. He told the most wondrous tales, he made her laugh, he surprised her with his insight.

And if he braced his hands against the rail on either side of her, effectively holding Alys in his arms, well, she was certain there was naught amiss with his ensuring that she did not lose her footing on the wet rolling deck.

Brigid was pale when they disembarked, for she had been violently ill for all of the journey. She closed her eyes in relief when her feet were on solid ground again, her fingers clung to Alys, and a ghost of a smile curved her lips.

"No more ships," she declared, and Alys felt guilty for having enjoyed those days with Burke while her cousin suffered.

There was an even more marked bounce to Edana's steps these days, her smiles cast at Kerwyn more often than not. Alys did not doubt that they two had spent considerable time together as well. She could not chide the maid for seizing happiness and, indeed, wished she shared Edana's cheerful optimism.

Burke strode back to the small company, Beauregard lumbering in his wake. Behind, Kerwyn coaxed Moonshadow onto the gangplank, that steed looking less than amused by the journey he had endured.

"Dame Fortune smiles upon us," Burke said with his own smile for Alys. "The Templar sergeant asks us to take some horses to Paris for him. He was pleased with our aid, though much of his gratitude is likely due to Beauregard's skill with salt fish and dill."

The former cook of Kiltorren had taken to the ship's galley when Brigid fell ill, determined to see her regain her health. The sea, though, had undermined all of his efforts and, indeed, had won most of them.

"One must eat with dignity, regardless of one's circumstance." The large man sniffed. "What I could have done with a plump hen! Lady Brigid would not have faded so had I more than fish at hand."

Brigid groaned and clutched her belly. "I beg of you, do not even *speak* of fish!"

"It occurs to me that a night with finer fare might be welcome." Burke tossed a wink to Alys, and she guessed what he would suggest. When she was privy to his plans, she found she had no objection to his turning matters his way. Indeed, this might lead Brigid to happiness, and Alys could hardly wait to see the result. "A friend of mine lives not far from our path. Indeed, if we rode with vigor, we could reach his abode this very afternoon."

"If this keep had even an old hen to spare, 'twould be good for Lady Brigid," Beauregard muttered protectively.

"Indeed." Burke smiled. "I have no doubt that there is much that will be good for Lady Brigid at Crevy."

Alys answered his smile with her own, hoping against hope that he was right.

The towers of Crevy-sur-Seine rose before them in the fading sunlight of the late afternoon. 'Twas not a small estate, by any means, and Alys realized at the sight of it just how paltry Kiltorren must have appeared to Burke.

Was Montvieux as fine as this? A new doubt joined the legion already occupying her thoughts. Indeed, Alys could not imagine that any man could shun so wealthy a holding and not come to regret its loss.

Or blame the woman on whose credit he cast aside his prize. Would bitterness come between herself and Burke over his surrender of Montvieux? Alys nibbled her bottom lip and studied the towers rising before them.

The four tall square towers of Crevy's keep were joined by high walls, then encircled with yet another high wall. Within this space were the stables and workshops, the village spilling around the road outside the portcullis. A low flat river flowed behind the keep, the gently rolling pastures were a verdant green, and the forest in the distance was filled with cool shadows.

The sentry let out a hoot of recognition when he spied Burke. At his cry, people spilled from the stables and the armory, calling greetings and waving with abandon. Half a dozen children ran behind the horses, not a one of them as ragged as the most prosperous villein at Kiltorren.

A finely dressed man strode out of the keep, both his authoritative wave and the way all turned to him telling Alys his identity. He was indeed slightly shorter than Burke, lighter of hair and darker of eye, though he looked to be of the same age. His build was muscular and trim; he moved with a warrior's ease.

"Do you think he will do?" Burke murmured, and Alys could only nod before the man halted beside them.

"Brother Burke!" he cried, though Alys could make no sense of the appellation. "What an unexpected pleasure!"

"Aye, Guillaume, 'tis good to see you as well." Burke dismounted, the two shook hands, grinned at each other, and then abruptly embraced. They laughed and exchanged pleasantries in the manner of old, good friends.

In the meantime, a short woman with silver hair made her way across the bailey with tiny steps. She let out a cry of delight when she saw who had arrived and ran the rest of the way. Burke laughed and swept her into a hug when she reached his side. She giggled at his embrace, kicking her feet when he lifted her high.

Then she clicked her tongue and framed his face in her hands, though she had to stand on her toes to do so. "You handsome rogue, 'tis too long since you have shared our company." She kissed his cheeks three times.

Burke bowed deeply, pressing a kiss to her hand. "Lady Crevy, you look younger and more beautiful than ever."

"Pshaw!" The lady blew out her lips at him with endearing familiarity. "You have not changed in the least little bit, always a drop of honey from your lips." To Alys's amazement, she reached up and pinched Burke's cheeks with affection. "Have you brought a bride this time, *chevalier*? Truly, I despair of the two of you!"

Guillaume rolled his eyes at his mother's comments and glanced over their party, his gaze lingering on Brigid.

Then Burke turned to smile at Alys and she forgot anything

else. "I have brought a lady," he said quietly, a glow dawning in his eyes as he offered her his hand. Alys pushed back her hood, grateful that her bruise had all but disappeared, and smiled. "Might I present Lady Alys of Kiltorren? Alys, my friend Guillaume de Crevy and his mother, Lady Crevy. And Lady Alys's cousin . . ."

Guillaume's eyes widened. "Did you say Lady Alys?"

"*The* Alys?" his mother demanded, her gaze bright as she stepped closer.

To Alys's amazement, Burke looked slightly discomfited. Indeed, there was a dull flush rising on the back of his neck. "You need not make such a fuss," he began, but Guillaume hooted with laughter.

" 'Tis her! 'Tis *the* Alys!" He clapped Burke on the back and stepped forward to offer Alys his aid in dismounting. "Forgive my manners, Lady Alys, but we had begun to doubt that this marvel of feminine virtue existed. Welcome, welcome to Château Crevy."

When her feet were on the ground, Guillaume kissed her hand with a flourish. "I am very glad that you have seen fit to grace this knight with your company. Indeed, his lofty tales did not do justice to your beauty."

Burke had told his friends of her?

Lady Crevy captured Alys's hands with a firm grip and her eyes sparkled merrily. "Ah, *si belle,*" she whispered with approval, then kissed Alys's cheeks as she had Burke's. "*Bienvenue,* Alys. As you may guess, we have heard much of you. 'Tis good to finally meet you."

Guillaume winked. "Truly, Brother Burke's moping grew tedious."

Burke had moped in her absence? Impossible!

All the same, there was something so genuine about this pair that Alys could not have doubted them. They certainly regarded Burke with open affection, their teasing manner making Alys conclude that they were both loyal friends and good company.

"You gild the lily, Guillaume," Burke complained gruffly. "Alys has no desire to hear your empty flattery."

His very manner gave credence to his friend's claim. "But I should like to hear of this moping," Alys said lightly. Burke shot her a dark look and she marvelled at his mood.

Guillaume could not hide his amusement as he glanced between the two of them. "He is not assured of his success as yet," he confided to his mother, and that lady nodded agreement.

"Aye, and his legendary charm wins him naught." She leaned forward and rapped a fingertip on Alys's arm, her eyes sparkling. "I like a woman who knows her own value." She indicated Burke with her thumb. "Indeed, 'tis good to see something not come readily to this one's will."

"Enough already!" Burke declared with rare impatience. "Must we linger in the bailey while you gossip about naught?"

"Naught?" Guillaume echoed and Burke averted his gaze. Their host knight did not move, his lips quirking with amusement. He leaned closer to Alys, his tone confidential. "Has he confessed to you the reason why we call him Brother Burke?"

"Guillaume!"

Alys shook her head, intrigued as much by Guillaume's confession as Burke's agitation. "He is no monk."

Lady Crevy laughed. "Nay, indeed!" She shook a finger at Burke. "She has eyes in her head, your Alys."

Burke folded his arms across his chest and looked doubly grim. 'Twas clear he did not believe he could halt his friend and equally clear that he did not like that fact.

Alys wondered what Guillaume knew that she did not.

"But Burke has been as chaste as a monk," Guillaume supplied, his smile a merry one. "At least since the day three years past that he rode to tourney at one Castle Kiltorren."

Alys blinked. Burke had been chaste? There must be some mistake!

"Three years?" she asked, her astonishment so evident that Lady Crevy laughed again.

" 'Tis impossible, *non*? That this knight who could have any woman he chose—and more often than not, *did* choose— should avoid all women." She smiled at Burke with affection. "Such is the power of *amour*."

Burke's complexion turned yet more ruddy. "I hardly think this is fitting conversation among ladies," he said with a huff. "If you shall not see to the horses, then I shall be compelled to do so myself."

"Aye, there was naught to be heard from him, save Alys this and Alys that," Guillaume continued, apparently untroubled by Burke's manner. "He regaled us with tales of Alys's beauty, Alys's sweet nature, Alys's heavenly kisses. Indeed, there were nights he seemed determined to empty my cellars, bemoaning the absence of marvelous Alys."

Could this be true? Burke cast a lethal glance at his old comrade and Alys could only conclude that he did not like having his amorous history—or its recent lack—paraded before her.

"He would look at no woman, and I confess that we began a small wager." Guillaume winked at Alys. "We set every whore in Paris after him, and no small number of ambitious ladies, not to mention widows skilled in the arts of seduction." He shrugged. "No result, save the lightening of my purse. Indeed, my own sister tried to tempt him on a dare, but without success. I must tell you that she was much put out by her failure, for Eglantine puts great stock in her charms."

Burke exhaled mightily. "I shall see Moonshadow stabled while you recount such frivolity, for 'tis clear that you do not intend to see to customary measures of hospitality." He grasped the steed's reins and strode off to the stables, the very image of male displeasure.

"You have embarrassed him," Lady Crevy chided, her tone unrepentant. She turned a sparkling glance on Alys. " 'Tis good for him, *non?*"

"And he will survive." Guillaume squeezed Alys's hand, dismissing Burke's displeasure with a wave. "You cannot imagine what a delight 'tis to finally meet you," he said, his gaze sincere. "Truly I am glad you two have found each other again. I know that you will be happy together."

"Do not be fooled by your knight's flattery," Lady Crevy added with equal seriousness. "But one glance at his pride when he rode through these gates told me all I needed to know, for I have known Burke since he was a boy." Lady Crevy patted Alys's cheek with affection. " 'Tis you he loves, Alys, and no other, and 'twill be thus for all his days."

Alys glanced after the rapidly departing Burke and knew she had once again done him a disservice. She had believed his attention would be fleeting, when indeed he had remained committed to her all these years, even when they were apart. There had been no pledge between them—indeed, Burke thought himself declined—yet he had been faithful to her memory.

'Twas more, far more, than she could have expected.

But then Burke consistently was far more than Alys might expect. He always kept his pledge and if they exchanged vows, his commitment would only be more than it had been these last years in the absence of one.

'Twas true enough that matters might change between them in the years ahead, despite good intentions. But 'twas equally true that Alys could lose Burke simply because of her own fear of accepting what he offered. If she took no chance, there could be no gain—but taking that risk could grant her all her dreams came true.

Alys had more wits than to lose a dream, simply for failing to reach for it. She loved Burke. She would show him the truth of it by facing her deepest fear.

Alys would step directly into the error that her mother had made, the error that had wrought Alys's life as it was, and she would put her trust in Burke to keep his pledge and make all come right in the end.

No lesser deed would do.

❖

Brigid felt decidedly ill.

Her stomach rolled, though 'twas empty beyond all. The magnificence of Crevy wavered around her as if she saw it through a curtain of water.

"Well done, *Maman*," this friend of Burke's declared to his mother after Alys excused herself and fled after Burke. "Am I wrong that you knew from the first who she was?"

"But one look at his face and I guessed the truth," the older woman declared. "And Alys's evident dismay when he flattered me told all too well what was awry. The poor *demoiselle* did not know to trust Burke."

"But now 'tis fixed." Brigid could hear the smile in Burke's friend's voice.

" 'Twould have been fixed at some point, if I know our Burke," his mother declared. "The man has a rare conviction."

Brigid closed her eyes and felt herself sway in the saddle. She grasped at Edana but missed. All tipped dangerously and Brigid cried out as she felt herself slipping toward the ground.

"My lady!" Edana squealed, and snatched at her.

"My lady!" Cook bellowed, and Brigid heard his heavy footfall.

Then she fell.

But Brigid felt herself snatched out of the air and cradled against a masculine chest. To her surprise, she opened her eyes to find that 'twas Burke's friend who held her, not the cook. This knight's dark eyes were filled with concern.

"Burke's friend," she murmured, as if that explained everything, and closed her eyes against the weakness coursing through her. She leaned her head against the knight's shoulder because 'twas there and decided he had quite nice shoulders.

They were broad and strong.

"Aye, and a man devoid of manners," he said ruefully. "I can only apologize for my failure to see you at ease, Lady . . . Lady . . ."

"She is Lady Brigid of Kiltorren, the cousin of Lady Alys," Cook supplied, his voice close to Brigid. She could feel him hovering protectively. "She was taken ill on the ship, but I know that a good broth of chicken would do wonders to aid her recovery."

"No fish," Brigid insisted quietly. She thought the knight holding her laughed under his breath.

"No fish, my lady," he agreed in an undertone. "You have my personal guarantee."

Brigid opened her eyes at that to find the knight watching her. He had kindly eyes and he smiled slightly when she met his gaze.

Just the sight was fortifying. Brigid took a breath and tried to recall her manners. She waved vaguely at the keep surrounding them. "Your home is l-l-lovely. Thank you for welcoming us."

" 'Tis a poor welcome that leaves a lady falling from her steed in a faint." He grimaced, though apparently not at her stammer.

"But you were r-r-right. Alys had to know that Burke l-l-loves her," she insisted. She smiled wanly for the knight's mother, who watched her carefully.

The lady smiled and came closer. "You are a sweet one to ignore your own discomfort for the sake of your cousin. Such selflessness is rare indeed." She reached to touch Brigid's shoulder. "But you have no more to fear, *ma petite*. Now they will wed and you shall have your broth."

But Brigid frowned and shook her head. "Nay, nay, they cannot." She tasted again her certainty that she alone would stand in the way of Burke and Alys's love. Even her illness delayed matters further, for Brigid could tempt no man in her current sorry state. For two weeks Brigid had fretted aboard the ship, and now she was fairly bursting with concern.

These people seemed so nice—surely they would understand?

Maybe they knew a man who would feel sympathy for her plight. That single thought sent Brigid's confession spilling forth.

"Alys cannot wed before me and I have no betrothed," Brigid admitted in a rush. "Burke said he would find me a husband, he would take me to P-P-Paris, but Mother said no man in Paris would have me." She took a shaking breath and dared to look to the older lady again, who frowned worriedly as if she shared Brigid's concerns.

Brigid heard her own voice rise in her anxiety. "I have no fine P-P-Paris manners, I will not find a husband, and Alys will not be able to wed Burke. 'Twill b-b-be all my fault!"

Shaking in the wake of the longest speech she had ever made, Brigid began to cry. She leaned against the knight's shoulder and wept from the depths of her soul, as ashamed of her behavior as her ineligibility yet unable to stop.

"Oh, *ma petite*. You are so tired that all hangs heavy on your shoulders." The lady brushed the hair back from Brigid's brow with unexpected tenderness, her voice low and soothing. "But rest assured, fine manners are not such an asset as that."

Brigid sniffled and, compelled by the certainty in that woman's tone, looked at Lady Crevy. "Nay?"

The lady smiled warmly. "Nay, *ma petite*. You have a gen-erosity of heart that is far more compelling than any manners could be." She flicked a glance to her son. "Do you not think so, Guillaume?"

"Indeed," that man said with unmistakable resolve. "Perhaps you might be persuaded to linger a few days at Crevy," he suggested with a quietude that Brigid found very appealing.

But protest rose immediately to her lips. "But I cannot linger! Alys and Burke—"

"Cannot expect you to travel when you are ill," the knight interjected firmly. "Indeed, I could not countenance your departure before your health is restored." He lifted one brow and smiled, just for her. "Please agree to stay."

Brigid found herself wanting very much to do precisely that. She looked to Lady Crevy who nodded vigorously, then smiled shyly for the knight. "I should like to linger here. 'Tis very pretty."

His smile flashed brighter than the sunlight. "Good!"

Before Brigid could respond, he strode toward the keep, calling for stablehands to take the horses. Brigid was amazed at the way all leapt to do his bidding. His mother called for a chamber to be made ready, and the bailey burst into activity. Cook and Edana ran behind them, Cook muttering about stock, Edana gasping in delight as they stepped into Crevy's hall.

But Brigid was watching the knight who carried her and thinking that he was not only handsome but very noble indeed. She liked how his eyes sparkled when he smiled at her.

But a knight like this must have a beautiful heiress as a betrothed. Brigid chewed her bottom lip and worried that she truly would be the cause of Alys's unhappiness after all.

Chapter Sixteen

BURKE!"

Burke spun in the shadows of Crevy's familiar stables to find Alys silhouetted in the portal. She was slightly out of breath and her cheeks were flushed, her hood cast back.

"Again I owe you an apology," she said with a fleeting smile. "But this I hope will be the last. I am sorry that I did not trust the fullness of your intent, I am sorry that I feared you would lose interest in me over time, I am sorry that I have always heeded the endorsement of others before your own pledge, and I am sorry that I doubted your fidelity."

Burke blinked, astonished by this confession.

"I have not trusted you fully, Burke, and that is no way to begin our match." Alys stepped closer, her eyes gleaming. "And I would seal my apology with a kiss."

Burke's pulse pounded at the prospect. Alys smiled as if she read his very thoughts, casting her arms around his neck and lifting her lips to his. Burke pulled her to her toes, slanted his lips across hers, and kissed her fully.

Alys trusted him fully. 'Twas all the more of a marvel for its unexpectedness—and perhaps worth the embarrassment Guillaume had extracted.

Their kiss quickly became incendiary, the tangling of their tongues setting a fire in Burke's blood that threatened to burn out of control. Alys pressed against him, her hands gripping his hair as if she would urge him to eat her whole.

And Burke was sorely tempted to do that. Ye gods, but Alys learned quickly! Everything within him clamored that he claim a stall in this very stable and bolt the door until they had had their fill of each other.

But 'twould be a dishonor to her.

Instead, Burke dragged his lips from hers and took an unsteady breath. Alys too was out of breath. Her eyes were wide and dark, her lips were swollen. More of her hair than usual hung in tendrils against her neck.

She was the most beguiling woman he had ever seen.

And she would be his bride.

"What is amiss?" she asked unevenly. "Why did you halt?"

"All is aright, Alys." Burke lifted a hand to her jaw, struck anew by her mingled softness and strength. "But as before, I would not dishonor you. We will wait for our nuptial night."

To Burke's surprise, his lady shook her head with vehemence. "Nay, Burke. We have waited long enough, you and I." She stretched to brush her lips across his. "I do not want to wait any longer."

Burke caught his breath. "But, Alys . . ."

"But, Burke, I trust you to do as you say in this," she insisted, her eyes filled with conviction. "I *trust* you to wed me as you have vowed, and I would give you evidence of that trust. Indeed, I have doubted you too long."

"But, Alys, there could be a child."

She smiled up at him, confidence lighting her features. "Then you have best keep your pledge soon."

Burke could not refuse her. He captured her hand within his and glanced over the stables, seeing only now that there were many watchful eyes.

"Not here," he said under his breath, then suddenly recalled the perfect trysting place. None would disturb them and he had oft envisioned Alys in that very spot.

He kissed her palm, then wordlessly lifted her to Moonshadow's saddle. Burke swung up behind her and gave the destrier his spurs, not caring who saw them depart together.

◈

'Twas on the eve of his scheduled wedding that Talbot left Kiltorren. Indeed, it had taken that long to induce Cedric and all those around him to drink themselves to a stupor.

Talbot glanced back only once, and that from Kiltorren's own gates. He paused beneath the open portcullis—Godfrey's objections silenced with a quick blow to the back of the guard's head—and felt an uncharacteristic pang of guilt.

For Malvina would not have the wedding day she so desired. 'Twas more than her disappointment at root, though. Talbot had taken the maidenhead of a noblewoman, and his very flight left that woman compromised. His uncle would not approve of that, and indeed, a corner of his own heart felt the shadow of shame.

Malvina would likely *never* have a wedding day, and that troubled Talbot much more than he had thought it would. To be sure, the woman was a virago when denied her desire, but Talbot could well understand her frustration with that circumstance.

Aye, there was something about Malvina that intrigued him, that Talbot could not deny. He had savored her lust, he liked that she strove to win what she desired, regardless of the cost.

And he could well understand her sense of inadequacy.

But there was no question of abandoning his uncle's quest or even his own agenda. Talbot had to ensure his own future. He could not let this Alys challenge his legacy.

He had to leave Kiltorren.

But 'twas with surprising reluctance that Talbot turned his back upon that keep, snarled at Henri, and rode with all haste for the coast. He had to return to France, and with all speed possible, for his prey was two weeks' ahead of him in this.

Nay, Talbot did not imagine for a moment that any man would be fool enough to cast aside a wealthy estate in exchange for naught. Burke—and Alys—would be at Montvieux.

Talbot could only hope he arrived there in time.

Burke dismounted when Crevy's keep was lost behind a bend of the river and reached to lock his hands around Alys's waist. The sky was a perfect hue of blue overhead, there was not a cloud to be seen, the river gurgled and splashed to their right. Even the village was out of view, the tolling of the church's bell echoing distantly over the land. Crevy's fields sloped away from the river on either bank, and the shadow of the forest loomed just ahead.

Burke folded his hand around Alys's own and led her into the shadows of the woods. There, by the river, the trees did not grow as densely and the sunlight scattered on the forest floor. Alys watched as he tethered Moonshadow within the shelter of the trees, where the beast could reach both river and undergrowth. Burke took his great fur-lined cloak, smiled for Alys, then led her onward.

Within a half-dozen steps, it seemed as if they two were alone. Alys heard the distant movement of small creatures, the call of birds, the incessant chortling of the river. Burke led her to a sun-dappled glade where the branches arched high overhead and the pale green leaves fluttered against the azure sky. She could see the flash of the river through the shrubbery on one side and knew she had never visited a more peaceful spot in all her days.

Burke cast his cloak upon the ground and turned to her with a smile, propping his hands on his hips as he glanced about himself. "What do you think?"

"I think it most odd that you knew exactly where this place

could be found," she teased, bold with new confidence that he cared for her alone.

Burke grinned. "I *have* visited here before."

"In those years before you came to Kiltorren?"

"Nay, 'twas Eglantine's choice when she sought to win Guillaume's wager."

"Without success."

Burke glanced at Alys, as if amused by her certainty that he had been faithful. "Aye." His lips twisted. "You shall mock me if I confess that the sunlight through the trees reminded me of the gloss of your hair."

Alys sobered. "And that is why you declined her."

Burke's smile faded in turn and he lifted one finger to her jaw. "I could only think of you, Alys. I have oft imagined you here, with your hair loosed over your shoulders." He stroked her cheek, heat dawning in his gaze and beneath Alys's flesh. There was a catch in his voice when he continued. "Will you unbind your hair?"

Alys kissed his fingers, removed her circlet and veil, and entrusted them both to Burke. He carefully laid them aside, and she unknotted the tie securing her braid. Burke watched her so avidly that Alys found herself smiling as her hair was worked free. She ran her fingers through its wavy mass, shook her head, and let it cascade over her shoulders.

The wonder on Burke's features was all she could have hoped for. He lifted a handful of her hair and let it spill over his fingers, watching with a smile as the sunlight glinted in its waves.

" 'Tis so very soft," he mused, flicking a glance to Alys's eyes. He stepped closer, then speared his fingers through it and cupped her nape in the strength of his hands.

Alys caught her breath, the intimacy of his touch making her heart race. "Gilded sunlight," Burke teased, and she laughed before he kissed her.

Then there was naught to laugh about. Alys could taste the difference in Burke's manner, for his kiss was languorous and thorough, seductive and purposeful. This time he would not halt at kisses, this time he would hold naught back. Alys felt a flicker of anticipation, for she trusted Burke to ensure her pleasure in this mystery of the intimacy between men and women.

Indeed, she could hardly wait to know more.

Burke's tongue eased between her teeth, the surety of his touch making Alys's knees melt. She leaned against him, surrendering all as his hands drifted down her back and lifted her against him. Alys revelled in the strength of him. She clutched the corded strength of his neck and felt the imprint of his hauberk through both his tunic and her own kirtle.

"It seems to me that we are too heavily garbed," Burke murmured. "Will you aid me with my hauberk this time?"

Alys chuckled and shook a playful finger at him. "Aye, if you do not vex me overmuch."

Burke's eyes flashed, then he kissed her with a lazy deliberation that left her breathless. "Are you vexed, my lady fair?" he whispered into her ear, his breath making her shiver.

"Aye," Alys declared, enjoying the flash of surprise in his eyes. "For we are too heavily garbed."

Burke chuckled, then kissed her quickly before he stepped away. He unbuckled his belt and laid his sword and dagger aside. He hauled his tabard over his head and cast it aside, then granted her a significant glance.

Alys stepped to his side, and between the two of them, the hauberk was quickly dispatched. Burke flexed his shoulders when its weight was removed, the way his hair was tousled and, indeed, the very breadth of him, making Alys tingle. He was so very masculine, so very different from her.

'Twas as if he understood that she might be shy about her own nudity, for Burke seemed bent on baring his own flesh first. He kicked off his boots and pulled his chemise over his head, casting it into the pile with a flourish.

"You are not very careful with your garb," Alys commented when he stood before her in his chausses alone.

"I make haste on this day," he confessed with a warm glint in his eyes. "But do not fear, I shall show exemplary tidiness when we share quarters."

With that he lifted her hands and placed them on the tangle of dark hair in the middle of his chest. Alys inhaled sharply to find that warm flesh so suddenly beneath her fingers, but Burke smiled down at her. "Alys, I am all yours."

The implication made Alys catch her breath. Burke granted her the chance to satisfy her curiosity.

Emboldened by the admiration in his eyes, Alys did precisely that. She slid her hands across Burke's chest, exploring the differences between them with her touch. She grazed the flatness of his nipples with her fingertips, surprised by the way he stiffened. Alys repeated the move, then gently slid her nails across them, enjoying how Burke caught his breath. She glanced up to find his gaze shimmering with heat.

The sign of her effect upon him was intoxicating. Alys ran her hands over him with increasing boldness. She felt every ripple of muscle, ran her fingertips over the contour of each rib. She found the precise spot where Burke was ticklish and returned to it mercilessly. He chuckled and watched her, perfectly content to let her take her leisure in exploring him.

And Alys did. "You are uncommonly patient."

Burke grinned. " 'Tis not without its own reward," he replied silkily. "Indeed, I am glad you persuaded me to this course."

Alys kissed him lightly, then examined his arms, his shoulders, his neck, his back; she circled behind him and ran her hands over his flesh. She slid her hands up the middle of his back, speared her fingertips though his hair, and felt him shiver. Alys pressed herself against Burke's back, his buttocks fitting against her belly, and leaned her cheek against his shoulder blade. She wrapped her arms around him and let her hands rove over his chest, retracing their course over his ribs to his lean waist.

Alys's hands hesitated at the top of Burke's chausses, knowing what was there and uncertain she was brave enough to touch. Burke waited for a long moment, then gently guided her hands to the drawstring.

Then he waited anew.

Alys closed her eyes, breathed deeply of his scent, and let one hand wander over his chausses below the drawstring. 'Twas easier in a way to examine him blindly, with her fingertips, and without Burke being able to see her maidenly blushes.

Although Alys had no doubt that he could feel the heat of her burning cheeks. Her hand eased down from his waist and encountered the hard shaft within his chausses.

Burke stopped breathing.

Alys let her other hand follow suit, her fingers closing around this part of him and squeezing experimentally.

"Ye gods!" Burke muttered, as if his teeth were clenched.

Alys peeked around his shoulder, relinquishing the grip of one hand to have a better look at his strained expression. "Is that painful?" she asked, her fingers repeating the deed more gently.

Burke gasped, he blanched, but there was no mistaking the heat in his eyes. " 'Tis exquisite torture,' he said with a rueful grin.

Alys knew her lack of understanding showed, for Burke shoved a hand through his hair, looking truly troubled in a most attractive way. "I shall show you the meaning of that soon enough," he said with a growl. "But look first at what you have wrought."

Alys unknotted the drawstring, then gave it a tug. Burke's

chausses, though, did not fall of their own accord, for they were caught upon the part of him she held.

And 'twas clear the man would do naught to aid her in this. He folded his arms across his chest and waited anew. "You leave me all the labor," Alys teased.

Burke grinned. "You demanded no less of me. And trust me, my Alys, you shall have your due."

Alys eased the dark wool free, running her hands beneath it to work it over his buttocks and thighs. She gasped when she saw what she had freed. " 'Tis so big!"

Burke's eyes twinkled with vigor. "That would be your fault."

Alys touched him with tentative fingertips and that part of him seemed to swell to her touch. "Is it always thus?"

Burke inhaled anew at her touch, then his smile turned rueful. "Only in your presence, or when I think of you."

"Is it painful?"

"Only when left in this state for prolonged periods."

And the man had desired her for three years. Alys bit her lip. She glanced at Burke and was unable to dispel the impression that he was mightily amused. She propped a hand on her hip to regard him, her blush rising again. "No doubt you find this amusing—"

"On the contrary," Burke interrupted smoothly, "I find your innocence totally enchanting."

He smiled with a warmth that made Alys flush yet more. She caressed him again, fascinated by his response to her touch, then looked to him anew. "How do you ease its state?"

"Ha!" Burke's grin flashed. "I thought you would never ask!"

Alys laughed and danced away from him when he might have caught her in his embrace. She shook a finger at him. "I shall guess that it has to do with the shedding of my garb!"

"Not necessarily," Burke declared in a low voice, then

kicked his chausses aside to lend chase in the full glory of his nudity. "But 'twould only be chivalrous for me to offer my aid, if you so desire."

Alys tossed her hair and held her ground. "I shall save a drawstring for you," she declared with a smile. Burke halted to watch as she shed her cloak.

Alys untied the girdle knotted around her waist and kicked off her shoes. She untied the garters of her stockings and peeled them off, then unfastened the neck of her kirtle. Her trembling fingers untied the lacings along its sides. Alys watched Burke as she shed the wool garment, hoping against hope that he found her as pleasing as she found him.

But the glow in his eyes when she stood only in her chemise was undiminished. "I certainly hope that you will fold your garments with greater care when we share quarters," he commented with a quirk of his brow.

Alys laughed, appreciating his attempt to set her at ease in this moment. She flicked the ends of the drawstring tie at him, and her mouth went dry. " 'Tis your task," she managed to say.

Burke frowned. "And my chemise, unless I miss my guess." Alys chuckled in acknowledgement.

He closed the distance between them with a single step, lifted his hand to the tie, and gave it a gentle tug. Her laughter fell silent as the bow untied, the gathering eased, and the chemise gaped. The warmth of Burke's hands closed over Alys's shoulders, his gaze fixed unswervingly upon hers, and he eased the linen away with one smooth gesture.

Alys felt the cool air against her skin. She shook the chemise free of her wrists, then Burke folded her against his warmth. The feel of his skin bare against her own made Alys gasp, then his lips closed over hers. Burke lifted her softness against his strength, his hardness pressed against her belly, and Alys could not get enough of his kiss.

Suddenly Burke lifted his lips from hers and swept her into his arms, his eyes glinting with mischief. Alys made a little sound of protest, for she was far from finished with kissing him.

"I did vow to teach you of exquisite torture," he reminded her with a wicked grin.

Alys could not wait to learn more. Burke lay her on the fur of his cloak and stretched out beside her, his hand cupping her breast. His thumb eased across the nipple, and Alys gasped at the tide of pleasure he awakened.

Then Burke bent to take that sensitive peak in his mouth. He suckled with increasing ardor, and Alys could not believe his wondrous caress. The tingle he had long ago awakened became a roar of demand, though Alys did not know how to sate it.

But Burke, she was certain, did.

His tongue worked against her with a diligence that she had come to trust in this knight. Alys clutched at his hair, the soft tickle of the fur beneath driving her to distraction, yet Burke continued undeterred.

He slipped his supporting arm beneath her, his fingers closing on the back of her waist. Alys was trapped against him and could imagine nowhere else she would rather be. He slipped one muscled thigh between her own, his free hand abandoning her breast and easing lower.

When his finger slipped into the nest of curls at the apex of her thighs, Alys thought she might burst with pleasure. She cried out at Burke's sure touch, then gasped as he caressed her with persuasive ease. Burke ran a teasing row of kisses up her neck, until he nibbled at her earlobe.

"Trust me, Alys," he whispered, the fan of his breath taking her desire to new heights. "The reward is well worth the journey."

Alys did not think the journey was without merit either, but she could not find the words to tell her knight as much. She gripped his broad shoulders, eagerly returning his long slow kiss. Alys felt a wetness spread between her thighs as he caressed her and a tension build beneath her skin. She writhed against Burke, loving the brush of his chest hair against her taut nipples.

'Twas unlike anything she had ever felt before and Alys wanted only more. Burke's fingers worked with an undeniable deliberation as Alys kissed him with all the ardor she was feeling. She felt faint and shivered when his fingers slid inside her, his thumb still easing across the sensitive pearl that drove her to distraction.

" 'Tis there I will go," he murmured. Alys's fingers wandered between them to touch his hardness in understanding, and Burke nodded against her throat. "Aye, Alys, within you is the only relief for this state."

"Then come within me," she whispered.

"Not yet." Alys looked into his silvery eyes once more and he smiled crookedly. "First I will see you touch the stars."

Alys was on her back, Burke leaning over her. His fingers teased with renewed vigor. Knowing that she alone stood in the way of his relief, Alys surrendered to the sensation building within her.

The dragon in her belly roared, Burke caught her close, Alys twisted but knew she would find no escape from this knight's loving touch. She loved Burke and he loved her. They would make their way together, secure in the circle of that love.

For Burke, Alys knew well enough, would surrender to no challenge that stood in the way of what he believed.

He slipped two strong fingers within her in that very moment and Alys clutched his shoulders at the resulting surge of pleasure, her love for him touching the flame to the tinder.

And she cried out in delight as the fire ripped through her veins, gasping when Burke's lips closed demandingly over her own. She saw naught but a blinding flash of light, she felt naught but Burke, she tasted those stars.

Exquisite torture, indeed. 'Twas exactly as Burke had promised her.

But then Alys had learned to expect no less.

"Why the smile?" Burke murmured when Alys's eyelids fluttered open again. He did not know how long he had simply held her, watching the crimson fade from her cheeks, watching her doze within the circle of his embrace, watching the sunlight toy with the majesty of her hair.

The moment he had dreamed of for so long was here, and Burke did not intend to miss any of it.

Alys's smile broadened, her eyes echoing the sun-flecked hues of this secret glade. She brushed his hair back from his forehead, her movements languid. Burke bent to brush his lips across hers and she sighed.

"Dare I hope you were pleased?"

"Sweet torture," she confirmed, and looped her arms around his neck. That dimple reappeared, her eyes twinkled with mischief, then suddenly she rubbed herself against his erection. "Yet you are still in such troubled state."

'Twas a marvel to see the understanding sweep over her and a new confidence color her every movement. Burke knew he would never tire of watching Alys, nor, indeed, of tempting that smile.

"We could see to that now," he whispered against her throat. Her sigh filled his ear as he kissed her creamy flesh, and she arched against him in a way that made him nearly explode with desire. Burke eased himself between the lady's thighs as they kissed and braced himself on his elbows above her.

When their lips finally parted, they were both breathing quickly. Alys ran her hands over Burke's shoulders, then flicked a nervous glance down between them.

"You truly go there?"

" 'Tis easier than one might expect, but the first time may

be difficult." Burke touched the tip of his nose fleetingly to hers. "You must promise to tell me if there is pain."

Alys nodded and bit her lip in trepidation. But Burke did not want her to be afraid. He captured her lips beneath his own once more, entangling their fingers as he eased closer to his goal.

She returned his kiss hungrily, her legs parting to accommodate him as she braced her feet on the back of his calves. The imprint of those toes on his own flesh nearly sent Burke surging forward, but he gritted his teeth and moved with excruciating slowness.

His Alys. She was so very wet and warm. Burke closed his eyes when his erection nudged against her softness. He eased closer and met resistance, then broke his kiss to watch his lady.

"Tell me," he urged, and Alys nodded quickly, her wondrous eyes wide. He moved again and she caught her breath, her fingers tightening on his own.

But the warm embrace of Alys surrounded him so sweetly that Burke had no breath of his own to ask. Indeed, he touched his brow to her shoulder and closed his eyes, aware of naught but her beguiling softness beneath and around him. Eventually he opened his eyes, only to be greeted by the lady's gentle smile.

" 'Twas just a twinge," she whispered, then wriggled her hips encouragingly.

Burke gasped and slipped further into her welcoming grip. His own tension eased when Alys's fingers relaxed their hold upon his. Finally buried to the hilt and certain paradise could be no more than this, Burke paused for a moment to let the lady become accustomed to him.

"That was not much," she confided. "Indeed, I had expected more . . ." Alys got no further before Burke tentatively moved. She gasped with pleasure, her eyes widened, and she clutched his shoulders once more. "Burke!"

He moved again and again, knowing he would not last long

and wanting to ensure she found satisfaction in this. He could not resist the creamy length of Alys's throat, the perfection of her ears, the ripe invitation of her lips.

She kissed him so demandingly she nigh drove him wild, her ardor rising with every stroke. Burke extricated one of his hands and managed to work his fingers between them, his thumb caressing Alys anew as he sought a rhythm to please them both.

Alys twisted and writhed beneath him again, her every move driving Burke onward. He felt the heat build but grimly hung on, waiting for Alys's release. He felt sweat bead on his back, his legs were clenched, he was bigger and harder than he had ever been in all his days.

Alys pumped her hips demandingly beneath him, she clung to his hand, she whispered his name. Burke felt her tremble begin, and as she parted her lips to cry out, he buried himself within her one last time. When Alys tightened around him, he heard himself shout her name, then he too tasted the stars.

Long moments later Burke opened his eyes to find Alys breathing as heavily as he. He had collapsed atop her and feared suddenly for her comfort. Burke rolled to his back, Alys still clasped in his arms, and savored the way she giggled as she sprawled across him.

"Ah, Alys, I do love you so," he murmured, then pressed a kiss into her hair.

Alys sighed and leaned her head on his chest, her breath fanning across him. "I shall never doubt you again," she whispered.

"Aye? Why?"

"Because you were right once more," she confessed drowsily. "One must match the rhythm of one's steed."

Burke chuckled despite his exhaustion to find himself compared to Moonshadow. Alys propped her chin in her hand, bracing her elbow against his chest, and looked down at him with a cocky smile. "And was this worth three years' wait, sir?"

Burke studied the unkempt vixen lolling on his chest and knew that Alys would never fail to stir his blood. He traced the line of her lips with a fingertip and smiled into her eyes. "I would wait a lifetime for you, my Alys, and that without complaint."

"More sweet words," she teased.

"And every one of them the truth."

"I know." When Alys leaned down to claim a kiss, her hair spilling all around them, Burke thought his heart would burst. He caught her close and kissed her deeply, and only then recalled another tale he would lay to rest.

To his relief, one glance to his cloak confirmed what he had suspected he would find.

"Look there," he bade his lady fair. Burke knew the very moment that Alys saw her own blood, for she frowned as if disbelieving the evidence of her own eyes. Burke slid her weight to one side, pointing to the mark of her maidenhead left upon him.

"And there," he urged.

Alys touched the smear upon his flesh, then met his gaze hopefully. " 'Tis blood."

"And not just any blood. 'Tis your virginal blood, Alys, and the mark of your maidenhead." He squeezed her waist. "Another of your aunt's lies proven for what it was."

Alys turned a smile upon Burke that fairly curled his toes. "And what of your lie, sir?"

Burke could not hide his astonishment at this, though Alys's manner was teasing. "I thought you knew I told you no lies."

"Aye, I know it well." Her smile did not fade. "But on this day, you at least were *misguided*." Alys ran her fingertips down Burke's chest, then across his lingering erection. The member returned to life once again and the lady laughed.

"You told me this would be resolved by our play, Burke," she jested, her fingers closing around him with newfound confidence. "But 'tis as swollen as ever. I would not see you so tormented."

Burke could not hold back his smile. "You abandon innocence with ease, my temptress."

Alys laughed again. "And you would complain of this?"

"Not at all," he declared, then sat up and gathered Alys quickly into his arms. She nestled against him quite contentedly, her head on his shoulder, her legs curled so that her feet were on his thigh. Burke captured one foot in his hand and leisurely ran his thumb across the soft flesh of the arch. "I should be delighted to offer my assistance in your quest."

Alys's eyes sparkled. "In the name of gallantry?"

"A man of honor can do no less," Burke agreed easily, then bent his head to claim another leisurely kiss before Alys could laugh once more.

Lady Crevy was a practical woman. She had not survived so long and so well by missing opportunity when 'twas cast into her lap.

Lady Crevy liked this pretty child who fretted so for her cousin's happiness. No less, she knew that Guillaume could trust such a tender woman with his heart. And she knew also that her son, still nursing his heart's wounds, would do little to make the most of the matter.

He could be so like his father at times.

She clucked her tongue as she marched up the stairs. A sensible woman had to turn opportunity to advantage, when others might let it slip away.

Lady Crevy rapped once as she entered the chamber she had granted to the visiting women and smiled to see that Brigid's color had returned. The young maid straightened from serving broth to her lady.

"Do not let me disturb you, *petite*," Lady Crevy declared warmly. "I would assure myself only that you are restored."

"Aye." Brigid smiled. " 'Tis good to b-b-be in a soft bed."

Lady Crevy sat on the edge of the mattress and felt the young woman's brow, satisfied that her skin had cooled. "You will join us at the board this night."

Brigid's smile faltered, but Lady Crevy was not about to let her decline. "I tell you why, *ma petite.* I have a concern for my son with which you might aid me."

"M-m-me?"

Lady Crevy patted her hand. "He is so shy with the ladies that I fear Crevy will never have an heir. It pains me to think that he will be alone when I pass away, for he is kind and not the manner of man who should be alone."

Brigid bit her lip, her eyes wide with sympathy.

"But you can help, *ma petite,* if only you will."

"Oh, I would do anything. You have been so nice!"

" 'Tis a small thing, you have only to talk to him."

Brigid flushed. "But I will st-st-stammer."

Lady Crevy leaned closer. "Ah, to believe that, you must know little of men. They love to talk of themselves, and my son, for all I love him, is no different in this. You have but to ask him of himself, of Crevy, then listen avidly to him. You must laugh at his jests, and thus, you will aid him to believe in his own desirability."

Brigid's gaze dropped shyly. "I think your son is m-m-most handsome."

"Aye, he has his looks from me, *non*?" They laughed together, then Lady Crevy clapped her hands. "Ah! This could help you as well, for you can cultivate those fine Paris manners you are so certain you lack. My son has been to Paris many times—ask him of this!"

Brigid's eyes widened, then she smiled, obviously entranced by the possibility. "I c-c-could do this. For Alys and B-B-Burke."

"Of course you could, *ma petite.*" Lady Crevy snapped her fingers. "I have another idea. You must be bored with the garments you have brought all this way. There is naught like a new kirtle, even one borrowed from an old woman like me, to brighten a lady's mood, *non?* And a bath, hot and deep."

"A bath!" Brigid breathed.

"I shall see it done." Lady Crevy rose and clapped her hands, her commands sending servants scattering. She noted with pride that Brigid already sat straighter, anticipation in her eyes.

'Twas then that a tousled Lady Alys entered the room, her hair easing from beneath her veil. Aye, Lady Crevy knew that manner of flush, that beguiled smile, as well as the root of both. Burke de Montvieux was a rogue, there was no disputing that, but she could hardly blame the man.

Three years! 'Twas *contre nature.*

"Alys! I am to aid L-L-Lady Crevy's son!" Brigid evidently knew naught of what had put such a smile upon her cousin's lips, and Lady Crevy marked innocence in that girl's favor.

"How wonderful." Alys flushed in a most telling manner and Lady Crevy knew that 'twas no accident Burke halted here, Brigid in his entourage. Lady Crevy's heart swelled that Burke should be so thoughtful, and she knew she could not let Burke's generosity go unrewarded.

He was a man who did not forget his friends, and Lady Crevy would reward such impulses.

She crossed to Alys's side and looked her in the eye. "Aid me in this," she insisted quietly, "and I shall aid you."

"Me? But how?"

Lady Crevy turned to Brigid and smiled. "Your *cousine* has agreed to aid my son in overcoming his shyness. I believe she will do a wondrous job, with such charm and such a sweet smile. Do you not agree, Alys?"

Brigid looked hopeful for her cousin's approval and Alys smiled warmly. "What a wondrous idea! Why, Brigid, he could assist you in learning Parisian manners."

'Twas no small thing Alys and she thought similarly, Lady Crevy concluded as Brigid beamed. "I c-c-can do it!"

"But of course!"

When Lady Crevy went to summon the bath, she caught Alys's elbow and made some excuse of needing her counsel. "I see your hand in this, and it shall not go unappreciated," Lady Crevy confided in an undertone. "I shall turn a blind eye upon you and Burke sharing a chamber in this keep." She shook a finger at a delighted Alys. "But understand that if Margaux de Montvieux believes I approved of such behavior, I shall deny it to my dying breath."

Alys laughed and threw her arms around the older woman, thanking her with a resounding kiss that boded well for this couple's happiness. "You are most kind!"

"Pshaw! Burke would do as he would with or without my approval—I would know only who sleeps where in my hall." Lady Crevy winked. " 'Tis clear he has a store of ardor to share." Alys's flush deepened and Lady Crevy smiled. "You had best share your cousin's bath, *petite,* and I shall find you new garb as well."

Burke turned at the sound of the women on the stairs, though he could never have prepared himself for Alys's radiant entry. She wore a different kirtle, one finer than any she had possessed thus far, though 'twas her smile that made his heart pound. She crossed the floor to his side with quick steps and laid a kiss upon his lips that made Burke marvel that he had ever been able to conceive of chastity.

He did not know how he would survive until their nuptials, for one lingering taste of his lady only tempted him yet more.

She smiled up at him, as if reading his thoughts. "Rogue!"

she whispered with sparkling eyes, then pointed across the hall. "Watch this."

Burke reluctantly looked up in time to see Brigid, not only similarly arrayed but apparently buoyed with new confidence. Guillaume met her gaze, then might have retreated to the board, but Brigid, to Burke's astonishment, lifted her chin. She and Lady Crevy exchanged a smile, then the girl swept toward Guillaume with rare purpose. She smiled at him, then clasped her hands together before herself.

"Sir, would you t-t-tell me of Crevy?"

Burke stifled his smile as his friend was visibly enchanted. As usual of late, matters proceeded markedly well.

⬦

Alys savored Burke's rare surprise when Lady Crevy insisted on seeing them to their chambers that evening. The chatelain frowned but withdrew at his lady's command. Guillaume and Brigid were so deep in conversation that they barely noted the trio's departure.

Alys elbowed Burke as they climbed the stairs, keeping her voice low so that their hostess did not overhear. "It seemed you have known best yet again." Burke glanced down in surprise. "I think your friend is an admirable choice for Brigid."

"One can only hope they two share our conviction."

"Surely you would compel them to share your view," Alys teased. "You are not one to welcome objections."

Burke grinned. "And you have complaints of this?"

"Nay," she conceded, then winked at her knight. "Indeed I could grow used to your determination—no less your lessons in the amorous arts."

Burke chuckled, then feigned sternness. "I cannot recall that we agreed to further tutelage," he mused so solemnly that Alys almost laughed aloud.

Lady Crevy paused ahead of them, then indicated a door on her right. "Alys, I hope this will suffice."

"Oh, 'tis a lovely chamber. I thank you so much."

Burke hesitated in a decidedly obvious manner. Lady Crevy propped her hands upon her hips and surveyed him. "Is it not fine enough to suit your taste, *chevalier*?"

"Of course! Alys will enjoy . . ."

"Then get yourself within before all of Crevy sees my indulgence of you two!" And Lady Crevy shooed him with her hands. Burke's eyes widened, but Alys seized his hand when he hesitated and dragged him into her chamber.

Lady Crevy winked. "I like a woman who knows what she desires," she murmured, then closed the door behind them.

Alys leaned her back against it just as Burke's laughter burst forth. "You cheeky wench!" he charged, admiration gleaming in his eyes. "You planned this!"

Alys propped her hands on her hips to regard him. "Oh? Did you not mean to wed me, after all?" she teased, and found herself in Burke's arms with satisfying speed.

"Indeed, I would not dare to let you go," he declared warmly, then arched a brow. "What was this you said about lessons?"

"I demand to know all you can teach me." Alys twined her arms around her knight's neck. "Continuing this night from this afternoon."

Burke smiled down at her, his gaze intent. " 'Tis an investment I doubt I will regret."

Alys smiled and stretched to her toes, ensuring that he had very little to say for a very long time afterward.

She could not, after all, leave the man with any doubts of her trust.

Chapter Seventeen

O N THE MORNING FOLLOWING BURKE'S ARRIVAL, Guillaume paced the breadth and width of his own hall anxiously. He knew he did not have sufficient charm to win a lady's affections, but Lady Brigid's attention the night before encouraged him. He kept one eye on the stairs and deliberately ignored his mother's humming as she spread honey on her bread.

Indeed, he scowled at the floor, telling himself he was a fool even to hope for shy Brigid's favor. She had simply been polite, nodding at her host's tales and smiling at his jests. It had been so easy to talk with her, the wine loosening his tongue, but this morn he half feared it had been a dream.

Aye, 'twas all too readily in the morn's harsh light that Guillaume recalled how many times he had presented a suit, his heart in his hand, and been mocked by the fine lady in question.

Perhaps this was a poor idea. Perhaps he should let Brigid proceed to Paris, perhaps he truly should live out his days alone.

Perhaps he should not be such a coward. 'Twas not a flattering realization, and it set Guillaume to more concerted pacing. He ran a prosperous estate, he could command an army when needs demanded, yet he worked himself to a frenzy over one damsel's potential refusal.

"Ah!" his mother cried. *"Ma petite!"*

Guillaume spun and his heart skipped a beat when he spied Lady Brigid hesitating on the last stair. She smiled shyly to his mother, then glanced at him and flushed. Indeed, she bit her lip in the most fetching manner, as if she found him rather fearsome. Her blush made her freckles even more winsome, her tentative manner prompted Guillaume's protectiveness.

Indeed, he was halfway across the floor, wanting only to reassure her, before he realized that he had taken a step. The lady did not move away, her gaze did not waver from him. She did not seek him out as she had done the night before, but neither did she flee.

Guillaume smiled and summoned every vestige of his charm as he came to a halt before her. "Did you sleep well?"

"Aye." Brigid looked as if she could not decide what to do. She seemed to hover, like a young bird uncertain of what *he* might do.

Guillaume hastened to reassure her. "Was there anything of which you had need? You have only to ask to see your will done in this place."

"Aye. I mean nay." The lady's cheeks turned crimson. "All was f-f-fine." Then her expression turned pained. Guillaume did not imagine that she glanced at his mother as if seeking escape.

This was not proceeding well, to his thinking, and was a bit too reminiscent of his experiences at the king's court to be encouraging. All the comments Guillaume had practiced in his chambers cruelly abandoned him as his confidence in his charm faded to naught.

But all the same, he felt compelled to say *something*.

When he spoke, his disquietude summoned an old plague, one that he had thought banished for good.

"Good, then. I suppose, I mean, I should suggest that, um, perhaps . . ." Guillaume gritted his teeth at his own idiocy when the lady looked at him in astonishment, then he swore softly under his breath. If only he had Burke's way with flattery, just for this one moment! "I should like to invite you to um, to join us to um, break your fast, Lady Brigid."

She said naught.

Guillaume knew he had made a muddle of this. Now she knew he was a fool! Indeed, he should do best to pretend this exchange had never occurred and spare his guest further embarrassment.

But he could not refuse himself one last glance at the lady.

Guillaume was surprised, for Brigid regarded him with undisguised delight. Indeed, she stared at him as if he were the most marvelous man in Christendom.

Knowing his own allure to women and the foolishness of what he had just uttered, Guillaume glanced over his shoulder. He fully expected to find Burke lingering behind, but no one was there.

The lady giggled, her hands landing on his forearm. Guillaume turned to find her leaning toward him, her eyes sparkling. "You almost stammered!"

Guillaume felt his ears heat to have his inadequacy pointed out to him. "Well, I cannot help it. Sometimes I just cannot, well, the words do not, um, when I want to make a good impression . . ." He heaved a sigh and shoved one hand through his hair, stared at his boots, and decided simply to state his case.

"This is the root of the matter. I want to ask you to remain at Crevy," he declared flatly. "I do not want you to seek a husband in Paris, for I should like the chance to court you, and I know well enough that I cannot compete with the men in that fair city. I am sorry to be blunt, but I cannot think of the words to ask your favor more graciously."

Now he had done it. Guillaume glanced at the lady carefully, certain she would turn and flee his boorish company. But she giggled and dimpled in a most charming way, her gaze dancing to his watchful mother and back to Guillaume.

"Oh, I like you too," she breathed, to his astonishment. "And I should like to know you better."

Guillaume stared at her in wonder. "Then stay," he urged.

The lady bit her lip and nodded quickly.

Guillaume dared to take her hands within his, a thrill running through him when she did not pull away. "Will you spend this day with me? We can talk, I can show you Crevy."

In truth, he did not want this fair flower to escape.

"Aye, I shall laugh at your jests." The lady leaned toward him, her fingers tightening over his. "But I did not have to try."

Try? Guillaume glanced to his mother. She hummed more loudly and spread honey with a determination wholly unnecessary.

He knew he had no reason to challenge what she had done. Indeed, it made Guillaume want to laugh.

In fact, he would not have put it past Burke to have . . .

"I am so hungry," Brigid whispered.

"The board awaits your favor," Guillaume declared gallantly.

His mother looked up with an approving smile and patted the bench beside herself. "Come here, *ma petite*. I have saved the comb of the honey for you. 'Twill build your strength anew."

"Oh, I love honey," the lady declared, eyeing the comb laid upon her bread as if 'twere a crown jewel. "We never have it at Kiltorren."

"*Non*? Perhaps 'tis too cold there for the bees. *Ma petite,* at Crevy, you may break your fast on honeycomb each morn. 'Tis a fine holding my son commands, and all its treasures lie at your feet."

"Oh, 'tis a fine holding indeed!" Lady Brigid granted the lord of Crevy-sur-Seine a smile that fairly curled his toes.

Ah, to think that Burke had plotted this and he had stepped into the scheme so unwittingly. Guillaume chuckled as he tore into his own bread.

"*Maman,* I believe we owe Burke a debt." He recalled Brigid's earlier confession and realized that his friend's own ends would be served by this courtship. But Guillaume was more than willing to aid Burke, in gratitude for choosing Crevy to showcase Brigid's charms. "And I know precisely the way to see it paid."

◆

Now that Alys's hand was securely within his own, Burke could not help thinking about Montvieux. As pleasurable as Crevy could be, and as delightful as the companionship was in this place, he began to chafe under the weight of the last uncertainty before himself and Alys.

She must meet his mother.

Burke was not looking forward to the confrontation, for he knew his mother would find no woman an acceptable mate for him. He did not care for Margaux's opinion, though he did not want Alys hurt by some cruel comment. And he did not want to leave Crevy before Alys's concerns for Brigid were laid to rest.

Yet 'twas becoming cursedly awkward to be without coin. Burke had never been without anything to his name, and he found the experience more troubling than he had expected. He wanted Alys adorned in silks, he wanted a ring of gold upon her finger, he wanted to exchange vows before a priest—but all of these endeavors took the expense of hard coin.

And he had none.

'Twas ironic that he had spurned his legacy for the chance to win Alys's hand, yet now Burke wished he held Montvieux, if only to see his lady garbed and pampered as she deserved. It chafed upon him to see her wear the same kirtle day after day. It troubled him even more to know that there was naught he could do about it.

Alys accepted whatever came to her hand, happy in small victories and shouldering burdens with ease. She had a strength

that could not be shaken by worldly lack, and 'twas a trait that
Burke greatly admired. Indeed, the fact that she chose to be
with him, despite his having naught, was an endorsement of
rare power. It meant Alys would be steadfast by his side, regardless of the state of his fortunes. Burke found that seductive indeed, even if the lady had yet to confess her feelings.
'Twould take time, Burke knew it well, and he would wait,
secure that he had already claimed the prize of her trust.

'Twas Alys who had taught him the treasures that could
come to him with patience.

'Twas indicative of his thinking that when Burke found an
errant piece of silver in his saddlebags the day after their arrival, he had promptly spent it in Crevy's village on a gift for
Alys. He waited only for the perfect moment to present his gift.

At least part of her could be garbed like a queen.

But still there remained the sole disagreement that continued
between them. Alys did not welcome the risk of the great tourneys, yet Burke knew that he could not face year upon year of
mock warfare. He would make his victories quickly and withdraw from competition, for indeed, he grew no younger.

And 'twas only the great lords who could afford to offer
the prize Burke coveted beyond all else—a manor, however
humble, to call their own. For truly, a life unfettered by responsibilities lost its allure with Alys by his side.

There would be children soon enough, if they two continued in such merry fashion. They must be wed, the children
must have the certainty of a happy home with a full larder.

Aye, the tourneys beckoned, though hurdles aplenty blocked
Burke's path.

First, Guillaume had to propose. Whenever possible, Burke
urged Guillaume to greater boldness, for that man's manner
was cautious enough in matters of the heart to ensure a
decade-long courtship.

Burke did not have a decade to ensure Brigid's nuptials,

and so he was more than pleased when—a mere five days after their arrival—Guillaume dropped to one knee before Alys at the midday board.

"Lady Alys, would you do me the honor of acting as representative of your family?"

Another piece moved into position, another obstacle crumbled in the path to his own nuptials! Burke barely restrained himself from hooting with glee.

"But Brigid is the daughter of the Lord of Kiltorren," Alys protested. "I am merely my uncle's ward."

"But 'tis of Lady Brigid I would speak."

"Oh!" Alys gasped in sudden understanding. Guillaume grinned and Brigid flushed mightily. Lady Crevy clicked her tongue in approval and cast a conspiratorial wink Burke's way.

"I would ask your indulgence in permitting me to wed your cousin, Lady Brigid of Kiltorren." Guillaume presented a nuptial contract to Alys with a bow, but she turned to her cousin.

"There is only one opinion of merit in this matter," Alys insisted. "What do you say to this suit, Brigid?"

Brigid smiled, clasped her hands together, and gazed at Guillaume with adoration. "Oh, I say aye, Alys. I would like very much to wed Guillaume."

"My son will treat you well, *ma petite*," Lady Crevy assured her, "or I shall give him such a shake."

Brigid smiled at Guillaume. "I know." Guillaume grinned back at her, and Burke smiled to see his friend so happily smitten.

"My family can have no protest against your circumstance," Alys continued, unfurling the document with a frown. She turned to Burke, a question in her lovely eyes as she offered him the deed. "You know more than I of such matters. Would you?"

"I should be honored," Burke agreed smoothly, wondering whether his lady could read. He pledged to teach her, if she

had the interest, and cursed the family of Kiltorren for denying her yet again.

Then he cast a mischievous glance at his friend, still kneeling before Alys. "Shall I negotiate on behalf of the bride?" he
suggested wickedly, and Guillaume snorted.

"You shall see me beggared, no doubt!" he retorted.
"Though 'twould be a small price to pay for such a lady's
favor."

"Guillaume!" Brigid blushed, yet she still reached to kiss
his cheek when that knight rose to take his place beside her.

Lady Crevy clapped her hands. "Then all is settled, and
most favorably. There is but one deed we have to see done."

Burke could not imagine what that might be, and he noted
that Alys was similarly perplexed. The others, however,
looked so smug that Burke knew they had been in league.

Lady Crevy gave a summons and a bevy of servants spilled
into the hall. A minstrel plucked a lute for the procession and
Burke quickly noted that they carried a small trunk between
them. 'Twas a simple one, though he was surprised when
'twas laid before Alys.

Alys clearly did not know what to make of the presentation.
Burke silently vowed that he would ensure that she did not
find the receipt of gifts so startling.

Aye, his lady had lived too long with too little.

"This is for you, Alys," Lady Crevy declared. "You may
consider it an early wedding gift or, indeed, a gift of gratitude
for introducing your cousin to my son. Either way, 'tis a gift I
hope you enjoy."

Alys glanced at Burke, but he knew his expression supplied
no answer. Indeed, he was powerfully curious as to what Lady
Crevy might have chosen.

"I thank you," Alys said, but the older woman laughed.

"You do not even know what 'tis!"

"But, Lady Crevy, you offer us such hospitality already. 'Tis too much that you grant gifts as well."

"Pshaw." Lady Crevy flicked a hand, and the most senior maid in the group tipped back the lid of the trunk. The entire company leaned closer to look.

Burke saw only a vibrant shade of purple before two maids reached into the trunk. They lifted out a garment, indeed, 'twas a kirtle wrought of fine woven wool. Its hue was deep violet; its hem and cuffs were ornamented with gold and red embroidery, with the girdle woven of the same rich hues.

'Twas a kirtle of wondrous workmanship and one that would flatter his Alys's coloring well. Burke sat back and watched her eyes widen. The only marring of this event was his own wish that he could have granted Alys such a gift sooner.

A chemise of snowy white linen was presented next, followed by artfully knitted stockings of the same undyed hue. Red garters were included, with a veil of palest mauve, and a plain golden circlet. Alys gasped when the servant reached into the bottom of the chest and shook out a cloak of the same hue as Burke's own, though this one was lined in silver squirrel fur instead of his black.

There was a conspicuous absence of one item of garb and Burke's smile broadened, for he had no doubt that Lady Crevy had heard of his own acquisition. Indeed, 'twas as if she ordered all to match his gift.

The time was ripe for him to present it.

"I cannot accept such richness," Alys protested, her eyes bright with unshed tears. " 'Tis far too much . . ."

Lady Crevy, as Burke might have anticipated, would not take nay for an answer. She grasped Alys's hand. "I will not hear your protest, Alys, and I grant you no choice."

"But 'tis too generous! Burke, you must aid me."

"Nay, Alys. Lady Crevy does as she wishes alone." He

smiled at his lady. "And as I also believe the gift is well deserved, you will not win my protest."

Alys shook her head at him. "You are no help at all!"

" 'Tis what friends are for," Guillaume argued.

Burke captured Alys's hand in his. "Lady Crevy, I must add my own thanks to Alys's own. Your taste, as always, is exquisite."

"But I cannot . . ."

"Alys, this gift is one from the heart," Lady Crevy insisted. "Indeed 'tis well earned by both the happiness you bring to Crevy with Brigid's presence and the happiness you bring to a knight I have loved as my own son." Lady Crevy smiled encouragement. "Take the gift, *ma petite,* for you shall need every advantage to face Margaux de Montvieux."

Alys turned to Burke with alarm in her eyes and he could not halt his grimace. " 'Tis true enough, Alys," he admitted heavily. " 'Tis true enough."

⬥

Later that evening, in the chamber they had come to share, Alys noted Burke's pensiveness.

They had talked of tourneys at length this week, comparing the merits of one against the other. Alys liked that Burke always spoke to her and took her readily into his confidence.

But on this matter they differed. Burke had an annoying inclination not to think of himself as mortal and so would choose the largest contests, which boasted both the fattest purses and drew the most experienced competition. Alys feared for his hide. But each time she voiced her objection, Burke was so pleased by her concern that the discussion seldom proceeded any further.

She wondered now whether he considered their path anew, since Brigid's match was secured. He had been troubled ever since Lady Crevy's comment about his mother.

She braced herself for another difference of opinion on the surety of his skills. "Is something amiss?"

"Aye, one could say as much." Burke admitted. He pushed a hand through his hair and surveyed Alys as if he would divine her thoughts. "We must go to Montvieux, and I would rather 'twas sooner than later."

Dread rose in Alys. "And I must meet your mother."

Burke winced, his expression a perfect echo of Alys's feelings on the matter. "Aye, 'twill not be a joyous occasion. The tourneys call, Alys, though we must visit my mother first. Now that Brigid is settled, would it trouble you if we rode out in the morn?"

Alys's mouth went dry. What would she do if Burke's mother scorned her? She had no dowry, no lineage, no talents that would make her a compelling choice of bride.

Indeed, 'twould be surprising if his mother did *not* disapprove. "How far is Montvieux?"

Burke shrugged. "A long day's ride. If we begin early, we can make Montvieux village and seek accommodation with the miller by tomorrow eve. Then with Sunday's first light, I shall ride to the château. Perhaps if I find my mother on her way to Mass, she will be in a more charitable frame of mind."

Alys blinked. "You do not intend to take me?"

"Alys!" Burke closed the distance between them and caught her in his arms. He smiled down at her, though the shadows in his eyes were far from encouraging. "One of the great benefits of being disinherited is that no one holds a sword over my head."

"Burke, this is no jest. I thought you intended that I should meet her."

"Nay, 'tis not a jest. But I must speak with my mother alone first."

"Why? Are you so certain she will spurn me?"

"Nay, but she may spurn me!" Burke sighed, and when Alys looked up, his smile turned rueful. "Alys, I have not seen my mother since declining Montvieux. 'Tis an estate of which she is vigorously proud. I have no doubt that she has much to say on the matter, and I would spare you such a first encounter. 'Twill not be pleasant, that I guarantee." He tipped her chin up with a gentle fingertip and brushed his lips across hers. "Though truly, I should welcome your strength beside me."

"But, Burke, you cannot be so concerned!" Alys chided, certain he merely tried to make her smile. "She is your blood."

The knight smiled crookedly and touched Alys' cheek. "And you,, of all people, should understand that blood who offer naught deserve naught in return."

He bent then and captured her lips beneath his own. Alys leaned against him, savoring his strength and his tenderness. When Burke finally lifted his head, his eyes were gleaming, though a wicked sparkle soon appeared in their depths. "I almost forgot that you are owed another gift this night."

"Another gift? Burke, you should not let them do this . . ."

"Alys, you shall have to become accustomed to receiving gifts." He tapped her nose lightly with one fingertip. "You have been with naught for far too long."

"But . . ."

"But naught. I have indulged myself in indulging you."

"You? But you said yourself that you had no coin," Alys argued. She knew it troubled him to be without coin. "Why would you waste any upon frivolities for me?"

" 'Tis no frivolity, but a matter of serious import." Burke's manner was solemn, but that twinkle in his eyes remained.

Alys surveyed her knight skeptically. "I doubt that."

He laughed and pointed to his saddlebags. "Look within it and mind your manners."

Alys was curious despite herself. She crossed the room and opened the saddlebag, well aware of Burke watching her.

Within the depths of his bag lurked a pair of feminine slippers the like of which Alys had never seen. They were wrought of leather so soft that she could not believe 'twas real. The toes were embellished with an ornate design, the leather had been dyed to the color of garnets.

Alys picked them up with wonder and turned to face Burke. He stood with his arms folded across his chest, smiling indulgently.

"These are for me?"

Burke grinned. "They would not fit me." He cast a glance over his own garb. "And I do not think 'tis a good hue for me."

"But, Burke, they are so beautiful!" Alys studied the marvel of them. "I have never seen shoes so wondrous. Indeed, I did not guess that such workmanship was possible." She looked at him again, the glimmer of his eyes reminding her of his jest. Alys bowed deeply, the shoes clasped to her chest. "I thank you, sir, for this marvelous gift."

His lips quirked. "It seems you learn quickly in all matters."

"All?"

Burke grinned outright. "All, indeed."

Alys laughed, crossing the floor to his side once more. She reached up and granted him a kiss, then looked at the shoes in amazement once more. "But why shoes? I have this other pair, after all." She held up one foot, the roughly sewn shoe nearly slipping from her foot for the hundredth time this day.

"Which fit you so poorly that they fairly fall off your feet," Burke said with unexpected heat. "And do you know, Alys, what effect the sight of your bare feet has upon me?"

Alys could not understand his manner. "Nay."

Burke held her gaze with resolve. "I believe, my lady fair, that you have the most exquisite feet in Christendom. These fleeting glimpses of them are torment!" He grinned suddenly. "Perhaps 'tis for the sake of my own hide that I grant you these."

"What does that mean?"

"If you flashed those toes during a tourney, I might become so distracted that I could well be injured beyond repair."

"Truly?"

"Truly." Burke's single word was firm.

Alys playfully kicked off her old shoes and lifted the hem of her kirtle, deliberately wiggling her toes against the floor. Burke caught his breath in a most notable manner, and Alys knew enough of such matters in these days to watch the silhouette beneath his tabard.

When she saw results, she smiled up at him. "Perhaps, sir, you might aid me in ensuring the fit of these new slippers?"

" 'Twould only be chivalrous."

Alys laughed, then tapped her finger on his chest, taking great delight in leaning against his erection. "I shall make you a wager, Burke, since you find the unexpected sight of my feet so distracting. I, too, have interest in seeing you leave the tourneys whole."

"Aye?"

"Aye. I shall never shed these slippers without your aid." Her boldness was more than compensated by the passion that lit Burke's eyes. "You can ease them from my feet each night and caress them back into place each morn."

"I shall take your wager, temptress," he said with a growl, and swept her into his arms. The shoes fell to the floor, momentarily forgotten. Burke rolled onto the bed, his kiss making her blood thunder, and Alys considered how she might torment him with her toes.

Fortunately, she was a lady possessed of creativity. And Burke did not complain at her efforts, for one could not count his moans of pleasure throughout that night as complaint.

Indeed, 'twas a long time before the slippers were fitted to her feet.

'Twas still dark when Edana heard Alys's whisper in the stables, the unexpected sound feeding her curiosity. Edana pulled from the warmth of Kerwyn's embrace and crept closer to listen. Alys stood with the Lord de Crevy as Burke de Mont-vieux saddled his steed.

But that was Kerwyn's task! Edana poked her toe into her partner's ribs and his eyes flew open. One glance at her expression and he crawled to her side, donning his chausses as he obviously tried to listen.

But the trio kept their voices low. Edana followed Kerwyn's lead and donned her kirtle, fastening the lacings with hasty fingers. There was no time to concern herself over her hair.

Moonshadow tossed his head, setting his harness to jingling, then the two knights shook hands. They embraced, then Alys kissed the lord's cheeks thrice in quick succession. Burke lifted her to his saddle and there could be no doubt remaining.

"They are leaving!" Kerwyn whispered.

"And *without* us." The pair exchanged a glance, their thoughts as one in this, and stepped out into the stables hand in hand.

"Sir, I pledged to serve you," Kerwyn declared. Though his voice was low, his words carried clearly through the quiet stable and halted the departing knight.

"Kerwyn, I am honored by your pledge, no less your intent to hold it. But 'twould be irresponsible to welcome your services when I cannot ensure that you will be housed and fed."

"You need me," Kerwyn argued. "As does your steed. And I am not the manner of man who does not keep his word."

"And you need me!" Edana cried to Alys. "How can you be a fine lady without a maid?"

"But, Edana," Alys shook her head, "Guillaume will assure your safety and your care. He has vowed it to us. Crevy welcomes you as free men."

"If I am free, then I can choose to leave," Edana argued. She eased closer to Kerwyn. "And we choose to come with you."

"Indeed," Kerwyn added, "we owe you no less loyalty than this."

Edana nodded. "I owe you *all* for freeing me from Kiltorren."

Silence reigned in the stable for a long moment and Edana knew they had surprised this pair with their determination. But she had not come this far to leave a debt unpaid, and she was not afraid to match her path to that of Burke and Alys. This knight would not be penniless for long, and Alys would always be a thoughtful mistress. Brigid would find another maid to braid her hair.

The knight shook his head, casting a smile at his lady. "I do not think we shall manage to leave without them."

"Nay, they are most stubborn," Alys agreed with affection. "Though I have a fondness for persistent souls." The couple exchanged a meaningful glance that left the knight chuckling and the lady's cheeks pink.

"Collect what you will, then," Burke urged. "We must make haste to reach Montvieux by dusk."

"The Templars' palfreys must be returned," Kerwyn observed. "Is Paris on the way?"

"Aye, more or less," Burke agreed, then frowned as he evidently planned their course. "We shall part company en route, if you have no objections. You can deliver the horses and meet us in Montvieux, for I am anxious to arrive there on this day."

"I shall ensure their delivery," Kerwyn declared.

"Aye, I know it well."

Edana felt her man straighten with pride at the knight's trust in him. Aye, they would be a good master and mistress, these two. Edana would be proud to serve them.

Perhaps, when the knight won a holding, she could even persuade them to raise goats.

"Take one of my palfreys for your squire's own," the lord insisted. Burke might have argued, but the other man silenced him with one hand. "A wedding gift, early," he insisted. "Take it and do not argue. After all, you leave me with a gifted cook."

" 'Twas the scallions that seduced Beauregard," Alys commented. "And the extent of your kitchen garden."

The lord smiled with pride and inclined his head in acknowledgement of the compliment. "I have no doubt that his presence will be an ongoing comfort to my betrothed."

And so 'twas settled, the sun rising red and hazy as the four of them took to the road, a dozen palfreys running behind. Edana raised her face to the wind, never having imagined that her life could hold such promise as this. Kerwyn winked at her and she knew a happiness beyond all expectation.

'Twas no small thing that 'twould always be hers.

Alys listened to the rain throughout Saturday night, keenly aware of Burke's absence beside her. She had a sense of great decisions being in the wind, though 'twas not until the following morning that she understood why.

There had been no mistaking Burke's tension all the day before. He rode in grim silence behind her, and Alys could fairly feel him summoning his resources to meet his mother's "formidable" will.

They took their rest in the abode of the miller of Montvieux, Alys in a chaste bed upstairs, Burke below. She slept poorly, missing her knight's warmth through the night, no less his low chuckle. Even the twilight sight of Montvieux's wealth had been enough to prompt troubled dreams.

Alys rose and dressed early, restless though she knew not why. At the sound of Moonshadow in the courtyard, she tore open the shutters, not caring a whit for her unbound hair. 'Twas raining fully this morn, neither the misty threat of the day before or the light patter of the night past. The rain fell in steady sheets and cast Montvieux in a thousand shades of grey.

Alys discerned Burke's silhouette in the same moment that she heard the rumble of his voice. He swung into his destrier's saddle, a dark shadow against the silver of the rain, his hood drawn over his helmet. She raised her hand expectantly, certain he would glance to her window, but Burke turned the steed and abruptly rode away.

Alys's hand fell back to the windowsill, a shadow of dread falling across her heart. She looked to the distant hill, where she had glimpsed the lights of Montvieux's hall the night before. Even the falling rain could not hide the size of that place, and Alys imagined she could feel the will of Burke's mother summoning her son to her side.

And what would that mother demand of her only son? Repentance, of course, and a return to his birthright. The formidable Margaux would bend Burke to her will. Burke had already shown doubts in the wisdom of his course, and now he would be confronted by the splendor of all he had cast aside.

Alys's fingers clenched. She stared after Burke as Moonshadow's hoofbeats faded to naught and cursed herself for not uttering the three small words that could have made the difference in his choice.

She had never told Burke that she loved him. 'Twas the only factor in her favor, and he did not know the truth of it.

The village chapel bell rang in a mournful summons to Mass as Alys felt the weight of her own foolishness. But there was naught to be done now. She closed the shutters and turned back to the room, wondering how she would bear the solitary wait.

But Talbot d'Annoceaux leaned in the portal, smiling cheerfully at her shock. "Good morning to you, Alys of Kiltorren," he said. "Are you truly the daughter of Isibeal of Kiltorren?"

"Aye," Alys admitted, edging away from the man she had instinctively distrusted from the first. What was he doing here? What did he want from her? And why had the miller let him climb the stairs unchallenged?

"Then you will have to come with me."

"Nay, I will not go anywhere with you. Burke is here . . ."

"Burke has left. I watched him go and you are at my mercy." At her obvious doubt, Talbot beckoned to another out of sight. His squire appeared, holding a knife to the miller's throat. Alys gasped as the squire's blade dug deeper and the miller began to beg for his life in barely coherent French.

"You cannot injure him!"

" 'Tis your choice." Talbot shrugged. "Accompany us and he will live."

Alys looked to the miller, then to the squire's shaking hand. Talbot was determined, though Alys could not imagine what this was about. She had to think of some way to save everyone involved.

She could fool this man, she was certain of it.

"Of course I shall come," Alys agreed, snatching up her girdle, veil, and circlet, She forced a smile, hoping she could disarm Talbot. "Indeed, I have worried of your fate since Kiltorren!"

Talbot's eyes widened. "Indeed?"

"Why, you must know that I noted you." Alys let her glance slide over him, hoping she managed some shred of sensual allure. She let her voice drop. "From the very first moment our eyes met, I thought you were a knight of rare charm."

Talbot smiled slowly. "I *knew* you were a whore."

Alys deliberately rolled her hips as she walked across the room, and Talbot devoured her every gesture.

"I thought you favored Burke."

"Him?" Alys waved dismissively as if scornful of Burke's abilities. "In truth, I have had better from an ostler."

Talbot chuckled and elbowed his squire. "I shall see you ridden as you have never been before."

Alys rather doubted that, but she smiled. "And then?"

"And then you shall win the fate you so richly deserve." Though Talbot tried to be ambiguous, there was a glimmer in his eye that did not bode well for Alys. She might have stepped back, but he snatched at her hand and hauled her roughly toward the stairs.

This was no jest and Alys tasted new fear at Talbot's harsh manner. She could smell the ale on him and wondered if he even knew what he did. Alys managed to kick off one of her shoes, casting it into the middle of the room she had occupied as a signal to Burke of her distress.

Talbot swore at her for impeding his progress and tugged at her arm, the sudden move making Alys's kirtle snag on the door latch. The metal dug painfully into her flesh. She heard a tear but did not even have time to look back.

In the chamber below, Alys watched helplessly as the squire hit the miller in the back of the head with the hilt of his blade. That kindly man slumped to the floor and was promptly shoved behind a trunk.

Alys could only hope he was not dead.

Talbot's expression did not bode well for her own survival, though his motive was a mystery. Burke would follow her, Alys knew. Burke would come in time, she had to believe that.

Alys had to keep herself alive, and she had to leave her knight a clear trail. Burke's insistence that she could not lie to save her life rang in her ears as Talbot dragged her out into the rain.

Alys hoped that for once in his life, Burke was wrong.

Chapter Eighteen

CONTRARY TO BURKE'S HOPES, MARGAUX DE Montvieux was not in a charitable mood.

He was ushered into the hall by her thin-lipped chatelain, that man's gaze barely flickering in recognition. He was not offered even the courtesy of his cloak being removed, Moonshadow was left wet in the stables, and Burke did not doubt his mother's anger.

Indeed, her eyes snapped like jewels. She sat in her great wooden chair, its arms carved in the shape of snarling griffins, her hands braced upon the knob of the cane she needed to walk in these days. Her hair had silvered completely since he last saw her, every vestige of ebony gone. But there still was a force of will that emanated from his mother, and 'twas one with the impact of a buttressed wall.

"You will ensure that my steed is brushed and dried," Burke informed the chatelain.

That man had the audacity to lift his brows. "Will your squire not see to it?" he asked mildly, knowing full well that Burke had arrived alone.

"This quarrel is between my mother and myself," Burke declared tightly. "There is no need for the beast to suffer."

The chatelain glanced to his mistress.

"Do it," she said tightly, her hearing obviously as sharp as ever. " 'Twill not be said that Margaux de Montvieux is unkind."

The chatelain scurried away, leaving mother and son. Burke was hardly in the state he would have preferred, but he shook off his sodden cloak and laid it over a bench as if untroubled.

Then he crossed the floor with leisurely steps to meet his mother. She rose as he drew nearer, bracing herself on her cane, lifting her chin. Though she stood on the dais, they were eye to eye, for Margaux had never been tall.

"If you come to beg my forgiveness, 'tis past time you fell on your knees," she said coldly.

Burke smiled at the very thought. "And why would I seek forgiveness?"

Margaux's eyes flashed with fury. "For your disregard! Your father told me of your foolish choice and, indeed, I expected to see you much sooner than this! On your knees, *chevalier,* and I might consent to grant you your inheritance once again."

"I have no desire for Montvieux," Burke said with a shrug. *"What nonsense is this?"*

"As I told Father, the price of your approval comes too high. I surrender Montvieux for the chance to follow my own will."

His mother sat down heavily. "You will think little of the merit of your own will when it compels you to watch that woman starve."

Burke's surprise must have shown, for his mother smiled coldly. "Naught happens on this holding without my knowing of it. You should know that."

"Indeed, your grip has tightened since last I was here."

" 'Tis naught but a reflection of my concern for you."

Burke smiled sadly at his mother. " 'Tis Montvieux alone that concerns you. Do not pretend that this fury is born of anything else. My rejection of Montvieux leaves your beloved estate without an heir apparent, and that is the only issue between us."

She eyed him for a long moment, her anger fading slowly from her features. "You truly believe that," she commented finally.

Burke shrugged. "I have spent my life fulfilling the dreams of others. I have a dream of my own and you will not undermine it."

"Then why have you come?"

"I believe 'tis courteous for a man to introduce his bride to his family."

"Courtesy." Margaux snorted. "You have had women before and they have never filled your head with such nonsense."

"This is different. I love her."

"A fine claim to make without a denier to your name." His mother rolled her eyes. "You could come back to Montvieux and offer this woman a finer life than you will win otherwise."

"And be subject to your every whim once more?" Burke shook his head. "I shall take my chances at the tourneys."

"The tourneys will see you dead!" Margaux snapped. Her lips pinched tightly together. "Who is she?"

"Her name is Alys."

"And her parentage?"

Burke smiled, knowing his answer would not win approval. "Is obscure."

His mother caught her breath and swore softly. "A *bastard*. You throw all away for a bastard, who is probably no better than a whore. Did I raise you with no more wits than that?"

"I would expect you to have the wits to refrain from addressing my betrothed in such terms."

His mother's eyes narrowed anew. "You mean to wed her."

"Of course."

Margaux straightened. "You have a lineage that makes you

worthy of wedding royalty. You would have an inheritance to back any such claim, if you were not so stubborn as to accept it. Yet you would discard all to marry some woman born of naught. I assume she brings you naught."

Burke folded his arms across his chest. "She brings me happiness, and that is no small thing. I shall wed her, with or without your approval, though I had hoped that you might stir yourself to welcome her to the family."

Margaux laughed, a chilling sound that echoed in the empty hall. "*Welcome* her! Have you taken a blow to the head?"

Her mockery angered Burke as her indifference had not. "Nay, I have not. But I have seen well enough what comes of a marriage wrought of fleeting desire and fitting circumstance." His mother's mirth faded abruptly. "And I will not spend my days and nights in a match such as the one from which I sprang." He glared at her. "I do not care what I must sacrifice to ensure that end."

His mother caught her breath. "You have set a price on welcoming your intended, unless I miss my guess."

Burke straightened. "You have a choice to make, Mother. You may greet my betrothed appropriately, you may welcome her to Montvieux and embrace her as befits the mother she has never known."

"Do not hold your breath on that account." She surveyed him. "What of my other choice?"

"Bluntly put, spurn my lady and you spurn me." Margaux sat up at this, but Burke did not cease. "Understand this, Mother. Alys and I have cleaved to each other as surely as if we had pledged before a priest. I love her and her alone, and naught you can say will change that. All you choose in this meeting is whether you will ever see me again."

Burke watched the color drain from his mother's features. She said naught and the stubborn set of her chin did not ease.

Well. He had said his piece, she had denied him. He should not have hoped for more.

'Twas time to leave.

"I wish you well, Mother, and many years of health and prosperity." Burke turned on his heel and strode across the hall where he had played as a boy. Silence crackled in the air behind him, but he scooped up his cloak without a backward glance.

He and Alys could leave for Champagne as soon as Kerwyn and Edana arrived.

"Wait!" his mother shouted just before he left the hall. Burke turned slowly to find her once more on her feet, though she trembled with anger. "You *cannot* choose this woman over me. I will not permit it!"

" 'Twas you who made the choice."

Margaux de Montvieux swore thoroughly. When she had exhausted every expletive Burke had ever heard, she used her cane to descend from the dais and leaned heavily upon it to cross the floor in his wake. When she paused before him, her will blade-bright, Burke was stunned by how tiny she had become.

"Tell me of this obscure parentage," she demanded. "Who is her mother?"

" 'Twas Isibeal of Kiltorren."

"And her father?"

"No one knows."

Margaux inhaled and her lips nigh disappeared. But she did not stride away, and Burke was struck by a sudden idea.

"Indeed, Mother, you might be able to aid my lady in this." His mother looked infuriated by the very thought, but Burke continued smoothly. "The tale is that Alys's mother, Isibeal, met her lover in Paris, that her guardians did not approve of him as a match for he was a younger son with no holding to his name."

"People of good sense do not permit men to wed when they have naught to their name," his mother said testily. "What is amiss with this Isibeal's wits?"

"She is dead," Burke declared, and his mother made a sound that might have been construed as a halfhearted apology. " 'Tis why no one knows Alys's father's name. This Isibeal was convinced he would treat her with honor, though he never came to claim her hand. 'Twas also said that he was likened to a unicorn and she the maid who seduced the beast with her sweet manner."

"Romantic nonsense," Margaux muttered under her breath.

Burke was undeterred. "Think upon it, Mother, for there is little that occurs in Paris without your awareness. Alys is twenty summers of age, her parents met at the king's own court. Perhaps you might recall the man's identity."

Something flashed in his mother's eyes before she abruptly turned away, and Burke knew 'twas anger at being denied her way. "I will not aid you in this course. You cannot wed this woman and shun Montvieux!"

"Then, 'tis farewell, Mother," Burke said without apology. Indeed, she cared for him only when he did her bidding. Burke was finished with all such ties. "Be well." He donned his gloves, pivoted, and stalked out of the hall, disappointed but not truly surprised by his mother's rejection of Alys.

"You shall return on your knees, Burke de Montvieux!" she cried behind him. "You will come to your senses and know that Montvieux is all you desire. *You will regret this course!*"

Burke did not even pause, and he certainly did not look

back. He went directly to the stables, mounted Moonshadow, and left Château Montvieux forever.

Margaux de Montvieux waited.

She stood in her hall, her hands braced upon her cane, fury alone keeping her upright. She knew Burke would come back, she knew he would reconsider, she knew he would not be such a fool as to turn his back upon the prize she had protected for him alone. He wanted only her agreement to meet some wench of whom Margaux knew she would not approve.

How could she approve of some lowborn bastard who had turned her son's head, then turned his heart against her?

Nay, Margaux would wait. Burke would return, contrite; he would surrender this nonsense and make a suitable match. Burke had always been a good son, after all. He had always done what he was bidden, he had never disappointed.

But Margaux stood there long and her son did not return. Her back began to ache. She recalled what Gavin had confided, that he had never seen such defiance in their son, that he had waited outside Tullymullagh's gates for Burke's return, but to no avail.

She did not like to have even this in common with the foul man who still held the empty title of her spouse.

Margaux heard the fading of a destrier's hoofbeats and her heart chilled. Burke mocked her, he played a game, he would see her fretful when he returned. She would not weaken.

Though 'twas Rowan who oft teased her thus, never Burke. Margaux gritted her teeth.

But as the silence stretched longer and longer, Margaux began to tremble. She closed her eyes and 'twas Burke she found in her mind's eye, Burke insisting that she cared only for Montvieux.

'Twas typical of a man to completely miss the point. Margaux cared for Montvieux only because 'twas destined to fall under the hand of her beloved son.

Her only true son. The sun, the moon, and the stars, the very fixture of the firmament, the only child of her own womb, 'twas Burke alone she cared for.

Margaux had raised him to be a man of honor, a prince among knights, a man who granted women an appreciation his own father could not. She had raised him to understand responsibility and to hold his head high. She had raised Burke to be an exemplary example of knighthood and all she had ever believed in.

And he would cast it all away on a worthless woman of mysterious lineage. Margaux was not about to let that happen.

Though it seemed she would have little choice. As she stood there, ramrod straight, Margaux began to think of what her son had said. Romantic drivel, to be sure, though that name was not readily dismissed.

Indeed, the name Isibeal was sufficiently uncommon that it struck a chord within Margaux's mind. Her memory was not what 'twas, but she remembered a knight seeking a woman of such name. She could fairly see his visage, but could not think of his name.

She was almost certain his standard bore a unicorn rampant.

"Arnaud!" Margaux bellowed with a volume that might be unexpected from a woman of her size. The chatelain scampered into the hall.

"I want half a dozen runners dispatched this very moment," she instructed crisply, quickly summoning the names of all the finest gossips she knew. "I want them to go to Agathe d'Orcy, to Magdalene de Nonces, to Constance who joined the nunnery of Des Lumières . . ."

"The Mother Superior will not permit conversation . . ."

"Then tell her that she can expect no contribution to her coffers from my harvest this year!" Margaux snapped. "She will permit one question or I shall withdraw my support. You may be certain that she will be persuaded." She frowned in thought. "There is also Marie, the one who aids the queen herself . . ."

"And the Bishop of Sainte-Madeleine, of course," Arnaud suggested, obviously seeing the direction of her thoughts. "He has a great memory for scandal."

Margaux snapped her fingers and spun to face her chatelain. "The *Bishop*! Aye, Richard d'Annoceaux was of a good family, and he had a younger brother. They bear a unicorn on their standard, as I recall. Do you remember the younger brother's name, Arnaud?"

"Let me see." The chatelain tapped his finger upon his lip. "The elder brother and heir was Michel d'Annoceaux, who of course wed the Roussineau heiress in that vulgar display of wealth that had all talking for a year . . ."

"The younger brother was Millard!" Margaux crowed with triumph. " 'Twas *Millard*! They were the sons of Theobald d'Annoceaux."

"A much-esteemed warrior and crusader." Arnaud frowned. "This Theobald wed Alys de Blois, did he not, and she bore him those three sons?"

"Alys!" Margaux hissed through her teeth, knowing the name could be no coincidence. She pointed a finger at her chatelain. "Find Millard d'Annoceaux, Arnaud. I do not care where he is or what he has become, I do not care for excuses, I do not care if he is *dead*. Bring him here, with all haste, or I shall have the head of every runner who fails."

Arnaud bowed. "Your will, as always, shall be done, madame."

"Alys!" Burke's call echoed through the miller's abode in a most unsettling way. Indeed, even the miller did not seem to be about, though Mass was over. Burke called again, to no response, and continued up the stairs.

His sense of alarm grew as the quiet of the house pressed around him. He ran to the chamber Alys had used and stopped short. The abandoned shoe in the midst of the floor taunted him.

It would seem Alys was gone.

And she had abandoned his gift, the shoe she had pledged never to remove without his aid. Something was clearly amiss.

Had she left him?

Did she leave suddenly, afraid of his future? Of Margaux?

Where was she? Burke surveyed the chamber again and saw something he had not noted sooner.

A tuft of cloth clung to the latch of the door.

He crossed the room, freed the cloth, and recognized its distinctive color immediately. 'Twas a piece of the wool from Alys's new kirtle, the violet one that she loved so very well.

Burke's fist closed over the thread. Alys loved this kirtle. She would not see it torn, she was not careless with her treasures. He bent and looked closer, the tinge of blood on the latch making his heart stop cold.

Alys had not left by her own choice!

The shoe was a message, and he was a fool for doubting his beloved.

Burke swore, lunged out the door, and thundered down the stairs, his hand on the hilt of his sword. How long since Alys had been dragged from this place?

Only now did he find the miller lying behind a trunk in the room below. Burke touched the man's pulse and bruised temple and suspected he would have no more than a headache to show for his experience.

The miller stirred and opened his eyes, clutching Burke's hand when he recognized him. "*Chevalier!* Your lady was taken!"

"Who? Who did this thing?"

"He said his name was Talbot d'Annoceaux. They took a knife to me and he called her a whore." The miller frowned. "Her manner changed then, but 'twas not right. She is no whore, your lady, and she did not feign it well."

Burke shook his head. "Ye gods, that would be Alys."

"She said she desired him from the first moment they met, that she did not favor you for she had had better from an ostler." The miller frowned. "I think he believed her, but many a man sees only what he desires to see in a woman." The miller clutched Burke's arm worriedly. "*Chevalier,* he means to injure her, I am certain!"

"Not if I have anything to say of the matter," Burke said grimly, and pushed to his feet. "Will you be well enough?"

"Go, sir, go!" the miller urged. "Do not waste a moment! They have been gone nigh as long as you."

Burke needed no further encouragement to bolt from the room. He sprang into Moonshadow's saddle, cursing the rain. Aye, if Burke were so fortunate as to see Alys safe, he would ensure there was not a single doubt left between them.

Better from an ostler. Burke snorted beneath his breath. He could only hope he had the chance to demand a toll for such an impudent remark.

Burke reined in when Moonshadow reached the road, uncertain which way to go. He spied something red in the mud far to the right. Burke urged his steed closer, dismounted, and picked up the mate to the shoe he still held. Relief surged through him, for clearly Alys meant to leave him a trail.

Ye gods, but he was glad his lady was a woman of good sense!

✥

Alys had discarded everything except her chemise and kirtle, taking care to mark each turn Talbot made even while she tried to do so unobserved. She feigned a desire to relieve herself as often as she dared and broke great quantities of growth when she did so.

Yet it seemed that Talbot deliberately took a circuitous path, and Alys's hope faded that Burke would truly be able to follow.

The rain halted just as they drew into a clearing occupied by a lone, dilapidated hut. They were miles from the village, the horses were steaming, and Alys could hear naught but distant birds. The sun was obscured behind the thick veil of clouds.

" 'Tis here we have awaited news of you," Talbot declared with pride. "For I knew that your knight would ultimately return to his home estate. What good fortune that we checked the village this very morn."

He dismounted, then tugged Alys from the saddle when she did not move quickly enough to suit him. He caught her against him and kissed her hard, the move so surprising Alys that she did not manage to hide her revulsion.

Talbot trapped her between himself and his steed. "Am I not good enough for you, whore?" he whispered.

"I did not expect your embrace to be so passionate." Alys tried to sound coquettish and knew she failed. She smiled despite the fearful clamoring of her heart and reached to kiss Talbot of her own volition. "You are indeed handsome," she whispered, hating how her voice trembled over the lie.

"Liar!" Talbot cried. "You think of him!"

"Nay, I . . ."

"Lying bitch. I shall make you forget him."

" 'Tis done!"

"Get the rope," Talbot bade his squire tersely. "See she cannot escape."

This would be her last chance. Alys screamed and slammed her knee into Talbot's groin. He roared in pain, his grip slackened, and Alys tore free of him. She ran, her wet kirtle and the tall growth conspiring against her. Her breath came in desperate gasps as Talbot's footfalls echoed behind. Alys ran as fast as she could, even knowing she could not flee to freedom.

She almost made the encircling trees when Talbot's weight landed upon her. Alys fell, but she fought the entire way down. She managed to scratch the knight's face, she bit him, she kicked his privates more than once.

But in the end she was bound hand and foot, and 'twas Talbot who stood over her, one booted foot braced on her belly. He took a deep breath and glared at her, hatred shining in his eyes.

"I shall make you pay for that," he declared softly. "But first I shall let you imagine the worst."

He whistled to his squire and stepped away, brushing his tabard as he strode toward the shack. "See that she is silent and helpless," he bade the boy. "I have need of a rest before I see this matter resolved."

Alys screamed with all her might as the squire wound a length of linen between his hands, though she knew 'twas to no avail. When she was silenced and frightened, there was only one thought in her mind.

Where was Burke?

Burke was on all fours in the undergrowth, in a frenzy to discern the direction his lady had gone. He had found her embroidered girdle in the midst of the road and knew they had made a turn, but could not be certain whether 'twas to the left or the right. He sought some hint in the wet grass, painfully aware that each passing moment could be critical.

Indeed, it might already be too late.

He was so absorbed in his task that he barely noted the canter of hoofbeats on the road and he did not look up before he was called.

"Sir!"

Burke straightened in shock at the familiar voice. "Kerwyn! And Edana. How did you find me?"

"The miller told us of your lady's fate and your direction," the younger man declared. "We thought you might need help."

"But I have taken a twisted course."

"And there were a multitude of signs of your passing along the way," Edana said.

"Signs?"

"In the grass, on the road, in the branches of the trees," Kerwyn said easily. "A steed such as Moonshadow does not pass without making a mark. I assumed there were few of his ilk running alone on the same course."

Edana smiled at Burke's astonishment. "Anyone who has ever tracked an errant goat knows how to read the land."

Truly 'twas a godsend to have these two find Burke now.

"Then aid me!" he cried. "They made a turn here, but I cannot guess which way." The pair dismounted and strode toward Burke.

"That way," Edana declared.

"There are two steeds," Kerwyn affirmed, "a palfrey and one slightly larger."

"Talbot's mare," Burke concluded.

Kerwyn studied hoofprints so faint that Burke could barely discern them. " 'Twould be the right size. She is tired, by her gait." He walked a dozen steps onward, then peered at the line of forest not far away. "The undergrowth is broken there," he said, indicating one point.

"Why would they cut through fields like this?" Edana mused. "No one of sense would take shelter in the forest when it rains. And all the dwellings are along the road."

Burke bit back a comment about Talbot's lack of intellect as he made a sudden and intuitive guess. He had followed this trail blindly and only now sought to discern his precise location. Burke spun in place, calculating the distance to the village, the particular copse of trees that must lie before him. It had been years since he had travelled this small road.

But he knew it well.

"The woodcutter's cabin," he concluded. The pair looked to him in surprise. "There was a woodcutter once who lived as a hermit in the hunting forest, despite all attempts to evict him. He was reputed to be a madman, though he is long dead. I visited him once, on a childhood dare from my brother Rowan. His cabin lay this way."

He turned and mounted Moonshadow. "If I am right, 'tis not far."

"I shall come with you, for you may need aid. They are two, after all," Kerwyn decided quickly. "Edana will remain behind."

"But . . ."

"But naught," the squire said savagely as he mounted his own palfrey. "I would see you safe." He bent and kissed her soundly, the move effectively silencing Edana's protest.

When he turned his horse, the goatgirl bit her lip, wringing her hands together. "God be with you," she whispered.

But Burke had already ridden toward the trees. The branches were indeed broken and a single golden hair hung like a beckoning thread from one branch.

Alys!

He would peel Talbot alive for that hair alone.

The rain eased as they made their way through the woods, the horses' footfalls muffled by the ground's cloak of fallen leaves. Kerwyn pointed to each broken branch of significance, and soon Burke, as well, could discern the path. Anxiety dogged his steps, for the time since Alys's abduction dragged long.

What if he were wrong? What if they had ridden hard beyond the woodcutter's hovel and, even now, were racing beyond his reach?

But when they paused in the shadows of the last trees surrounding the clearing Burke recalled, he immediately spied a familiar mare lazily grazing. A smaller palfrey was tethered beside her, the pair still saddled and damp from their exertion.

They were here.

The woodcutter's shack was more decrepit than Burke recalled; there was a sizable hole in its roof, and the forest had advanced. The clearing that had once been stamped clear of growth was now hip deep in wild grasses and meadow flowers.

A measure of them moved and Burke stiffened, his eyes widening when a figure separated from the darkness beneath the far trees. Talbot's squire sauntered to the wriggling grasses and spat.

"Save your strength," he advised. "You shall have need of it when my master awakens."

The grasses moved with great agitation and the squire laughed. Outrage rolled through Burke at this treatment of his lady, then settled into a cold kernel of resolve.

Talbot's unsuspecting squire strolled back to his place, leaving Alys safely undisturbed—whatever her state—in the middle of the clearing. Burke surmised that Talbot himself must be within the hut.

"Yours," Burke mouthed, indicating the squire.

Talbot would be Burke's.

Kerwyn nodded, and his eyes narrowed. Mercifully, the hut was too simple to sport even a window and it had only one door, which faced into the clearing. Its back was nestled against the forest.

Burke conferred quickly with the younger man, mapping a plan in near silence with his hands. The squire nodded understanding. They parted, slipping from their steeds and disappearing into the shadows of the forest on silent feet.

Burke eased around the hut, straining his ears for some sound from within. He focussed on the task at hand, not daring to let himself be distracted by looking for Alys. She was alive, he knew that much, she was unscathed enough to struggle. She was silent, which meant she must be gagged, her very inability to move indicating that she was bound.

He could only hope that that was the worst of it.

Burke drew his sword as he eased around the last corner and let it flash in the wan light.

Talbot's squire bounced to his feet, his mouth working in shock. He pointed across the clearing at Burke.

"You! What in the name of . . ." He got no further, for a lean shadow loomed behind him and raised a hand. A single blow sent the squire crumpling to the ground.

But Talbot had heard his squire's cry, as Burke had planned.

"What is amiss?" Talbot roared from within the hut. Burke stepped quickly along the wall, his timing perfect beyond belief.

"Can I not trust you to do a simple task . . ." Talbot bellowed as he threw open the door.

The bite of Burke's sword at his throat silenced his words.

"Good afternoon, Talbot d'Annoceaux," Burke said smoothly. "You have rendered an insult to my lady fair and I am here to take an accounting from your own hide."

Talbot blanched, his gorge worked beneath the blade's point.

Burke divested the knight of his dagger with one hand, his sword never wavering. "Perhaps you might do me the courtesy of unfastening your belt," he suggested amiably. "But be warned, my patience runs thin on this day." He pushed the tip of the blade a little more heavily against Talbot's flesh.

The man's fingers shook as he shed his belt, the scabbard attached falling to the ground with a clatter. "You do not understand, I simply could not allow her to ruin all I have labored to win."

"Nay, I do not understand any man's desire to abuse a woman."

Talbot closed his eyes, whimpered, half recounted a prayer memorized by children. "She is unharmed, I swear it to you."

"By virtue of my timely arrival alone." Burke traced a path across the man's neck with the tip of his blade, drawing a thin line of blood, and Talbot paled. "I am guessing that your abduction would not have ended well for my lady otherwise."

"I shall do penance."

"Indeed, you shall. I shall ensure it." Talbot's eyes widened, but Burke cared little for the man's fears.

"I did not hurt her!"

Burke spoke with all the conviction he felt. "I shall kill you slowly if you did." He ignored the other man's dismay. "Kerwyn?"

"Aye, sir?"

"How fares the lady?" Burke could guess his squire's progress by the movement of Talbot's eyes. He heard Alys gasp and knew her gag was removed, heard her murmured thanks as Kerwyn aided her.

"Burke, I am fine," she called, her voice the only sound that could have reassured Burke so well.

"Nay, there are chafes upon her wrists and ankles from the rope, sir," Kerwyn corrected.

How like Alys to understate the indignities served to her. Burke wanted this sorry excuse of a knight to taste a measure of the fear he had forced upon Alys.

"What bad fortune for you, Talbot," he said deliberately. "For I have a great fondness for the perfection of my lady's ankles." Burke shrugged as Talbot swallowed with horror. "It seems that I shall have to kill you, after all."

Chapter Nineteen

S ALYS WATCHED, TALBOT BLANCHED AND A DARK stain spread down the front of his chausses.

"He pissed himself!" Kerwyn declared in disgust.

"Burke, he is not worth killing," Alys insisted.

She watched her knight's jaw set stubbornly. "He must pay for treating you thus, Alys. I am not inclined to be indulgent this day."

Alys guessed that Burke had not had an easy exchange with his mother, though 'twas not the time to ask. "He may have influential ties and the deed cast a long shadow."

"He hurt you, Alys, and for no good reason." Burke drew his blade across Talbot's throat.

"I had every reason!" Talbot cried. "She could have ruined me!"

"Alys?" Burke sounded as astonished as Alys felt. "How?"

"My uncle thinks Isibeal of Kiltorren is the lady he long sought, and he will think that Alys is his own daughter. I cannot permit her to interfere in my inheriting all he owns." Talbot grimaced and his voice rose high. "Have you any idea what I have endured from this man over the years? I have worked for this legacy!"

"Who is this uncle?" Burke demanded.

"Millard de Villonne."

The name meant naught to Alys, but Burke whistled through his teeth in admiration. "Remind me of his standard."

"A unicorn rampant, of course!" Talbot began to whine, even as Alys's hand rose to clutch her pendant. "Are you going to kill me?"

Burke's blade marked a course slowly. "Nay, I have a much worse prospect for you, Talbot."

"Worse than death?" that man squeaked.

"Aye." Burke grinned. "You shall meet my mother." He took a step back. "Sadly for you, she is likely to be in rather foul temper. She did not take well this morn to my refusal to bow to her will."

Talbot looked puzzled even as relief raced through Alys. Burke had denied his mother!

Burke smiled. "I told her that an insult to my lady was an insult to me. How unfortunate you did not guess as much yourself."

Burke sheathed his sword and Talbot sagged bonelessly against the hut, but his relief came too soon. Burke quickly landed a trio of punches—two blows to the face and one to the belly—the sum of which left Talbot hunched over in pain and moaning.

"Burke!"

That knight flicked a telling glance to Alys. " 'Tis better than he deserves and less than I would have preferred," he said grimly. "As always, my lady, you speak with good sense."

Burke offered his hand to her, dropping kisses upon the marks on her wrists before anxiously studying her face. "You are otherwise unhurt?"

"I am fine," Alys insisted, and leaned against his welcome strength with a sigh. "I knew that you would come."

Even if she had not known Burke would reject his mother's

command. Alys thrilled at this sign of his love and cursed herself anew for doubting him. Never would she err that way again.

Talbot moaned pitifully, but they both ignored him.

"I nearly did not," Burke confessed, his fingertips trailing her cheek. "For I feared you had abandoned me."

Alys knew her astonishment showed. "*You* had a doubt? *You* feared the power of your allure? No less, that you did not know best?"

A ruddy flush rose on the back of Burke's neck. "I thought perhaps you tired of my determination."

Alys could not permit him to continue. " 'Tis your determination that won my heart, Burke, and do not doubt the truth of that."

His eyes shone silver for a heartstopping moment, he kissed her brow, then he gestured quickly to Kerwyn. "Let us bind their hands and feet and cart them back to Montvieux. We shall have the truth from them soon enough."

And Talbot groaned, as if he guessed the import of that.

Indeed, Alys suppressed her own shiver of trepidation, for the moment of meeting Margaux was upon her as well.

Burke did not permit his mother a single moment to celebrate his return. Her eyes lit up at the sight of him, but he dragged Talbot across the hall and cast the man at her feet. "He says my Alys is the blood of Millard de Villonne. I thought you would care to know this."

But his mother was unsurprised; indeed, she did not cast a glance to Talbot's whimpering form. "I suspected as much."

Burke surveyed the hall warily, then stepped back to join Alys. He watched his mother fix her gaze upon his lady and felt Alys stiffen. She stood regally straight, though, despite the fact that her hair was unbound and her kirtle stained.

Ye gods, but he was proud of her.

"She stands tall enough," Margaux conceded. She eased closer, leaning heavily on her cane as she circled they two, her gaze bright. "And I suppose she is pretty. But too slender by far."

"Alys is perfect." Burke won a quick smile from his lady for his endorsement.

But Margaux snorted. "But likely too thin to bear sons."

"I am not a broodmare." Alys's golden eyes fired with annoyance, and Burke stifled a smile at his mother's start of surprise.

"She has a tongue in her head," Margaux said softly, bracing her hands atop her cane.

"And *she* prefers to be addressed directly." Alys met Margaux's gaze steadily. "Here I had thought manners were finer in France."

Margaux inhaled sharply and Burke could restrain his chuckle no longer. His mother glared at him, then at his intended, then stalked to her customary seat. She surveyed them in poor temper.

"I could respect a woman with steel in her spine," she acknowledged, then inclined her head. "Alys."

"As could I," was the lady's soft reply. "Lady Montvieux."

His mother, for the first time that Burke could recall, smiled.

Talbot squirmed restlessly against his bonds. "What about me?" he demanded. "What shall happen to me?"

Margaux actually chuckled. "I have a gift for you, Talbot d'Annoceaux. Or perhaps you shall be a gift for my guest."

Talbot's eyes widened, Burke frowned, Alys looked to Burke.

And suddenly a roar carried from the far side of the hall. "TALBOT! Trust you to have made such a mess of matters!"

"God's blood," Talbot muttered, and squeezed his eyes closed. "Anyone but Uncle."

An older knight strode into the hall, his silver mane catching the light, his green tabard graced with a unicorn rampant. His eyes snapped with fury and he shook his fist. "Aye, and you should be quaking to see me, for if ever your mother had a thought that I should make you my heir, 'tis scattered for good on this day. What excuse of a man are you to take a noblewoman hostage . . ."

"She is a whore," Talbot argued weakly.

"A *whore*?" the older man roared. "You spend so much time in their company that you can see naught else! Not all women are whores, you witless fool, and this one may indeed be my daughter!"

Alys clutched Burke's hand.

"I am Millard de Villonne," the arrival declared, his survey of Burke curt. "And you must be Burke de Montvieux."

"Indeed."

Millard's gaze swept over Alys and he nodded. "I have a matter to resolve before we speak." He drew his dagger and cut the bonds on Talbot's ankles, hauling that knight to his feet.

Talbot's knees quivered. "Please, Uncle, I beg of you . . ."

"You have the right to beg naught of me," Millard snapped. "I sent you on an errand to fetch Isibeal of Kiltorren, or indeed her child, but you were not bringing this woman to me. You intended to break your pledge to me, which is no small thing."

Talbot shuddered. "Nay, Uncle."

"Aye! You saw only your own advantage. In hindsight I perceive the twisted course of your thoughts—you intended to kill this woman to ensure your own legacy of Villonne."

Talbot squeezed his eyes shut, but Millard leaned closer. "But I would never have made such a sorry excuse of a knight my heir. You would never have inherited Villonne, even if there was no fruit of my union with Isibeal. I would have granted it all to the Church, if only to spite you and my sister for expecting otherwise."

"But—but . . ."

"But you are a fortunate man, Talbot." Millard exhaled heavily. "For I saw fit to follow you to Kiltorren and thence to Montvieux, where Alys was said to be destined with her betrothed. You are fortunate that I travelled swiftly and saved you from the wrath of a warrior like Burke de Montvieux, no less that of his mother."

The older man paused and all held their breath.

"Indeed, 'tis a mercy that you have to deal only with me." Millard lifted the blade with cold intent, and Talbot began to babble for forgiveness.

◆

As Alys held her breath, uncertain what this older knight would do, another party spilled suddenly into the hall.

"Do not kill him!" cried a woman.

"Malvina!" Alys gasped, and Burke turned in her wake.

"Do not kill him, I beg of you, sir!" Malvina pleaded as she flung herself at Millard's feet.

"The Lord and Lady of Kiltorren," Montvieux's chatelain announced belatedly. "And their daughter." He bowed and retreated.

Millard looked astonished to find Malvina at his feet.

"We followed you, sir, for I had to find Talbot," she declared. "He is my one true love, he is my betrothed."

Talbot looked more than ready to faint.

Deirdre strode across the hall. "He took my daughter's maidenhead, sir, then fled on the very eve of their nuptials."

"Aye, 'tis true," Cedric affirmed.

"We demand he pay his due!" Deirdre cried.

Millard looked to his nephew. "What excuse have you for this unseemly behavior?"

Talbot licked his lips. "I thought she was a whore, sir."

Alys heard Burke's unwitting chuckle and did not dare to meet his gaze for fear they should both laugh aloud.

Millard drew himself up taller. "Is there any vestige of honor in your soul?" Clearly he expected no answer, for he pivoted to face the family of Kiltorren. "Know that I despair of this knight and his lack of honor. Know that on this day he has abducted a noblewoman, intending no good to her person. Know that his heart is blackened with greed and that you may never safely turn your back upon him. Know all of this and tell me whether you still would have him wed your child."

"Aye!" Cedric cried. "We shall take him and willingly."

"Aye, he is perfect for Malvina," Deirdre agreed.

Millard seemed stunned by this, but he turned to the prostrate Malvina. "And you? What have you to say of this?"

"I love him, sir." Her smile turned as cold as her following words. "And he will cross me at his own peril."

"God's blood," Talbot whispered.

Millard chuckled in surprise. Then he voiced the very thought in Alys's mind. "Indeed, Talbot, you may oft wonder whether you truly were saved this day." Millard waved to the family of Kiltorren. "Take him, and welcome."

They descended upon the sagging knight with glee, Malvina landing a smacking kiss upon his lips. Talbot staggered away, surrounded by them and looking somewhat dazed.

Millard turned then, shoving his dagger into his belt, and fixed a gaze upon Alys so bright that it stopped her heart. "The question remains now as to who this lady truly is."

Alys straightened, reassured by the solidity of Burke's presence behind her. "You spoke of my mother, Isibeal of Kiltorren."

Relief lit the older man's features. "Then you are her child!"

"Aye."

The older knight took a step closer, his expression intent.

"I loved my Isibeal," he admitted, a catch in his deep voice. "And she was stolen away from me, her family name hidden that I might not retrieve her. Though I sought her from sea to sea, I never did find her. I never meant her any dishonor, though I can only wonder if our two Isibeals were indeed the same."

"My mother died when I was young," Alys confided. Millard's expression saddened immediately. "Heloise said 'twas of a broken heart."

"Heloise! My Isibeal had a maid name of Heloise!"

"Heloise was my mother's maid." Their gazes held for a moment and Alys felt a tantalizing possibility.

Or was it just coincidence? How many maids named Heloise had served how may ladies named Isibeal?

"*There* was loyalty," Millard conceded. "The Heloise I knew did much for your mother and me, and I never had the chance to thank her. Dare I hope that she at least is with you? Perhaps she might recognize me and solve this mystery."

"She died recently."

Millard looked suddenly older. "And you were too young to remember much of your mother, no less anything she might have said." He rubbed his temples and Alys felt a sympathy for all he had lost. "You cannot possibly recall what she looked like, or the sound of her voice. Either way, my Isibeal truly is lost to me."

How would Alys feel if she lost Burke in this moment? She could not imagine the heartbreak of seeking him without success for twenty years.

"I know one thing," she offered, wanting to ease the other man's pain. " 'Twas a tale that Heloise told me of my father and mother, a tale of their love for each other."

The older knight's head snapped up. "Aye?"

"Aye." Alys fumbled with the neckline of her chemise. "Heloise said my father granted this token to my mother as a sign of his esteem." She pulled the chain over her head and offered her pendant.

Millard caught his breath as if he did not believe his eyes. He stepped closer, raising a shaking hand. "*My* Isibeal," he whispered brokenly, and his tears began to fall.

Then he looked to Alys with new intensity. "How old are you?"

"Twenty summers."

"And your name?"

"Alys, Alys of Kiltorren."

"God in heaven, she named you for my own mother." Millard shook his head as if incredulous, his gaze raked over Alys. "You are *my* daughter. Isibeal of Kiltorren was my own Isibeal."

Alys was stunned to find this old tale to be the truth.

"My daughter," Millard declared with growing conviction. He grinned and opened his arms to Alys, and she stepped forward.

"My father," she whispered, and touched his cheek.

"My daughter!" Millard roared, and swung her in the air with undisguised delight. Alys did not know whether to laugh or cry; she had never imagined she would know such a moment, so she did both.

"Aye, you have your mother's smile, child." With Alys's hand clasped in his own, Millard turned and bellowed to the entire assembly, "My daughter is Alys of Kiltorren!"

He spun with startling speed to face Alys again. "And you are an heiress, child, *my* heir. All I have is yours. Come, come to Villonne, and see what I have built."

Margaux rose to her feet. "That will be impossible, Millard. My son's betrothed must remain at Montvieux."

Millard squared his shoulders and faced Margaux undaunted. "Your son has spurned Montvieux, from what I heard. Indeed, he may not be a fitting match for my daughter, given her new status."

Margaux inhaled sharply. "My son is worthy of a queen's hand."

"And Villonne is a king's prize. Whosoever my daughter weds shall be a mighty man indeed."

"Ye gods," Burke muttered under his breath. " 'Twas far simpler, Alys, when I was disinherited and you had no parents."

Alys laughed, but their respective parents turned a common blaze of fury upon Burke. "I heard that!" they cried as one.

"You shall remain at Montvieux!"

"You shall come to Villonne!"

"We remain at Montvieux on this day, for my lady has need of a rest." Burke captured Alys's hand and pressed a kiss to her knuckles. He winked at her. "After that, who shall say?"

"How can you propose to wed my daughter?" Millard demanded. "You have no legacy!"

Burke shrugged. "We are en route to the tourneys in Champagne."

"Tourneys!" Millard spat into the rushes. "My daughter will not wed a knight with no better prospect than that."

"And I had thought," Burke mused, "that Isibeal's family declined your suit because you held no land."

Millard blanched; he caught his breath, and glared at Burke. "You could be killed. Then what would become of Alys?"

"Burke would not need to tourney, if he were to be heir to Villonne," Alys dared to suggest. "I am certain he has the skill to administer it . . ."

"Of course he has the skill," Margaux snapped. "He was raised to command Montvieux."

"A much *smaller* holding," Millard observed.

"If he spurned Montvieux, he might well spurn Villonne," Margaux observed coldly. "Do not hold your breath in this, Millard."

"Burke?" Millard asked, all eyes turning upon the knight.

But Burke looked only to his lady. "Alys?"

"What of freedom from burdens?"

"In truth, I miss the security of knowing my responsibilities." Burke smiled in that slow way that heated Alys from head to toe. "And I would welcome the chance to indulge you fully, as the lady of an estate should be."

"You would not tourney?"

Burke grinned. "I know you will be woefully disappointed."

There truly was no choice. "We should do this," she decided.

"We accept," Burke informed Millard, folding Alys's hand into his own.

"And we shall be wed," Alys added.

"In a fortnight," Burke clarified.

"The wedding must be a rich one," Millard argued. " 'Twill take three months to be arranged as befits the sole daughter of Villonne."

"And the son of Montvieux," Margaux added.

Millard shook a finger at the couple. "I will have no rumor dogging this match. There will be no cause for counting fingers when your first child arrives, or you, sir, will have much to answer for."

Burke smiled easily. "Your concern comes too late."

Margaux caught her breath, Millard swore. They exchanged a glance.

"Two weeks, then, and not a day less," Margaux charged. "We shall be ready, one way or the other."

"And you shall be wed at Villonne!"

"Nay, they shall be wed at Montvieux!"

Burke and Alys exchanged a glance. "We shall decide." And leaving their parents all aflutter, he led Alys away.

"You are incorrigible."

Burke grinned, then sobered. "And you would change this?" He looked at Alys, hope in the silvery depths of his eyes, and she knew 'twas past time she made her confession.

"Nay, I love you, Burke, just as you are." Alys framed his face in her hands, resolved to leave him no doubt of her feelings. "Though I may take issue with you, you will know the truth of it. Rest assured that you shall endure my company for all your days."

Burke laughed. He kissed her with abandon, his arms tight around her, then withdrew with a grin. "And what of all my nights?" he jested. "And your mornings? Indeed, I understand that you had a most busy morn on this day, my lady fair."

"This morn?"

Burke's eyes twinkled so merrily that Alys wondered what he was about. "Aye, I hear that you have had pleasure beyond any I could grant from an *ostler*. I know that you had no chance to tarry with any ostler at Crevy. It must have been this morn that you sampled some ostler's charms."

Alys laughed, and before Burke could tease her further, she granted him a kiss meant to curl his toes.

His eyes gleamed when he finally lifted his head. "Ostler or no ostler," he muttered, " 'tis high time I showed you the merit of a honeyed tongue."

Alys could hardly wait.

Epilogue

I N THE END, THEY WERE WED IN A FORTNIGHT AT Villonne, Margaux planning a fête for Midsummer at Montvieux, one of suitable richness to impress a king.

For Margaux had learned of Brianna's pregnancy and insisted upon summoning Luc and Brianna to Montvieux, necessitating a wait for their arrival. She would not hear of her first grandchild—even a grandchild not hers in the strict sense of reckoning bloodlines—being born in the "uncivilized wilds" of Ireland.

Burke refused to accept a delay in the nuptials, for he did not believe Brianna would abandon Tullymullagh. Sparks flew at Montvieux, each as stubborn as the other, though Alys's suggestion of the dual celebration seemed to satisfy all.

And it suited Alys well enough to be wed quickly—to keep those busy fingers from counting—but also to have the chance to become acquainted with her father at Villonne. He proved to be a man of marked honor, filled with tales, who sang *chansons* in a marvelously deep voice.

Aye, Millard would be a perfect grandfather.

Villonne lay to the west of Paris, situated on the Loire, its hall still being built. Burke took to the administration like a duck to water, he and Millard agreeing so frequently on how matters should be that it became a jest they were but two peas from the same pod. And Alys became accustomed to all that was expected of her, as lady of the keep, including an insistence that Edana and Kerwyn be suitably wed.

Alys learned to ride better with Burke's assistance, and her father's first gift to her was a fine chestnut mare with an easy gait. Alys was not the only one enchanted with the gentle creature, for Burke had to restrain Moonshadow with a vengeance whenever they rode together.

Burke commented that he had never intended to learn the art of breeding destriers but clearly would not have much choice.

And so 'twas they rode to Montvieux in June, already wed but prepared to celebrate their match anew. Luc and Brianna were indeed there, Brigid and Guillaume made the journey, and even Margaux thawed enough to kiss Alys's cheeks thrice in succession.

"My brother Rowan," Burke murmured to her when a russet-haired man sauntered into the hall crowded with guests.

"Typically late," Luc added. Margaux immediately waved her cane at her errant son and summoned him with a shout.

"I would not be in his hide," Luc commented.

Burke grinned. "He takes no notice of her at all. Watch."

Alys did watch as Rowan nonchalantly plucked a sweet from a nearby table and assessed a serving maid's charms. 'Twas as if he were blissfully unaware of his mother's approach.

"His manner drives her mad," Burke confided to Alys.

She grinned. "To be incorrigible seems a family trait."

"No doubt." Burke winked just before Margaux roared.

"A pox upon you! Late for your own brother's wedding fête and not a word of apology from your lips."

Rowan saluted Burke with a wave, then turned an engaging smile on Margaux. "You would not want me stealing the bride's affections, would you, Mother?"

Margaux poked the butt of her cane into his chest. "You had a woman on her back, and I know it well. Look at you! You smile as if there were naught amiss with that . . ."

Rowan spread his hands. "And what is amiss with that?"

"The lack of wedding vows!"

Rowan scoffed. "You cannot say as *you* have not taken lovers without the benefit of wedding vows. And indeed I am testimony alone that Father did not feel inclined to adhere to his."

Luc's brows rose and Burke gave a low whistle at Rowan's boldness. The assembly noted the exchange now and turned to watch.

Margaux hissed through her teeth. "The cheek of you! We have an entire hall of guests, the estate celebrates the nuptials of my only son, and you can do naught but embarrass those who have taken you in." She drew herself up taller. "You have a charm, Rowan, but truly you grow too old to trade upon that alone."

Rowan looked at Margaux, clearly startled by her words.

"Now she has his attention," Luc murmured with a smile.

Rowan hid his surprise very quickly. Alys sensed that he was not one to readily give hint of his own feelings. Nay, he was one to cover all with a smile and a jest.

He smiled now and he jested, propping one hand against a table to grant Margaux a cocky grin. "And what shall you do, Mother? Further embarrass your house by casting me out?"

"Nay, I shall grant you one last chance." The tension eased immediately from Rowan's features, but Margaux shook her head. "Do not be so relieved before you know my condition."

Rowan folded his arms across his chest. "And what is that?"

"You were sent on a bride quest by Brianna of Tully-mullagh. Your brothers have both found brides yet you have none." Margaux stepped back. "You will return to Montvieux with a bride before the Yule or I shall wash my hands of you."

"You would not!"

"I would. Do not doubt me this time, Rowan."

"But you cannot do this!"

"I most certainly can. By the Yule." Margaux turned away with satisfaction and beckoned to her guests. "Come! The meat grows cold!" At her signal, the minstrels began to sing, the wine was poured, and the guests moved to the board in a swirl of fine cloth and glittering jewels.

Rowan stood unmoved as if he could not believe Margaux's decree. Then he shook his head and strode to meet his brothers.

"See what a fix you have made for me," he complained amiably, bowing low over first Brianna's, then Alys's hand. "I shall have to find a way to persuade her to dismiss this task."

"Why do you not simply seek a bride?" Luc suggested.

Rowan glanced at him in surprise. "Tell me that is a jest."

" 'Tis not to Margaux," Burke observed.

"A bride?" Rowan grimaced, then flashed a smile to Alys. "No offense intended, of course, but some men are not made for matrimony." His expression brightened. "I should bring home a dancing girl, with a dozen brats to her name already. That would teach Mother not to challenge me thus."

"And leave you in the cold all the same," Luc concluded.

"Aye, the way you indulge yourself, you should wed an heiress," Burke jested.

"He *should* wed an heiress," Luc repeated as if sampling the idea and finding it favorable.

"Wait a moment!" Rowan protested. "I will wed no heiress!"

" 'Tis fair enough, for no heiress of sense would wed you," Burke observed.

"Nay, 'twould be her father who would protest the match," Luc corrected. The foursome chuckled at Rowan's expense, while that man feigned insult and looked between them.

"You do not think I can do this!"

"Of course not!" Luc agreed.

"We should challenge him," Burke declared. "Rowan loves a dare."

"Now, wait a moment! I do not even want a holding!"

"I did not seek Tullymullagh." Luc spread one hand to Burke.

"I did not expect Villonne." They smoothly turned on their dismayed brother. "She must be heiress to an estate larger than either Tullymullagh or Villonne," Burke concluded.

"An Irish heiress," Brianna amended.

"And you will wed her before the Yule," Luc added. "We shall meet you here on Christmas Day when you present your bride."

"You do not think I can do this."

Burke chuckled. "We *know* you cannot do this."

Rowan appealed to Alys. "Do you see what manner of family you have joined? To imagine that a man's own blood could think so little of him."

" 'Tis shocking," Alys agreed, barely holding back her smile.

"Do you think I can do it?"

Alys laughed aloud. "Nay, I do not!"

Rowan chuckled, then threw his hands skyward. "Neither do I!" he declared recklessly. "But a man who lives without risk does not truly live at all." Rowan pivoted and shouted across the hall, his cry halting the minstrels' music. "Mother! I shall wed an Irish heiress by the Yule or never darken your doorstep again!"

Margaux stared at him dumbfounded, but Rowan waylaid a servant and snatched up a chalice of wine. "I drink to my brothers' fair brides!" he called to the company. He bowed to both women. "And I drink to the bride I am pledged to find!"

The assembly applauded, then began to laugh, whispers spreading through their ranks as Rowan drained the chalice in one long gulp.

"Will he truly do it?" Alys whispered to Burke.

"With Rowan, one never knows. The man's life is a feckless adventure." Then Burke captured her hand and placed it in the crook of his elbow. "Forget Rowan and his need to have the eye of all upon him," he advised. "This is a celebration for you and me alone, the culmination of all we have sought these three long years."

Alys smiled as they reached the place of honor on the dais and Burke turned her to face him. She loved this man as never she had imagined 'twas possible to love another. They had pledged to each other for all eternity and had already begun their romantic tale.

'Twould be even a finer one than Nicolette shared with Aucassin. The assembly roared for a show of affection, and Burke smiled slowly, his eyes a piercing silver.

" 'Tis time for a salute to the bride," he whispered, his words so low that only Alys could hear them. Burke touched her chin with one gentle finger, and the crowd cheered as he bent to kiss her leisurely. Alys's heart sang as she slipped her arms around her knight's neck.

Aye, Alys had hold of the only dream she had ever wanted, and she would never let him go.

Prologue

London, July 1172

ROWAN DE MONTVIEUX WAS IN A FOUL MOOD.

Not only had he been ill beyond belief on the journey from Le Havre, but he was not where he had intended to be. Indeed, the last Rowan had heard, the Thames was *not* in Ireland.

Which meant that he had to endure another sea voyage, no doubt even less pleasant than this last, and that he must do so immediately in order to meet the challenge he had accepted from his brothers.

Nay, he was not in a fine mood. He strode through the tangle of merchants on the docks, retrieving his horse and finding his squire Thomas with no small effort. They badgered him from every side, these hagglers with their shoddy goods, and he braced himself against thieves in the crowd.

He had need of a measure of ale, some song, a bit of the sorry excuse for food in this country warm in his belly—and then blissful sleep. That would restore his interest in bucking his brothers' expectations. Rowan loved a challenge—at least when he was feeling hale—and the more desperate the stakes, the better.

An Irish heiress, for the love of God. What had possessed him to take such a dare? On a morn like this, with the taste of his own bile ripe in his throat, Rowan doubted he could charm even the most ancient and desperate crone alive.

Or that he wanted to.

"Oho! A fine knight just into port!" a slavemonger cried. The man was unshaven and unkempt, his dark hair hanging in his eyes and more than one tooth missing from his mouth. "I have just the wench for you, sir, and she is a bargain on this day of days." He leaned closer to whisper, his breath even more foul than Rowan's own. "I shall make you a special deal, sir, on account of your knightly status and recent arrival."

Rowan growled a dismissal and made to push past the man, his gaze drifting disinterestedly to the woman in question.

And then he stopped to stare.

'Twas not the bright red gold of her hair that captured his attention, nor even that her tresses were cropped short. 'Twas not the deep hue of her tan, nor even how that tan made her eyes appear ethereally blue. 'Twas not the ripeness of her breasts fairly spilling from her chemise, not even that she wore a boy's chausses, which hid none of her copious charms.

Nay, 'twas that she feigned insouciance nearly as well as he.

The woman did not even blink. Her stance remained unchanged, her arms folded across her chest, her bare feet braced against the ground. She was nearly as filthy as her owner, a rough length of rope knotted around her neck and tethering her to that man. Rowan swallowed as he noted the chafed skin.

"I have no need of a slave," Rowan said mildly, finding himself disappointed that the woman's steady stare did not waver at his refusal.

The would-be seller grimaced and turned away, muttering something uncomplimentary under his breath and giving the woman's rope a savage tug. She made no protest, obviously accustomed to his abuse, and strolled behind him with her head as high as a queen's. Rowan could not help but watch them go.

He imagined the man taking his pleasure with this woman,

his sweaty bulk heaving atop her as she stared fixedly at the rafters. His stomach rolled mutinously and Rowan felt ill again, though his boots were on dry land.

Though 'twas true he had no use for a slave.

"How much?" he called impulsively.

"Three silver deniers," the man cried, spinning to jab a finger at Rowan. "*Two* for you!"

"Outrageous," Thomas murmured.

'Twas a shocking price but Rowan found himself digging for the coins. "My mother will be proud of me," he muttered. He fired a glance at Thomas. "Be sure to tell her of this. I may well be in need of her favor."

Thomas nodded. A mere heartbeat later, Rowan's purse was lighter and he held the end of the distasteful rope in his hand. The seller marched away, whistling.

But the woman surveyed him with the same cold manner. If Rowan had thought she might thank him for winning her release from that old creature, he was clearly mistaken.

And that irked him. He had just bought a slave, for no good reason, a slave he did not want, expending coin he would have preferred to keep or at least spend on some amusement.

She could at least appreciate the gesture!

"For a smile and a word of thanks, I would release you," he declared pointedly.

Her gaze flicked over him. "Gratitude for paying him for his crimes?" she asked. "You will not have that from me, nor a smile."

"A smile would cost you naught."

" 'Twould cost me that very freedom you promise," she retorted dryly. Her eyes narrowed. "Or have you not noted the fine company we keep?"

'Twas true enough that the docks were swarming with unsavory characters, more than one of whom had a thorough study of what filled her chausses.

" 'Tis your own fault for wearing such garb," Rowan felt compelled to observe.

The hint of a smile crossed her lips. "The embroidery on each and every one of my kirtles is being repaired."

Thomas laughed, then looked to Rowan and fell silent. Rowan fixed the woman with a dark glance, not liking that 'twas she who made the jests instead of he.

His look did not seem to trouble her in the least, which was doubly vexing.

"At some point," he said sternly, "you donned that garb of your own choice."

"True enough."

"Why?"

Now she did smile, although the expression was sadder than might have been expected. " 'Twas born of an innocent trust, lost long ago and far away."

"Why?" Rowan repeated, determined to have one answer from her.

Her smile disappeared. "I thought to disguise myself as a boy."

"You? A boy?" Rowan laughed. He could have done naught else. "A man would have to be blind to doubt your gender!"

The woman glared at him and Rowan felt a measure of pride for stirring some response from her. "I thank you for observing my foolishness. I might have doubted it otherwise, given my current exalted status."

Thomas snickered even as Rowan's smile was snatched away.

" 'Tis the mark of maidens in a convent to imagine that they can deceive the world simply by donning boy's chausses and cropping their hair . . ." Rowan's voice faded as he stared at her in sudden comprehension. "You speak too well to have been raised in a gutter. Who are you?"

The woman's eyes flashed so quickly that Rowan almost

missed the telltale sign that he had found a truth. "I am no one," she declared.

"You have studied in a convent," Rowan insisted.

"I labored in one," she corrected hastily, though Rowan guessed 'twas a lie. She shrugged, her composure in place once more. "Until I ran away."

"Shunning the compassion and care of the nuns for the charms of that one." Rowan jerked a thumb in the direction her former owner had taken.

"I did not expect . . ." she began hotly, then caught herself and said no more. She folded her arms across her chest again and glared at Rowan.

"You made a mistake," he acknowledged softly. "And I think you have already paid for it. Pledge to me that you will not flee and I will remove the rope."

"So much for your fine offer." She turned to Thomas. "Are your knight's words worth so little as that?"

Before Thomas could answer, Rowan clarified the matter. "I offered an exchange, but I have yet to have thanks and a smile."

Her full lips tightened. "Do not hold your breath."

"Then 'twill be a year and a day of labor from you," Rowan declared as if he made such arrangements all the time, "for I must have something from my coin."

In truth, he could not have cared less for the coin, but he did not want to give her the satisfaction of knowing she intrigued him.

She visibly gritted her teeth. "I shall not labor on my back."

"I would not expect you to."

"Nay?" Her skepticism was more than a little grating, and Rowan had the urge to provoke a response from her.

"Nay," he retorted. "I like my women lean and lithe."

Her eyes flashed dangerously and Rowan darted backward, not the least bit certain that she would not strike him. Instead she loosed a string of Gaelic so potent that he knew 'twas naught she could have learned in a convent.

Ha!

Rowan grinned at her. "Your pledge, *ma demoiselle*?"

"If you touch me, I shall flee."

"Fair enough."

She considered him for a moment, her eyes narrowed. "Then I swear it to you," she said finally, her reluctance to accept his very generous offer more than obvious.

Rowan gently unknotted the rope, catching his breath when he realized the chafing was more extensive than he had guessed. "This must hurt," he murmured.

She averted her gaze. "One can accustom oneself to anything." She was cold and composed again, though Rowan yearned for another glimpse of that fire in her eyes.

"Have you a name?"

Her blue gaze flicked to his and away. "Ibernia."

"A lie," Rowan concluded with a smile of appreciation for her quick wits. It meant literally from Ireland, something he would guess to be true judging by her earlier spate of Gaelic. "But 'twill do. And if you truly are of Ireland, then you can be of assistance to me without rolling to your back."

"How?" One more sensitive than Rowan would have construed her suspicion as an insult.

"I seek a bride, the most wealthy heiress in Ireland." He grimaced comically. "Sadly, I do not know her name."

"You seek a bride for her wealth alone?" she demanded with one fair brow arched high. "How very romantic."

Thomas, curse him, chuckled again.

Rowan folded his arms across his chest, his good humor dispelled. "I seek her to answer a challenge from my brothers."

"Oh, I should like to see you lose," she murmured with unexpected heat, "for you are too confident by far."

Rowan grinned that she once again revealed her thoughts.

"Indeed 'tis the near certitude of failure that made me risk this quest."

Ibernia blinked. "Truly?"

"Truly." He spared her his best smile, to no discernible effect. "I *like* a challenge."

She straightened, a daring glint in her eyes that made Rowan's pulse quicken. "Then you will be delighted to know that the wealthiest heiress in all of Ireland is one Bronwyn of Ballyroyal."

"Why should that delight me?"

Ibernia smiled fully then. The result was so fetching that Rowan nearly lost the thread of their conversation, and he considered the challenge of winning this woman's favor.

"Because she will not have you," she declared with resolve. "There is no doubt of the matter."

Rowan would not take that to heart so readily. He leaned closer and winked, well aware of his own good looks. "Because she likes her men less handsome? Less charming? Less amusing?"

Ibernia snorted with unwilling laughter, then lifted one hand to her lips to halt the sound. "Because she is already betrothed," she said with satisfaction, "and will be wed by summer's end."

"Perfect!" Rowan cried, laughing at his companion's startled expression. He gripped her waist and swung her into the air. " 'Tis completely hopeless! We must find passage with all haste." He set Ibernia on her feet and touched one fingertip to her nose. "And you, my lovely *demoiselle*, shall guide us directly to Ballyroyal."

She shook her head, clearly marvelling at his response. "I will do so, if only to witness your failure."

"Do not be so certain of it as that," Thomas counselled in an undertone. "Matters have a way of turning unexpectedly in this knight's presence."

"Aye," Rowan agreed with a wicked wink for Ibernia. "By the end of this, even you will not be able to resist me."

And that made Ibernia laugh outright for the very first time. There was a kind of satisfaction to be had in seeing her so surprised. Indeed, Rowan guessed that this year and a day might provide a very interesting pursuit, one beyond his brothers' quest.

Aye, he liked the sense of chance mounting against him. Rowan would woo this Bronwyn of Ballyroyal to be his bride *and* he would seduce Ibernia before they parted ways. And there, Rowan knew well enough, would lay the greater challenge of all his days.

He could hardly wait to begin.